KASEY SAFFORD

The Amulet of Undoing

First published by Independently Published 2025

Copyright © 2025 by Kasey Safford

All rights reserved. No part of this publication may be reproduced, stored or transmitted in any form or by any means, electronic, mechanical, photocopying, recording, scanning, or otherwise without written permission from the publisher. It is illegal to copy this book, post it to a website, or distribute it by any other means without permission.

This novel is entirely a work of fiction. The names, characters and incidents portrayed in it are the work of the author's imagination. Any resemblance to actual persons, living or dead, events or localities is entirely coincidental.

Kasey Safford asserts the moral right to be identified as the author of this work.

First edition

ISBN: 9798312179279

Cover art by Sarah Moon

This book was professionally typeset on Reedsy. Find out more at reedsy.com

Contents

Dedication	1
Chapter 1	2
Chapter 2	13
Chapter 3	21
Chapter 4	34
Chapter 5	42
Chapter 6	56
Chapter 7	62
Chapter 8	72
Chapter 9	84
Chapter 10	96
Chapter 11	108
Chapter 12	113
Chapter 13	119
Chapter 14	124
Chapter 15	132
Chapter 16	143
Chapter 17	150
Chapter 18	161
Chapter 19	171
Chapter 20	183
Chapter 21	190
Chapter 22	198
Chapter 23	209

Chapter 24	216
Chapter 25	222
Chapter 26	231
Chapter 27	240
Chapter 28	248
Chapter 29	259
Chapter 30	266
Chapter 31	279
Chapter 32	286
Chapter 33	296
Chapter 34	304
Chapter 35	315
Epilogue	325
Luna's Lavender Tarts Recipe	329
Acknowledgments	332
About the Author	334

Dedication

This book is dedicated to my father who once told me he would write me a check for the amount of my choice if I stopped reading fantasy books.
I'm not just reading them anymore.
Sorry, Father, but this is priceless. I love you.

Chapter 1

I dip the gold-laced measuring spoon into the canister of lavender powder a third time, still certain that its predecessors weren't as exact as they ought to be. To others, baking lavender tarts might not be of large importance or a matter that requires such exact measurements.

"Eh, yeah. That looks like about a half teaspoon or so," someone might say as they carelessly toss the imprecise portion of ingredients into the bowl, but I certainly will do no such thing.

It's important to be precise. If you don't control the ingredients, you don't control the outcome. I strive for a perfect outcome. Therefore, my ingredients must be perfect.

"Lita! Come back here please."

I hear the quick titter-patter of feet before her small figure darts around the corner. Her simple maid's dress flows ever so slightly as she halts to a stop under a stream of light from the upper window. In the sunlight, with her pale skin and white shoulder-length hair, she looks almost ghost-like.

"Yes, Your Highness?" Her yellow-tinted wings shimmer as she stands at attention.

I hold the measuring spoon of powder at eye level, close to my face, peering. "Do you think this measurement looks precise?"

"I trust Your Highness's judgment. If you believe it to be precise then I agree it must be so."

"Lita, please. I want your honest opinion."

She shifts her body weight slightly, rocking onto the toes and then the backs of her feet. "Well then, Your Highness, I honestly believe that your previous measurement was the most precise."

"That's exactly what I feared!" I say, exasperated, dropping the spoon into the canister with such force that a purple cloud erupts. "What if I am never able to recreate my second measurement and have detrimentally damaged these tarts? They have to be ready for the coronation ball this evening. Important people are coming. Even representatives from the sprite kingdom and we've never had them at a palace event before! It has to go well."

"It will go well, Your Highness. A dessert by you has yet to turn out poorly. I'm starting to lose all belief that it's even possible. There aren't many steps left. How about I have someone from the kitchen staff finish this up for you so you can go relax a bit before the party?"

Both my arms fall slack at my sides and I let out a small sigh. "I suppose that's for the best. I could use a bit of downtime before the festivities. Thank you for the suggestion, Lita."

"My pleasure, Your Highness."

Taking off my apron and hanging it on the nearest hook, I flash Lita a smile as I fly up and out of the kitchen and down the hall toward my bedroom. I take a deep breath in as if I can smell the hustle and bustle of fairies preparing for the night's celebrations. Tomorrow, I will be Queen of Celestia. Just the thought makes my heart race in the oddest mixture of both excitement and fear.

I bring myself to a slower, fluttering speed as I make a detour down the hall of family portraits, the thoughts of tomorrow's coronation having gotten my emotions in a nostalgic tizzy. I peer at the first painting, a portrait of me done by one of our local watercolor artists in honor of my coronation. I overheard a maid say that it is to be displayed at the ceremony tomorrow shortly after the crowning. I'm not sure how I feel about that.

I'm not a vain person by any means. I mean, I'm aware of my beauty. I come from a long line of beautiful women, but my looks aren't something I can take credit for. After all, I had no control over them and I'm old enough now to understand that it takes far more than a pleasant appearance to live up to the expectations set on you.

If looks were all it took, the birthing fairy would have held me up and said, "She's beautiful. A perfect Queen!"

However, no such thing happened. I wish it had been that easy. If anything, inheriting my mother's appearance has only placed extra expectations on me. I continue down the hall slightly further until I'm in front of a family portrait from when my wings were only half-grown. I still remember the itchy fabric of the gown they stuffed me in that day and how my mother kept telling me not to squirm.

Gazing at the portrait, it's easy to see all the ways I take after my mother. The hair is always the first thing your eyes go to since red hair only runs in the royal family. I'm often thankful that the shade is more of an orangish red rather than a deep rose. A dark red with my pale skin would have washed me out profusely. Instead, the slight addition of orange in the coloring complements my porcelain complexion and makes my light blue eyes stand out. I also have my mother's eyes. Although, I think they are too light. When I was little, and still attending fairy school, a boy in my class told me my eyes looked stupid and cloudy.

I hit him over the head with my textbook and then proceeded to tackle him till he begged for mercy. I'm pretty sure the next day was when I started private tutoring at the palace. Can't have the future Queen causing a scene. I was allowed no discrepancies even as a child.

Chapter 1

I still don't regret tackling him though.

Why couldn't they have been a rich blue? The kind of eyes that would have a man falling in love with me just from a glance. I suppose that kind of power would go straight to my head though, so maybe it's for the best.

Hair, eyes, and then, of course, the freckles. Oh, the freckles. While my mother's are scarce and scattered like constellations across her cheeks, mine resemble something closer to a meteor shower. I have freckles scattered all across the bridge of my nose and sides of my cheeks with a few stragglers above and between the center of my brows. On other fairies, they might stick out like a sore thumb, but Mother says I wear them well like she does.

While most of our features are similar, there are a few I don't take after her.

My eyes drift slightly upward to where my father's face is looking lovingly down at my mother and me in the portrait. He wasn't alive when the portrait was painted, but mother had insisted that she wanted one of the three of us. I've looked at him in this so many times; sometimes for hours.

Since he married into the royal family, he doesn't share my fiery hair, and his amber eyes are a contrast to my own. However, I share his bone structure. Small nose, slightly upturned at the end, with a strong, sharp jaw. On him, a strong jaw looks natural and simple. On me, it looks like my face is more acute than other fairywomen around with all their graciously rounded faces.

He looks like he was kind. Handsome, for sure, but not an arrogant handsome. Most fairymen who know they're good-looking wear it proudly, like a badge. While I can't know for sure, I doubt he was like that. I bet he was humble. Humble and sweet. The kind of man my mother fell easily for.

Their love story is one I never tire of hearing.

Mother came down with a terrible sickness and he was the healing fairy that was assigned to her. Mother says he later told her he knew she was the one when he first laid eyes on her. She says he must have been crazy because she'd probably never looked worse than when she was sick.

Through all his visits, they fell in love. Mother says she kept pretending to be sick for at least a week after she felt better just to keep him around. He told her he'd known the whole time when she finally confessed. They got married shortly after and mother was soon pregnant with me. It's crazy to think that my mother was married at my age, the age of 20, before she was even Queen. Mother says their marriage could have stood the test of time if it hadn't been for the fire.

With the thought of that horrific night, I float further down the hallway till I come to the last portrait on the wall of my mother and Aunt Amyra.

They look so alike that it's uncanny. The pale skin, scattered freckles, and light eyes, but my mother has softer features. Amyra's eyes have an almost unsettling look to them. It's hard to describe. It's like if you match gazes with a wild animal and even though you're looking right into its eyes, you have no clue what it's thinking or what its next move will be. Mother looks so delicate standing next to her. Amyra was always destined to be Queen per her birthright as the eldest, but it was never easy for her. Everything was lost that night. She and Dad were both lost in the fire, which palace officials suspected was started by sprites. Thus, launching the estrangement between Celestia and Durand.

"Luna?"

"Ah!" I turn quickly, accidentally smacking Rhea across the face with my wings.

She makes a pained wincing sound. She's wearing her lilac-colored dress today, contrasting her cocoa skin and dark eyes. She pushes a strand of her short, curly, black hair behind her ear to rub her right cheek. "You know, you have got to be the least graceful Princess ever."

"And you have got to be the cruelest best friend ever. I've told you before not to sneak up on me like that!"

Rhea loops her arm through mine as she sweeps me away.

"I wasn't sneaking in the slightest. I was tempted to, of course, but I didn't. I said your name twice before you heard me. You were so lost in thought. What were you all sucked into? I don't know if you've heard, but I'm a great listener."

I chuckle. "Whoever told you that must not have known you well."

"Perhaps we were just mere acquaintances, but let's not dwell on details shall we? How 'bout we get to the bottom of what's on your mind? Tell Rhea everything. Your secret is safe with me."

I tilt my head towards her.

"Okay, somewhat safe. Now, spill," she says, nudging her elbow into my side.

"I don't know. I've just been in my head a lot lately with the coronation ball tonight and then the ceremony tomorrow. It's a lot to take in and flying down the portrait hall, I saw the one with my dad and then Aunt Amyra. Even though I never had the chance to know them, I still wish they could have been here."

"I know how you feel, but you can't dwell on the past right now when the most exciting event of your life is happening! Now, more than ever is the time to be present," Rhea says as we flutter through the entrance of my room before dropping back onto our feet.

I allow myself to release a small breath. My room has always been my safe space. My oasis where everything is in its place. A large, triangular stain-glass window with shades of fuchsia and rose sits on the far wall with one pane open to let in the fresh air. To the left is my wooden, ceiling-high bookshelf filled to the brim with novels I've already read multiple times over. Then there's a light blue vanity desk with a mirror beside my bed which sits under the overhang of a giant, glowing, spotted mushroom. Small beads of yellow crystal hang down from the ceiling in scattered traces and wildflowers are tucked into every nook and crevice available.

"Look at me." She holds a hand on each of my shoulders and turns me to face her. "I am so proud of you. No one knows how hard you've worked to prepare for this day more than I do. You deserve to soak up every minute of this happy time! I know Amyra and your father can't be here, but I'm here, and your mother's here, and we are all so excited to watch you be crowned tomorrow, okay?"

I smile and embrace her. "Thank you, Rhea. I'm so lucky I have you."

She flips her short, black hair over one shoulder. "You sure are, aren't you."

We laugh.

I don't know what I would do without Rhea in my life. Life at the palace would be so incredibly lonely if it wasn't for her companionship. She has such a feisty and confident spirit. She's so sure of herself. The day she joined me here at the palace was probably the best day of my life.

"You're staring. It's freaking me out."

"Can't I just think about how much I love my best friend?"

"Of course. However," she lifts an index finger, "now is when you should be focusing on getting ready for the party! Let's call Lita in here and get you all gussied up. Guard!"

My guard enters from his post outside my room. "Yes, Lady Rhea?"

Rhea gives a fake cough to indicate that she's waiting for him to address her using the "official title" she gave herself long ago.

He sighs and gives a slight eye roll. "Yes, Lady Rhea; Incredibly Beautiful and Talented Best Friend to the Princess of all Celestia."

Rhea flashes a pleased grin and flips her hair again. "That's better.

Chapter 1

Don't forget to change that last part to Queen after tomorrow though. We require assistance to prepare Her Highness for the coronation ball. Please fetch Lita for us."

He bows and says, "Right away," before flying off.

Once he's gone, Rhea flops down onto my bed, lying on her stomach with her head propped into her hands. "How did the tarts turn out?"

I lean against my vanity and let my head fall back with a groan. "I got too stressed so Lita had the kitchen staff finish them for me."

"Well, I'm sure you did all the hard work. Your stuff's always delicious. I can't wait to try one tonight." She pauses before flashing me a mischievous grin. "Speaking of tonight, have you heard about the sprites that will be attending?"

I tilt my head thinking. "Well, I know we have about three or four of them coming. Although, I'm not aware of what their positions are in Durand."

"Is the Sprite King coming?"

"I'm not sure. If he was, I most likely would have been notified by now."

Rhea starts alternating letting her feet go up and down as her face takes on a look of wonderment. "Well, I sure hope he's there. I heard he's dreamy."

I guffaw at her. "Rhea! Where did you hear such a thing?"

"I'm afraid she heard it from me, Your Highness," says Lita as she flies through the entrance of my room, coming to stand beside me.

"Oh, so you're to blame for putting this nonsense in her head," I say.

"I apologize for gossiping, Your Highness, but I've been hearing rumors about him from the other maids and palace staff all week."

I flop down onto my bed beside Rhea as Lita goes into my closet to fetch gown options for tonight's party.

"What else have you heard?" Rhea asks, impatient with curiosity.

Lita emerges from my closet holding three dresses. "Oh, Lady

Rhea. I'm sorry, but I don't think Her Highness wants me gossiping anymore."

Rhea turns her head quickly to face me with a pleading look. Big eyes, pouty lips, the whole works. I'm defenseless against her tactics.

"I suppose I could allow it just this once. Only to appease Rhea, as I know there's no stopping her until she gets her way."

Rhea grabs my hand in hers and gives it a tight squeeze. "You know me so well," she says, smiling. She then quickly drops my hand and spins back to Lita, demanding, "Now spill, you fairywoman!"

Lita holds up a dress for my consideration. A deep indigo blue gown with long layered material and short sleeves. It's too much. I shake my head and she moves on. "Well," she says, "I heard he has mesmerizing eyes. They say one look and you're a goner."

"A goner in a good way or a bad way?" Rhea asks with wide eyes.

I slowly turn to her with furrowed brows. "You ask the oddest things sometimes."

Lita lets out a small laugh. "I'm not quite sure, but you'd be a goner either way," she says before holding up the second dress. This one is a light pink with swirls of a red, shimmery material that glistens in the sunlight from the open windows of my room. It's pretty. Of that, there's no doubt, but I'm unsure of the color. Pink isn't usually my go-to, and I still feel like tonight requires something with a bit more simplicity. I shake my head.

"More, more!" Rhea chants.

Lita's face takes on a mischievous smirk. "Oh, did I forget the most interesting thing I heard about him?"

Rhea lets out a long groan as I laugh at Lita. "You're enjoying this far too much," I say.

Lita holds up the third dress. Fitted around the chest, it then billows out into a short, yet modest length. Accompanied by two long sleeves of semi-translucent material that hang off the shoulders, the cream satin material carries a heavily regal look. I nod my head, excitedly, which makes Lita smile as she hangs it on the hook beside my vanity.

Rhea throws her head face down into my comforter with another groan. "I fear I may die of unfulfilled curiosity. What a pitiful way to go."

Lita and I share a laugh at her dramatics. "Alright, alright," I say. "Let's hear it. What's the most interesting thing you've heard?"

Lita takes a moment of silence to truly optimize the effect. She then glances towards the entrance of my room before turning back to us with a lowered voice. "He's very muscular *and* tall."

Rhea and I both fall silent to process this. Fairymen are not tall. They're known to even be slightly shorter than most fairywomen. This poses no problem, as height has never truly been one of the main sought-after features of fairyfolk. However, I have heard brief rumors that sprites tend to be taller; some even much taller. As for the muscles, guards are truly the only people of strength in the kingdom. Fairymen tend to average on the slender side since fairies never really engage in hard labor. Our way of life is far too gentle and simple.

"Wow," Rhea finally breathes out.

"Okay, okay, enough gossip. I'm done wasting energy on silly sprite talk. I need to look perfect for tonight," I say, rising and going to sit in the chair of my vanity.

"And you will, Your Highness. The kingdom will be in awe of their new Queen," Lita says, reassuringly.

I hope so, I think to myself.

"While I arguably already look fantastic, I suppose I should go get gussied up as well," Rhea says, dragging herself off my bed. She turns back to yell, "Tonight's going to be magical," before she turns and flies out of my room.

As Lita does my hair, I do my best to not let my anxious inner thoughts take over. I have known this night would come since I was just a wee child. It's foolish to be so stressed about something so long awaited. Why am I bothered with nerves over tonight's festivities anyway? Tomorrow's ceremony is the main event. If anything, *that* is what should be the cause of my jitters.

Perhaps it's because I know that tonight's event will be more personal. More conversation, laughter, dancing, and fellowship to be had. The conversation usually worries me as it's laced with so much pressure. Every comment, every sentence, and every word I breathe must portray the strength and conviction of a new ruler.

I created my tarts to have the perfect, casual conversation starter. I'll ask if they've tried them yet, explain that I made them, and then let the lingo take its natural course. With all of my incredibly precise ingredients, I'm positive that they've turned out delicious. I allow my tense shoulders to fall with the release of a breath I didn't quite realize I was holding. All I have to do now is look perfect, charm the representatives from the sprite kingdom, and make my mother proud.

How hard can that be?

Chapter 2

I hear the distant sound of laughter mixed with music and clinking glasses as I make my way to the party. Wearing the satin gown I selected earlier, I've paired it with a pair of gold flats that have silk straps lacing up my legs to the top of my kneecaps. My long flaming hair has been pulled back and tied into a loose braid that trails halfway down the length of my back. Small gold-painted leaves have been woven into the braid like ivy that perfectly matches the small golden vines that twist and twine from my lobes up to the peaks of my ears. I feel confident and gorgeous. Lita has practically rendered me ethereal. Both my excitement and nerves are ever-growing as I enter.

The great courtyard has always been one of my favorite places in the palace, but I think it never looks more beautiful than it does at night. Overlooking the liveliest area of the kingdom and covered overhead by dazzling stars and constellations, the regular flora and fauna of the courtyard are now intertwined with tables and chairs of varying colors. Each table has a lace tablecloth over it accompanied by tall, regal-looking centerpieces of baby's breath, peonies, and forget-me-nots. Rose petals of all different shades have been scattered across the grassy pathways, around the tables, and the vast display of palace delicacies. But at the center of all the festivities lies the round dance floor of ivory-colored tiles. The overcast moonlight makes the already stunning decor seem even more magical.

I'm still absorbing the atmosphere when I feel someone step up behind me and place a hand on my shoulder. "You look lovely, my dear. Every bit as lovely as a future Queen should," my mother says.

I turn to face her and we share a quick embrace. She looks enchanting in a magenta gown with fabric that's been sown into cascading ruffles that run down the length of her figure before billowing out onto the mossy grass of the courtyard. The top of the gown gathers all the fabric toward her neck in a halter design, which perfectly complements the low bun that her hair is gathered into. Her wings, a gold shade similar to mine, glisten in the starlight.

"Thank you, mother," I say, as we both turn to look out upon all of the attendees already settling into a festive collection. "I can't believe this night has already come."

She holds my hand in hers and sighs a deep breath. "I couldn't agree more. Where has time *flown?*" We share a laugh at her clever wordplay before she takes on a more sincere expression and tears begin to bud in the corners of her eyes. "I'm so proud of you, darling." She takes a short, haggard breath before adding, "And your father would have been, too. So, so proud."

I squeeze her hand, trying my best not to allow the tears brimming my own eyes to fall. "Thank you, mother."

Someone from our far left calls to her and she kisses me on the cheek before making her way over.

Immediately, Rhea finds me, flying through the laughing crowd to be by my side. She gives me a quick twirl before striking a pose that looks anything but natural. "Well?"

I laugh, my lips pulled tight in a genuine smile. "You look positively radiant." And it's true. She does. Tonight, she's donning a short dress

Chapter 2

that's tangerine orange. It's sleeveless and fitted around her torso before breaking into a poof of fabric that curls underneath itself to provide an almost bubble-like effect. The top part of the material moves in a thick strap across the back of her shoulder blades leaving a giant open cut out beneath it, emphasizing her beautiful red-toned wings.

She finishes twirling, soaking up my compliment before her mouth falls open in awe. "I'm sorry, but why are we even wasting breath talking about me when you look like that?"

My cheeks shimmer. "You think so? I told Lita to do her very best work. Tonight has to go well and I need to look perfect."

She smiles. "You are the picture of perfection. Now, let's begin making the rounds. I'll be your wingwoman."

We begin gradually making our way across the courtyard, but don't get far before a group quickly approaches us.

"Your Highness," the first fairyman says, "I can't tell you how excited we are to be here. This is a spectacular party."

"Why, thank you. I agree. The palace staff outdid themselves. Their hard work has certainly paid off."

The rest of the group murmurs in agreement before there comes a short lull in the conversation.

"Has anyone tried the lavender tarts yet?" I ask. "I made them myself specifically for this evening."

"Oh," says a fairywoman among us. "I do love a good lavender dessert."

"Then you must go try one. I assure you they're divine." *They have the most precise ingredients*, I want to add.

"Her Highness is the most amazing baker in Celestia," Rhea says, giving them unrealistic expectations I fear.

"Well, then we must try some," says the fairyman.

The group scurries off to the dessert table and I sigh. Thank goodness for those tarts.

Rhea looks at me. "I don't know why you put so much pressure on yourself. You're a natural!"

"A natural?" I ask. "That anecdote about the tarts was entirely planned. I'm afraid there was hardly anything natural about that."

* * *

I don't understand how the orchestra is still playing so lively after so many hours. Their fingers surely must be raw by now. Rhea left my side about an hour in to allow me to make the rest of the rounds myself and the rehearsed, mechanical conversations have been immensely draining.

I can't pretend to ignore the fact that I'm well aware not everyone in Celestia is excited for me to take over as Queen. It's understandable. My mother truly has been the perfect ruler. The people adore her. Due to that fact, they are apprehensive about whether I can adequately fill her role.

That doubt constantly weighs on me; pushing me to be and do better. Aiming for the best in all my conversational efforts tonight has been exhausting. I'm so quick to answer exactly as I ought to. I even go as far as to ensure that my posture, tone, and demeanor are all adequate. I feel like every time I simply converse with someone, it's some kind of test.

Sometimes I hear myself and wonder if that's me speaking. Every response sounds so premeditated. I often wonder what it would be like to speak openly and honestly; and let people know me.

The thought of speaking honestly makes me think of my encounter about an hour ago with two of the sprite representatives from Durand. They stuck out like sore thumbs among the crowd with their tall, built figures, pointed ears, and lack of wings. Two male sprites in simple garments, not exactly meeting the formal party attire, muttering and barely touching the food on their plates. I went up to them and introduced myself. They both nodded curtly, acting quite uncomfortable.

"Is something wrong with the food?" I asked.

They exchanged a look before the blonde one on the left spoke up, saying, "Yeah. The food is horrible."

"I beg your pardon?"

"It's true," said the other one. "It's all *so* sweet."

"Fairies love all things sugary. Our culture includes sweets as a sign of celebration," I attempted to explain. "So, at fancy events, it is customary to have plenty of desserts."

They both groaned.

I spotted Rhea a short distance away and tried to give her a pleading look in my eyes. She ran over immediately.

"Hello, spritemen!"

"Whoa," said the blonde one, gawking at Rhea as he eyed her from top to bottom. "*Hot.*"

"What the—" Rhea started before I quickly grabbed her arm and started hauling her away.

"Please excuse us. I hear someone desperately calling us over, but it was so nice to meet you both," I half-called back to them as we made our quick escape.

Once around a nearby tree, Rhea turned to me and said, "Wow. So, those are spritemen."

"Correct," I said. "About as ill-mannered as one could expect. But at least now, we've made our dutiful 'small talk' and can avoid them the rest of the evening."

"True."

Rhea then left to go speak to someone she knew and that was how I ended up here to finally catch my breath.

Sitting in my chair now, it occurs to me that I haven't tried one of my lavender tarts yet. I make my way from my chair over to the dessert table, passing groups of laughing fairyfolk and couples spinning across the dance floor. I graze the table, walking the length of it, taking in the array of sweets. Pomegranate caramels, moon spell pies, candied tangerines, and more make up the beautiful spread. While they all look delicious, they're not what I'm searching for.

Suddenly, I see the gold tray up ahead with only one remaining tart. I smile to myself, so pleased that there is one left for me to try. It must be fate.

I'm so concentrated on the tart that I don't even notice the man across the table from me, who reaches for it at the same moment, until our hands graze.

"Pardon me," I say, as I quickly pull my hand back.

"No problem," he says, taking the tart off the tray.

I lift my face to meet his in surprise, only to realize how towering he is.

Standing almost a whole foot taller than me, I almost strain my neck looking at him. A spriteman, surely, based on the lack of wings and exaggerated height. Dressed in a sage-colored, shirt with long sleeves that bulge from the muscles beneath, and wearing dark brown pants, he sticks out like a twig among the flowers in the colorful courtyard. Tan and long, his face ends in a sharp jaw. His black hair is cut shorter on the sides and longer on the top, making the image of him look very low-maintenance. As if his appearance takes simply no effort and you can jolt him out of bed when the moon is still high and he'll appear just the same. He turns his head, gazing at the tart in his tanned hands which gives me a clear view of one of his pointed ears.

I clear my throat and when he turns his eyes to mine I feel like all the air in my lungs suddenly disappears. It's like staring into nothing, but yet everything, all at the same time. The darkest shade of brown

Chapter 2

I've ever seen.

Finally, after a quick second, my air returns. "Excuse me, but a true gentleman would allow the lady the pleasure of the last tart."

"Oh," he says, "is that so?"

I nod, smiling politely. The poor sprite just doesn't know his manners.

"Too bad I'm no gentleman," he says, his lips pulling thin into a grin one could only call devilish since it makes you feel like you need to keep your whims about you, or else they might vanish at any given moment.

The nerve of this man. As if not being gentlemanly is something to brag about. He should be embarrassed by the fact. "If you're no gentleman, then what are you doing at a palace event?"

"I was invited," he says, matter-of-factly.

"Is that so?"

"Yes," he says, before pausing and using his free hand to stroke his strong jaw. "Or did I sneak in?" His hand drops back down to his side as he once again meets my eyes with a mischievous look. "I can't remember exactly."

My mind immediately starts filling with all the possible scenarios in which he would be able to sneak into the party without being detected. But then all thoughts flee my mind as he begins to eat the tart.

He's looking straight at me; right into my eyes now as he takes a second bite.

I fear my blood may begin to boil from the audacity.

We maintain this intense eye contact in utter silence until he finishes his last bite. It's only when he starts to lick the remaining crumbs off his fingers that I avert my gaze momentarily; overcome with rage.

"How is it?" I can't help but ask since he ruined the one chance I had at finding out for myself.

"Delicious," he says. "Such a shame you weren't able to try one."

I turn back to face him. "I made them," I say, proudly, crossing my arms across my chest.

I take such pleasure in seeing his pompous expression stagger for a brief moment before he regains his arrogant demeanor. "Did I say delicious? They're actually quite bland. I was just trying to be polite."

I peer into him. "Why would you bother being polite? You're no gentleman, remember?"

With that, I quickly turn and walk away at a brisk pace, swearing off sprites for all eternity.

Chapter 3

I'm fuming so much that I fear actual smoke is being produced from my nostrils as I storm off. The nerve of him! I groan. I tried my best to remain calm and polite, but after his comment about my tarts being bland, I sort of threw all of that out the window.

Stupid, *stupid* sprites. The whole lot of them. I hate them. And not in the way that I hate other things; like when I stub my toe or get a sliver. Oh, no. This is a newly unlocked level of hatred unlike anything before. For him to speak to me that way- to me! The *Princess*! He clearly isn't in any sort of high position in Durand with that lack of respect and decorum. It's too bad I never did get to meet the Sprite King tonight because then I would have had the chance to tell him myself how incredibly undignified his court is. I'm sure we'd bond over it and then swap our stories of dealing with that unruly sprite.

I see Lita bringing out a vase of flowers to a nearby table and scurry over to her.

"Forget everything you were told," I say, crossing my arms over my chest as I lean back against the table.

Lita sets the vase down before turning to me with a puzzled expression. "About what, Your Highness?"

I flail my arms out in a messy circle. "About sprites! They're rotten; the whole lot of them. I don't know who exactly told you sprites were such a catch, but they couldn't have been further from the truth. First, I met two of them. They were awkwardly picking at their food and blatantly told me it was all too sweet. Incredibly rude. Then, Rhea came over to try and save me only for one of the sprites to gawk at her and utter the word 'hot' before I pretended someone was calling me away just so Rhea and I could escape."

Lita's mouth falls open slightly. "Wow," she says. "That's bad."

"Oh," I say, almost laughing with disbelief that I even have this experience to recount. "That was nothing. The third sprite was supremely worse than the prior two. Remember the lavender tarts I made specifically for tonight?"

She nods.

"Well, after many polite introductions and such, I realized I hadn't had the chance yet to try my tarts to see how they turned out. I went to the dessert table and saw that there was only one left."

"Oh, how perfect that one was left for you to try!"

"That's what I thought, too!" I exclaim, exasperated. "But then, when I went to reach for the tart, this spriteman was suddenly there and he took it! Even after it was perfectly clear that I was already reaching for it!"

"Well, that's not very gentlemanly of him."

"I know!" I let out a groan, happy that Lita understands exactly where I'm coming from. "I told him it wasn't gentlemanly and he said he's no gentleman. He then proceeded to eat the tart in front of me, incredibly and purposefully slowly, only to tell me that it was bland. Were they really bland, Lita? If so, I'll have to hide from embarrassment since I recommended them to a multitude of fairies tonight."

Lita's face takes on an apologetic expression. "I'm sorry, Your

Highness, but I've been so busy working tonight that I haven't had the chance to try one."

It suddenly hits me how inconsiderate I'm being. I place my hand on her shoulder and let out a small sigh. "Of course. I'm sorry, Lita. Here you are trying to work and I'm ranting to you about a rude sprite and lavender tarts."

"No need to apologize at all, Your Highness. I'm honestly disappointed I wasn't able to try your tarts. Your desserts are always delicious. I still have dreams about the candied lemon drops you made for me for my birthday last year," she says with a light giggle.

I smile. "Well, then I promise I will make them again for you."

Her face lights up. "Really?"

"Of course," I say. "You do so much for me. It's the least I can do."

"Thank you, Your Highness." She says, right as Rhea quickly flies over to stand beside us.

"Wait, what's happening? You two look like you're dishing something dirty over here," Rhea says, upset at the thought that she's been left out of fresh gossip.

"Her Highness has been having an unfortunate evening sprite-wise," Lita says with a slightly cringed expression.

Rhea rolls her eyes. "Ugh, don't remind me of those two."

"They don't even come close to the sprite I met at the dessert table," I say with a huff.

Rhea's eyebrow rises inquisitively. "Go on."

Lita dips her head at me before making her exit to continue her work.

Rhea leans back against the table beside me, surveying the party, as I recount my tale to her.

"Wow," she says, dumbfounded, once I finish. "Well, first off, I tried your tarts and thought they were divine so don't believe a word he says. Secondly, he sounds dreadful. Where is he? Point him out for me. I wanna know who I gotta pounce."

My eyes scan the crowd before I see him speaking to the other two sprites near the dance floor; probably collectively complaining about the food some more. "There he is. The one in the sage shirt."

Rhea's eyes land on him and go wide. "Um, yeah. I'll gladly pounce on him."

"Rhea!" I smack her arm. "Did you not listen to a word I said? He's practically horrid!"

"Yes, but he looks horridly *handsome*," Rhea says, gawking ridiculously. "I'll never be able to look at a fairyman the same ever again."

"You're ridiculous," I huff.

"You're being ridiculously *blind*," Rhea says. She grabs my shoulders, giving me a slightly jarring shake. "Wake up and smell the petunias, Luna. That right there is a *masterpiece*. The muscles, that height, those eyes."

I gaze at him as she trails on beside me, her voice tuning out till it's somewhat of a murmur in the background. The moonlight is giving the top of his black hair an almost blueish tint as he turns and explains something to the other two sprites. His face is animated as he talks, gesturing towards the courtyard doors, no doubt planning their escape. I suppose you could say he's handsome, but what good is that when he acts like such an ill-mannered snob?

"Looks go to complete waste when he opens his mouth," I say, assuredly.

"What a shame," Rhea says just as the musical group starts a new song, signaling that it's time for "Gaiety," the traditional fairyfolk dance that I am required to participate in.

"Ugh, let's go," I say to Rhea. I straighten my posture, plaster on my best Princess smile, and we make our way over to the dance floor.

Gaiety is a dance that goes back as far as the tales of fairyfolk are told. It's a dance of merriment, and not too complicated of steps, involving a graceful melody that is interspersed with bursts of lively harmonies at which time each fairyman must rotate around the sphere of dancers to a different partner as the ladies twirl in place. The tune is composed mainly of harps, violins, and flutes.

A fairyman finds his place before me as the music begins. He is about my height and sporting an almost blindingly yellow suit jacket. He seems to know the dance well at first, his hands respectfully on my waist, leading; acting as a shadow of my steps. Although, the beads of sweat on his forehead indicate that it's a struggle for him. His concentration is keeping him silent as we dance aside from the occasional "One, two, three. One, two, three," that he mutters.

The harmony erupts, signaling the time to swap. I spin around as he moves on, finally stopping as I face my new partner.

Him.

He sees that it's me and lets out a groan; his dark eyes rolling back into his head.

"Are you alright?" I ask, glaring.

"Oh, yes. It's nothing," he says, playing off his initial reaction. "Just some tart left in my teeth from earlier."

I let out a burst of exasperated air at his insolent response.

He moves forward to begin dancing with me and I take a step back, unwilling.

He looks to each side before leaning in slightly towards me with a lowered voice. "I do believe I overheard that it is customary for the royal family to partake in Gaiety. It'd be such a shame for you to bow out now with so many people watching."

I curse whoever originally developed that custom with a huff. I will myself to breathe slowly and maintain my smile, knowing that, unfortunately, he's right.

I flash him my best fake grin and step back up in front of him. He gazes down at me from his towering height and I swear I hear him hold his breath as his hands reach out, landing on my waist, before he then pulls me the rest of the remaining distance into him. My breath catches at the realization that his hands are so large that they cover a sizable span of the fabric of my gown, his fingers curling slightly around my lower back. My breaths suddenly feel ragged and I force the air to smooth.

I hold my arms high above my head and begin flourishing them about in their choreographed movements as he spins me slowly, his fingers tracing along the soft satin of my dress. I try not to focus on the heat of my skin that I feel there under his touch. When I'm finished turning, we fall back into the simpler steps of the dance. Of course, just as I'm hoping we'll finish our whole turn of the dance in silence, he speaks.

"I was actually quite impressed with your baking skills," he says not meeting my eyes; instead peering clear over my head with his neck straight. My face is level with his chest, the top of my head ending slightly under his jaw. I can feel his breath grazing over the top of my hair.

"Is that so?" I ask, trying not to give away any hopefulness in my tone.

"Oh, yes. I never knew that someone could take all the flavor out of a dessert, yet still maintain that odd mealy texture. Truly astonishing. I assure you everyone will be hearing about these tarts back in Durand."

I step on his foot.

"Ow!"

"Oops, clumsy me," I say, playing off what was deliberate as accidental.

"They'll be hearing about that, too," he adds, under his breath, just loud enough for me to catch.

"I could care less what you sprites think of me."

"You sprites? Wow, Your Highness. You're too kind," he says, dryly.

"You don't deserve my kindness," I say, matching his tone.

"All because I'm a sprite, I suppose. You shouldn't judge, Your Highness. It's quite unbecoming."

I scoff. "I am perfectly allowed to judge based on actions and your actions, sir, have not well-portrayed your character in the slightest."

"Likewise," he says, plainly.

"Excuse me?"

"You're excused."

I huff, irritated.

"You hate that you're so easily read?" he asks tilting his head down at me with a mocking smirk.

"I am not easily read," I say, determinedly.

"Is that so? So, you're not some privileged Princess that acts perfect all the time, and the fairy people don't adore and worship you even though you were gifted this role by birth rather than having to earn it?"

I'm thrown aback at his words but decide not to let him see how much he's shaken me. "I don't act perfect. I am perfect," I say, tipping my chin slightly towards the sky.

He scoffs, rolling his eyes.

I don't know what comes over me and propels me to add, "And the majority of fairyfolk don't worship or adore me."

He looks down and we lock eyes for just a brief moment. I wait for him to inquire further into my remark, but I'm grateful when he doesn't.

When the silence starts to border on palpable, I speak. "It's quite unfair of you to hold my birthright as Princess against me. After all, it's how all rulers assume the throne."

He makes a tsk sound. "Maybe in Celestia, Your Highness, but not in Durand. Sprites respect a position that is earned more than simply handed down."

"Simply handed down?" I repeat with a tone of question. "I assure you the process has been anything but simple. My whole life has been spent in training so that I may develop the proper makings of a Queen."

"And do you feel ready to be Queen now?"

His question surprises me and I hesitate. "I—" I begin to speak, but then stop when I realize that I can't say for certain. After all this time, I still feel unsure of myself. Years of training, and at my core, I still feel incapable. Tears brim my eyes and I decide not to give him the satisfaction of seeing them fall.

"Excuse me," I say, before quickly darting away. I notice the turns of people's heads in my direction as I pass them, but I don't care. I'd rather have them see me leave than cry. I fly up and out the courtyard doors back into the halls of the palace. Thankfully, the ongoing party has drawn everyone outside, leaving me some solitude. I turn around the corner of the hall of portraits and slump to the floor; the tile cold against the knees of my skin. It's only then that I allow the tears to fall.

They start slow. A first and then a second tear fall down my cheek before the flow becomes a fountain of my sorrow. I pull my knees to my chest and bury my head in my hands. Squeezing my eyes shut, I will the tears to cease. My breaths are staggered and keep catching deep in my throat.

I've been trained to be Queen my whole life. How do I *still* not feel ready? What more could my mother and the palace tutors have done to prepare me? I feel all of the doubt of the people in the kingdom fall onto me, atop the heaviness I already feel from tonight, and it becomes too much.

My chest feels constricted like my lungs are trapped in a firm grasp that can't be loosened. I begin to gasp for air, my heartbeat feeling too fast to keep up with. I force myself to feel the tile with my fingertips, smell the stale air of the hallway, and close my eyes. Focusing on the different sensations helps, and before I know it, my heartbeat returns to normal.

When I open my eyes, I notice that one of the frames on the wall in front of me is slightly crooked. Even though I'm still enduring the lingering sensation of my emotional panic, I can't leave it be. I stand and make my way to the portrait. I breathe my first full breath in a good few minutes once it's straightened. I step back and peer at the painting. It's of Celestia. A low-cast sun spills a golden light across the kingdom with flying fairies frozen in moments of conversation and laughter. The portrait truly brings the beauty of Celestia to life—my beautiful, beautiful kingdom.

The colorful, lush landscape is filled with crystals and plants while giant mushrooms are scattered about with spotted tops and rainbow underbellies. Vibrant, evergreen treetops spring upwards as if reaching for the sky with vine-covered bridges connecting the various tree limbs in arches. Circular fairy homes dangle down, suspended from the treetops, with stained glass windows depicting the flower attributed to each family's lineage. But below it all, the illuminated river lives; glowing as if bathed in by a million lightning bugs. Its turquoise hue pulses like the sparkling heart of the land.

A few straggling tears fall and I wipe them away with the back of my hand and tilt my chin upward. This is the kingdom my family line has cared for. The smiles of the people in this portrait and the beauty of the land exist because my family sacrificed their lives to care for all the fairyfolk and prioritize the good of the people.

The people may not think I'm ready, but I suppose I'll just have to be.

* * *

As I enter the courtyard once again, I take a deep breath in an attempt to center myself. Rhea finds me, grabbing my arm gently as she approaches.

"Hey," she says, happily, before taking in my face and asking, "Are you okay?"

"So, I do look like I've been crying. Great," I say with a sigh.

Rhea tugs me slightly over towards the corner of the courtyard so we're not so surrounded by other wandering fairyfolk. "Why were you crying?" she asks, sincerely, before her face suddenly becomes pinched with anger and she adds, "Was it that sprite again? I don't care if he's handsome. I'll kick his ass!" She turns and immediately starts scanning the room for him while taking off her earrings. "Here! Hold these."

I grab her wrist gently and turn her back to face me. "No, no, no," I start, but then stop when I remember this did involve him to some degree. "Well, I wasn't crying because of him specifically, but something he said just really got to me."

She stalls amidst taking off her second earring, looking borderline disappointed. "I don't need to kick his ass?"

I chuckle slightly. "No. Not yet at least, but I appreciate your willingness."

"Of course," she replies, putting her earrings back on now. "What did he say to you?"

I consider telling her about his question and not feeling ready to be Queen, but even thinking back on it now makes me feel the same weight of that insecurity and pressure. I don't want to allow myself to get all worked up again, so I decide to do my best to move on and not let it continue to spoil my evening. This is supposed to be a happy time after all.

"Nothing worth rehashing. You know. Just stupid sprite stuff," I say. Rhea gives me a look that says she knows it was something bad if it

Chapter 3

made me cry, but that she can tell I don't want to talk about it right now, and will just get it out of me later. It's amazing to have a friend I know so well. Our glances always allow us to speak in silence.

"But you're okay now?" she asks, reaching out to squeeze my hand.

"Yes."

Her eyebrows raise in question. "You promise?"

"I promise."

Suddenly a chorus of clinking glasses begins. Utensils tap the rims of cups all around the courtyard signaling a speech. I turn around with Rhea to where my mother is now standing to address the room. A vision of me in my older years, she looks so regal and confident. Why did she have to make the biggest shoes for me to fill?

She raises her hand gracefully to signal an end to the cacophony of clinks. Once they are fully diminished, she begins.

"Greetings, my people," she starts with a smile. I look at everyone's faces as they watch her; pure adoration in their eyes. "I'm delighted that you were all able to spend this evening with us. Tomorrow is a day long-awaited that calls for much celebration and tonight truly has been magical. Everyone, please join me in a round of applause for our palace staff whose hard work has made tonight so wonderful."

Applause rings aloud as the palace staff scattered across the terrain of the courtyard soak in their moment of recognition. Rhea and I search until we find Lita so that we can face her as we applaud to show our direct thanks. She stands tall and proud with her hands behind her back at the side of the room, beaming. Not only did she work wonders with getting me all pampered earlier for the party, but she's worked during the whole event as well. Her work ethic is something I shall always admire and aspire to achieve myself. I truly must make her those candied lemon drops again very soon.

The applause dies down and we turn back to face my mother.

"By this time tomorrow, Celestia will have its new Queen!" she announces proudly. The slight decrease in the previous amount of cheer does not slip past me and I take a deep breath to steady myself.

I am strong, trained, and in control, I remind myself. *The people will learn to love me. Soon I'll be able to prove myself. I'll show them that I'm good enough.*

I know Rhea has noticed the slight decline in applause, too, when she gives my hand a gentle squeeze.

To most, my mother looks composed and unshaken by the crowd's reaction, but I know her too well. She's noticed, but won't address the negativity and ruin the merriment of the evening. Instead, she opts for positivity and reassurance. "I cannot wait to see my dear daughter ascend the throne," she says confidently, turning until she meets my eyes and flashes me a heartwarming smile. "My sweet darling, it has been truly mesmerizing to see you grow into the beautiful fairywoman you are today. I cannot wait to see what you will accomplish as Queen. I love you, my dear Luna."

Tears bud at the corners of my eyes from her kind and reassuring words and I mouth, "I love you, too," back to her. If all else fails, at least I know that my mother has faith in me and my capabilities as Queen.

"In light of this very special occasion, I can't help but think about those who did not receive the gift of being present for this day." She pauses, taking a deep, steadying breath. "My mate. The love of my life and the object of all my desire and affection." Her light eyes take on a look of both utter happiness and sorrow as she thinks of my father. "Holden was a light unto this universe. Too good for this world, he was taken from it. My spirit cannot wait to join him across the rainbow someday where I know he will be waiting with open arms so I may tell him of joyous times such as this."

I wipe away the warm tears that cascade down my cheeks and even hear Rhea and some others sniffle around me in shared emotion. The

Chapter 3

way my mother speaks of my father is the epitome of love. I'm sure of it, even if I've never experienced it firsthand. I hope to find a mate who I can share those thoughts and feelings with. Someday.

It's been hard and I've hated seeing mother alone all these years without my father. She has never even looked at another fairyman with a morsel of interest. Her heart is forever claimed. Even though their time together was short-lived, she's so lucky to have experienced the kind of love most fairyfolk only dream of finding.

"He will be so proud to hear of you, my darling. I see more of him in you every day," she continues and her words settle into a spot in my heart where I pray they will remain forever, never to be forgotten.

"I also want to take this time to think of Amyra, my dear sister, who was also taken from us far too soon. If it weren't for the tragedy that struck our palace that night long ago, I would not even be standing here as Queen before you today; a place that was supposed to be hers to hold. It's a heart-wrenching shame—" she stops speaking in an instant. A look of shock and disbelief consumes her face.

"That I wasn't able to become Queen?" calls a distant voice in the back. "Why, yes. Yes, it was."

I hear gasps and sounds of shock ring out as people move to make way for someone walking through the crowd. Rhea and I push slightly forward from where we're standing, trying to see, when she suddenly emerges into sight. I feel my hand go ice cold in Rhea's.

It can't be.

Aunt Amyra.

Chapter 4

Complete and utter silence falls over the courtyard as Amyra emerges from the front of the crowd to face my mother. I've spent so much time memorizing the portrait of her and mother in the palace that I would recognize her anywhere; even if her vivid red hair wasn't a dead giveaway to her royal heritage. Her skin is wrinkled and creased in all the places that age tends to wear you down, but her eyes shine in an indication of much life left beneath them. She looks tired. Not in a literal, fatigued sort of way, but her spirit seems expelled as if she's been through truly tasking experiences.

Where has she been?

Her expression is one of complete relief as she lays her eyes on my mother and says, with open arms, "I've returned, sister. Oh, how I've missed you." Her eyes turn watery.

Mother's own eyes begin to tear up as she runs into Amyra's open arms. They hold their embrace. Two sisters, torn apart by fate, finally reunited at last.

They finally pull back from one another and Mother wipes her tears. "In all my wildest dreams, I never imagined—" she starts.

"I know, I know," Amyra says, cutting her off, but reaching out to

Chapter 4

squeeze her hand.

A giant smile consumes my mother's face as she lifts the hand she holds with Amyra into the air before the crowd and announces, "My people! It is time for a truly great celebration. My long-lost sister, Amyra, has returned!"

For the first time since Amyra's grand reappearance, I turn to peer at the crowd to gauge their reaction. It's only then that I realize, they're not reacting.

They're not happy, joyous, or celebrating.

They look *indifferent*.

How can they be so insipid? This is the happiest of days!

Seemingly unphased by the crowd's lack of reaction, Amyra speaks. "It's true," she begins. "I have returned to Celestia!" She tilts her chin up slightly and her eyes turn to slits as she smiles. "And I'm ready to be Queen."

I blink. My breath feels haggard. I must have misheard her.

I am to be Queen. Not her.

Mother's happy face has turned to one of disbelief. She turns to look at Amyra. "To be Queen?"

Amyra lets go of my mother's hand and turns to face her fully. "That's right, sister. I was deprived the chance of the proper timing by that dreadful fire, but I have returned, and I am ready," she proclaims, victoriously, as if this is the answer everyone should so obviously see. "Thank you for taking care of my kingdom, Marigold, but I will take it from here." She turns and faces the onlooking fairies and proclaims, "Are you ready for your true Queen, my people?"

This can't be happening.

"I am to be Queen," I hear myself say, surprised that I have found my voice to speak up.

Aunt Amyra's head spins in my direction and takes on an expression of wonder. "Luna, is that you? You're so grown up."

I try not to think about all of the fairies watching as I speak. "Yes, and my coronation day is tomorrow. We are happy you have returned Aunt Amyra, as we all thought you were lost in the fire, but plans are already in place."

My chest feels tight and I have no clue how I'm finding the courage to speak right now.

Amyra suddenly tilts her head to the right and whispers, "Don't worry. A technicality." She laughs. "Everything will be fine!"

She spins her face back to me and says, "Apologies for crashing your party dear niece, but you're unfit to rule, and I am the true ruler." Her head ticks to one side in a jittered movement. "True ruler, true Queen, true everything. It's all true but untrue."

My blood turns cold and I swear I can feel the chill that runs through the air as we all collectively realize what's happening.

She's hearing *voices*.

"Unfit to rule? My daughter is more than ready. She's been trained—" mother starts in my defense before Amyra cuts her off with a cackling laugh.

"Training or not. Who cares? The people don't *want* her," Amyra spits.

Sweat is beading on my brow as I spin to peer at the fairy folk around me. They all cast their eyes away from mine, some taking small steps backward away from me, confirming Amyra's claims.

"I may have only just returned, sister," Amyra says, "but I picked up on everything quite quickly." She takes a slow step towards Mother, who takes one backwards in turn. "You see, it all just felt a bit too familiar."

Familiar?

Amyra notices my confused expression and turns to my mother with a smile that makes my blood run cold. "Does she not know?" she whispers back behind her to no one, "She hasn't heard!"

Chapter 4

She creeps towards me slowly, the fabric of her long navy gown trailing across the courtyard grass beneath her. Her head tilts to the left. "You and I are the same, dear niece."

I pray to the rainbow that isn't true.

"You see, I was the eldest daughter. I was to be Queen; just like you. Every expectation was put on me. I carried the weight of the kingdom on my back and I was trained to be perfect at everything. I stood tall, I was well-spoken, and I knew all about our culture and diplomacy. I was ready and prepared to be Queen. I could feel it in my blood. I was—" she stops, muttering under her breath quietly, "in my prime."

She peers back up at me. "But was it enough?" She throws her head back, laughing so maniacally that Rhea and everyone around me takes a few steps back. She meets my eyes again and her expression is crazed. "No! It wasn't. The kingdom had me, prepped to perfection and willing to sacrifice my whole life for their goodwill, and what happened? They didn't *want* me."

Amyra turns and points a crooked finger toward mother with a look of rage. "They only wanted *her*." She spins towards the crowd and begins pacing in front of them. "You insolent fools had a Queen standing in front of you, but you never saw me. You never saw the potential of what I could do; the kind of ruler I could be. You only looked right past me. I knew it." She groans. "I felt it every day. No one cared for me. You only praised *her*!"

She screams suddenly; a piercing, ear-deafening screech that catches us all off guard as we rush to cover our ears. "When that fire happened and I escaped, I was just outside the kingdom." She whispers to imaginary companions, "I was so close. They didn't look. They didn't look for me. If they had, they would have found me. I was so close. So close!"

She whips her head back up and meets my mother's eyes. "Too hurt to travel back on my own, I waited two nights for all of you to find me and bring me back."

She turns to me at a rapid speed. "I thought they would be so happy to see me return safely. Then they'd want me as Queen! Then they'd appreciate me! Then I'd be good enough." She mutters to herself, "But no. Instead, on the morning of the third day, I heard the coronation bells ringing. Signaling that my younger sister had been crowned and I had already been forgotten. I thought I'd spend my life away. Give the kingdom what it wanted. But one day, a thought occurred to me."

She suddenly comes up in front of my face; so close that I can feel the heat of her breath. Her eyes look wild and send shivers down my spine. It takes all of my self-control not to pull back away from her. "I still wanted to be Queen," she spits at me. "I wasted my whole childhood on it. It was all I had. So, I decided to come back and take what's *mine*."

She walks over, grabs the glass out of the hand of the person nearest to her in the crowd, and downs its contents in a single swig, before shattering the glass in her hand. I flinch at the sight of the glass shards now piercing the palm of her skin; blood dripping red onto the mossy ground. She peers at the blood, unphased.

"Oops," she says, with a chuckle. She turns, noticing our shocked faces. She makes eye contact with me and slowly closes her fist tight. More blood gushes out from the glass now running deeper through the tissue of her hand and I feel like I might vomit at the sight. "I feel *nothing*," she says, smiling madly.

Suddenly, Amyra turns towards mother. "Give me my throne! It was never supposed to be yours. Celestia is mine. If you won't hand it over, I'll take it myself!" She screams before suddenly lunging at mother, arms out in front of her, aiming for the throat.

I gasp.

It all happens so fast.

I begin running towards mother, having no idea what I will do, but

Chapter 4

just knowing I need to get to her. I'm not quick enough, but the guard is. I watch as he runs from nearby, placing himself between mother and Amyra. I watch as Amyra's hands wrap around his neck. Her fingertips turn black and something unspeakable happens.

He begins to *wither*.

As soon as Amyra's black-rimmed fingertips are on him, his entire being begins to wrinkle and crease. His eyes roll back as his body falls from her hands to the floor where he writhes until he has completely shrunk in on himself. I hear people screaming. I see them running in scattered directions in my peripheral, but I can't look away. I watch as the guard's skin turns ashen. I watch as blood begins to trickle from his nose. I watch as he turns frigid and the life leaves him till he's left looking like nothing more than the shedded skin of the fairyman that once was.

"It works. It worked. It's working," Amyra mutters to herself, running her hands down her face, smearing the blood from her palm like paint splattered across her crazed expression.

Mother looks frightened beyond belief staring down at the sight of the guard, her face a sheet of white.

Amyra turns towards me, bloody and wild. "Now for you, dear niece."

She lunges towards me so fast that I barely have time to begin moving away backward from her. I crouch and place my arms above me in an attempt to shield myself. I'm braced for impact when I feel a shadow cast over me suddenly. It's only when the body falls, withering into itself, and I have to slide it off of my back and onto the ground that I realize it's Lita.

"No! *No!*" I scream as I begin sobbing uncontrollably. Not Lita. Not dear, sweet, innocent, hard-working Lita. Not the Lita who only did good; who only yearned for good. *No. No. No.* I wrap my arms around her body trying to steady her, but she continues to writhe;

fighting uncontrollably against me. I cry as I hold her and watch her spirit fade.

"Lita!" I cry. *"Lita!"*

She'll never get the lemon drops like she hoped. She'll never get anything out of life now that she hoped for. The limpness of her delicate figure tells me her spirit has left her and I fear my heart may crack and splinter into a thousand shattered pieces.

I thought I was sobbing before, but it's nothing compared to the unbridled cries that escape me now. Holding Lita's cold, shriveled body, I whip my head to Amyra. "What have you done?" I cry, demanding. "What is this?"

Amyra cackles. "It's withering, dear," she says, proudly. "The dark power of withdrawing all the life from something till it's nothing more than a frigid shell. Now that you have seen what I am capable of, do not hesitate again to give me my crown. It is not one touch and done, girl. It is everything according to my bidding and control. I can take it all or I can take just enough."

My mind is aching with the struggle of trying to comprehend what's going on. How is this happening? None of this makes any sense. How can she do this? With Lita's cold frame still in my arms, I rotate my head around, trying to find my mother. Through the panicked fairies desperately flying about in an attempt to escape, I see her over in the corner behind some guards. Tears stream down her face as we lock eyes.

"Run," she mouths once to me, but I can't move. I'm frozen in my fear. I can't run without her. Mother's face turns more urgent when Amyra spins and begins heading in her direction. The guards turn to try and rush mother out of the courtyard.

"Run, Luna!" Mother screams now. Flying fairies block my view of her as she's taken out of the courtyard, Amyra hot on her tail.

I can't run. I can't leave Lita. I can't leave my mother; my home.

Chapter 4

Not with Amyra loose in the palace to take even more innocent lives. I feel a set of hands begin to pry me from where I'm wrapped around Lita. "No!" I cry, fighting. "I can't run! I can't leave her!" Even as I say it, I'm not sure if I mean my mother or Lita. I suppose I mean them both.

"Luna, you have to come with me! Please!"

I twist my head and see that it's Rhea. Still tugging at my arms, her head is darting all around the room on the lookout for more danger. When she turns back to me, her voice takes on a commanding tone that I didn't even know she was capable of. "Luna, come with me. *Now!*" It's the urgency in her voice that manages to shake me out of my shocked state and regain the use of my extremities.

I gently remove my arms from around Lita, still crying, and bend down quickly to give her a quick kiss on her forehead. *I'll never forget you. I'm so sorry*, I say in my mind as a message to her lost spirit. I make a vow to see her over the rainbow someday.

I stand and turn to Rhea. "I'm ready," I say, having to shout now for her to hear me over the panicked mayhem of the palace. She nods, grabbing my hand in hers and taking flight. "Fly as fast as you possibly can!" she yells.

And I do.

Chapter 5

Rhea and I fly through the palace at a dash I didn't even know was possible; the adrenaline unlocking new speeds. Fairies are flying everywhere in a panicked state of mayhem. Screams blur in the background as we do our best to zig-zag our way through the palace halls. I search for my mother as we go, praying that I'll spot her somewhere, but I never do. I count two or three more shriveled bodies scattered on the floor of the palace as we fly and will my stomach not to heave up all its contents. Rhea has a firm grip on my hand and directs me. I have no clue where she's taking me, but I trust that she must have some sort of plan since she's flying with such a sense of direction.

"Down here," Rhea says, suddenly jerking us down to the floor and pulling me over to the nearby wall. She begins to shove a wooden table away from its current placement. Seeing her struggle, I jump to her aid and together we move it out of the way. She quickly throws back the rug that had been underneath it, revealing a thick slab of wood in the center of the tile floor with a round handle. Rhea grabs the ring-shaped latch and pulls upwards, opening a small square that drops down into darkness.

Chapter 5

I don't even have time to register my surprise at the hidden space before she spins, motioning me in with her arm. "Get in. Hurry!"

I quickly get on my knees and then proceed to lower myself down through the square's dark entrance. I let go once my feet touch the floor beneath and Rhea then climbs down herself, closing the entrance's wooden door as she descends. Once we're both inside, immersed in the darkness, Rhea twists the inner circular latch of the slab till she hears a click. She breathes a heavy sigh. "There. It's locked."

We both take a moment to slow our quickened breaths, but the faint sound of screams from above us prevents me from fully calming down. The total darkness gives me no indication as to where I am. However, I am still fully confident that I would rather be here than anywhere above us.

"What is this place?"

Rhea is still panting heavily as she answers. "It's a secret tunnel. Your mother told me of it in case you were ever in danger."

The mention of my mother makes my heart ache.

"There's a handful of them hidden throughout the palace, but this is the only one I could remember in my panic," Rhea continues. "All of them lead somewhere outside the kingdom, but I can't remember where specifically this one leads. I'm sorry."

I reach my hands out into the dark until I feel her and I pull her into me, holding her close. She wraps her arms around me. "Don't you dare apologize," I tell her. "Your quick thinking saved us. I can't thank you enough."

She gives me a quick squeeze before drawing back. "It's too dark to see, but I can push my arms out and feel the sides of the walls. It's a pretty confined space; no room for flying. And since I don't remember where this tunnel leads out, I don't know the distance it might take to get to the exit," she says, sounding apologetic at her uncertainty.

"That's fine," I say. "Let's just get out of here."

She reaches out into the dark and finds my hand. Our fingers intertwine and we do something fairies don't often do.

We walk.

* * *

I feel like we've been walking forever, but at the same time, not long at all. With no way to tell time, the aching on the bottoms of my feet is the only way I know we've already accomplished a decent distance. The tunnel has been at a slight downward angle the majority of our way so far, which only makes the venture even more strenuous. I'm so grateful to Lita for picking out flats for me to wear today as heels would have made walking more uncomfortable.

Lita.

The thought of her conjures up the image of her withered body; nothing left but thin, shrinkled skin on bone. Her small figure was so lifeless in my arms, her spirit drained. It's an image I wish I could erase from my mind, but deep down I know it will stick with me forever. Her good life deserved a better end.

I hear Rhea let out a small sniffle beside me as we continue walking forward in the tunnel.

"Is it Lita?" I ask, softly.

"Yes," she answers back.

"I feel like it's my fault," I say, sadly, tears brimming. "If I had just moved out of the way instead of cowering in place, she never would have jumped in front of me to try and block Amyra. I should have been quicker."

Rhea gives my hand a firm squeeze. "Hey. Don't even think like that. It wasn't your fault. Lita was the one who decided to get involved.

Chapter 5

You didn't make her. It was her decision. And you and I both know she would never want you to blame yourself."

Deep down, I know she's right. "Lita was always so selfless."

"Till the very end," Rhea adds, solemnly.

Suddenly, we collide with a firm wall, letting out cries of both surprise and pain as we fall backward onto the ground.

"What just happened?" Rhea asks, confused and dazed from the sudden impact.

"We hit a wall," I say, reaching up to rub my left eyebrow. Something warm coats my fingertips. "I think I'm bleeding."

Concern rises in Rhea's voice. "Where? How much?"

"Near the end of my left eyebrow and not too much I don't think. I'll be fine. Does the tunnel end here?"

"It can't be a dead end. Maybe it's a divet."

I begin moving about, slowly, trailing my fingertips along the cool stone walls in front of me, until I feel the wall give way to my left. I move around in that direction and breathe an excited sigh when I see the tiniest bit of light emanating from up ahead. "It turns to the left!" I say, grabbing Rhea's arm and dragging her over. "Look! There's a light up ahead!"

Rhea lets out a small gasp when she sees the small dot of light and we both hasten our steps towards it, anxious to escape the dark. I feel my heart get lighter and lighter with each increase in the size of the light as we near it. The light blooms into a full opening and we pass through it into a woodsy clearing. Sighing with relief, we slump down onto the textured ground where we then lay for a good few minutes. I close my eyes, focusing on breathing in and out.

I'm snapped out of my moment when Rhea sits up suddenly and turns to me. Her feet are stretched out straight in front of her and she leans back onto one arm in her bright tangerine dress on the mossy ground as she wipes the sweat from her forehead with her free hand.

"If it's daylight, that means—" she starts.

"We've been walking all night," I say, finishing for her. I sit up, pull my legs into me, and remove my shoes. I'm not surprised at all to find my feet red and aching; the beginning of a blister budding on the back of my right heel. I try to rub the tension out of my feet with my thumbs in circular motions, but it only produces an even greater ache. I look up and find Rhea staring at my feet.

"I'm not even going to look at mine," she says, flatly. "I know they aren't going to be pretty."

She's got a point.

I lean back on my hands and peer up around us, taking in our surroundings. The tunnel juts out of a stoney mountainside into a small clearing with mossy ground and a few scattered trees; a mixture of pine and birch. Wildflowers lay in beautiful patches near the base of the trees and if I lean my head back, I can see a few straggling clouds interrupting the blue of the sky. A part of me feels like the land shouldn't be allowed to look so beautiful on a day so horrific.

"What's our game plan?" Rhea asks. Her hopeful eyes tell me that she's praying I have a plan because she sure doesn't.

I give it some thought. "Well, while I'd love to go back to the palace and wreak havoc on Amyra in every possible way, I know that I have nothing at my disposal that is capable of putting up any sort of fight against her dark gift. I won't be able to go back and help my mother, or my people, unless I have some sort of help."

Rhea scoffs, gesturing to herself with a fling of her wrist.

"Besides you," I say.

Rhea strokes her chin. Her dark skin takes on an almost golden hue from the morning sunlight that streams across the clearing as her face suddenly grows into an enlivened expression and she points her index finger up towards the sky. "I know! Let's go ask the Sprite King for help."

Chapter 5

My mind recoils at her suggestion, recalling all of my awful encounters with sprites so far. Their lack of decorum, bluntness of speech, and complete inability to act civil all come together in my brain to tell me that they offer no form of helpfulness. I open my mouth to tell Rhea this, but then stop. Perhaps the Sprite King is different. Perhaps he has the manners and decorum that his subjects lack. I have yet to meet a royal who doesn't meet the standards of their station. However, the sprites and fairies have been estranged ever since that fire long ago. Would he even be willing to help me?

"Alright," I say. "We can try going to Durand. Hopefully, the Sprite King is nothing like his representatives we've met so far and won't mind helping the soon-to-be ruler of a kingdom estranged from his own."

Rhea nods, happily; excited that I like her suggestion and she has been useful in some way to our cause.

A thought occurs to me. "Although, perhaps I can use the fact that I am soon to be Queen to my advantage in bargaining for his aid. I can't promise that fairies and sprites would fully make amends, but I could hint that if he were to help me, I, the future Queen of Celestia, would be very, very grateful to him and would remember his kindness."

"That sounds perfect!" Rhea says, standing now. "I'm sure he'll be willing to help in some way. If there's anyone who can convince him, it's you. Now, how do we get to Durand from here?"

I rotate my gaze, slowly surveying our surroundings once more. I try to conjure up the last time I looked at a map of the kingdom in my mind. "Based on the lightly scattered trees, I think we're on the far left side of the kingdom's outskirts. If we keep walking this way, we should reach a portion of the glowing river."

"Then we just follow the river to Durand! Great plan. Let's fly," she says, standing and grabbing my hand to hoist me up.

We take flight, but make sure to stay low to the ground, so as not to be seen, since we have no clue where Amyra is, or if she has anyone working with her who might be looking for us. It feels so good to use my wings and give my feet a break after all that walking.

After a decent amount of flying, a view of the glowing water begins to peak through the scattered trees. We drop down to our feet beside it and I crouch to dip my fingers into the illuminated, moving current.

"You can touch it, sweetheart. It won't hurt you. Don't be afraid," my mother said to me when I was small and she first brought me to the river's edge. I had been scared to touch the water and she was very patient with me.

"Why does it glow?" I demanded to know, my little face and baby wings peering up at her intently as I squeezed her pinkie finger with my whole hand. "Why does it do that?"

My mother sunk to a sitting position along the side of the river and pulled up her long dress. She sunk her feet into the glowing pool before turning to me with a smile.

"See? Nothing to be afraid of," she said, wiggling her toes for emphasis. "It feels good! Come join me."

She held her hand out in invitation, but I hesitated. It took turning and peering at her toes, confirming that they were still safe in the water, for me to allow her to pull me over. I sat beside her and pulled off my shoes. Holding my little legs straight out across the top of the water, I turned to her for one last moment of reassurance. Her eyes were full of optimism as she gave me a nod.

"Go on, sweetheart."

I slowly lowered my feet into the glowing current, toes first. I flinched a little as soon as the water touched the tips of my toes and closed my eyes tight before peeking them open again to happily confirm that they were still intact. Feeling a tad less scared then, I proceeded to fully submerge my feet under the water.

"Ha! It doesn't hurt at all!" I giggled, joyfully.

Chapter 5

"I told you it wouldn't!"

"Wasn't I brave, mommy?"

Her eyes and proud smile warmed my heart. "You were so brave, darling."

I think I can feel my heart breaking. I won't let Amyra ruin everything. I will fix it. I don't know exactly how, but I will fix it. I have to.

"Luna? Hello?" Rhea's voice clips me from my thoughts.

I shake my head, regaining my sense of reality as I remove my fingertips from the water. "Sorry. Yeah?"

Rhea tilts her head and puts her hand on her hip. "Girl, I need you to focus here. What's the plan? The river flows down this way," she says, pointing, "for miles before it reaches the sprite kingdom. I've never been there, but from what I've heard, it's kind of a long journey. It'd be a tiring flight."

I sigh, my shoulders slumping. "Well, better a long flight than another long walk, right?"

Now, it's Rhea's turn to sigh. "All I want is a long nap."

I nod, exhausted. "That makes two of us, but we gotta keep moving—" my words halt as I catch sight of something flowing downstream towards us from over Rhea's shoulder.

It's a raft.

Logs laid flat and strapped together with a thick twine-twisted rope make up the base while a single log pole in the center holds a small, white sail at its peak. There's a spriteman standing towards the front of the small vessel and using a long wooden oar in his hands to guide the raft downstream. The raft isn't much at all.

But it looks large enough for two extra passengers.

"Excuse me, sir!"

Rhea's head spins behind her to see who I'm addressing.

The spriteman comes up alongside us, riding the stream, and cocks his head at me. It's then that I recognize him. He's the blonde one from the pair of sprites who mocked the food and hit on Rhea at the party. I see him recognize me at the same moment I recognize him and his expression turns sour.

"Rhea, look who it is! It's the lovely spriteman from the party!" I say, emphasizing every word in mock joy. "Weren't you just talking about him?"

His face turns into a smirk as he glances over at Rhea and puffs out his chest, leaning his weight onto the hand at the top of his guiding pole. "Is that so?"

Rhea starts to laugh. "What? No! I was—." It's then that I grab her arm and squeeze it. She looks at me and I do my best to convey with my eyes to play along.

Just trust me.

"I mean, I wasn't talking, so much as rambling!" she says, catching on.

I let out a short laugh and throw an arm around her. "That's right. Couldn't get her to shut up about you! Hey! Since you're here, would you be able to give us a ride down the river?" I ask, tilting my head and flashing my biggest smile.

His proud expression takes on a doubtful look. "I don't know."

"Please?" Rhea asks, batting her lashes. "I'd be very grateful for your help."

This perks his pointed ears right up.

Well done, Rhea.

"I suppose that'd be fine," he says, using the pole to push the raft over alongside the bank.

"Thank you!" Rhea and I both exclaim in unison. We both hop onto the raft. I'm pleased to find that it feels sturdier under my feet than I expected. Maybe it's built better than I had previously thought.

Once we're both onboard, he uses the pole to push away from the bank and set us both on course. He wastes no time in flirting with Rhea. We're all still standing as we make our way downstream and he slides closer to Rhea in front of me, placing his hand on her back. She does her best not to shy away from his touch.

"You know I built this raft myself," he says proudly, clearly trying to impress her, before I notice him trying to slide his hand lower.

"Do you hear that?" I ask quickly, causing his hand to freeze.

Rhea releases a small sigh of relief.

"Hear what?" he asks, dropping his hand, and taking two steps over to where I'm standing now near the back of the raft.

"I think it's coming from under the back of the raft. It sounds bad! You better check it out."

He stands beside me and listens for a moment before growing impatient. "I don't hear anything. Crazy fairy." He rolls his eyes.

"No, really!" I say, urgently. "I think you just have to get closer to hear it. It's coming from right under that last log," I say pointing to the last log strapped in at the back of the raft. "I can hold your pole for you if you want to inspect it. I'd just hate for it to be something really bad since you put in so much hard work making this raft."

He groans and gets on his knees, crouching forward to listen.

"Closer!" I say.

He leans forward slightly more, his ear pressed firmly to the log now.

It's then that I use my foot to tip him over and off of the raft. His yell of surprise becomes quickly overshadowed by the loud splash he makes as he tumbles into the glowing water.

"Go, go, go!" I shout to Rhea as I try to push us further downstream with his guiding pole; knowing our escape needs to be quick.

Rhea looks around the raft, scatterbrained, before spinning back to me with an exasperated face. "What am I supposed to do? You have the only stick!" she yells at me wailing her arms about.

"I don't know! Just something! Anything!" I'm maneuvering the guidepost quite poorly, having never done this before, but after two tries, I finally manage to grasp the way to push it off the river's base and project us forward at a faster speed. It's not fast enough though.

"You stupid fairies! Give me back my raft!" He grabs onto the back of the raft now, trying to pull himself back onboard.

"Oh, no you don't!" Rhea yells as she quickly grabs the guiding post out of my hands before using it to shoo him off the raft. "Off! Off the raft!"

"It's my raft!"

"Not anymore it isn't!" she yells, smacking his hands with the end of the stick now.

"Ow!" he yells when one of her smacks lands straight on his knuckles. He lets go of the raft, flopping back into the water, when suddenly an idea hits me. It just might work.

"Rhea, quick!" I fly to the back of the raft, lowering myself, careful not to get my wings wet, as I begin to use the momentum from my wings to propel the raft faster downstream.

Rhea quickly catches onto my plan, laying the guide post flat on the base of the raft and then using my same winged technique while holding on to the side of the center pole. Together, we successfully accelerate the raft's speed and continue until the spriteman's cries fade into the distance.

Once he's out of sight, we finally relax; slumping down to sitting positions at the base of the raft's center pole. We're both panting, but I can't tell if it's due to the adrenaline of the situation or the physical strain of flying at full speed while also pushing a small vessel.

I'm staring up at the sky peeking through the tall tree tops around us, trying to catch my breath, when Rhea thumps onto her back beside me.

"Did we really just steal a raft?"

Chapter 5

I turn to face her. "I believe we did."

"We stole a raft," she repeats.

"That was bad," I say, a slight hue of guilt settling into where the adrenaline previously was.

"Then why did it feel so, so good," she says, turning to me with a suppressed smirk. Then, suddenly, we're laughing and we just can't seem to stop. We laugh till tears bud in the corners of my eyes and Rhea is curled into herself on her side, clutching her stomach. "Stop! Stop! It hurts!" she gasps through her giggles.

Our laughter diminishes slowly from hysterics to chuckles, and finally to simple smiles.

Rhea sits up and turns towards me with a proud smile. "You were brilliant back there."

I sit up, leaning back on my hands, palms flat against the logs of the raft. "You were great! You went along with everything so well."

"Well, of course. We're like one brain, but it was your quick thinking that got us out of there," she says, giving my shoulder a gentle squeeze.

I feel my cheeks shimmer in reaction to her words. "Well, I'm just glad we are officially on our way to get help." I take a breath before adding, "Sweet sugar, I'm exhausted."

"Me too," Rhea says, chest heaving with a sigh.

"Since we don't know exactly how far down the river Durand is, one of us should stay awake at all times to make sure we don't accidentally travel past it."

"You're right." Her eyes light up. "I know! Let's sleep in shifts," she says excitedly, as if that wasn't already my original idea.

I smile. "Sounds great. Do you want to sleep first—"

"I call the first turn sleeping!" she yells, quickly flopping onto her side, facing away from me as if, once again, that wasn't what I was already going to say.

I can't help but chuckle to myself. "Alright, sweet dreams."

I breathe in deep through my nose and out my mouth as I spin where I'm sitting cross-legged now to face forward off the front of the raft. The water is taking us at a slow, gradual pace down the river. I can feel the soft lull of the current gently rock the raft. Remembering the bash to my head earlier, I lean slightly forward over the edge of the raft, just enough to glimpse my reflection. Sure enough, there's a small gash on my forehead. The small patch of blood has dried just above my left eyebrow. I scoop up a bit of water and use it to clean the small wound.

I don't deserve this. People died today. Innocent people. People like Lita who didn't have a bad bone in them. They lost their lives; their spirits dispelled from their bodies. Yet, somehow I managed to escape with a small gash to the forehead. It seems so unfair.

I lay down on my back and straighten out the length of my body with a stretch. The raft is long enough for most of me, but the tips of my feet still stick off the side. I gaze up at the blue sky ahead.

Rhea's comment about me being brilliant in the heat of the moment with the sprite was flattering, but it doesn't sit right with me. I wasn't brilliant. I was just acting on impulse. I didn't have any real plan. In fact, I don't think I've done a brilliant thing all day. What happened when Amyra showed up and she came for me? Lita jumped in my way because I was too cowardly to run or fight. It was like I went into a state of shock. A part of me always wondered what kind of response I'd have in a scary or dangerous situation. How would I react? Would it be flight or fight?

Well, it turns out it's not flight or fight. It's just fright. It renders me absolutely and positively useless.

If I truly was brilliant like Rhea suggests, then today would have taken a completely different course. I would have acted promptly in response to Amyra's hostility and formulated some kind of plan to apprehend her before the situation could escalate.

Chapter 5

Perhaps then Lita would still be alive.

I gasp and bring my hands up to my face. I hadn't even realized I was digging my fingernails into the palms of my hands; an old bad habit from when I was young. I thought I'd outgrown it.

The crescent moon imprints on my palms say otherwise.

I press my hands flat out at my sides, feeling the rough texture of the logs beneath me. I close my eyes and the sunlight paints my eyelids a hue of cherry red; the sun too bright to block completely.

I pray to the rainbow that the Sprite King will help us. He has to. He's my only hope.

Chapter 6

It's only when the sun's position in the sky has significantly shifted, and I'm barely able to keep my eyes open, that I wake Rhea.

"Rhea," I say, softly, nudging the shoulder of her sleepily sprawled out beside me. "It's time to wake up."

One of her brown eyes pops open before quickly shutting again accompanied by a groan. "It wasn't all a dream then. Fantastic." She lifts her hand and uses the back of it to wipe across her mouth. Her eyes pop open and her face contorts as she registers how much drool she just captured. "*Ew. Gross!*"

I tilt my head towards her with an encouraging smile. "You're not gross."

She throws an arm dramatically over her eyes. "You're right. I think I achieved 'gross' back in that dark tunnel when I got sweaty in places I didn't even know I could and developed blisters on the heels of my feet that while I haven't seen, I'm certain are there. Now, with this amount of drool, I have officially crossed over the line into 'disgusting.'"

I roll my eyes. "The only thing you are is *dramatic*. Can I please take a turn sleeping now?"

"I suppose," she says, sitting up and stretching her arms out above

Chapter 6

her head now.

"Thank you," I breathe with a sigh. "I didn't even know my body was capable of reaching this level of exhaustion."

I lay down flat on my back first before deciding to turn onto my side and curl into myself. I face off the side of the raft, the view of the passing nature fading as I close my eyes. I thought sleep would find me immediately, but it doesn't. Every time I close my eyes, the events of the last 24 hours replay in my mind. Amyra lunging for me, Lita's limp body in my arms, the depth of the darkness in that tunnel, and the thought of my mother. *Is she safe?*

It's only when Rhea absentmindedly begins to hum the melody of an old fairy tune that my anxious thoughts dissipate and I'm able to fall asleep.

* * *

The timer of the oven makes a ding; signaling my tarts are finished baking.

I grab the closest woven cloths from where they're sitting on the counter and use them to carefully remove the tray. I sigh as I inhale their heavenly scent and place each tart onto the cooling rack.

"Those smell divine, Your Highness." Lita's kind face pops around the door of the palace kitchen.

I usher her over. "I'll let you have the first one."

Her smile widens and she walks over, grabbing a tart from the rack in her small hands. She begins to lift it to her mouth, but she hesitates. "Thank you, Your Highness," she says.

"Lita, it's nothing. You've done so much for me. This is just a very small token of my appreciation. Now go on, but be careful. It may be hot," I say, excited to witness her reaction to the tart's delicious flavor.

She lifts the tart to her mouth and takes a small bite before letting out a delighted moan.

I grin proudly. "You like them?"

She takes a second and then a third bite before she answers. "These may be your best tarts yet, Your Highness."

My heart flutters. "Really? Even better than those candied lemon drops I made before that you said you love?"

Lita laughs; a calming twinkle of a sound. "I said the best *tarts*, not dessert entirely. Those candied lemon drops are too good to beat!"

I place a hand on her shoulder as we share a laugh now; the chorus of our giggles echoing down the palace hall.

Suddenly, the tart falls from her hand and she takes a faltering step back with wide eyes.

"Lita?"

She begins to make a gasping noise and her skin begins to crease and wrinkle as if aging in fast forward.

"Lita!" I scream at her now, grabbing her shoulders.

Her eyes roll back into her head as her body falls limp to the cold floor. I drop to my knees and hold her as I cry out for help. She begins to writhe in my arms; her body shrinking in on itself. I realize I'm sobbing as I register the hot tears spilling down my face.

Why has no one come to help? Where is everyone?

Her skin turns ashen and blood begins to trickle in a small trail from her nose to her upper lip.

"Lita! Lita, what's happening?" I cry, helplessly.

Her withered hand wraps around my wrist suddenly and she whispers in a pained and accusatory voice, "The tart. *You.* You did this to me."

"No," I demand as I feel my body begin to shake. "No, I didn't. I didn't mean to! No, no, no!" I watch as she turns frigid and her spirit fades. Her skin remains ashen like a faint shell on her bones and her

Chapter 6

eyes sit sunken in her head. She's dead.

I killed her.

"Luna!"

I jolt awake, gasping with beads of sweat on my brow. "What? What?" I ask, trying to slow my breathing.

Rhea's face is hovering over me, pinched with concern. "Are you alright? You started jerking around. Did you have a nightmare?"

"Possibly," I say slowly, dragging out the word.

Rhea's lips take on a thin line. "Okay, so that means you definitely did," she says before placing a caring hand on my shoulder. "Do you want to talk about it or move on?"

While Rhea's offer is kind and sincere, I'm in no hurry to rehash the contents of my nightmare to reveal to her just how much I blame myself for Lita's death. She already told me once in the tunnel that it wasn't my fault, so I know I can only expect a similar response if I talk about my dream with her now. I know hearing it again won't likely be enough to make my heart listen, so I opt out. "I'd rather just move on."

"I understand," Rhea says, sympathetically. "But," she leans down and gives me a quick hug, "I'm here if you change your mind."

I give her a small smile. With my heartbeat finally reduced to a more regular pace, I stand up beside her on the raft, stretching my wings, and surveying our surroundings. It's a useless feat. "These trees and everything look the same to me."

"Preaching to the choir," Rhea says, with an exasperated fall of her tense shoulders. "Hopefully, we're close to Durand because if I keep staring at this scenery, I'm gonna lose my mind." She turns to me, crossing her arms over the top of her tangerine dress which sticks out against the deep greens of the forest. "It can't be much further, right?"

"How should I know?"

"Good point."

"Hey," I say, plopping down into a sitting position with my legs crossed beneath me. "Let's take this time to formulate a plan for when we get to Durand. I don't think I need to reiterate to you that this is our only option for help so we have to execute a plan perfectly. If even one of our components is miscalculated, we may not get the help that we need."

"Roger that!" Rhea says with a salute as she drops down to sit across from me. She raises an inquisitive eyebrow. "So, what's the plan?"

I rub my freckled temple as I think. There are just so many factors to consider and having never met the Sprite King, or been to his kingdom, I feel like I'm going in blind here. Nevertheless, I must devise a plan as precise as possible.

"Well, let's begin with our entrance to the Durand. As soon as we arrive, we will ask the nearest, unidiotic-looking, sprites for help."

"They might be difficult to find if our previous encounters have been any indication of their kind," Rhea interjects, flatly.

I nod. "That may be true, but I'm sure we'll find someone relatively stable-minded eventually. Once we do, we'll explain that we are here on behalf of the fairy kingdom, on important business, and must have an audience with the King. Once they lead us to the palace and we meet him, I will explain our situation and ask that Durand offer us aid. I'm not sure exactly what kind of aid I'm hoping he'll offer up, or what might actually help combat Amyra's evil powers, but hopefully, he'll have something in mind that might work."

"What if he isn't willing to help us? I mean, our kingdoms *are* estranged after all. He may not think helping us is a worthy cause. Like our problem isn't directly affecting him, so why bother?" Rhea asks, her angled eyebrows bunched together.

"Well, inviting some sprites to the party means he may already be aware of what's happened. Although, I don't recall seeing any sprites once the mayhem started. Maybe I could make it seem like

Chapter 6

Amyra might come for him next," I think out loud. "She very may well attempt to cause corruption in the sprite kingdom once she's finished wreaking havoc on the fairyfolk."

"She does seem power-hungry. That's for sure."

"Agreed," I say with a nod. "I think that's our best bet. I'll insinuate that this is his opportunity to kill a problem before it becomes his own. An urge for preventative action, if you will. How does that sound?"

"Well," she says, tilting her head, "I've never met this King, but I know you would do anything to keep your people safe." She waves her arms about, gesturing to our situation. "Exhibit A."

"Hopefully, he shares that priority," I say with a sigh before plastering on a forced smile of confidence. "Okay! We've got ourselves a plan. Now we just have to—" my voice cuts off as another one rings out.

"Aren't you fairies a little far from home?"

And just like that, my well-formulated plan is rendered kaput.

Chapter 7

Rhea and I both whip our heads in the direction of the voice. Standing on the sandy bank shortly ahead of us along the length of the river is not one, not two, not three, but four sprites. Three boys and a girl. Two of the spritemen are clearly twins as they are the perfect mirror image of one another with their brown buzz cuts and pale skin. The other sprite man, a blonde fellow, has his arm flung around the shoulder of the girl in a protective manner. They must be an item. I squint my eyes. He looks so familiar, yet I know I've never seen him before. It's the oddest sensation.

The girl speaks again. Her messy, black bob of hair swaying as she tilts her head and raises her brows. "You ladies look lost."

This earns her a few snickers from the group.

Rhea and I both stand up on the raft now to face them. I tilt my chin high. "Actually, you're just who we were hoping to see."

"That so?" the blonde sprite asks now.

"Yes," Rhea chimes in. "We need an audience with the Sprite King."

The whole group of them chuckles. "He won't wanna talk to any—"

"—fairies," one twin starts, and the other finishes.

"Okay, that was creepy," Rhea mutters under her breath beside me.

Chapter 7

I use the guide post to take us to the water's edge. We hop off the raft and use the post, driven into the floor of the river, to keep the raft steadily parked along the small shore. "I don't care if he wants to or not. We must see him. It's a matter of great urgency," I state with a firm tone.

"Great urgency?" the girl echos. "How about you fill us in on what this is regarding and we'll decide if it's actually important enough to bother the King about?"

I hesitate. Telling them about our situation means it could get out to the entire sprite kingdom if they go and blab to everyone. "I'm afraid I can't share it with you. The matter must remain private between dignitaries."

"Dignitaries?" the girl repeats in question before a look of realization dawns across her round face. "You're the Princess, aren't you? The one with the tarts?"

I swear, to all the rainbows, that I will kill that sprite if he ever so much as shows his face to me again.

I clear my throat. "Yes. May I please see your King now?"

"Wait a second," the blonde spriteman says, removing his arm from around the girl and approaching the raft. He reaches down and trails his fingers along the front side log of the small vessel. His expression changes when I realize he is looking at etched marks in the wood. He snaps his head to us. "This is my brother Gire's raft. Why do you have it? Where is he?"

I swear I can hear both mine and Rhea's breaths catch in our throats in perfect unison.

Think, think, think.

"Well, you see," I say. "Gire and Rhea here," I gesture with my hand beside me to Rhea who gives a nervous wave, "really hit it off at the party we had! Didn't you Rhea?"

"Oh, yes," Rhea says, nodding her head. "He was so very," she hesitates. "Um, so very," she falters again. I shoot her a look with my eyes. "So very *charming*! Yes," she clears her throat. "He said he liked my dress and then my heart was his!"

There's a pause as Gire's brother looks down and takes in Rhea's tangerine gown. "Orange *is* his favorite color."

"Exactly!" Rhea shouts, excited at lucking out. Then her face takes on a long, heart-strung look. "You see, because Gire and I became bewitched by each other, I confided in him the urgent matter of what we must discuss with the King. He said the King would need to know about this important issue at once! So, he gave us his raft and sent us on our way. He said he would find other means back because he had some business to attend to before he returned."

I'm sending up prayers as she concludes her tall tale that the sprites will believe it and she hasn't inadvertently given away anything to its true falsehood. The sprites are all silent for a moment with quizzical looks. Gire's brother straightens his stance and takes two steps up to Rhea, flopping a callused hand onto her shoulder. Just when I think he sees through us and is about to have us arrested and thrown into some kind of jail, he smiles.

"That does sound like him; the hopeless romantic."

The rest of the sprite group nods and rolls their eyes in agreement.

"Well, then future sister-in-law, let's get you to the King." He wraps his whole arm around Rhea now.

She turns back to me with a wide smile on her face and a clap of her hands. "Yay!"

I smile back and fall into step with the group as they begin walking. Rhea and Gire's brother have stricken up a conversation so I make my way over beside the girl sprite. "I'm Luna," I say.

"Tinsel."

"Can I ask what your King is like? I'm afraid I haven't heard much about him and I would really like to gauge his character before I meet

Chapter 7

him."

"Well," she says, "I suppose I should begin by letting you know that rule is no longer established here as it is in the fairy kingdom. Our old King was terrible. He treated ruling our kingdom like it was a game. He treated lives like they were meaningless and," she hesitates, "expendable."

"I'm so sorry."

She acknowledges my sympathy with a curt nod. "He came into rule because our old laws stated it was a birthright, such as the system your kingdom operates with. However, when the King was killed, he had not yet married or been able to provide a true heir for the kingdom. His only surviving, true-blooded relative in the royal line was his mother; a terrible woman. She was far too old to rule."

"What happened?" I ask, curious what next course of action the kingdom could conduct.

"With her ruled out as an option, the sprites decided it was time to do away with the birthright system and vote a new ruler into power." She turns to me with a smile now as she says, "No one even hesitated to select our King. The whole kingdom voted unanimously."

I don't even know this King and yet I am more envious of him than he can dream. To think that his people chose him, picked him, to rule over everyone in the kingdom? It's such a stark contrast to the way my situation is. I wonder if anyone in my kingdom would choose me if it had come down to a vote. "That's quite impressive. Admirable. Has he proven to be the great ruler you all assumed he would be?"

She faces forward again but remains smiling. "He has. Ever since he became King we have had nothing but peace in our kingdom. He took all of the cracks and calluses caused by our previous King and polished them with a fair hand and a protective spirit."

Her admiration for his rule shines through her words. I hope to someday make at least one person speak as proudly of me and my

The Amulet of Undoing

time as Queen as she does of him.

"This urgent matter I must bring up to your King," I begin, "involves me asking him for a form of aid for my kingdom. I know you don't know the details of the situation, but do you think he may be willing to help?"

Her face scrunches in thought as she takes a moment to ponder this. When she seems to have finished, she turns to face me. "I can tell you this. He always puts his people before anything else. If helping you will hurt his kingdom, then he probably won't. But if helping you will protect the kingdom, then he probably will."

I find some relief in her words. If what she says is true, then the remaining portion of my plan should work swimmingly. If I make it seem like Amyra might come for the sprite kingdom next, which is a very real possibility, then he will most likely help.

"Thank you. I appreciate the information."

For the first time since we began talking, I turn my gaze from Tinsel. I feel my breath catch in my throat as I take in the view of Durand straight ahead. It's a collection of homes and huts built and burrowed into the rolling hills of the land; lit windows and doorways peering out from stone and dirt. Wooden roots snake and crawl, curling around the deep green, moss-covered rooftops. Lanterns hang on wooden posts every few yards or so, dimly lighting the rocky, cobblestone pathway that winds through the rustic gathering. Sprites mill about on foot in various directions. A wide, swampy moat encircles the kingdom for as far as I can see. A drawbridge is pulled up across the mucky moat ahead of us where I see two sprites posted on either side. The air feels sticky as we come to stand at the moat's edge.

"Who goes there?" yells one of the sprites. I see a sword strapped to his hip, although I'd say he looks far too young to be carrying it and far too frail to ever wield it.

"Brick, you know it's me. You can see us," says Gire's brother.

Chapter 7

"I meant them two," says the guard with a nudge of his head. "They got them wings I've read about at school."

Rhea and I both instinctively lower our wings flat against our backs, out of sight, and offer up our best we-promise-we're-not-threats smiles.

"They're with us. They came to see the King," says Gire.

The young man still seems skeptical. "I'm still not sure 'bout them."

Gire's brother drapes his arm around Rhea's shoulder and uses the index finger of his other hand to point up at her face. "But this one's gonna be my sister-in-law." He turns his head towards Rhea, hoping she'll chime in.

"Oh, yes," she says, taking on that look of love-struck wonderment again from earlier. Her long lashes bat against her brown eyes and she plays shy at confessing her feelings. "Gire has my heart. He's bewitched me, body and soul." Then she takes on a look of slight pain. "I must merely count the hours, minutes, and seconds until we are reunited."

This earns her an adoring sigh from Tinsel. Wow, she's really selling it.

The young man frowns. "That makes me trust you even less."

Gire's brother huffs now and removes his arm from around Rhea to wave his fist at the guard. "Don't make me come up—" but before he's finished uttering this threat, the bridge is being lowered.

The bridge is so wide the six of us can easily cross it walking in step with one another. It appears to be constructed of thick wooden planks held together by some sort of tree sap. Two rusty, metal chains are attached to either side to raise and lower it. They remain stiff, fully extended as the bridge is lowered for us to cross. The young man stands at attention as we walk past him, but I know both Rhea and I sense him staring at our wings as we pass and enter into the official territory of the sprites.

The coarseness of the cobblestone path is easy to feel beneath my feet thanks to the soles of my shoes being worn thin from all the walking in the tunnel. I trail behind Rhea who's walking with her mouth brazenly agape as she takes our surroundings in. The air is heavy from the surrounding moat and forest and I feel it settle onto my skin like a blanket. The lanterns perched every few yards or so cast a cozy hue of gold over the mossy floor and rooftops. I pass an open door into one of the homes and surprisingly take in the sight of a staircase descending in a spiral wave below the ground.

Are there more homes beneath the ones I see here? How far are they burrowed down?

"Mommy, why is that lady growing petals from her back?"

I turn to find the culprit of the voice. The young girl stands, ears pointed, behind me, clutching her mother's hand and pointing at me with the other.

"That's a fairy. Those are wings, not petals," her mother says, quickly pulling her arm to try and drag her away.

The girl holds firm, clearly unwilling to budge until she gets answers. "But how do they work?"

The mother lets out a sigh now.

"I can show you," I offer with a friendly smile.

The mother looks hesitant. I drop down slowly to my knees a few feet from the girl and turn away so my wings are facing her. I give them a flutter which causes her face to light up. She lets go of her mother's hand and rushes over to me to get a closer look. Her mother gingerly creeps forward, too.

"You can move them," squeals the little girl excitedly.

"I sure can. They budded when I was even younger than you and grew slowly, but they're fully grown now. I can control them as easily as I would an arm or a leg." I show her a short series of different flutters of various speeds and how I can also flatten them on my back. She watches in a mesmerized state. Then I offer to let her touch one.

Chapter 7

"Please, Mommy!" Her blonde pigtails bounce with her little hops of excitement. "Can I touch the fairy lady's wings? Oh, please, please, please—"

"Alright, alright," says the mother before looking up at me. "You don't carry any diseases on those things, right?"

I try my best to refrain from showing how taken aback I am by her question. "No. No need to worry."

She nods and the little girl reaches out her hand to gingerly poke my right wing. She does this with one eye closed. Once she sees it's nothing to be afraid of, she touches it again more slowly. "Wow. It feels so soft," she says, eyes glazed. She retracts her hand and begins to clap and hop in place. "Now, fly! Fly! I wanna see you do it!"

I stand, noticing the small crowd that has gathered around us to observe. "Alright. Are you ready?"

She nods, excited and impatient.

"Okay. Here I go!" I push up onto the tips of my feet, flapping my wings, but don't catch air. My efforts feel strained. I try again. This time, I put all my strength into it, but my wings only flap slowly, a sense of heaviness on them that prevents me from generating speed with my flutters. I give up with a pant, my feet flat on the ground.

What is going on?

"I'm sorry," I say to the little girl who looks quite disappointed. "I don't know what's wrong. I only can't fly if my wings are wet, but even while traveling along the river today, I've been very careful to keep them dry."

"Could it be the humid air?"

"Pardon?" I ask, not understanding.

"The air," the girl's mother says again. "We're in a deep part of the forest and the low elevation and surrounding water makes the air humid. It means there's a lot of water in the air. The air collects moisture and it can feel heavy."

The heaviness I felt settle on my skin when I arrived. That must be the humid air. "Perhaps, there's so much water in the air that it's coating my wings."

She nods. "That's probably it."

I turn back to her daughter. "I'm sorry I can't fly for you with the humidity, but I promise I can fly high and fast."

She smiles wide.

"Thank you," her mother says, taking her hand and heading off.

"You're welcome."

As soon as they leave, the small crowd that had gathered dissipates and it's then that I realize I don't see Rhea or our group anywhere. They must have gone on without me. I turn to the nearest sprite who backs away a few steps to maintain a safe distance between us.

Do I look that scary?

"Sir, can you please point me in the direction of the palace? I need to speak with the King."

He nods and, arm fully extended, juts a finger in the direction of a winding path that continues through the town.

"Thank you."

I pass along more homes and come into what appears to be a market or collection of small shops when I smell a delightful aroma. I let out a small moan and trail around till I find the culprit of the scent in a display box set beneath a nearby lantern post. The woman behind the display startles as I approach.

"These smell divine. What are they?" I ask.

She calms a bit at my compliment and offers me a bashful smile. "They're rosemary bread loaves. It's my grandma's recipe from when she ran the stand long ago."

I nod, still enchanted by the scent emanating from the fresh bread. "I'd love to try one," I say, "but I don't have any money on me." In my haste to get away from the palace with Rhea, I didn't think to grab

Chapter 7

any.

Do sprites even have the same currency here?

"I can help you with that," says a low voice from behind me. But if it's who it sounds like, I don't even want to turn around.

Chapter 8

The feeling of breath grazing over the top of my head is all too familiar. Of course, I had to run into the one sprite I'd like to avoid during my first fifteen minutes in the kingdom. Screw politeness. I refuse to turn around. "No, thank you. I'm quite alright."

"You just said you were broke."

I look down, pretending to be suddenly interested in smoothing out the cream satin of my dress. "I did not say I was broke."

"You said you had no money," he states, matter-of-factly.

"Well, yes," I begin, but he interrupts.

"Isn't having no money the exact definition of broke?"

I huff and force a smile towards the bakery woman. "Thank you. They look delicious, but I'm actually not that hungry after all."

This is, of course, the precise moment at which my body betrays me and my stomach broadcasts a very audible rumble to remind me that I haven't eaten anything since we fled the palace.

I hear a low chuckle behind me.

I nod my head to the woman with a quick, "Good day," and hurry on down the path to the palace.

My feet can't move fast enough. Oh, how I wish I could fly away

Chapter 8

right now. Instead, I'm forced to do this awkward half-run, half-walk that I'm sure makes the nearby sprites think I have to pee, or perhaps that all fairies are this odd and walk like they have no control over their extremities.

The cobblestone path continues once the houses and shops have cleared, breaking into a field of sorts with scattered trees and vines. Moss continues to blanket each rock and protruding tree roots jut out near the bases of different trunks that I pass. The path rounds up ahead around a short hill. Surely it can't be much farther past that till the palace.

I slow my stroll now to a more leisurely pace. That stupid sprite. Every time he's there, he makes me feel like such a fool. It's like he baits me; saying things he knows will get me to say other things that will make me look ridiculous. Like making me look broke in front of that woman!

All of the pent-up energy and frustration from both the last five minutes and the last 12 hours becomes all too much and I let out a combination of groans and shrieks as I punch and throw my arms about as if hitting all of my obstacles away. A moment of this gets my pent-up jitters out and I take a deep breath.

Okay. Think, Luna. Pull yourself together!

I take a slow, deep breath and resume walking. Alright. I can use this time to reformulate my plan for talking with the King. First, I will find Rhea to give her hell for leaving me behind, and then—

I hear a twig snap behind me and whip my head to see the culprit.

It's him. Standing as tall as ever, with his tan skin and sharp jaw, he's in the same sage-colored shirt and brown pants as the party, except now he's added a leather vest. His black hair is slightly ruffled on the top above his pointed ears as if he just recently ran his fingers through it. His raven eyes meet mine and he offers a grin, halting mid-step.

"I promise I'm not stalking you. I just also happen to be headed this way," he says, holding a loaf of rosemary bread in each hand, which I pretend I don't notice.

"Your promises mean nothing to me as we have established no trust in one another," I say, quickly turning on my heel and continuing in my desired direction.

He waits briefly before I hear his steps continue behind me. "I don't see the need to get upset with me. It's not my fault you have trust issues."

I spin back, angrily huffing with both hands at my sides. "I do not have trust issues!" I say before realizing I'm letting him get me all worked up again. I clear my throat and un-clench my fists. "I don't have trust issues," I repeat, this time at a much lower and calmer volume.

"Just anger issues alone then," he says with a nod.

I groan and begin walking again. He catches up to me in a mere moment without even hastening his pace since his steps cover more ground than mine, even with the somewhat infuriated march I'm now maintaining. He walks alongside me without a word. I vow to walk in silence as long as I must. I will not be the first one to speak after his most recent comment.

He begins to eat one of the loaves of bread. His first bite removes a chunk from the perfect crust and the bread uses the opportunity of the opening to push its heavenly scent in my direction. He catches me peering at the loaf out of the corner of his eye and turns to me. I quickly look off in the other direction as if something very interesting is taking place over there.

"This is so delicious. I mean, it's no tart—" he drawls.

I roll my eyes with a groan.

"—but sprites do make the best bread."

I wrap my arms around my stomach suddenly when I feel another rumble coming on, but it's of no use. The gurgle is loud enough I'm sure everyone back by the houses and shops heard it.

His face takes on a sympathetic look now and he holds the other loaf out to me. "Here."

Still facing forward, I shake my head. "No, thank you. I can't take your food."

"You're not taking it if I'm offering it to you."

"I can't accept it."

He stops walking suddenly. "Oh no!"

"What?" I ask, stopping to turn towards him.

I watch as he pulls a white cloth from the pocket of his vest and lays it flat on the ground.

"What are you—"

"Shhh," he says. He then takes the uneaten bread loaf and sets it onto the cloth. He stands and peers back up at me, making a sad face. "I've dropped my bread."

I tilt my head, narrowing my eyes at him. "You did not drop it."

"Um, I think I know perfectly well when I've dropped something. Thank you very much."

"You set it there," I insist.

"No. You're misunderstanding. You see, first I accidentally dropped the napkin, and then I accidentally dropped the loaf of bread. If one happened to land perfectly atop the other, that is purely a matter of coincidence."

"You are ridiculous," I say, turning and continuing onward.

He falls into step beside me, eating his bread.

I stop. "What are you doing? You're just going to leave it there?" I say, pointing back to where the uneaten loaf rests on the forest floor.

His eyebrows come together in a quizzical look as if I've asked the silliest of questions. "I dropped it on the ground. I no longer want it."

Is he serious? "Are you serious?"

"Of course. If an animal, something, or *someone*," he draws out this third option, "was to come along and eat it though, it would be theirs for the taking." He continues walking forward.

I see what he's up to now. I stand looking at where the loaf sits on the ground. On one hand, I, the Princess of Celestia, can't be seen eating food off the ground; food from a stranger, no less. It would be highly undignified and I fear people would never look at me the same.

On the other hand, there aren't any fairies here. With this sprite as my sole witness, I have no reliable witnesses to recount the story. If he talks of this later on, I'll simply deny anything he says. Then, there's the fact that I haven't eaten anything since the party.

Now that I think about it, I didn't eat anything at the party. I had been too preoccupied greeting guests and making small talk to enjoy the food and then when I finally made my way over to the table, I, of course, wasn't able to try my tarts.

My stomach rumbles again and with it goes the last of my restraint; hunger winning out. I rush over to where the bread is and snatch it up. The first bite is so heavenly I let out a moan.

The sprite clears his throat.

I ignore him, picking up the white cloth. I close the gap between us and hand it to him, munching on the bread in my other hand. He shoves the cloth back into the pocket of his vest and walks beside me. "This path leads to the sprite palace."

I nod. "I'm aware," I mumble, my mouth full of bread.

"What business do you have there?"

I swallow my current bite and respond before taking another. "I have to speak to the King about something urgent."

He nods, slowly. "I see. What is it regarding?"

If he's asking then that must mean he and the other sprites did not witness Amyra's wicked mayhem. "Did you and the other representatives leave my coronation party after the dancing?"

He nods again.

Chapter 8

"Well," I begin. "Something horrible happened and many of my people are now dead. Including," my voice shakes, "a very dear friend of mine."

He looks genuinely sympathetic when he turns his head and meets my eyes. "I'm sorry you lost your friend and others. May I ask what exactly happened?"

I hesitate. "It's rather painful to recount. My Aunt Amyra was the eldest daughter and was supposed to be Queen long ago. Everyone thought she was dead. She showed up, out of the blue, at my party shortly after you left. She went on and on about how growing up, she always knew people preferred my mother over her. When the fire happened, I guess she escaped and was not far from the palace. She waited to be found but said the next thing she heard was the sounds of festivity in the kingdom as they crowned my mother Queen. It was clearly a very painful experience for her, but she's changed now. She's not right, you see. She ticks and jitters about. She talks to herself, too, and can be rather frightening in her mannerisms. She demanded to have my crown. When my mother and I made it clear that was not going to happen, she exposed her dark power."

At this, he stops walking entirely and turns to face me with a worried expression. "Can you describe it to me?"

The horrid images of Lita and the guard flash through my mind. "It's hard to describe. Amyra called it withering. Her fingertips turned black as she touched a guard. He fell on the ground and the tissue and muscle of his body just started dissipating. His nose bled and he was gasping for breath. His body spasmed so violently that it was like you could see his spirit being taken away from him even though he was fighting it as hard as he could. When I knew he was gone, his eyes sat wide open, sunken into his skull and his skin was shedded on his bone."

At this description, his face grows pale and distraught. I force myself to take a deep breath so I don't cry. Even as I recount the occurrence to him, it hurts and feels like I'm seeing it all again for the first time. It's heartbreakingly sad that this is a memory I have now that can plague me forever.

I don't even know why I'm telling him any of this. Perhaps, I just needed to talk to someone about it more than I thought I did.

"He was first," I continue. "My maid, my friend, Lita, was killed next. I saw more bodies too, as I escaped the palace."

"So, you have no idea how she came to possess this power?" he asks, hesitantly.

I find this an odd first question to ask after all that I've just rehashed, but I'd be lying if I said I hadn't wondered the very same thing. "No. She didn't say, but I've never seen or heard of anything like it."

He clears his throat, gingerly placing a hand on my shoulder. "I'm sorry that happened to your people."

"Thank you," I say.

His dark eyes peer at me and a warm sensation begins to build where his hand still rests on the bare skin of my shoulder. I suddenly realize just how alone we are. I quickly shrug his hand off with a fake yawn and shake out of the emotional funk brought on by my story.

"Anyways, I'm here to meet the Sprite King in hopes that he'll be willing to offer me some form of aid."

He winces. "I don't know if that's possible."

I roll my eyes. "Why not? I can be very convincing. I'm sure I can get him to help. He sounds like a noble ruler from what I've heard of him."

I swear his pointed ears perk up even higher. "Oh? And what have you heard?"

"I heard he's very protective of Durand and about how he's brought nothing but peace to the land since he was voted onto the throne after the previous and merciless King was killed."

Chapter 8

"And while gathering all this intel, no one mentioned his wicked good looks?"

I turn to flash him a bored expression. "No, because that's irrelevant information. I only cared about obtaining the important facts."

He faces forward with a suppressed smile. "I think it's important."

"I can assure you it isn't. He could be as ugly as a toad and I wouldn't care. What matters is simply if he's willing to help me or not."

"I don't think—" he begins when suddenly we round the corner and I spot Rhea sitting cross-legged on the ground in front of the sprite palace.

The palace is constructed differently from the sprite homes we've passed. While the previous homes were all built burrowed underground or into hillsides, this building stands of bricked cobblestone. Vines snake in between and around the components of the structure and moss lines the windows in vibrant patches. The palace is significantly smaller than ours in the fairy kingdom, but I know I'm only seeing what is above ground. Perhaps there is more beneath.

It's so funny seeing all the ways that while fairies took to the sky, sprites were becoming one with the land.

The structure stands high, surrounded by tall grass and green and black ash trees with long vines for leaves that hang down like hair to shield the palace in a secluded shadow. The large doorway Rhea sits in front of is shaped like a circle and has the outline of an overlapping tree and crescent moon carved into it. Two guards stand on either side of the entrance.

Rhea is looking down, poking at the ground absentmindedly with a twig. I clear my throat and her face snaps up. Her expression is filled with relief as she runs over and wraps me in a quick hug.

"Finally, you're back!" she exclaims before pulling back and planting her hands on her hips. "I told them I wouldn't go in without you." It's at this moment that she registers my walking companion. Her face turns from delight to irritation. "Well, if it isn't *Mr. Tart.*"

He suppresses a smile and gives a curt nod. He glances at me as he walks past us. The guards both nod and open the door to let him in. I never asked what his business was at the palace, but whatever it is he's bringing to the King's attention, I hope it doesn't take up too much time. I have mixed expectations now about how things will go with the King after Tinsel's words of encouragement and then that sprite's discouragement on the matter.

Rhea glares at him. It isn't until the guards close the door behind him, that she finally turns back to me. "Did you walk all this way with him? Ugh, I'm sorry. I should have never left you."

"Yeah!" I say, shooting her a how-could-you look. "We were in the kingdom for only a few minutes. I turned around and you were gone. You left me!"

"I know, I know, and I'm sorry!" Rhea says as she exasperatedly fluffs her hair. "Truth is that Gire's brother was going on and on about recipes that Gire likes that I could make for him when we're," she pauses to fake a gag, "*married.* At first, I wasn't listening, but then he started talking about these honey pinwheel rolls that sounded so good so I started listening quite intently. I thought maybe I could convince you to make them for me if I still remember the recipe when all this is over." She grins sheepishly.

I roll my eyes.

"Next thing I knew, we arrived at the palace and I turned and realized you were nowhere to be seen. I started freaking out, but Tinsel said she saw you stop to talk with a little girl and that you were probably close behind us. Tinsel and everyone left after dropping me off. I didn't want to go in there without knowing you were okay and I wanted a chance to talk to you first about what exactly we're going to do when we head inside."

"Yes, I did stop to talk to a little girl. I—" I begin, but Rhea interrupts,

Chapter 8

grabbing me by my shoulders and giving me a good shake.

"Oh! I can't believe I almost forgot, but I think something is wrong with my wings! I can barely fly a foot off the ground!"

I place a comforting hand on her shoulder and her breathing slows. "I know. The same thing is happening to me. A woman I spoke to said it may be the humidity."

Rhea's eyebrows rise. "Humidi-what?"

"Humidity. Apparently because of the big swamp all around the kingdom and how deep we are in the forest, the air is thick with moisture. That's why it feels heavy and muggy. I think the air must be wet enough here to prevent us from flying."

Rhea puts her hands on her hips and huffs, processing this while looking at the ground. After a moment, she faces me again with a decided face. "I do not like humidity."

"Me either."

"How are you feeling about going in there?" she asks now, crossing her arms. "I mean, let's face it. I'll just be a mere decoration in there. I'm leaving all the talking to you."

"Well, when we were first walking to Durand from the river, Tinsel told me a lot of encouraging stuff about the King. Apparently, their old King was killed and had been a horrible ruler. His mother was the only true-blooded relative left, but she was too old for the throne. The people decided to vote their next ruler into power and unanimously voted for the new King."

"Wow."

"I know," I say, nodding. "She said he's brought them nothing but peace and safety. She also said he would probably help us if it also helped the sprites."

"That's great!" says Rhea, clapping her hands together.

"But then—" I start and watch her expression fall.

"But?" she echoes.

"But then I talked to that annoying sprite who ambushed me at a bakery display and he said it's unlikely that the King will help us."

"I like Tinsel's answer better."

"Me too, but the spriteman seemed very certain."

"So? He said your tarts were bad. We can't trust his opinion."

"You're right. Regardless of anything I've heard about the King, I must talk to him. I'll go inside, ask to speak to the King, and then I'll tell him of what's happened and that it could potentially happen to Durand next. Are you good with the plan?"

"Yes, ma'am."

"Alright. Let's do this."

* * *

Rhea and I are ushered into the throne room of the palace where a group of other sprites are already waiting; presumably to see the King as well. A large wooden throne sits on a slightly raised platform and there's an utter lack of decor. Besides a few hanging lanterns and a rug, there's one portrait on the wall. I walk over to inspect it closer and see that it's of a beautiful woman who looks about my age. She has dark brown curls that cascade down her back and perfectly plump lips compose her smile. Her long lashes surround her hazel eyes and her tan skin sets her apart from the light blue backdrop of the painting. I'm sure this must be the King's lover as it's the only portrait in his throne room. I suppose he considers himself lucky to have such a lovely mate.

The group of sprites start to stare. What business fairies could possibly have with the king is what I'm sure they're all pondering.

Rhea clears her throat and turns to me. "Guess we're not the only ones needing to see the King today," she says under her breath.

Chapter 8

"I just hope we are seen first. Time is of the essence. Amyra could be claiming more lives by the minute."

"Well, just in case he does chat with them first, I'm gonna use the bathroom now. I don't think I can hold it much longer," she says, doing a slight dance with her legs.

I chuckle. "Okay, just don't be gone too long."

She nods, rushing out.

Rhea is gone for only a mere moment before suddenly, the double doors on the right of the room open wide and a guard walks in, standing at attention. "Introducing His Majesty, King Caspar."

I quickly fix my posture and plaster on my best smile. I have to make a good first impression.

A figure comes around the corner. "Thank you, Lennox."

My heart sinks into the pit of my stomach as I realize it's *him*.

Chapter 9

I squeeze my eyes tightly shut, convinced they must have deceived me, but when I open them again, I'm greeted with the same horrible sight.

His tall frame strolls past the guards and takes his seat on the throne at the front of the room. While he'll look everywhere, but meet my eyes, I still know the suppressed smirk on his face is meant for me. The group of waiting sprites quickly run over to flock about him, all chatting away about the business they want to discuss.

How on earth could he be the Sprite King? He has utterly no form of manners or decorum. His pompous attitude has certainly never hinted at him being in any position of authority. Oh, but it all makes sense now. Like with how he thought it was important I knew of the King's wicked good looks? What a ridiculous game. He took advantage of my naivety about him and Durand and played me like a fool.

Great goodness, what am I to do? He surely hates my guts, as I do his, but nevertheless, I need his help. I will simply have to do my best to start fresh, play nice, and remedy the situation.

"Ahem," I clear my throat. When no one pays any heed, I offer it up

Chapter 9

again at a slightly heightened volume. "Ahem!"

He pauses in his discussion and tilts his head, looking about the room, but still not meeting my eyes. "Did you hear something?"

Oh, for fairy's sake.

I suppress the urge to roll my eyes at his childishly coy attitude and raise my hand with a smile. "It was me, Your Highness."

He sits up straighter in his throne and the people about him move to the sides and face me so they can see who the king is addressing. His dark eyes finally meet mine with a fierce yet playful gaze. "And you are?"

Is he really going to keep up this ruse? "I am Princess Luna of Celestia and I—" I begin, but he cuts me off.

"I thought you royal fairies were supposed to have red hair."

I guffaw and flip one side of my hair. "I *do* have red hair."

He shakes his head slowly. "No, I'd say it's more of a dirty orange. You bathe in your kingdom do you not?"

I can feel a vein pulsing in my temple. If he wants to play it that way, then fine, I can play it that way, too. "I can promise Your Highness that my hygiene is not of his concern, but that *his* certainly is because that stench has been quite disturbing. Tell me, how do you get anything accomplished with that odor? Does it bother you or have you simply grown immune to it?"

I see the gaping faces of the sprite people, but pay them no heed. He may have started this, but I'm not afraid to finish it. However, what was said to rattle him, seems to only have spurred him on as his face takes on a grin.

Challenge extended and accepted.

"What you're smelling is the scent of a good leader," he states.

"I'm afraid it can't be because it smells nothing like the perfume I wear each day. My scent is that of one *born* to be a ruler." I stand proud.

Holding our gaze, he stands from his throne and slowly walks towards me with his hands clasped behind his back, chest broad. I maintain my stance. He comes up directly in front of me, peering me down. He tilts his head down towards the side of my neck and I feel him breathe in. My breath becomes snagged in my lungs, but I will my face to remain indifferent. After his inhale, he releases deeply, as do I, and we lock eyes again. I know he's smelling the perfume Lita made me of rose hip oil and vanilla. It's a magical concoction; almost hypnotic.

An even darker look takes over his eyes for a moment before he suddenly gives his head a shake and stands back, running a hand through his hair. "All I smell is burnt tarts."

Okay, *now* he's crossed a line. "I never burn my tarts and the tart you tried was not burned!" I can feel my blood boiling in my veins. Jokes about hygiene are one thing, but I will not have him mock my art.

He smiles, clearly happy to have struck a nerve. I will not give him the satisfaction any longer. I'm here on business and must reroute the conversation back. I take a deep breath and lower my voice back to a normal register. "Is there perhaps somewhere more private we could talk, Your Highness?"

He nods, his face taking on that devilish grin of his. "Lennox," he calls, never breaking my gaze.

"Yes, Your Highness?"

"The Princess wishes to finish this discussion in private. Please show her to my chambers and I will be there shortly after I finish business with my other guests."

His *chambers?*

"Um," I begin with an awkward cough, my shock making it hard for me to remember how to breathe. "Is there perhaps somewhere else we could speak?"

Chapter 9

"You just asked for somewhere private. I assure you my chambers are very, *very* private," Caspar says, tilting his head at me, teeth flashing in his grin now.

A shiver runs through my body.

"Perhaps outside?" I persist, my throat feeling dry. "I could use some fresh air."

His eyes take on a gleam of something wicked. "Yes, it is getting rather hot in here, isn't it? Lennox, take her to the garden. I will be there soon."

I breathe a sigh of relief. I nod quickly in Caspar's direction with averted eyes before Lennox ushers me out of the throne room and down a long hallway. I follow shortly behind Lennox, taking in as much of the palace as I can as we walk. Since all the doors we pass are closed, the only thing I notice is a couple more portraits of the same woman from the painting in the throne room. Whether she is the Queen, Princess, or whoever, I doubt she would have appreciated the King's blatant flirting in the throne room. I'll have to add unfaithful to his list of bad qualities. A list that's quite ever-growing, might I add.

Suddenly, Lennox stops and opens a door to the left. "This way please, miss."

"Your Highness," I correct him.

He smiles. "This way, *miss*."

I'm beginning to lose all faith in this kingdom. I stare him down as I walk past and through the door he holds open for me which accesses what appears to be a small, private garden. A high cobblestone wall surrounds the grassy space. Two weeping willow trees stand side by side with long leaves that hang down over the garden like stilled rain and there's a pond at the base of a small, trickling waterfall that's produced out of the top of a nearby rock fixture. A wooden bench stands next to the pond's edge and I take a seat. My right hand grazes along the top of the wood. It's old and chipped in certain spots, giving away its secret of having visits with a constant companion.

I must admit it feels good to finally have a moment alone to myself. Everything has changed so fast. I thought I had weight on my shoulders before when I was all anxious about becoming Queen, but now I have problems beyond my worst nightmares. Lita and so many others are dead, I don't know where my mother is, the whole kingdom is in peril with Amyra still on the loose, and I have no idea what to do about any of it. I am always the girl with the plan. But Amyra came out of nowhere and now everything's gone to hell. I don't know if I've ever felt so helpless.

I begin sniffling now. Tears brim my eyes and for the first time in as long as I can remember, I don't fight them. I allow them to fall and I cry. I cry for Lita and every fairy person lost. I cry for my mother and the stress and fear she must be feeling if she is still alive. I cry for my kingdom and for how scared I feel.

"Ahem."

I snap my head up and quickly do my best to smear away my tears. "You could at least announce yourself."

"That was my way of trying," says Caspar from where he stands across the pond looking at me.

I read his expression. "Don't look at me like that. I don't want your pity."

He begins walking slowly over towards me. "I wasn't looking at you with pity. I was merely wondering if these tears were because of our repartee in the throne room earlier."

"A repartee you coerced me into," I demand.

"I don't believe I forced you to form any comebacks of your own. You did that quite organically." He pauses and sits on the bench beside me, facing the opposite direction. "So these tears are because of my actions?"

I sigh. "No. As frustrated as you made me in there, I wouldn't give you the satisfaction of tears."

This earns a chuckle out of him. "I'd expect nothing less. Is it your kingdom then?"

"Yes," I answer quietly. I turn to face him, serious now. "Why would you play me like that? All this time, you never told me you were the King."

"I didn't want to tell you."

"Why?" I question.

"Well, at your party I didn't want to tell you because you were being rude."

"I was not—"

"And then when I ran into you here in town, I didn't want to tell you because I thought it might relieve some of the pressure for you if we were able to discuss your concerns between peers rather than dignitaries."

This stuns me for a moment. "But that would mean you were nice to me."

He shoots me a wink. "Don't tell anyone."

I chuckle before I stop, remembering his comment during the walk to the palace. "Wait, you said during our walk that the King was unlikely to help me. Why do you not want to help?"

He sighs; his face taking on a determined aura. "To put it plainly, this is a fairy problem; not a sprite problem. While I am sorry for the pain your kingdom is experiencing, it is still unrelated to my people so I view it as a waste of my resources."

I've seen that look before but on my mother. I grew up hoping I'd develop that look of protection, pride, and determination on my face when I became Queen. While I'm still nowhere near perfecting it, here he is doing it so effortlessly.

I could be upset that he just called helping my kingdom a waste of resources, but the truth is I understand where he's coming from. I feel his sincerity for the pain my kingdom is going through, but I also understand his refusal isn't personal. Perhaps, there is some sort of aid he could offer that wouldn't take many resources.

"Amyra seemed very power-hungry. Signs point to her coming after Durand as soon as she conquers Celestia. What if I didn't ask for soldiers or any large resources of that kind? Is there perhaps something smaller you could offer that would still be of great help?"

He ponders this, seeming to take the matter more seriously now that I've insinuated Durand being next. "What exactly do you have in mind?"

"How about information? Do you know of anything that might help me beat Amyra? With her magical power, I feel like we might need some magic of our own. Perhaps a legend or something?"

"Another legend?" echoes a voice I don't recognize.

I turn from Caspar to face our new visitor. It's a rather studious-looking sprite fellow in a plain cream-colored tunic with evergreen pants. Slightly shorter than Caspar, with green eyes and ashy, messy hair, he stands just inside the garden's entrance clutching three different books under one arm. He uses his other hand to push his glasses further up the slope of his nose and gives me a nod.

"Greetings, Your Highness."

"Hello," I say, nodding politely and turning to Caspar for an introduction. He looks oddly nervous and clears his throat before he speaks.

"This is Atlas, my royal scholar."

"I'm also His Highness's best friend," says Atlas, standing tall with pride.

Caspar sighs with a smile. "And that."

Atlas marches over to me and takes my hand, kissing the back of it with a quick peck. Finally someone in this kingdom with a sense of manners.

"Your hands are very soft. Do you moisturize often?"

I slowly retract my hand. "Umm."

"Atlas, what have we talked about?" asks Caspar, shooting him a look.

"That edict about forest nature?"

"No."

"Those spicy eggs we had for breakfast two days ago?"

"No."

"That weird dream you had where you woke up all—"

"No!" Caspar drags his hands down his face.

Atlas lights up. "Oh! About saying things in my head before I say them out loud?"

Caspar sighs. "That's the one."

"Oh," says Atlas, realizing now what Caspar means. He stares at the ground. "I'm sorry I asked you about your moisturizing routine, Your Highness."

I chuckle. "It's alright. King Caspar here tells me that you are a scholar. Something horrible happened in my kingdom and I have to fix it. Do you know of any information, or legends, that could help me?"

Atlas shuffles the books in his arms till he finds a specific one. "Here you are," he says, handing it out to me.

Caspar quickly reaches out, pushing the book back towards Atlas. "I think she'll need you to read it to her."

I narrow my eyes at him. "I most certainly do not. I am perfectly capable of reading it myself."

Caspar retracts his hand and folds his arms across his chest with a smile.

The leather-bound book feels worn with age as I take it in my hands. The cover contains no markings, only adding to the mystery of its contents. Eager to read what it holds, I gingerly open the pages.

It's a different language.

I know Caspar sees the moment I realize this because he lets out a suppressed chuckle.

"Go on," Atlas urges, excitedly.

I clear my throat. "Actually, would you mind? I think I will have you read it to me after all."

"I thought you said you were perfectly capable of reading?" Atlas asks.

"I am," I assure Atlas, "just not whatever language that is."

"I see," he says. "Well, we actually don't have a name for it and I only learned how to read it because we have two other books in the same language. I cross-referenced them with one another until I figured it out. This is the diary of a man who went after the Amulet of Undoing."

"Amulet of Undoing?" I repeat quizzically. "What does that do exactly?"

Atlas shrugs. "Well, we can't be one hundred percent positive, since we have never actually seen it in person. However, the gentleman in this journal notes that it is believed to be a magical object that has the power to undo anything you wish."

"That could work! How do I get it?"

"There you are!" Rhea comes jogging through the entrance of the garden but stops in her path when she sees Caspar and Atlas. She shoots Caspar a glare before turning to Atlas. "You're new."

Atlas nods towards her. "I am Atlas, miss. I'm the King's royal scholar and best friend."

At this, Rhea smiles. "I'm Rhea. I'm the best friend of the Princess! We're gonna be fast friends you and I," she says with both hands on her hips as if proclaiming the statement has already made it true.

Atlas smiles in return and pushes his glasses upwards once again.

"Rhea, Atlas was just telling me about this diary they have about an

Chapter 9

Amulet of Undoing that has the power to undo anything—" I begin.

"By speculation!" Atlas interjects.

"By speculation," I continue. "But it sounds like it might be just what we need to stop Amyra."

"Amyra?" Atlas repeats with a confused look.

Caspar clears his throat, drawing the group's attention back to him. "Atlas, her Aunt Amyra, who was once thought to be dead, showed up at Princess Luna's coronation party with evil powers and demanded the crown. She killed many people with this odd withering ability and Luna and Rhea were forced to flee here. Got it?"

Atlas nods slowly.

"That's correct. So, Atlas, how do we get this amulet?" I ask, leaning forward intently.

"Well," he begins. "As I said, all we know about the object is from this diary. The entries entail that you must venture into the Bog—"

This earns a gasp from both Rhea and myself.

The Bog is an enchanted forest known as a plague upon the realm. It's rumored to be filled with death-defying creatures, unpredictable magic, and obscene horrors. Only the truly desperate enter.

Atlas continues, unphased. "And it appears there are three objects you must collect and bring to the final destination to obtain the amulet."

"How do we get these objects?" Rhea asks.

"It appears you collect them by completing a certain series of different challenges; all quite dangerous. They're complicated and difficult to explain," says Atlas.

"But they're doable?" I ask.

"Well, he completed the three challenges and obtained the required objects just fine, but he never got the amulet."

"Why not?" Caspar asks now.

"I'm not quite sure. The last entry is him arriving at the final destination where you are supposedly tasked with trying to exchange the collection of objects with a creature for the amulet. Since the entry was started but never finished, and a wandering sprite just found this book with two others and brought them to us, I'd say it's safe to assume he died."

At this, Rhea's mouth hangs open. "He died?"

"I'm just assuming," says Atlas, plainly. "I think it's safe to assume that conclusion since most explorers would certainly take the time to finish logging their expedition if they had completed it. To stop at the pinnacle point would be a waste of intellectual intent."

I blink, processing this. "So, let me get this straight. You're saying the only object that can help me could easily cost us our lives if we go after it?"

"Death is always a possibility. There's no escaping it."

"Gee, that's morbid," says Rhea with a shiver.

"It's just a fact," says Atlas.

I stand and take Rhea's hand, leading her to the corner of the garden. "Excuse me. I just need a moment to consult with Rhea alone."

"You think this is as crazy as I do, right?" I ask her, once we're out of earshot.

"One hundred percent," she begins. "But, isn't it pretty much our only option?"

"No, I'm sure we could find something else if we—"

She cuts me off. "Luna, this is it. An Amulet of Undoing?"

Deep down, I know she's right. An amulet with the power to undo anything could mean not only undoing Amyra's evil power but perhaps bringing Lita back to life as well. It might be nearly impossible to obtain, but it really would solve all our problems if we were successful.

"I know. You're right. This is it. But Rhea, I just lost Lita. I can't lose you, too. If something happened to you, I'd never be able to forgive—"

"Don't even think like that," she says, squeezing my hand. "The diary man could have gotten sick, or just been so old his time was up. We can't be certain of what killed him or if he even died at all."

I squeeze her hand in return and a thought occurs to me. "It sounds like the man in the diary was by himself. If you and I go together, we'd have twice the odds. Plus, we have our wings and the ability to fly is sure to prove helpful."

"Very true."

"I'm scared, but I have no other choice. I have to do this for my people."

She sighs with a smile. "And I have to because you're going to do it and I have nothing else to do."

I chuckle. "Okay, then it's settled."

We walk back over to where Caspar and Atlas sit on the bench together.

"Rhea and I have decided to go after the amulet," I announce. "It's the only way to stop Amyra."

Caspar nods and then stands with his hands in the front pockets of his leather vest. "Okay. Then, we're coming with you."

Chapter 10

"Umm, yeah. I think not," says Rhea, crossing her arms.

"Yeah, I don't think so," I echo.

Caspar takes a step forward till he's towering over me.

"Must you always tower so?" I ask, eyes narrowed. He smells of pine needles and fireplace smoke.

He smirks. "I can't help it that you're small. Now, how do you plan on reading the diary if you go on your own? Oh, wait. You can't."

Rats, why didn't I think of that? "Well, then Atlas can come with us to interpret. I see no need for you to tag along."

He folds his arms across his chest now. "You tell me that Amyra is coming for Durand next, this amulet is the only way to stop her, and you don't think I'll want to come and make sure it's properly retrieved?"

I know exactly what he's insinuating with this statement. "You're saying you think we'll fail?"

He stays quiet.

"Well, that's a yes," Rhea huffs from behind me. "And very rude might I add!"

"All I'm saying is it significantly raises our chances for success if I

Chapter 10

lead the mission," says Caspar.

Mission? Lead?

"Okay, listen here," I say, pointing the tip of my index finger into his chest. "I am leading this quest because it is *my* kingdom that is *currently* on the line. If you come, which I'm expecting you will because I don't anticipate you letting this go anytime soon, then you need to understand that *I* will be leading and we will do this according to *my* plan. Got it?"

He smirks and I notice his dark eyes dip momentarily to my lips. "You're cute when you're feisty."

My cheeks shimmer with heat. Suddenly beside me, Atlas drops all of his books and wrestles a small notepad and pen out of his pocket. He begins to write furiously.

"What are you doing?" I ask, turning my head towards him.

"Just making note that it's true fairy cheeks shimmer instead of blushing. I had yet to confirm it in person, myself. What a discovery!"

Rhea slaps a hand to her forehead and I roll my eyes.

"Is it also true that your wings glow when you're kissed?" asks Atlas.

"Yes," I huff, "but that's not important right now." I spin back to Caspar with my arms crossed. "We'll need to head out immediately. Time is of the essence."

"No."

Rhea guffaws behind me.

"Excuse me?" I ask, placing my hands on my hips.

Caspar takes another step towards me, forcing me to tilt my head back about as far as my neck will allow. "I said, no. We'll head out first thing tomorrow morning." He then turns and begins walking around me back towards the interior of the palace.

I spin at him. "No. That's a waste of time! We should—" He cuts me off.

"Lennox."

The guard appears at the door's entrance, ready for orders.

"Take Princess Luna to the crescent room and her companion to the pine room. Then prepare dinner."

Lennox nods to Caspar who turns back to face me. "You won't be of any help on our quest without proper food and sleep. We will all rest up tonight and head out tomorrow." I begin to protest, but he makes a shushing noise and holds his arm out, ushering both Rhea and me to the door.

* * *

I tuck in the edges with a huff.

"He's coming along with us? And his scholar?" I groan. "They're just going to slow us down!"

"I know," Rhea mumbles from where she's sprawled out, face down on the nearby couch in my room which consists of a simple bed, a writing desk, and a large window beside the couch. She lifts her head to meet my eyes where I stand fluffing one of the pillows on the bed.

"Their not being able to fly will double our traveling time," she supplies before plopping her face back down again.

"This is just the last thing I need right now. He drives me crazy."

"I think *you* drive *him* crazy," Rhea murmurs, her voice dissolved in the couch's cushions.

I place the pillow back down in its spot and spin towards her. "Oh, please."

She props her head up in her hands to peer at me. "You gotta admit he's hot."

I ignore her gaze, continuing my work. "I'll admit to nothing."

"That 'you're cute when you're feisty' line?"

I roll my eyes. "He just said that to frustrate me even further. I

Chapter 10

swear, all he does is find ways to annoy me. You should have seen him in the throne room after you went to the bathroom. He acted like we'd never met and said rude things to me. He asked if we bathed in the fairy kingdom and said that my hair was dirty orange and not red."

At this, Rhea starts to laugh.

I put my hands on my hips. "It's not funny!"

Her laughter finally slows and she smiles. "You gotta admit, that's a little funny."

I roll my eyes, again.

"Did you fire any remarks back at him?"

I purse my lips, coyly.

She smiles proudly. "Thatta girl."

I throw my hands up in the air as I move to fluff the other pillow. "Well, that's nothing compared to the fact that he's coming on this quest now. He's going to make me go insane, Rhea." I set the pillow back down. "The guy gets on my every last—"

"Nerve?"

I spin towards the doorway where Caspar now stands, smirking.

"Precisely," I say defiantly, crossing my arms. "And you could have knocked."

His gaze shifts from my eyes to behind me, puzzled. "Did you remake the bed?"

"No, I didn't," I answer, quickly.

"Yes, she did," Rhea half-whispers from the couch.

Caspar chuckles, amused.

"Gee. Thanks for that, *best friend*," I say, cheeks shimmering, shooting her a glare before spinning back to Caspar. "Everything in my life has become one big giant mess, so excuse me for wanting a little semblance of control."

"She also rearranged the flowers in the vase on the bathroom counter," Rhea supplies.

At this Caspar full-on laughs; a light, but full sound that sends a shiver down my spine.

I shoot Rhea daggers now. "Anything *else* you'd like to add?"

She opens her mouth, pointing an index finger upwards.

"*That was rhetorical!*" I say, quickly cutting her off. I huff, spinning back to Caspar at his place in the doorway. "Did you need something?"

"I just came to say that dinner's ready."

At this, Rhea bolts off the couch. "Say no more! I'm starving," she says, dashing past Caspar and down the right of the hallway.

"Other way," he calls, still facing me.

She passes behind him in the other direction now, muttering, "Okay, Mr. Know It All."

"Will you be joining us?" Caspar asks, his tall frame leaning against the inside of the doorway.

"Of course." That loaf of bread earlier barely did anything to suppress my appetite. I walk forward to make my exit, but just as I do, he moves into the center of the doorway, using his right arm to reach up and grab the top of the frame. I halt in my path and he peers down over me.

"Oh, by the way," he cranes his head down next to my ear, voice low, and I shiver at his breath. "I apologize, but my cook is fresh out of tarts."

While I'd refused to meet his gaze, I snap my eyes up to his now. "That's perfectly fine," I whisper back, feigning indifference. "All other tarts fall short of mine anyway."

"If we're speaking in terms of bitterness, then yes. That's correct."

I exhale an exasperated breath and attempt to make my exit, but he slides his arm down the right side of the door frame, so it's jutting directly in front of me, blocking my path.

"Must you always be so—" He cuts me off.

Chapter 10

"So what?" He brings his other arm up, gripping the frame on the opposite side of me as well now. Feeling trapped, I take a mini-step so my back is against the door frame to put some space between us. "Tall? Strong? Wickedly handsome?"

I narrow my eyes at him. "Irritating."

"Well, must you make it so easy?"

"I'm doing nothing of the sort and I doubt she would appreciate your flirting."

"Who?" he asks, looking genuinely confused.

"Gee, I don't know. Maybe the only woman whose portrait you have hanging all over this place?" I say. "Whether she's your lover, Princess, or whoever—" I trail off as he drops his arms and takes a step back.

"Those portraits are of my mother," he says, his demeanor changing entirely in a mere moment.

"Oh," I begin, but he cuts me off.

"We better get going or dinner is going to be cold," he says, turning and heading down the hall.

I fall into step a few paces behind him. We pass a portrait of his mother on our way and suddenly all I can see now are the ways they look alike that I didn't notice before: the slant of their noses, their tan skin, and the placement of their dimples. Now they look so alike, I can only see him in her face. I turn to see Caspar disappear into an open doorway on the left. I follow after him into a dining room where Rhea is picking at her food, looking half-asleep, with her face slack into an upright hand.

"So, you see," Atlas says, waving his fork about animatedly and holding an open book in the other, "the Hipira Beetle actually dies when it gets understimulated, or in simplified terms, bored. How fascinating!"

Rhea moves another piece of food around her plate, muttering,

"Lucky beetle," before she turns and sees Caspar and I approaching the table. Her face lights up with both delight and utter relief as I take a seat next to her. "Oh, my dear friend. I have never been so glad to see you."

I smile sideways at her with a knowing glance as I scooch in my chair and allow myself to take in the room. Small, but quaint, the dining room consists of plain walls and a roaring fireplace on the left side along with a medium-length table. It's long enough to give each guest proper arm space, but also isn't spacious enough to make it difficult to pass something to the person closest to you. This indicates to me that they don't have servants who wait on you at meal times as we do in Celestia. There are two chairs on each side of the table and none on the ends. So, with Atlas sitting across from Rhea, and me beside her, Caspar is forced to sit directly across from me. How lovely.

I turn from watching Caspar take his seat to look at Rhea. My eyes widen at the sight of her. "Rhea, what happened to you?"

"Don't eat the stuff in the brown bowl," she says, with a weak smile.

While I'd shot a quick smile her way a moment earlier, it hadn't been long enough for me to notice how bloodshot her eyes were. Red and puffy, it looks as if she's been crying for hours.

"I'm okay now, really," she adds.

I spin to the array of food lining the table until I find the brown bowl. It appears to be diced potatoes, but when I bring the bowl to my nose and inhale, a stinging sensation fills my nostrils.

"What is this?" I ask.

"Potatoes with cayenne," offers Atlas. "A sprite favorite due to the simplicity of its recipe and the fact that it's so versatile. Breakfast, lunch, or dinner, you can't go wrong with cayenne potatoes." He smiles, shoving a scoop of said potatoes from his plate into his mouth.

I turn to Caspar. "What is cayenne?"

Chapter 10

"It's a spice from a pepper. It adds a bit of heat to the flavor of the dish."

Rhea scoffs. "Yeah, sure. 'A bit of heat.' I felt like I'd set my tongue on fire."

"Oh, Rhea! I'm so sorry!" I say, rubbing her shoulder.

"I'm fine now," she says, taking a sip of a glass of milk that I notice has another empty one beside it. "But it was scary there for a moment. All I could think was that I would hate for everyone back at home to hear that I died from some freaking potatoes."

At this, I can't help but chuckle.

"Do you not have anything spicy in Celestia?" asks Caspar.

"No," Rhea utters with a thankful tone. "We don't have anything that tastes even remotely like that and rightfully so. I don't see how anyone could want to burn their insides to a crisp for a sense of flavor."

"Interesting," Atlas muses, jotting this down in his notebook that he once again pulls out.

I turn to Caspar who is filling up his plate across from me. "Is there anything here without spice that I can eat?"

His eyes graze the array of food before he nudges two dishes across the table in my direction. "This one," he says, pointing to the bowl, "is rice with assorted veggies." Then he moves on to the platter. "And this is grits with cheese and corn."

I'm surprisingly delighted at the flavors when I try a small tester bite of each before scooping full portions onto my plate; being careful not to let them touch. Caspar fills up his plate with an assortment of food, slopping things on top of each other in a very unorganized fashion, and as we both begin to eat, a wave of awkward silence falls. After a solid minute of only munching noises to fill the space, Atlas speaks.

"Should I perhaps take this opportunity to divulge more information about the quest we will embark upon tomorrow morning?"

"Yes," I reply at the same moment that Caspar says, "No."

I whip my head up from my plate and narrow my eyes at him. "It's important that we know what we're getting into tomorrow."

"We've all already agreed to go so the details don't matter."

"Of course they do. Without knowing all the details, how are we supposed to properly formulate a plan?" I counter.

Finally, he lifts his eyes off of his plate to look at me. "Don't worry about a plan. I've got it all under control."

At this, I put down my fork entirely. "I'm sorry, what part of 'I am leading this quest' did you not understand?"

He leans back in his chair, putting his arms up behind his head. The rippling muscles of his arms bulge in the position, but I pretend not to notice. "I understood what you were saying."

"Why are you being so difficult then if you agreed with me?"

"I never agreed with you."

"Yes, you did."

"No," he says. "I believe my only response was 'You're cute when you're feisty.'"

My cheeks shimmer and I act like I don't note Rhea's suppressed smile in the seat beside me.

"You know what, whether you agree with me or not, *I* will be leading this expedition. Therefore, I will be calling the shots and deciding what information is or isn't vital to our cause." I turn to Atlas. "Now, please tell us about the details of the quest."

"Well," Atlas begins, but Caspar raises a hand, cutting him off.

"Don't say a word."

I turn to Caspar, my patience for his antics running thin. "What?"

He leans forward, resting his arms on the edge of the table and bringing his hands together. "In case you've forgotten, he's *my* scholar."

"And best friend," Atlas leans forward to supply, earning him a glance from Caspar that makes him quickly lean back into his seat.

Chapter 10

Rhea sits beside me, sipping on her milk with wide eyes, watching all of this go down; clearly loving the drama.

"Well, in case you forgot," I say, leaning forward onto the table now with my arms to peer at him. "This is a dangerous mission—"

"That could potentially get us killed," Rhea interjects.

"Precisely," I continue. "You wouldn't even be going on this quest if it wasn't for me. So, how about you realize that and let Atlas here give me the information I need before I have to resort to getting it out of him myself?"

Atlas gulps and spins to Caspar with a nervous look.

Caspar's previous, serious face takes on a smirk now. "Very well. Atlas, tell her what she wants."

Atlas breathes a sigh of relief and turns back to face Rhea and me with the open journal. "The diary reads that once we travel into the Bog—"

Rhea shivers at the mention of it.

"—we must travel till we reach the garden of things to never forget."

"Never forget?" Caspar and I echo in perfect unison before shooting each other a glance; annoyed to have shared a similar thought.

"What does that mean?" I press.

"I have no further details on that part," says Atlas. "I can simply only relay what is here on the page."

"But—" Caspar begins, but Rhea jumps in, cutting him off.

"Everyone stop interrupting him so I can hear the rest!" she insists. "Continue, Atlas."

He appears nervous at her command, but compiles. "After we arrive there, we are to meet two wisps—"

"What the hell is a wisp?" Rhea asks, exasperated.

I spin to her along with Caspar who points a finger her way.

"You just said no interruptions!" he huffs.

"I meant from you two!" she spits back.

Caspar and I both roll our eyes at this.

Rhea leans onto the table towards Atlas. "Now, what is a wisp?"

Atlas shrugs. "I cannot say. Unfortunately, this diary is not very detailed."

I groan. "Oh, great. As if I wasn't already nervous enough about what we're getting ourselves into here, now I know we're basically going in blind. Perfect."

"You know, we don't have to know all the details, have a plan, and all that stuff. We can just go out and get it done. That's all it takes," says Caspar in my direction.

"Excuse me," I say, "but I will never share that opinion. Not when regarding little matters and definitely not ones of this magnitude of importance."

"That's fine," says Caspar. "You don't have to share my opinion. I just don't want your control issues getting in the way of our quest."

Rhea sucks in a breath beside me.

"Excuse me?" I ask, and he smirks. I lean forward at him. "I'd say it's also a control issue if you fear control and have to do everything on a whim."

"That's technically an accurate statement. You see—" Atlas begins, but Caspar hushes him.

"I don't fear control," Caspar states back at me now, folding his arms across his chest defiantly.

"Then why do you have to do everything on a whim?" I ask, peering.

"I don't have to. I just get to because it doesn't take a fat load of planning on my part to accomplish a simple task."

"A simple task?" Rhea jumps in. "That couldn't be more of an understatement." She points a hand in my direction. "She has her whole kingdom riding on this. Tell me I'm wrong when I say that if roles were reversed, and it was your kingdom on the line, you wouldn't want to do everything in your power to make sure it would go well."

Chapter 10

"Well, I—" he starts but then stops.

"You know I'm right. Now can everyone please just realize that we are all on the same team here?" Rhea asks, arms out to her sides.

"A team?" Atlas repeats with a wide grin. "I've never been on a team before!"

"Really? I can't imagine why," says Rhea, shooting me a sideways glance.

I turn and see Caspar's eyes fixed on me. Can we play nice? Are we capable of that? For the sake of my kingdom, we have to try.

"Truce?" I say, stretching out my hand.

He holds out for just another moment before he reaches out to shake my hand.

"Truce."

His hand is so large it envelopes mine like a blanket and while my hand is soft, his is covered in rough calluses. His dark eyes go from our handshake to meet mine and he's looking at me so intently that I feel frozen. The warmth of his hand in mine vanishes as Rhea quickly stands up and yawns.

"Okay. Now that that's accomplished, I need some sleep," she says aloud before turning to me. "You coming?"

I nod and stand. "Thank you for dinner. Goodnight."

Caspar dips his head at me. "Goodnight."

"And sweet dreams!" Atlas adds with a smile.

I chuckle as Rhea and I make our exit. Dinner may have started rocky, but it ended well. I think our truce will help us avoid danger, but as I turn back while rounding the doorway, I see Caspar's eyes still on me, and feel that warmth in my hand all over again.

Maybe this quest isn't the dangerous thing I should be worried about.

Chapter 11

"I thought you two were going to launch into a full-on brawl right in the dining room if I didn't intervene."

I turn onto my side and roll my eyes at Rhea beside me on her bed, having come to her room after dinner to discuss the evening with one another, as we do everything.

"Oh, please. It wasn't that bad," I say with a nonchalant toss of my wrist.

Her eyes grow wide. "Wasn't that bad? Girl, your whole argument was escalating faster than that cayenne pepper lit my throat on fire."

I chuckle. "Well, you get how he's so irritating, right? It's not just me?"

She grows serious. "No, you're right. I see why he's so irritating to you. You guys are polar opposites—"

"Exactly!"

"—and also so similar."

"Wait, what?" I ask, tucking my arm under my head to prop it up. "We aren't similar at all. How dare you insinuate that I share any similarities with that pompous sprite!"

She gets up and proceeds to sit cross-legged across from me. She

Chapter 11

tilts her head downwards with her eyes up at me. "Are you serious?"

Now I sit up also to convey my firmness through my stance. "Yes!"

"Luna," she starts. "You're both dignitaries, you both care a lot about your kingdom, and you are both very stubborn—"

"Hey!"

"It's the truth!" she finishes, flashing me a smile. "I love all those things about you. If you use those similarities properly on this quest, it could help us."

I keep my mouth shut, wanting to refute her statement, but knowing she's right. Caspar and I really do have to try and get along on this quest of ours or else it will be one miserable expedition for everyone.

"What have we gotten ourselves into?" I ask aloud, falling back and stretching out on the bed.

Rhea lays back and wiggles around till she's positioned directly alongside me. We stare up at the wooden ceiling together.

"I know," she says. "It's crazy to think we were just celebrating you ascending the throne and now we're in the palace of the kingdom estranged from ours and about to head out on an adventure with a King, whom you despise, and an odd, intellectual fellow."

"He is quite odd, isn't he?"

She nods. "I thought you were rather odd when I first met you."

I laugh. "Likewise."

Her face takes on a nostalgic smile. "You know, I don't remember much of my childhood. I don't remember my parents, but I remember this little gangly girl, with the brightest hair I'd ever seen, coming to my rescue."

"I remember that day," I say, quietly. "I can remember it like it was yesterday. Gosh, we were so little then. I was flying back to my room, after a Princess lesson in the library, when I heard guards yelling around the corner. I flew over to see what all the fuss was about and there you were, surrounded by three guards, with your arms full of food."

"Candies, cookies, chocolates," she trails.

"I came up to you and I asked why you were taking all that food."

"And I said it was because I didn't have anyone to feed me."

"Then I said, 'Well if you're going to steal food, why not steal it in town? Why go through all the trouble of sneaking into the palace?'"

She laughs; a melodic sound. "And I said because I knew the palace had the best treats and even though I was an orphan, I was still picky."

I reach down and grab hold of her hand, squeezing it. She squeezes back.

"Then," I continue, "I told you I would take care of you from now on."

"You took me by the hand and tried to lead me away, but the guards stopped you and said you couldn't just keep me. You said, 'Do you know who I am? I may be the Princess now, but one day I'll be Queen. So, if I say she's staying, then she's staying. She is now my best friend.' I couldn't believe it. You had saved me in the whole span of about one minute flat."

I squeeze her hand again. "The best minute I ever spent."

She smiles, rolling her head onto my shoulder. "In case I haven't said it before, thank you."

My eyes start to feel watery but with happy tears. "Don't even mention it. If anything I should be thanking you. My Princess lessons drove me crazy. Everything drove me crazy. I felt like I never got to do anything for myself. So, when I went to my mother and told her about wanting you to stay at the palace, I was surprised when she said yes. I thought she'd just see you as something to distract me from getting ready to be Queen. I was shocked she said you could stay and asked why she was so fine with it. She said she knew I needed a companion my own age, especially never having gotten a brother or sister."

Chapter 11

"I really am like the sister you never had."

"You sure are."

She sits up to turn and look at me. "While we may be in a crappy situation right now, just know that there's no one else I'd rather be in it with."

I smile, sitting up to embrace her. "Me either."

As we release each other from our embrace, she lets out a giant yawn.

"I'll let you get to bed," I say with a pat on her shoulder.

"Yeah, we should both get some sleep. *Big* day tomorrow."

"Love you," I say through the crack of her door as I close it.

"Love you too!" she yells through the door, making me chuckle as I head to my room.

I pass through the doorway and then stop in my tracks. Caspar is sitting at the base of my bed, relaxed, leaning back onto his hands, but he sits forward as soon as he sees me.

"What are you doing in here?" I ask, coming to stand across from him, arms folded.

"I just wanted to say you were right. I—"

"I'm sorry," I say, holding a hand up, stopping him. "I think I must have misheard you. I was what now?"

He scoffs with a roll of his eyes before peering back at me. "I said you were right."

I feign shock and give him a quick glance from bottom to top. "Okay, who are you and what have you done with the King?"

He laughs a low chuckle that rumbles through the air. "I walked right into that one."

I nod. "You sure did. Now what am I right about?"

"Me," he hesitates. "I do fear control."

I'm surprised he's admitting this to me and he must read it on my face because he quickly adds, "Just a little bit."

I uncross my arms to put them on my hips now. "Why are you telling me this?"

"Because I wanted to say that I meant our truce if you did."

"I did," I say, seriously. "This has to go well. I don't want our bickering to get in the way of that."

"Nor do I." He stands and approaches me. "You like to be in control and I don't share that same need, but I'm offering to be understanding of that difference of ours if you can be also."

I peer into his eyes and read his face. "It's hard for me to trust you after you led me on for so long before telling me you were the King."

He takes another step towards me, arms out as a sign of surrender. "I explained my reasoning behind that."

"You may have, but how am I to know you are being sincere?"

"I just told you that you were right. Do you know how painful that was for me?"

I smirk. He's right. "I can imagine. Alright, then. I can understand our differences in how to approach things."

He smiles. "Happy to hear it." He turns and begins to leave.

"I would have never expected you to wave your white flag so soon, Your Highness," I say.

"You'll find that I'm full of surprises," he says, turning back with that wicked grin of his, "and we can drop the formalities. Call me Caspar."

Chapter 12

"Okay. Here's one for you and one for you," Caspar says, passing around the leather satchels. "Each one has your reserve of food and water, as well as some light first aid supplies and a blanket."

Atlas accepts his bag from Caspar's outstretched hands and whispers, not quietly enough, "Did you pack my ointment?"

Caspar gives him a quick nod. Rhea and I share a glance and she lets out a quick burble of a chuckle.

Atlas turns to her. "Are you alright?"

I cover my mouth with my hand to suppress my laugh now.

"I had something stuck in my throat," Rhea says, pounding her fist to her chest once and then breathing slowly.

Atlas grows serious. "Well, if at any time you should need respiration assistance of any kind, just know that I am fully trained and qualified to assist."

Rhea nods with a suppressed smile. "Oh, thank you. Yes, I'll remember that."

Atlas smiles, happy to be of help.

I wear my satchel cross-body, as do Rhea and Caspar, but Atlas throws his lightly over his right shoulder. I turn to Caspar.

"Which way to the Bog?"

Rhea shivers.

He points a finger. "This way."

"Well then, let's be on our way," I say, leading the group.

Rhea quickly runs up to walk alongside me, leaving the men behind us. "I still hate walking. Do you think we'll be able to fly in the," she shivers, "you know what?"

I ponder this but come up with no definitive answer. "I'm not sure, but I hope so. Oh, hey," I say, lowering my voice to her now. "I wanted to tell you that I found Caspar in my room after we said goodnight last night."

She raises her eyebrows. "And?"

"And he told me I was right about him not liking control. He said that if I could be understanding on this quest of our difference in that perspective, then he would be too."

"Well I'll be darned," she says, eyes wide and blinking. "I didn't see that coming at all."

"Me either. I'm glad though because I don't want this whole trip to be filled with fighting."

She nods slowly before she makes a face. "Well, saying you want a truce and then actually acting on a truce are two very different things. You both may have agreed to be understanding, but we'll have to see just how well you mean it."

I lower my voice even more. "I am perfectly capable of holding up my end as long as he holds up his."

"What are you two whispering about up there?"

Rhea and I turn our heads towards Caspar in step with Atlas behind us. He smirks. "Is it something you can share with the group?"

I open my mouth to speak, but Rhea beats me to it. "Why, yes. We were just brainstorming what Atlas's ointment could be for."

At this, Atlas's face takes on a furious shade of red.

Chapter 12

"Like hell, that's what you were whispering about," says Caspar, his eyes narrowed.

"You'll never know," I say with a smirk.

Rhea and I face forwards again and we all walk in silence for a few minutes before Rhea speaks. "Okay, I think it's time to play 'pick one.'"

I let out a groan. "Rhea, please no."

"Is it a game?" asks Caspar.

"I'm unfamiliar with it," says Atlas, pushing up his glasses. "Can you please provide me with the rules? Once I learn how to play, I do plan to best you all."

I roll my eyes with a chuckle. "It's this game she and I always play when we're bored."

"It's simple," Rhea says. "We take turns asking the group to pick between two things and everyone shares their answers."

"That's it?" Caspar asks.

"That sounds oddly elementary," Atlas mumbles, suspicious. "Surely there must be some other element to it for the sake of complexity. This sounds like a child's game."

Rhea narrows her eyes at him.

"I don't know if I feel like playing," says Caspar, folding his arms across his chest.

"Yeah, me either, Rhea," I add, not wanting the pressure of asking questions to Caspar or having to answer them myself.

Rhea turns to meet the eyes of each of us in turn as we walk. "You'd all rather walk the entire distance to the Bog," she shivers, "in awkward silence?"

Caspar and I both release a breath.

"Fine," he says.

"Fabulous," Rhea says with a clap of her hands. "I'll go first. Sunrise or sunset?"

"Which do we prefer?" Atlas asks, clarifying before he provides his response.

Rhea nods.

"Sunrise then," Atlas says matter-of-factly. "There's more science behind them."

"Sunset for me," I say.

"Why?" Caspar prods.

"The colors," I say, but his eyes make this feel like less of an answer and more like a confession.

"Me too," he says, before returning his gaze to the ground.

"Sunsets for me, also!" says Rhea. "Okay, now it's your turn, Luna."

I take a moment to think. "Cooking or baking."

"Cooking," answers Caspar insanely quickly.

I turn my head to shoot him a glance. "You didn't even think about it."

He shrugs. "It's not a hard question."

"Yes, but because baking is the obvious answer."

"Oh yeah? And why is that?"

"Because of all the ingredients and the whole process. It's like an art."

"Cooking has ingredients, too. It can also be an artistic process," he says, standing proud at having rebuked my claim. "But cooking is better because it's done with more soul."

At this, I guffaw. "You don't think I put my heart and soul into my baking?"

"I didn't say that."

"You insinuated it," offers Atlas.

Caspar shoots him a glare that makes him retreat a step backward.

"Cooking is better because it's less by the book. You don't follow a recipe exactly. You measure with your heart."

There's no way he just said that. "I'm sorry. What did you say? How do you measure with your heart?"

Chapter 12

"Yeah, I don't get how that works," adds Rhea.

Caspar shrugs. "You just put in however much of the ingredient you want that feels right."

He can't be serious. "What? That's ridiculous," I say.

His eyebrows shoot up. "Ridiculous?"

"Absolutely." I continue. "If you are measuring each ingredient so carelessly, how are you ensuring the turnout of the final product?"

He gives a low chuckle. "You can't. That's the fun part of it all. You never know for sure how it's going to turn out and recipes can end up producing new flavors all the time."

I spin to Rhea and find her with a knowing glance, plenty aware of how much this differs from my firm stance on baking. "Is he serious?"

"I assure you I am," he says, plainly.

"Well, that's absurd," I state.

He rolls his eyes. "Let me guess. You think it's absurd because things ought to be done exactly according to the recipe. Am I right?"

While I know that he wants admitting this to feel like an embarrassing feat, I have no issue with it as I am proud of my stance on the subject. "That's absolutely correct because that's the only proper way to go about it. The recipe is there for a reason. Why, for fairy's sake, would you ignore the measurements that have been provided to you? If you control each ingredient, you control the outcome to make it match your desire."

"What if I desire to have a unique outcome every single time?" he asks, his voice taunting.

I open my mouth to rebuke him again, but Rhea speaks first, clapping her hands together. "Okay!" She clears her throat. "Waving the white flags, my ass."

"What?" asks Caspar, looking between her and me. I smack her arm.

"Nothing!" she says. "Atlas, I believe it's your turn now."

"Hmm," he muses and we walk in silence for a moment as he thinks. "I've got it," he says finally, excited. "Ecology or Environmental Science?"

"Umm," Rhea begins, but Atlas cuts her off by breaking into hysterical laughter and slapping his knee.

"There's no correct answer because they are the same! You couldn't possibly choose Environmental Science without also involving Ecology," he exclaims, cracking up.

We all watch him in silence until he finally catches his breath and looks at Rhea.

"Congratulations, Atlas," she says, plainly. "You've officially ruined the game."

His face slacks. "What? No, I—"

"Yes, you did," she says.

We all share a sigh. This is going to be one long trip.

Chapter 13

"I don't get it," says Rhea as she stands at the front of the group. "It looks normal."

We arrived at the outskirts of the Bog a few moments ago, but have been too hesitant to enter. While I wasn't entirely sure exactly what I was expecting, I know it wasn't this. It appears to be completely ordinary.

Rocks and twigs are scattered atop the mossy ground, and when I peer through the thick wall of pine trees before me, I see nothing special. It looks entirely identical to the forest Rhea and I wandered through on our way to Durand, minus the different tree types.

"Are you sure this is it?" I ask.

Atlas nods.

"But it looks like every other forest," says Caspar, speculatively.

"It really does," I agree.

"Well, maybe everything we've heard is all rumor," Rhea says with a hopeful tone.

I shoot her a doubtful glance. "You seriously think that the stories about the Bog that have roamed the realm for centuries and centuries have been mere fabrication?"

She sighs. "A girl can hope."

"Well, since it looks like nothing, I say we go ahead and get on with it," says Caspar, stalking forward.

"Wait!" I call, forcing him to a halt.

He turns back and peers at me.

"You can't just waltz in!" I insist. "We need a plan."

He strokes his chin in thought for a brief second before turning back to face me. "I mean, I planned to walk in, but did you want to jog or something instead?"

I glare at him.

"I see no reasoning behind the suggestion that our speed of entrance should affect the environment once we are inside the forest," says Atlas, with a tilt of his head.

Rhea groans. "There *is* no reasoning behind it, Atlas. Caspar was just being an ass."

Caspar opens his mouth, but she holds up a hand, silencing him. "You totally were, so don't even start with me."

He closes his mouth and folds his arm across his chest in defiance.

"Now, what is the plan, Luna?" Rhea asks.

"Well, we have no idea what awaits us in there and while it may look normal, let's not believe it until we are inside and have determined so for ourselves. I say we all form a circle, facing away from one another, so that we are protected from all sides, and then we can all walk very slowly into the forest."

I see Caspar roll his eyes, but to my surprise, Atlas speaks first. "I think that's a splendid idea. That way every angle is accounted for and we are readily prepared for any surprises."

A smile slowly creeps across my face. "Thank you, Atlas. Now let's all get together."

We all form a half circle near the forest's edge, locking arms with our backs to one another ,so we can have a wide view of our surroundings.

Chapter 13

"Okay," I begin. "Everyone ready?"

"Yes," Atlas and Rhea answer in unison as Caspar mumbles, "We could have been well inside by now."

I ignore him. "Alright, then. Let's go. Slowly."

We begin creeping forward at a snail's pace, and for a moment, I feel as though we're being silly and this precaution wasn't necessary. However, all my thoughts vanish as we cross into the Bog and the strangest thing happens.

It's suddenly nighttime. The same forest we were just peering into, which had looked entirely ordinary, is now cloaked in darkness with falling snowflakes. A blanket of thick fog lays atop the forest floor making everything appear even more ominous as the specks of white land on our wings and skin with a shiver.

We all stop walking and Rhea speaks first. "Okay, what the actual hell?"

Atlas pushes his glasses up his nose with a glazed look of wonder in his eyes. "Fascinating."

I turn to Caspar, arms out in question. "It's night?"

He looks around and then up towards the sky. "There's no moon in the sky."

"Yet it's night," I say, dumbfounded.

"That it is," he responds in awe. "And it's snowing."

"Well," Atlas begins, "the Bog is known for being a place of oddities."

"I know that," says Rhea, "but I still wasn't expecting this."

"Well, is everyone okay to continue despite the dark?" I ask.

Caspar looks surprised. "And here I would have pegged you as the one who would want to stop and make camp."

I put my hands on my hips. "Guess you're not the only one who's full of surprises."

He flashes me that grin of his that always makes me feel both thrilled and nervous.

"I'm good to go on," says Rhea. She turns and begins walking forward ahead of us. "Can't fly with the stupid snow on our wings, though," she mumbles with a huff.

"True," I say, before turning to Atlas. "Does the journal say anything about how far it could be till—" I begin, but a scream cuts me off.

Atlas, Caspar, and I twirl around, searching, but Rhea is nowhere in sight. My heartbeat quickens.

"Rhea?" I yell out.

No answer.

"Rhea!" Atlas and Caspar scream, joining in.

"Where is she?" I ask, panicked. "Did either of you see where she went?"

Atlas shakes his head. "No! I saw her start walking off in this direction," he begins, moving to where she'd been standing and beginning to replicate the steps she took. "She was right about here—" and suddenly, faster than a bolt of lightning, he vanishes down beneath the fog of the forest floor.

I let out a scream. Caspar and I both take off our satchels and quickly rush over towards where he disappeared, but as soon as we reach the spot, I feel the ground disappear beneath us and we begin to descend into a foggy pit.

I'm screaming and screaming at the top of my lungs and grappling about trying to find something to grab hold of as we fall. I know Caspar must be beside me somewhere, but it's so jet-black that I can't see a thing. When it feels like I've been falling forever, and my throat begins to hurt from screaming, I suddenly connect with a slap into some kind of liquid and the hard impact causes my skin to feel as if it's burning. With all my clothes on, I'm weighed down and the liquid feels thick around me. I struggle to propel myself up and grab gasps of air. I'm flailing about and screaming, but one of my screams allows liquid to lap into my mouth and I begin to gag. The taste is strong

Chapter 13

and metallic; the liquid of a thick consistency.

Wait. The metallic taste. The thick consistency.

It's blood.

Now, I begin to panic even more. I fight against the crimson fluid, trying with all my might to keep myself near the top of the surface where I take huge breaths of air like it's food and I'm starving. I keep falling below and then fighting my way back up. The blood is in my ears and eyes and if I wasn't in such a dire situation, with so much adrenaline coursing through me, I know I would surely hurl.

After another moment, I feel my limbs begin to strain. No, no, no, this cannot be how it ends. I can't die in a pool of blood, down in a mysterious pit, in a magical forest, while my kingdom's fate still rests in my hands. I'll never get to see my mother again. I'll never get to bake another thing in the palace kitchen. I'll never get to be Queen. I failed.

My legs tire and my thrashing slows as I begin to accept my fate. At least I'll be able to be with Lita over the rainbow now; the one light in this dark abyss. I sink below. The last breath I took slowly escapes my lips and I know it's the last air I'll taste. At least when I go in a moment, I won't notice the dark of death creeping in since my surroundings are already so dim.

Something grabs my foot and pulls me down further. I want to scream but know that I can't. Suddenly, I feel hands grab me by my shoulders and lips press to mine.

Chapter 14

My brain feels foggy as I struggle to register what's happening. I jerk and attempt to make the person lose their grip on me. My wings begin to glow faintly, turning the blood around me to a light pink. I dare to peek open an eye for a millisecond and see that it's Caspar.

Caspar is kissing me? Now is hardly the time! I try to pull back out of his grip, but he moves one hand to grab the back of my neck. His other twists around my waist to pull me against him. In his kiss, I feel a desperate urgency. He's scared and I am, too. I don't know if it's the fact that I'm mere seconds from death or a moment of pure insanity, but I decide to give in to him.

He feels the moment I relax and uses it to pull me even closer to him. We're practically smashed together, but his kisses are still gentle. When I wrap my arms around his neck and kiss him back, I feel him startle slightly, his shoulders tensing under my arms. But then he seems to sink into it just as I did. His grip on my neck becomes softer and I feel his hand slide up into my hair. Butterflies fill my stomach as I realize how intimate his kisses suddenly feel.

My wings begin to glow brightly now, lighting up our surroundings. He pulls away, peering at my wings and then over to the right of us,

Chapter 14

where we can see the blood flowing in a current towards and then out of a large hole.

The hand from my neck trails down my arm, afraid to let me go, and takes my hand. He swims over to the hole, pulling me along behind him, and I do my best to kick my feet and make it easier. Where it's going to take us, we don't know, but what other option do we have?

We get to the hole, but it's slightly too small for us to fit through. The wall is composed of thick rock and Caspar does his best to kick at the edges of the opening. I feel like my lungs are going to burst as I watch him try to widen our only exit and words can't begin to express the immense relief I feel when he finally manages to knock some rock away.

His work causes the current to grow stronger and it quickly sucks us in. I'm not expecting to fall again, yet that is precisely what happens. The hole leads to another pit, similar to the one that brought us to this horrible pool in the first place, and we are thrown from the blood and begin falling once again.

We both scream now and he's holding onto my hand so hard I fear I may break a finger, but I don't want him to let go.

I see a light up ahead and begin to wonder if it's death coming to greet us. Perhaps this pit is deep enough to go all the way to the underworld.

I strongly hope it isn't.

We grow nearer and nearer to the light, and I squeeze his hand as we finally collide with it. But instead of impact, we are shot out of the bright opening. I'm suspended for a millisecond, my eyes closed in fright, and it's only once I feel my body collapse onto the hard ground that I open them.

We're back in the Bog, but the sun is out, and the snow is gone. Caspar is sprawled beside me, moaning and rubbing his left arm, soaked in blood with his clothes and hair tinted ruby red.

I attempt to sit up but groan from the strain my muscles feel; everything aching from my panicked attempt to stay afloat. I continue moving ever so slowly until I'm standing. I turn to Caspar and offer him a hand.

"Here. Let me help you."

I feel so many things when his eyes meet mine, hooded by wet hair, as I help pull him to his feet. Once he's upright, I feel something drip onto my eyelid. I use the back of my hand to wipe it away. When I see the blood on my hand, I'm reminded of the horrible, metallic taste that had filled my mouth. And it's precisely that thought which makes me lurch forward and hurl right onto Caspar's feet.

My lower back muscles pinch and spasm as I heave up the few contents of my stomach. "I'm sorry. I'm so sorry," I attempt to say.

I'm so embarrassed, but I can't stop, the memory and stress of all that just occurred sending my body into overdrive. To my surprise, Caspar reaches out and gently gathers my hair back from my face with one hand and then rubs the patch of skin between my wings on my back soothingly.

"Just let it out," he says, softly. "You're okay."

After another moment, my heaving finally slows and I'm able to stand back upright, although it's a shaky endeavor with my body feeling so weak. Caspar looks at me cautiously.

"Are you better now?"

"A little, I think," I say, hands on my hips in an attempt to steady myself.

We walk around for a few moments till we find our satchels and put them back on. Caspar does a slow circle in place, taking in our surroundings.

"I think we're back in the Bog, but it's daytime now."

I nod. "My thoughts, too."

"Wait," he says. "Did you see any trace of Atlas and Rhea when we

Chapter 14

were down there?"

I feel my body tense with guilt. I'd been so caught up in my own peril, I'd forgotten we ended up there in the first place because we were looking for them.

He must read this on my face because he speaks again.

"It's okay. I sort of forgot about them too down there. That doesn't make us bad people. We just focused on our safety first. Anyone would have in our situation. It's instinct."

I nod slowly. "Yeah, I suppose, but," I groan, "what if they are still down there?" I ask, pointing to the large hole a few feet over that we shot out from. "What are we supposed to do? Go back down?"

He opens his mouth to respond but stops. His eyes widen as they lock on something behind me, and he looks both concerned and relieved.

"Caspar?" I turn to see what he's looking at. "Rhea!" I call out, running as fast as my sore limbs will allow until I reach her. While I want to embrace her, I stop when I see that both she and Atlas are dripping in something caramel colored and sticky.

"What happened to you guys?" I ask.

Atlas tries to use the bottom of his shirt to clean off his glasses and Rhea turns to me with an exhausted expression.

"I started walking ahead of you guys and I guess I must have fallen down a hole or something because suddenly I was sinking into the ground; just falling and falling for what felt like forever and then I got thrown into this pool of goo," she cringes recalling it. "The consistency was so sticky that it took all my strength to move. I felt like I was drowning in a bottle of syrup. Now, I'm pretty sure it was tree sap. Atlas fell down a moment later, which was a surprise." She sighs. "Long story short, we were able to get unstuck and then climbed out of the hole using these long vines. We did lose our satchels down there though, so we've lost our supplies."

I tilt my head at her and narrow my eyes. "How did you get unstuck?"

Atlas opens his mouth and holds up an index finger, signaling that he's going to speak, but Rhea slaps a hand over his mouth with an angry expression.

"You shut up!" She slowly lowers her hand and turns back to face me. "We just did, okay?"

I know there has to be more to this story, but I'll have to get it out of her at a later time because all I can think about now that I know they are safe, is how to get clean.

Atlas pushes his glasses up the bridge of his nose. He peers at Caspar and me, his expression bewildered. "What in the realm are you covered in?"

"We fell down the same hole going after you guys, but ours was pitch black and plopped us into a thick pool of," I try to say, but begin to gag at the memory and cover my mouth quickly.

Caspar pats my shoulder twice before turning to Atlas.

"Blood," he says, with a sigh.

Now it's Atlas's turn to cover his mouth.

Rhea gapes at us in horror. "Whose blood is it? Where did it come from?"

"All good questions, but unfortunately, it doesn't look like we're going to get any answers. What matters now is that we're all safe," answers Caspar.

"He's right," I say, finally calm again, the wave of nauseous past. "We're all back in one piece and that's the most important thing. Now, the next most important thing is to get clean. I say we keep walking onward to find that garden of things to never forget, and just pray and hope that there's a stream or something along the way." I hold out my arms in question. "Everyone with me?"

"Like we have any other choice," Rhea breathes with a sigh.

Chapter 14

* * *

We've been walking in silence for what feels like forever. Everyone is too exhausted to speak. Caspar and I have been walking side by side behind Rhea and Atlas and I keep thinking of our kiss; the way his hand felt in my hair and how my stomach was in knots. I keep waiting, thinking he'll reach out and take my hand or something.

Rhea suddenly stops walking. "Wait, how did you guys get out?"

The rest of us stop walking and Caspar and I share a glance. He runs his hand through his messy hair, the blood having dried and made it stiff now. "Well, we," he starts to Rhea but falters. "We, um," he looks to me, unsure of how to recount it.

"He kissed me," I begin. Rhea's eyes widen. "And the glow from my wings was enough light for us to see a hole leading out of the pool. We swam through that and fell down another hole, except this one took us up. We fell upwards, if that makes any sense," I say with a shrug.

"Well, well, well," Rhea says, glancing back and forth between Caspar and me with a smirk, arms crossed.

"That was genius!" says Atlas, clapping a proud hand on Caspar's shoulder.

Rhea turns to him, eyes narrowed. "Genius?"

"Yes!" Atlas says, excitedly. He looks to Caspar again. "He kissed her because he knew her wings would provide them with the light they needed to find a way out."

Rhea shoots me a questioning look and I will my face to not reveal the shock I'm feeling inside. I look down at my shoes.

So, that kiss wasn't a confession of feelings? A desperate attempt to have one moment together before we met our end? It was just part of a plan? How could I be so foolish?

I guess he's played me once again. I swear it'll be the last time.

Atlas pats Caspar's shoulder again. "Great, job, my friend. That was very quick thinking. Not everyone would have remembered that under such impending circumstances."

I see Caspar shoot a look my way out of the corner of my eye, but I refuse to make eye contact right now, afraid he'll see right through me. He shifts, stretching his neck out. "Happy it worked."

I feel my heart chip away a little. That smug sprite. Whether what he did saved us or not, he used me. Ugh, now I feel so incredibly stupid for kissing him back. He was just trying to save us and I got all sucked up into the moment. How could I have been so thoughtless? He couldn't possibly care for me, or I for him. We hate each other and have butted heads every moment since we first encountered one another. It doesn't matter how the kiss felt, or how it made me feel. One thing is certain. If I want to make it through the rest of this trip without losing my mind over my stupid heart, then I need to make sure he thinks I was in on his plan the whole time.

"Yeah, I was so glad to see you had the same idea when you kissed me because I was worried that if I kissed you first, you might get the wrong impression," I say, standing tall and plastering on my best smile.

Caspar ruffles his hair once more. "Yeah, no worries."

We all begin walking again.

"Does anyone see water or something anywhere?" Rhea asks, desperately. She throws her head back with a groan. "Disgusting doesn't even begin to describe how gross I feel right now." She pulls a strand of hair in front of her eyes. "See?" she says, showing it to me. "That tree sap turned my hair to solid rock!" She flicks the thick strand of hair with the fingers of her free hand, and sure enough, the hair makes a small whack sound and is completely unphased.

I hold up a hand to her. "Don't you dare even begin to complain to me. I would take tree sap over blood any freaking day."

She observes all the blood now dried onto me and cringes. "Yeah,

Chapter 14

you're right. That's definitely worse."

I nod and then peer ahead of me at Caspar's back and broad shoulders; hoping that he believes my lie. I will my heart to forget how good that kiss felt.

And how much I want to do it again.

Chapter 15

"Oh, sweet mercy!" Rhea cries, breaking free from the group and darting off to the left towards what appears to be a large pond of water among a giant collection of flowers. As soon as she reaches the pond, she wastes no time in jumping straight in, shoes, clothes, and all with a loud, "Woohoo!"

The rest of us are hot on her tail. Atlas, Caspar, and I ease ourselves into the pond, versus Rhea's outright cannonball, and I feel instantly better as soon as I'm submerged into the cool water. We all quickly begin scrubbing our skin and clothes and washing out our hair.

Gosh, it feels so good to get clean.

Atlas is leaning with his arms up along the side of the pond and Rhea floats on her back beside me.

It takes Caspar and I longer to get the blood completely off us; it having dried into every nook and cranny. I un-braid my hair to ensure that I get every last, little bit washed away.

Atlas sneezes; a loud noise that reaches a high pitch I wouldn't have guessed he was capable of.

"Shhh!" Rhea says, frustrated. "You're disturbing the one peaceful moment I've had since we entered this disaster of a forest."

Chapter 15

Atlas sneezes again.

Rhea turns back to an upright position now and juts a finger at him, angrily. "I'm serious, you smart-ass sprite!"

He opens his mouth to speak, but another sneeze escapes him.

"That does it!" Rhea yells, lunging forward in the water towards him, but I grab her by the arms, holding her back.

"Rhea, calm down! Please!"

Atlas sneezes another time and Rhea's face turns to rage. "Let me at him!"

I hold her tight. "Rhea, stop! You can't hurt him! We need him to read the map, remember?"

Atlas wipes his nose and looks frightened beyond belief as he scurries up and out of the pond.

Rhea's eyes narrow. "A little damage, but I'll steer clear of his eyes so he's still useful to us."

I loosen my grip on her and take on a wary tone. "I think this quest is changing you."

She shrugs me off and points at Atlas where he stands out of the water with a scared expression. "You owe me one peaceful moment!" she says. "Got it?"

He nods rapidly and I feel bad for the poor boy. He poked the beast at the wrong time.

Caspar chuckles, having watched everything go down.

I shoot him a look. "You're not helping."

"Sorry," he says amidst his laughter. "I can't help it."

I roll my eyes.

Caspar finally stops cracking up and hops out of the pond, turning to Atlas. "Why are you sneezing so much, bud?"

"I think I must be having a mild allergic reaction to all the flowers," Atlas says, covering his nose with his arm.

"You're allergic to blue daisies?" Caspar asks, confused, looking at all the surrounding flowers.

"Those aren't blue daisies," Rhea scoffs, hopping out of the pond with me. "Those are forget-me-nots." She turns to me and rolls her eyes at them. "Stupid sprites."

Realization hits me as her words sink in. "Wait, what did you say?"

She looks at me quizzically. "I said, 'stupid sprites.'"

"No," I say, tapping her arm, excitedly. "Before that! You said these are forget-me-nots and you're right. They are. Which means—"

"This is the garden of things to never forget," Caspar finishes for me.

Atlas sucks in a breath and grabs Caspar's arm, holding out his other hand openly. "Give me the journal!"

Caspar opens his satchel and hands the book to Atlas. "See?" Caspar says. "This is why I insisted on carrying it. If you'd had it, it would be sunken into a pool of tree sap right now and we'd be screwed."

Atlas stands tall and flips through the journal's pages. "I don't see how discussing hypotheticals is at all productive right now."

Caspar rolls his eyes.

"Aha!" Atlas says, pointing to the page he's selected. "Here we are. Once you reach the garden of things to never forget, you shall meet two wisps. They are very friendly, but beware of dishonesty or you shall pay."

Rhea groans. "Why does everything have to be so ominous and vague? Would it have killed him to write in some details?"

"For real," I add, sharing in her frustration. "They are friendly? Beware of dishonesty?"

"Quite vague indeed," notes Atlas.

"Okay, lack of detail aside, what do these wisps look like?" asks Caspar. "How do we find them?"

Atlas's eyes skim across the page before he looks up with a solemn face. "I'm afraid that information was not provided."

Caspar lets out a deep groan. "Of course, it wasn't. Because that would have actually been helpful."

"All we know is that we have to obtain a magical object from them in order to proceed with our quest," says Atlas with a shrug.

"Okay," I say, grabbing everyone's attention. "Let's just start looking around and see if we can find these wisps somehow. I know we don't know what they look like, but something tells me they'll be easy to identify."

Rhea puts her hands on her hips and turns, starting to peruse the flowered area. "Alright. Let's get cracking."

Caspar, Atlas, and I all spread out, too. I inspect the patch of forget-me-nots nearest to me, not sure what I'm even looking for. How am I supposed to find a wisp if I don't even know what one looks like?

After a few minutes of no progress, my body jolts with a startle as Rhea suddenly begins clapping her hands and yelling, "Here, wisp! Here, little wisp!"

Caspar throws his head back with a groan before turning to me with his arms out at his sides. "Is she serious?"

I'm still feeling mixed things about Caspar from our kiss, but one feeling I know for certain is in that mixture is anger. "She can search for them however she wants. She's definitely being more proactive than you."

His eyebrows bunch together, questioning my retort, but I act indifferent and return to searching the flowers around me.

"Come out, come out, wherever you are!" Rhea chants with more rhythmic clapping.

Atlas stands with a huff. "I don't believe they will simply come when called. What wild creature has that natural tendency?"

Rhea shoots him a glare. "Don't you give me any crap. I will search however I want to search. You just remember that you are on my list. Got it?"

Atlas takes a couple retreating steps away from her.

Having known Rhea for most of my life, I know that she doesn't usually get this irritated with someone so easily. There has to be a root cause for her anger. Perhaps it's related to how she and Atlas managed to escape the pool of tree sap they were trapped in before. If that involved him doing something to piss her off, then that would explain her short temper with him both in the pond and now. I make a mental note to ask her about it as soon as we have a moment alone without our traveling companions.

"Well, even if the wisps won't come out and greet us, I can at least beauty myself up a bit. Not that I need it," says Rhea, bending down and plucking a flower from its stem to tuck behind her ear. She spins towards the rest of us now, striking a pose. "Well? How do I look?"

A glowing being slowly and silently begins to manifest behind Rhea, the molecules of the air shaking and pulling to form together. It's shaped like one of us with its height and overall form of arms and legs, but its composition is comprised of what appears to be purple flames, and instead of hands and feet, the end of its limbs dissolve away into nothing. Its eyes are yellow and as bright as the sun itself, but its mouth is light pink. Its head is incredibly large and resembles the shape of a teardrop with the top coming together to a point.

We found a wisp.

The wisp finishes developing in what feels like slow motion, but I know it must all happen in a mere second. It's suspended in the air behind Rhea, two teeny-tiny, indigo wings sprouting from its back. While it doesn't look necessarily scary, I will assume that it means harm until I see proof of otherwise. I open my mouth to yell out to Rhea across the flower patch from the rest of us in warning, but the wisp speaks first.

"You look fabulous," says the wisp in a high-pitched screech of a tone.

Rhea whirls around towards the wisp and lets out a scream.

As if mirroring her reaction, the wisp spins around and frantically searches the area behind it, letting out an identical scream before running to hide behind Rhea.

"What!? What is it?" It flails its limbs about in fright.

At this, we are all stunned.

Rhea seems to find her words first. "Um, I thought I saw something, but it's gone now," she says with a nervous smile.

The wisp lets out a sigh "Whew!" A bright smile returns to its pink mouth. "Hi, there! I'm Seraphina."

"And I'm her sister Effie!"

Atlas twirls around and lets out a high screech at the sight of the mint-colored creature behind him. Effie resembles her sister identically in all things except color. Where Seraphina is hues of purple with facial features of yellow and pink, Effie's comprised of minty-teal tones with deep fuchsia features. Two equally small wings protrude from the top center of her back as she hovers laughing at Atlas who shies away. "What a girlish scream!"

This causes Seraphina to nod and laugh along, too.

Atlas frowns, yanking the bottom of his shirt downward and pushing his glasses up.

"I don't think my scream sounds girlish in the slightest," he says, offended.

"Is that so?" Seraphina asks, her voice dripping with doubt.

Effie turns to me and I will myself to not act frightened by how close she gets. Her eyes are glazed and foggy like coated in a winter frost. "Do you think his scream was girly?"

I know saying yes will hurt Atlas's feelings, so I open my mouth to say otherwise, but suddenly I remember the words of the journal: Beware of dishonesty. I don't know what price there is to be paid, but I don't wish to find out. Honesty it is. "Yes, it was."

Atlas's hand goes slowly to his chest, his mouth open.

"See?" Effie says, smiling as she turns back towards Atlas.

I lean to the right to see Atlas around Effie's frame. "I'm sorry!" I half-whisper.

He crosses his arms over his chest, clearly not letting it go.

Seraphina notices Caspar standing on the other side of me and her eyes shine even brighter.

"My, my, my," she says, floating over to him. She makes slow circles around him as he stands, looking confused, but trying to remain still. "You must be the Sprite King. Caspar is it?"

I see a look of confusion flash across the faces of Rhea and Atlas that's identical to my own.

Caspar looks equally befuddled. "How do you know me?"

"He matches her description perfectly, doesn't he?" She says to Effie.

I swear I see sweat suddenly bud on Caspar's brow. Did his mother travel through here?

"He's taller than she said, but besides that, it's a perfect likeness," agrees Seraphina with a nod.

"Thank you for your interest ladies. We're glad to finally meet you," Caspar says.

"Very glad," I say, interjecting myself into the conversation. "We are on a very important quest and require your assistance."

They both peer at me, curiously.

"Who are you?" asks Seraphina.

"My name is Luna and I am the Princess of Celestia, the fairy kingdom."

Effie's form shines even brighter with what appears to be excitement. "A King and a Princess? How romantic!"

Seraphina and her share a swoon.

"How did you fall in love? Oh, please, *please* tell us the story!" requests Effie, impatiently.

Chapter 15

Caspar and I both start waving our arms about in an attempt to somehow get a grip on the situation.

"Oh, no—" he begins.

"We're not—" I stammer.

"We're not together," Caspar finally utters.

At this, Effie's expression falters, before picking right back up as she flutters over to him.

"But why not? Don't you think she's beautiful?"

I swear all sound dies suddenly with Effie's question, the forest even hushing to hear Caspar's response. I can feel my heart pounding in my chest, unsure of what answer I'm even hoping to hear. If he disagreed, it would coincide very well with every other rude thing he's ever said to me. I'm sure he will since he is used to spritewomen with their pointed ears and olive, tan skin; nothing like me.

"Of course," he breathes, meeting my eyes.

Seraphina and Effie swoon, but I'm waiting; waiting for whatever price it is to be paid for his lie. Surely, he lied. I hold my breath, but nothing happens and I feel my heart grow even more confused.

He was telling the truth.

"Well, if you think she's beautiful, it's only a matter of time!" says Effie with utter glee before turning from Caspar back to me, forcing me to break eye contact with him and look at her. "Now, tell us about this quest."

"We are following the instructions of a journal that should lead us to the Amulet of Undoing," I say, happy to shove Caspar's answer into the back of my mind to examine later.

Effie makes a high-pitched coo of interest as Seraphina speaks.

"My sister and I are one with the Bog. We feel the energy of the forest around us and the tug of every magical object and creature within its walls. Your journey will be a hard one, but the amulet is incredibly powerful. Its great ability should prove helpful in whatever need you have for it. But you need something from my sister and I don't you?"

"Yes," I breathe, trying to not show how desperate we are.

"You need one of our hearts," says Effie.

"Your hearts?" Rhea asks, eyes narrowed in question. "How can you give us your heart? Won't you die?"

"Yes, but to die without sharing your heart with someone is a waste."

"We used to have another sister," adds Seraphina. "A man came through long ago and he took her heart. Now, it is our turn, but if you want to win our hearts, you must let us truly be friends."

Rhea, Atlas, Caspar, and I all exchange a quick glance with one another.

"Okay," Atlas speaks. "How might we win your friendship?"

"Tell us about yourselves," Seraphina says, mint and glowing from where she hovers.

Atlas stands tall and clears his throat. "Well, my name is Atlas and I am the youngest in a family of six. I was teased mercilessly when I was young for my intellect, which made me view it as a hindrance rather than an asset. I'm thankful to have learned the latter now. Once doing so, I decided to dedicate myself to furthering my education. However, with so many children to care for, my parents could not help fund my education. I went to the palace and I asked King Caspar here," he says, gesturing to Caspar beside him, "if we could make a deal. I said that if he paid for my schooling, then I would promise to work at the palace as a scholar for the rest of my life."

"What did he say?" asks Rhea curiously, earning a glare from the group.

"He said he would pay for my schooling, but that I only had to work at the palace upon graduating if I wanted to and that I could also leave at any time. It's a kindness I am still indebted to him for."

"You are not," Caspar says, placing a hand on his friend's shoulder.

Chapter 15

"You don't owe me anything."

Atlas smiles at him and Caspar drops his hand back to his side.

"I went to school and then came to work at the palace as soon as I'd finished. We formed a friendship and I have been working as a palace scholar ever since. Now, I am acting as a guide for our group and am providing directions via the journal."

"Wow, that's a lovely story," says Seraphina, gleefully. "Can I see this journal? I'm curious if it belonged to the same man who took our sister's heart long ago."

"Of course," says Caspar, hurriedly opening his satchel to retrieve it. However, he acts too fast and out with the journal, falls the bottle of Atlas's ointment.

Seraphina is too quick and she flies over to where it lays on the ground and peers at it. "What is this?"

"It's Atlas's ointment," Rhea says with a snicker.

"No, it's not!" Atlas yells at her and faster than my eyes can hardly register, both Effie and Seraphina lose all their vibrancy and turn to jet black, their eyes and mouths a deep red and they grow twice in size, beginning to hunch over in their stances, causing bony spines to protrude from their thin backs so clearly that I feel I could count every single one of their vertebrae; skeletons born from flame. We all back away in fright.

"Don't you lie to us!" Seraphina and Effie both shriek in voices sounding starkly lower and raspier than they previously have.

I watch in horror as they each raise a dark limb towards Atlas and he starts to scream; an ear-piercing cry of pain. He's grabbing at his throat and tears stream from his face.

No, no, no!

"What's happening to him?" Rhea cries.

Caspar runs in between Atlas and the dark sisters in an attempt to block whatever evil they are doing, but his presence between them makes no difference and Atlas continues to cry out.

"Stop!" I yell at the two dark wisps. "What are you doing to him?"

Effie's head spins all the way around to face me, though her body still faces forward and her eyes send a chill throughout my very bones; making me feel like I'm staring straight into the depths of hell itself.

"He shall never lie again!" she cries with a hiss.

Atlas's cries suddenly grow fainter and then even fainter and black smoke begins to drift out of his open mouth. Realization hits me. They're burning his vocal cords.

I think I'm going to be sick.

Rhea and Caspar hold him by his shoulders, yelling at the sisters to stop. I'm too frozen at the sight of it all to move. Atlas looks shattered in pain. Tears stream down his face and he continues to open his mouth and try to speak, but to no avail.

Everything is going wrong and I don't know how to fix it, but I have to do something. What if the sisters are so upset that they turn on the rest of us next? I can't let more people get hurt.

Think, Luna! Think!

Wait. The wisps said they die if they give you their hearts. I doubt they'll give them to us now.

So, we'll need to take them.

Chapter 16

Rhea has rushed over to join Caspar by Atlas's side where he now kneels on the ground among the flowers, but it's too late. The sisters have dropped their limbs and I see him trying to speak, but failing. The pain in his eyes cuts into my heart. The sisters stalk toward Atlas and continue to scold him.

"To lie is to spread falsehood in our forest!" screams Effie at him.

"Friends *don't* lie!" says Seraphina.

I make a motion with my arms to get Caspar's attention on me where I'm standing behind the sisters and use my mouth to slowly say, "Come here."

He cautiously looks at the sisters, who tower over Atlas, distracted in their fury, before he slowly walks backward over to me. Once he's reached my side, he whispers, "What?"

"I've got a plan and I need your help," I say, grabbing his arm to show my sense of urgency.

He nods. "What do you need me to do?"

"I need you to be prepared to run interference with Seraphina," I pause, taking a breath, "while I deal with Effie."

His eyes bulge. "Are you insane?"

"I'm going to rip out her heart."

He runs a hand through his hair. "Well, that's a freaking *yes*."

"Are you in or out?" I ask. "We have to do this now while they're distracted."

"Okay, fine." He says, heaving a breath. "Let's do this."

I turn and see Effie up ahead, the ridges of her spiny back before me. This is going to be difficult no matter what, but I do wish that she hadn't grown twice in size when she changed to black.

I take a deep breath. The fact that Effie is made of flames makes this tricky. If I touch her, I'll be burned. I stare at her back for a brief second, trying to figure out the smartest way to go about this. Suddenly, I remember that we got out of the large pond some time ago now. I do a quick small flit of my wings and confirm that they have air-dried and I am once again able to fly. Okay, this, I can work with, and at least I also have the element of surprise on my side with her distracted.

I quickly fly over to the pond and use my hands to cup as much water as I possibly can before I quietly fly up to Effie from behind, Seraphina and her both still yelling at Atlas over his dishonesty. Caspar has walked back to stand on the other side of Seraphina now, ready for anything. He slowly unbuttons his leather vest and pushes the sides back to carefully rest his hand on a dagger I now notice is strapped to his hip. If I'd seen he was armed earlier, I may have scolded him for not telling me, but now I'm just glad he's prepared in case this gets ugly. However, a dagger might not provide a huge help when the creature you're fighting is formed of flames.

I use my wings to fly silently upwards till I'm directly above Effie. Taking a quick deep breath, I utter a fast prayer to the rainbow. I fly down suddenly in front of Effie, catching her off guard. Shock plagues her face as soon as she registers it's me.

"What are you—" she begins, but I quickly throw the cupped water

Chapter 16

in my hands onto her chest.

She cries out in pain as steam emits; a splitting sound that's so loud I see Atlas, Rhea, and Caspar all attempt to cover their ears, but I can't. I don't have much time. I have to act fast.

I quickly shove my hand into Effie's chest through the singing hole until I feel her beating heart. Then, I clutch it firmly and pull it out with all my strength. The water only cooled her flames for a brief moment and as I pull my arm outwards, I cry out from the heat. I don't think it's enough to burn me, thanks to the water, but it's still incredibly painful.

Once my arm is fully retracted, with her heart in hand, she loses all color and drops into a pile of grey ashes on the forest floor. I'm using the brief moment I have to stuff the dark, mushy heart into my satchel when I hear a cry ring out, but I turn to see that it's Seraphina. She is clutching a limb; shorter now than the others as if her flaming arm has been severed, and I know it has been once I register the small ashes on the ground beside her and Caspar poised in a fighting stance with his dagger drawn.

Rhea and Atlas run over beside me and I turn to them, grabbing Rhea's shoulder with one hand and pointing at the pond with another.

"Both of you! Grab as much water as you can and help us!"

They nod, Atlas running over with Rhea flying beside him.

I turn back and watch in horror as Seraphina's limb slowly grows back to its full length and she lets out a hiss to Caspar. While I expect her to lash out at him for severing her limb, it's not what she does. Instead, she turns to me.

"You stole her heart!" she screams. "You stole it! And now you must pay for it with your own!"

She quickly flies toward me, but I fly out of reach, swerving off to her left. She turns, screaming out in fury, and lunging after me again. I try to fly upwards this time, but she grabs hold of my foot.

Thankfully, her flames only wrap around my shoe, but I can see the fabric starting to char by the second as she gives me a firm yank. I'm caught off guard by her strength as I'm thrown to the ground. I thud on impact, dropping at such a speed with her pull that I bounce a second time before finally skidding to a stop; feeling the rough forest floor scraping my knees and arms as I do. I flip from my stomach onto my back and try to get to my feet, but everything hurts and I struggle to catch my breath.

"This is for Effie!" Seraphina cries in rage. "If you are going to *act* heartless, then you shall *be* heartless!"

She lunges towards me, dark limbs outstretched and poised for my heart, but suddenly Caspar dives in front of Seraphina, landing in a crouched position before me and the ends of her flaming limbs connect with the leather of the vest overlapping his chest instead. He drops the dagger in his hand and lets out a warrior cry; pain and bravery all laced together.

Seraphina's face takes on a furious expression at his interruption, but she has no time to speak on it before I hear Rhea yell, "Take this, you flaming freak!" as both she and Atlas toss their water onto Seraphina.

Steam emanates off her body in reaction and she screams, furiously, spinning around to face them.

Caspar wastes no time. He quickly grabs his dagger off the ground and slices it into Seraphina's spine. She screeches in agony and I can't believe my eyes as I watch Caspar rip out Seraphina's heart, with his bare hand and arm, right through her back. As soon as he retracts his arm, Seraphina diminishes into a pile of ashes; just like Effie.

Caspar is panting where he still crouches in front of me; chest heaving from the adrenaline and the pain I know he must be feeling from his burns. Unlike a regular burn, the flames have left him scarred, singing him with dark black veins, that look like tree roots, which

Chapter 16

snake across his right hand and up under the sleeve of his shirt.

I push onto my feet and walk around in front of him.

"Are you alright?"

He gingerly touches the black markings on his hand and winces, squeezing his eyes shut before opening them again with a groan.

"Hurts like hell, but I'll be fine," he says.

I take his hand in mine and help him to his feet. We all stand side by side in a semi-circle for a moment; processing everything.

After a moment of silence, Rhea huffs. "Good riddance," she says, kicking the pile of Seraphina's ashes; sending them scattering across the ground in a flurry. She puts her hands on her hips, turning to me now. "What you did back there with stealing Effie's heart was," she waves her arms about her head in a disorderly fashion, "absolutely insane."

"I must have lost my mind for a moment," I say, with a chuckle.

"For real!" she insists. "I saw you do that and I was like who is she? It was like you became some alter ego! Like," she pauses, thinking for a moment before holding her arms out wide, "Lunatic Luna!"

I can't help but chuckle at this.

"And you!" she says, turning to face Caspar now. "You literally reached in there and took Seraphina's heart without even the help of water. You're just as insane, if not worse," she says, smiling.

He shrugs. "Thanks, I think? I was really just copying Luna's idea with Effie and hey, now we have two hearts when we only needed one. We got what we needed, so I'd say this was semi-successful." His eyes catch on Atlas beside Rhea and his face falls serious. "Well, in all ways except one. I'm sorry about your vocal chords, Atlas."

Atlas nods, eyes bloodshot; strained from his time spent crying. Rhea lays a hand on his shoulder and squeezes it.

"If you want, I can talk for you," she says, standing straight up, on her tiptoes, mimicking Atlas's height. She pushes a pair of imaginary glasses up her nose and takes on a voice that sounds, honestly, nothing at all like Atlas, but I think is supposed to. "Well, I can't see how standing around is productive to our overall cause. It is my formal suggestion that we travel onward per the journal's instructions to continue our quest." She drops back to her regular height and gives him a bow. "How was that?" she asks.

Atlas gives what appears to be a genuine smile and nods once.

Rhea beams.

Caspar walks to Atlas, laying an arm across his shoulders. "I'm sorry about your voice, dude. Why did you lie about your ointment? You knew the journal said to beware of dishonesty."

Atlas sighs and shrugs.

"He probably just got caught up in the heat of the moment," I say, looking towards Atlas before shooting my eyes to Caspar. "It's easy to do."

Caspar narrows his eyes at me in question, but I turn back to Atlas.

"I'm sorry you lost your voice, Atlas."

"Me too," chimes Rhea.

"It sucks, man, but it could have been worse. I mean, they could have killed you or burned your whole body instead of just your vocal cords," says Caspar.

Atlas nods in agreement.

"We're all still alive and we have not one, but two wisp hearts now," I say, cheerfully, the realization finally hitting me that our first challenge went pretty well. If we can get through a horrible interaction with two crazy wisp sisters and remain intact, then maybe we really can be successful in our quest overall and get the amulet. Optimism fills my veins for the first real time since Amyra resurfaced at my party.

"We did it!" Rhea says, gleefully, clapping her hands.

Smiles slowly form on Atlas and Caspar's faces as well.

"We can do this guys," I say, my optimistic attitude flowing through

Chapter 16

my grin. "Let's get on to our next challenge."

Caspar hands the journal to Atlas, who starts to open the journal, but then stops, face stricken. It only takes a second for us all to realize why.

He can't interpret the journal for us without his voice.

And just like that, all my optimism flees.

Chapter 17

"That clearly says gnome, not comb!" Caspar says, exasperatedly, dragging his hands down his face.

"Why are you always so quick to assume that I must be wrong, huh?" Rhea asks, voice raised to him, with her hands on her hips. "Is it because I'm a fairy or a girl?"

"What? It's not—"

"Either you're racist or sexist," Rhea says, folding her arms now, "but just remember that no matter what you say, you're still a pig."

Caspar balls his hands into fists at his side for a moment, taking a deep breath, before he speaks again. "All I'm saying is that I don't think comb makes sense here," he says, gesturing to where an exhausted Atlas sits scribbling words into the dirt of the forest floor with a stick.

The same place he's been for the last hour.

Atlas writing out interpretations of the journal for us seemed like a good idea at the time. However, as it turns out, Atlas has the worst handwriting in all the realm. I gave up trying to figure it out about five minutes ago since I couldn't think with Rhea and Caspar's incessant arguing anyhow.

"Finding the *comb* inside the biggest tree makes perfect sense!" Rhea

Chapter 17

yells now.

"Finding a *gnome* makes more sense!" Caspar yells back. "Why would we need a comb?"

Atlas rubs his temple with his non-stick-bearing hand.

I groan, standing up from where I've been sitting on a nearby tree stump. "Will you two quit it?"

They both point a finger towards the other.

"He started it!"

"She started it!"

They say in unison.

"Look," I say, giving Rhea a cautious glance. "I'm sorry, Rhea, but, as much it pains me to say it, I think Caspar is right."

Her mouth drops open and now she points her finger at me.

"*Betrayal*," she breathes out.

"What we are trying to decipher is what we must obtain another object from, right?" I say, turning to Atlas who gives me a nod. I turn back to Rhea and Caspar. "Then, getting an object from a gnome makes more sense than getting one from a comb because a comb is already an object."

I can see her realize that I'm right by the slight change in her defiant expression, but she's too stubborn to ever admit that she's wrong.

"Fine," she huffs. "We'll go with gnome for now, but when we get to the big tree and there is, in fact, a magical comb, I will be saying I told you so," she says, turning and stomping off.

I chuckle.

Atlas drops his stick and does a quick, light jog. Once he's caught up to Rhea, he gently lays a hand on her shoulder and points off toward the left with his free hand; signaling that she's stomping off in slightly the wrong direction.

"Oh," she says, adjusting her direction accordingly. Atlas walks beside her and Caspar and I fall into step behind them. After a moment of silence, Rhea leans to Atlas. "I bet right now, you'd be saying something about the forest vegetation or how peculiar it is that the weather here seems to have no regularity. Am I right?"

Atlas shrugs and I see the sun begin setting up ahead, casting low hues of purple and pink across the sky.

"You see, science never interested me much growing up. I mean, things just grow, right? It's not like there's any real system behind it."

At this, Atlas's brows furrow together furiously.

"I mean, let's be honest here," Rhea trails off as Caspar leans over to me.

"He just lost his vocal cords and now she's going to make him lose his mind? That hardly seems kind," he says, shooting a smirk my way, but I keep my gaze on the ground. We walk in silence for another beat before he speaks again. "Wisp's heart for your thoughts?"

At that, I can't help but chuckle and one escapes me. "Normally, that'd be a tempting offer, but I already happen to have one in my possession."

"Ah," he sighs, grinning. "I see. So," he pauses, "care to share your thoughts for free then?"

"Well, I've got a lot of them right now," I say, with a sigh. "How much time do you have?"

His dark eyes cast a slow glance across the evergreen forest around us before returning to mine. "Believe it or not, I've got about as much time as you need right now."

"Well," I begin, "my mind is all jumbled. I'm happy about getting the hearts, but I'm sad that Atlas lost his voice. I'm glad we're making progress, but I wish it was quicker. And finally, I'm still trying to process ripping out Effie's heart and what that felt like. I'm worried that's burned into my brain forever now."

"I know what you mean," he says, casting his eyes upon the visible portion of the black veins that now scar his hand and arm.

Chapter 17

"Does it hurt?" I ask.

"It did in the moment, but it doesn't anymore."

"That's good," I say before a thought occurs to me. I add, "You seem like you're more used to danger, or intense situations. I mean, you were already armed and I get the feeling that you usually are and that's not something new just for going on this quest."

He nods slowly. "It's true. I'm always armed and prepared."

"Always?" I ask, raising one brow in question. "What about when you sleep?"

"I keep my dagger under my pillow," he says, with a shrug.

"Hmmm," I muse. "I've never touched a weapon in my life. In fact, ripping Effie's heart out is probably the most dangerous thing I've ever done. I'm not usually like that. I mean, I tackled a boy in my class when I was younger, but besides that—" he cuts me off.

"Wait, wait, wait," he says, holding up a hand. "Why did you tackle this boy?"

I groan. "You're really going to make me tell you the story?"

"Do you have something better to do right now?" he says, gesturing to our surroundings before shooting me a wink.

I give him an annoyed glare but with a smile. "Well, when I was little, there was this boy in my class. He was always super annoying; drove me crazy. He was always acting out. He'd distract the teacher and disrupt the lesson when I was trying to focus so I could learn." I take a breath. "Anyhow, one day, during our break for lunchtime, I was around the corner near him and some other boys, and I heard them talking about all of the girls in our class." I turn to Caspar as I share this part. "They were rating us on a scale of one to ten."

He rolls his eyes.

"They were naming off girls and then one of them mentioned me. Tommy quickly said four."

At this, Caspar looks surprised, his brows bunching together.

"He said it with no hesitation and I got so mad."

Now, Caspar grins at me. "You had your temper even then?"

I smirk. "Some say I was born with it, in fact."

We both share a chuckle.

"What happened then?" he asks.

"I acted fast; didn't even think about it. I rounded the corner and marched straight up to him with my hands on my hips and I said, 'What's the matter with you, Tommy? Why would you give me a four?' Now, looking back, I know it was a stupid thing to ask. I basically set myself up and gave him the floor to hurt me. He looked straight at me and said, 'Because your eyes are stupid and cloudy looking!' and I felt a rush of two feelings. I felt angry and hurt."

"So," Caspar begins before shooting me a look. "I'm guessing the anger won out if you tackled him?"

I nod, slowly. "Yup, and they put me in private school lessons at the palace the very next day. My mother was worried I'd have another outburst and people would worry about me being Queen." *Although, it turns out they feel that way anyway.*

"How do you feel about it now?"

"What?" I ask; Caspar jolting me back from my thoughts.

"How do you feel about tackling him now? Like when you look back on it?"

"Oh, I'd do it again in a heartbeat," I say with a grin.

Caspar turns his head slightly to meet my eyes. "Good."

We both face forward again and a moment passes before he adds, quietly, "And your eyes aren't stupid or cloudy. They're more of a robin's egg blue. Tommy just hadn't learned his colors properly yet."

I feel my cheeks shimmer at his words. "Thank you."

This sprite is going to make me lose my mind. How can he say stuff like that? We kissed for fairy's sake. Yes, to get light to escape a perilous situation, but still. Does he not realize that a kiss opens up a whole new way to interpret comments like that? That sharing a kiss, for any reason, can take a simple compliment and turn it into something intimate? He keeps going back and forth from driving me mad to saying stuff like *that*, making me feel like my head is spinning. My heart is toddling on an axis and feels like it could fall completely at any moment.

Every time he looks at me, I feel this odd sensation in my chest; like I can't breathe, but in the best way. Even when we argue, I feel that there and it scares me because he's just becoming a distraction, and if my mother has taught me anything, it's that I can't get distracted when I'm working towards something important. And this quest is, quite literally, the most important thing I have ever worked towards. I need to shut my heart in the deepest part of my soul and keep my eye on the amulet. Caspar can't get in my way.

The sun has fully set now and we walk in silence for only a few more minutes before Rhea jolts to a halt in front of us, spinning around and declaring, "I'm too tired to go on. The sky is dark, so I say we stop and sleep."

Beside her, Atlas nods in agreement.

I turn to Caspar and he gives me a shrug, "Alright. Let's stop for the night," I say.

"We should take shifts," Caspar says as we all walk towards the middle, open section between a group of trees that lay naturally in a semi-circle formation. "That way nothing, and no one, can sneak up on us while we sleep."

"Good idea," I agree. "Well," a thought occurs to me, "we probably shouldn't give Atlas a shift because he's unable to yell if there's danger."

Atlas nods sadly, his shoulders drooping, inclining Rhea to give him a comforting pat on the back.

"I guess that leaves us and Rhea then," Caspar says, and the way he says "us" so effortlessly doesn't go unnoticed by me. "I can take the first shift," he offers.

"I'll take the next one," I say.

"Best for last then, I guess," Rhea says, walking over and opening my satchel.

I startle. "What are you doing?"

"Grabbing your blanket. Mine is in my satchel buried under tree sap right now, remember?"

"Oh," I murmur, remembering. "That's right."

"Don't worry, I won't hog it all," she says, laying the blanket out flat on the ground before spreading herself out on top of it; hogging all the space.

"Rhea, you're already hogging it!" I say, giving her a playful nudge with my foot.

"Am not!" she says, whining defensively, before rolling onto her side to face away from me.

I chuckle and turn to see Atlas casting pleading eyes at Caspar who lets out a groan. "Fine, but only because we have no other options." Atlas smiles at this and watches as Caspar lays out their blanket.

"I'm going to go grab some wood and make a fire before it gets even darker," says Caspar. "I won't go far. Be right back."

Atlas gives him a little wave before curling into a ball on the blanket across from Rhea and me with his back to us. Realizing this might be my only moment alone with Rhea for a while, I lay down beside her, poking her back with my index finger. She reaches an arm back to swat at me.

"Shhh! I'm trying to sleep."

Now, I grab her shoulder and shake her entirely. "Roll over! I have to talk to you," I whisper.

At this, she obeys; rolling over to face me. "What's up? Are you okay?"

I groan and tuck an arm under my head, propping it up. "I don't

Chapter 17

know," I answer, careful to keep my voice down so Atlas doesn't hear. "In the last day, I've had my first kiss, swam in a pool of blood, and ripped the heart out of a magical creature."

At the mention of the kiss, Rhea's eyes bulge and she grabs my wrists, shaking them. "That's right! Tell me all about the kiss. Don't you *dare*," she says, giving my wrists an extra-tight squeeze for emphasis, "leave out a single detail!"

I sigh and push some red hair out of my face once she releases me. "Well, I was drowning and I thought it was the end. My muscles grew too exhausted after trying to stay afloat and I couldn't fight anymore. I started sinking beneath the surface when suddenly I was dragged down by my foot and then I felt lips on mine."

Rhea covers her mouth with her hand as she imagines it all.

"I had no clue what was going on. It was the last thing I was expecting to happen, but it did! Then, my wings started to faintly glow and I peeked one eye open and saw that it was Caspar."

"Wow," Rhea breathes quietly before her eyes light up again. "Wait! Tell me about the kiss itself. What was it like?"

I think to myself, wanting to explain it properly. Finally, it comes to me. "Do you remember that guy you kissed last summer?"

She tilts her head, propping it up on one arm in thought. "The hot gardener?"

"No, the other one," I muse.

"Oh!" she says. "The hot gardener's hot cousin?"

"Yes!"

"Oh, that was a *good* kiss," she says, her eyes taking on a glazed look as she relives the memory. "It started slow, but I could tell in his kiss that he really wanted me, which made it really spicy, and then when I kissed him back, we kind of just sunk into it."

"That's exactly it!" I say, excited to have a good example to relate it to so she'll understand.

She looks at me in shock. "He kissed you like *that?*"

"*Yes*," I say, drawing out the word for emphasis. "When his lips first met mine, I was shocked."

"Obviously," she interjects.

"Obviously," I echo. "But the way the kiss felt," I hesitate for a moment. "It was like he was telling me something in that kiss."

"What was he telling you?" Rhea asks, before adding under her breath, "Cause all the hot gardener's cousin was telling me was that he wanted to take me right there in the petunias."

I chuckle, rolling my eyes at her before dropping my voice to an even lower register as I say, "It was like he was saying that he knew it was the end; like it was his last chance to share a moment with me."

"Seriously?" Rhea asks. "You're sure?"

I roll my eyes at her again, but this time in frustration. "Rhea, it was my first kiss. I'm not a master of the language of it, but that was what my gut felt."

"But that doesn't make sense then," she says, thinking out loud. "Atlas said Caspar kissed you to make your wings glow so you had the light you needed to find a way out."

I groan, quietly. "I know. That's why I'm upset, or confused, I guess I should say. He's saying that he kissed me because we needed light, but it felt like the complete opposite."

"Like he kissed you because he wanted to?" Rhea asks.

"Exactly," I breathe.

A beat passes before Rhea says, "Wait! Didn't you say something about how you were glad you guys had the same idea?"

"Yes, but that was just because I kissed him back once I realized it was him and how the kiss was making me feel. I only said that because I didn't want him to know that I thought the kiss was more than that."

"Well, here's the most important question," Rhea says, scooting so close to me that the tips of our noses almost touch. She looks into my

Chapter 17

eyes and in them, I find the sincerity only a friend could have. "Do you *want* it to be more than that?"

Her words send my mind into a tizzy. I thought the kiss was some kind of declaration of feelings when it happened in the moment. Was that because that's what I wanted it to be? For a brief second, I let myself remember the kiss and it feels like once the floodgates open, I'm reliving every millisecond of it in my mind. The urgency of his kiss, but the romantic sensation in it, too. The way his hand slid up into my hair. "Well, I've never been kissed before, but I will say that for my first kiss, it felt very natural."

Rhea raises her perfectly arched eyebrows at this. "Natural?"

"Yeah," I muse. "It felt like we'd done it before, or were always meant to, if that makes sense."

"I knew it!" she says, excitedly, slapping my arm, but quietly enough that only a small pat emits from the action. "I knew you two had the hots for each other! The way he bugged you, or still does, had to have an underlying cause. I just knew it!"

"But that's the thing," I say, my voice wavering a little; displaying my uncertainty. "What if it's not both of us? I mean, I know I'm feeling," I pause, "something, but what if that something isn't reciprocated?"

"Like what if he really *was* just kissing you for the light," she says, voicing her thoughts.

"Exactly," I breathe.

She thinks for a moment, before meeting my eyes again. "I don't know what to tell you, Luna. I mean, Atlas is the one who first mentioned kissing you to create the light you guys needed, but Caspar did agree with him. Then, you agreed on top of that. So, even if he did kiss you because he wanted to, he thinks you kissed him back because you did it for light."

I groan. Rhea's right. I didn't even think about that. "Everything is so messed up," I say, rubbing my eyes. "This is the last thing I need right now. I need to focus on our quest and getting the amulet so that we can save Celestia and stop Amyra. I don't need to be wasting my time on a silly sprite."

"Not even one who apparently kisses very, very well?" she asks, smirking.

I slap her arm lightly. "No. No distractions. I'm like 99 percent sure he did it just for the light anyway and I pretended I did, too. So, I just need to move on and focus on our mission instead of this nonsense."

"But he's—" she begins, but I use my hands to push her; rolling her back over to face the other direction.

"Sorry, can't talk! Need my sleep!"

She chuckles. "Love you."

"Love you, too," I whisper.

Chapter 18

I'm back in the pool of blood. Waves of it lap into my open mouth as I scream and cry out for help; the metallic taste making me wish my taste buds had lost their functionality. I feel my muscles straining from the effort to stay afloat, but I fight it. I fight it until my legs start to cramp and my arms go numb from flailing about. I begin to descend slowly beneath the surface; my whole life ended in such a perilous manner, with Celestia left in pieces as a result of my failure to follow through and save everyone.

I know it's not real. I know it's a dream. Still, I can't manage to shake myself from it and the fear feels just as real as it did when it happened. Once I sink below the surface into the thick liquid, I know it's time to feel Caspar's hand on my foot. When my foot is grabbed, I don't fight it. I'll kiss him again to create light or whatever the purpose. Of all the parts of this vivid dream, I'm not ashamed to admit it's the only part I'd willingly relive. But suddenly, I realize I'm being dragged too far down. *Why is he taking me so deep below?*

I look down below me at my foot and see Effie there; her figure glowing black with an evil smile on her face as she drags me further and further. There's a hole in her chest where I took her heart. She's come back to kill me. This is her revenge.

It's not real. It's not real! But even as I tell myself this, it feels hard to believe it; every element feels all too realistic. Her firm grasp on my foot, the dark of the pool around me, the exhaustion in my limbs from trying to stay afloat. Suddenly, she drags me past a form in the pool of crimson and the light from her dim glow allows me to see that it's Caspar, fighting in the firm hold of one of Seraphina's flaming limbs. She makes eye contact with me before she lets out a cry and shoves her limb clean through his chest from behind, ripping his heart out in the process.

My body begins to shake. *Wake up, Luna! Wake up!*

"Wake up, Luna!"

I jolt upright from where I lay on the blanket, lurching forward into Caspar's waiting arms. Hot tears spill down my cheeks and he holds me against his chest as I try to stop gasping for breath.

Finally, after a few moments, my breathing slows. He pulls me back from him by my shoulders and looks at me with concerned eyes. "Are you alright?"

"I think so," I breathe.

He uses his thumb to wipe a tear away from under my left eye and it feels so intimate my cheeks shimmer and I drop my gaze.

He lowers his hand from my face, using the other to reach up and scratch the back of his head. "I get nightmares, too," he says quietly.

"They're the worst," I say, brushing the rest of the tears off my face with the back of my hands before attempting to smooth my hair behind my ears. I don't know if it's because we're the only ones awake, or because I don't want to keep it inside, where it will fester as I constantly think back on it, but I continue speaking. "I was back in the pool of blood."

His head tilts back up to look at me. He leans back on his arms, stretching his long legs out in front of him. I keep my voice down so I

Chapter 18

don't wake Rhea next to me, though she's always been quite a deep sleeper.

"My muscles started cramping and I fell beneath the surface." I pause, drawing in a shaky breath. "It felt so real that I could taste the blood in my mouth all over again." I fiddle with my hands in my lap before pulling my legs under me. "I felt what I thought was you," I say, meeting his eyes for just a moment at the mention of him, "but when I looked down, I saw it was Effie. She was dragging me down. She was going to drown me. I just knew it. Then, out of the corner of my eye, I saw you trapped by Seraphina with one of her flaming limbs wrapped around you." I hesitate, not wanting to go on, but he's looking at me so intently that I know I can't stop now. "She ripped out your heart and then that's when I woke up."

"Wow," he says, his eyes flitting down before back up at me. "It sounds like everything that happened with those wisp sisters today is really bothering you."

"I guess so," I add with a quick shrug of my shoulders. "I mean, I've been in more danger in the last two days than I have been in pretty much my entire life. It's been hard having to think quickly on my feet and develop plans to try and figure out how to be safe."

"You don't have to have a plan. You just have to go with your gut. Follow your instinct."

"I don't think I've developed any instincts of that sort yet."

"Instincts, and that gut feeling, are what fighting and defending yourself is all about!"

"I've never fought anyone in my life!" I say, throwing my hands up in surrender. "Besides tackling Tommy, my life has been spent learning how to be a proper Queen."

At this, he stands up and extends his arm, offering me a hand. "Come on."

I peer up at him, confused. "What?"

"I'm going to teach you how to fight."

I guffaw. "Yeah, I don't think so."

He crosses his arms over his chest now and gives a knowing nod. "Ah," he says. "Sorry. I guess I just forgot that Queens are so delicate."

My mouth drops open and I narrow my eyes at him. "Excuse me? I literally ripped out a beating heart today! I hardly think that's delicate."

"Oh, I see," he says, stroking his chin now as if in deep thought. "So, you can do that, but fighting *me* is too intimidating for you. Okay. I understand it now." He puts his hands in the pockets of his leather vest and leans down close to my face with a cheeky grin. "And don't worry. There's nothing wrong with being delicate."

I am *not* delicate.

"For fairy's sake," I mutter under my breath before reaching up. "Give me your hand."

He flashes me that wicked grin of his as he pulls me up before nudging his head towards the right where a small fire glows in the center of the grassy area next to us. "Over here."

I follow him over by the fire so we're a ways away from Rhea and Atlas who are sleeping surprisingly soundly given that we're in possibly the most terrifying place in the realm.

He faces me. "First, let's just get something out of the way, alright? It's okay for you to hit me. I won't get pissed. I want you to give this your all."

"You want me to hurt you?"

"Okay, that's not what I said," he says with a roll of his eyes. "This isn't me saying, 'please let out your personal rage,' or anything. I'm just saying I don't want you to be afraid to hit me."

I take a deep breath and release it slowly. "Alright."

He lowers his legs, crouching ever so slightly, but still towering over me as he stretches his arms out to his sides.

"What are you doing?"

Chapter 18

"Copy my stance," he orders.

I bend my knees a bit and put my arms out at my sides, but slightly in front of my body. "Happy?"

"Yeah, 'cause you look pretty ridiculous."

I huff and step forward, swinging for him with my right arm, but he swivels his body to the left and dodges me. He flicks the back of my head once he rounds past me.

"Ow!" I say, throwing my hand up to the spot on the back of my skull.

"Do it again," he says, taking his stance once more.

"Okay, I'm sorry, but isn't the master supposed to teach the student how to do things first before making them do it?"

He grins at me, suggestively. "I'm your master?"

I groan. "Do you have to be so crude?" I ask, glaring at him.

"Do you have to make it so easy?" he says, with a wink. "Now, do it again."

I lunge at him again now, but this time I raise my right arm for a backhand. He somehow still deflects me though; this time, crouching down and grabbing me around the waist with one arm, picking me up, and throwing me over his left shoulder.

Gosh, this is high off the ground.

"Hey! What are you—" I yell, but he hushes me.

"Sh! Are you trying to wake up our comrades?"

I groan and lower my voice. "Put me down this instant!"

"Only if you're going to try harder."

"I am trying hard!" I insist, but this earns me a smack on my backside.

My mouth drops open with a guffaw. "Did you just—" I start, but he cuts me off.

"Don't lie to me. Now, are you going to try harder? Cause I'm ready to go for real."

If he wants to go, I'll go. "Fine! Let's go for real this time."

He slowly starts to lower me down from over his shoulder, but as he does, I flap my wings to use the momentum of the air as extra strength. I combine this with grabbing his left arm with both of my hands and use the mixture to flip him over and onto his back. He lands with a thud and narrows his eyes in a wince of pain.

I bend down over his head and give him a cocky grin. "I thought you said you were ready?"

"You cheated," he mutters.

I gape and throw a hand to my chest in mock offense. "I did no such thing," I say before putting a hand on my hip, leaning my weight onto it. "Sounds like you're just a sore loser." I grab his hand to pull him up but then drop him back down.

"Hey!" he says, annoyed.

I lean my face back down over his. "If I let you up are you going to try harder? Cause I'm ready to go for real," I say with a smirk, enjoying the pleasure of throwing his own words back at him.

He shoots a glare up at me. "The student hasn't become the master yet."

"Well, which one of us is on their back right now?" I ask with a tilt of my head.

He narrows his dark eyes up at me. "I could have you on your back in two seconds flat."

My cheeks shimmer furiously. *Are we still talking about fighting?*

"One good move does not make a good fighter," he continues, holding his hand out.

I help him up for real this time. "Oh, yeah?" I ask. "Then what does?"

"Learning all you can about your opponent and then using that to read them and predict their moves."

"Okay, so how do I do that?" I ask, hands back on my hips.

Chapter 18

"You want to gauge what their physical strengths are so that you're aware of what they'll be trying to utilize against you. Like for instance, your wings would be something an opponent would notice about you before beginning a brawl. They'd be smart to assume that you'd use your wings to your advantage against them."

"Then how come you didn't?" I ask with a suppressed smile.

He stands up taller. "I was distracted."

"I don't know much about fighting, but I'd guess that maintaining focus is like the number one priority."

He begins taking off his leather vest now as he speaks. "It's hard fighting and instructing at the same time," he says, tossing his vest over onto the ground. I can't help but notice how the muscles of his chest are highlighted through the fabric of his shirt in its absence.

Is he just trying to distract me now?

"Let's focus on the instructing portion," I say, tucking a loose strand of hair behind my ear. "So, when I see an opponent, I size them up and decipher the tools that they have to their physical advantage. Then what?"

"You use that information to predict their next move. Here's an example. Aren't you curious how I was able to perfectly dodge your first two shots at me?"

"I just assumed it was luck," I say with a sassy tilt of my head.

He narrows his eyes at me. "Don't sass your master."

I roll my eyes.

"When looking at you, aside from your wings, an opponent could see that you don't have a ton of upper body strength—" he begins, but I interject.

"Oh, I know you aren't downplaying these top-notch muscles right here," I say, flexing the biceps of my thin arms. "I'll have you know that I've lifted many heavy pots and pans out of the palace oven completely by myself and that strength doesn't just come from thin air."

He lets out a low chuckle. "Okay, okay. Then, let's just say you don't have as much upper body strength as some *other* people do. Are you going to argue with that?"

I fold my arms across my chest. "No," I say, drawing out the word, and tilting my chin up.

"Good," he says. "Well, your lack of upper body strength leads me to think that you depend on your legs. So, every time you were about to swing at me, you'd actually take a small step forward before you did. This let me know it was coming."

I open my mouth to reject his claim, but then replay our small brawl in my head. He's right. I do put my foot forward before I try to take a hit.

"Shoot," I say, shaking my head and looking down at the ground for a moment. I kick a small rock that lies near my foot.

"It's alright," he says. "There's nothing wrong with that. It's just good for you to be aware of it because opponents will be."

"Okay, I'll keep that in mind," I say. Both of us stare at the ground and a wave of silence falls over us. Finally, he meets my eyes again.

"Learning the basics is the easy part, but learning to put them to use in an actual fight is more difficult."

I draw in a breath before exhaling it slowly. "I don't know if I can do it."

His dark eyes pour into mine with sincere curiosity. "Why not?"

I fiddle with my hands, wondering why telling him anything feels like a confession. "Because I'm a lover, not a fighter."

"What if I told you that you could be both?"

"How can I do that?"

"By fighting for the ones you love," he says, softly.

He holds eye contact with me and I swear it's like he sees right through me; right through every wall, barrier, and border, I hide behind. Like he sees all my insecurities and weaknesses, the darkest

Chapter 18

parts of me, but doesn't care. How can he make me feel like that with a mere glance when everyone else I've encountered in my life has only made me feel the opposite?

He takes a small step towards me and I feel my breath catch nervously in my throat. "Luna, I—" he begins, but his voice fades out and he exhales a shaky breath.

Is he nervous?

"Yes?" I say, and I don't know why, but I take a small step closer to him too now.

"That kiss," he begins again, taking another step towards me, narrowing the space between us even more. "It was a mistake. I shouldn't have kissed you like that."

His words cut into my heart like a knife, forcing me to actually wince as if I've been struck. He must read this in my face because he reaches out to take my hand and I pull it back.

"No, Luna. What I mean is—" he starts, but I cut him off, not wanting to hear more.

"It doesn't matter, Caspar," I say, crossing my arms over my chest and breaking his gaze. "The kiss saved us and that's it, alright?"

"But I—" he begins, but then Rhea suddenly rustles from her spot on the blanket.

"Yes, I made out with the gardener, but not in the petunias!" she unconsciously yells in her slumber as she rolls to the other side.

Caspar makes a confused look her way before turning back to face me. I take a step back from him.

"Why don't you get some sleep? I'm up now. I'll start my shift," I say.

"Luna—"

"Goodnight, Caspar," I say, strongly and he knows from my tone that our conversation is decidedly over.

He picks his vest up off the ground and puts it back on.

"Goodnight," he says as he turns away and heads over to lie down beside Atlas.

I walk over and sit cross-legged on the ground beside the embers of the dying fire. The quiet of the sleeping forest all around me makes my thoughts even louder.

Kissing me was a mistake? Why would he bring that up? How could saying that do anything but hurt me?

I shake my head in an attempt to break myself from spiraling down that wormhole of thoughts. It doesn't matter. He said it was a mistake and that's that. I'm glad I cut him off. If I'd let him continue, he probably would have just elaborated on why our kiss was such a huge mistake, which I definitely don't need to hear right now.

Gosh, I feel so stupid for confiding in Rhea all of the mixed emotions I've been feeling about Caspar and our kiss. Now, I'll have to tell her that it really was just all me. All those feelings I had about our kiss, and the little moments here and there that we've shared, have utterly and clearly been one-sided.

I throw my head back and look up at the stars peeking through the tops of the trees above me. *Why?* I want to ask the universe. *Why did Amyra have to show up? Why did I have to go to Durand for help? Why did I have to go on this quest and let my heart get swept up in a bunch of nonsense?*

I know there's no point in asking because there will be no answer. There never are to hardships. You must simply persevere.

It's all I can do.

Chapter 19

"Rise and shine, everyone, for another day that could potentially be our last!" Rhea calls, clapping her hands and striding around the group of us on the ground. I rub my tired eyes while Caspar and Atlas sit up slowly on their blanket, stretching out their tired limbs.

I was glad when it was finally time to swap my watch shift over to Rhea so that I'd no longer be alone with my incessant thoughts. However, the time flew by and, although I know I slept, I don't feel like I did at all. Curse this wretched Bog for depriving me of even a decent sleep.

"What a positive thought to begin the day with. Thank you for that," Caspar says as he stands up.

"Reality is a hard creature to face, my friends, but best to face it than hide, and have it find you later," Rhea says, standing with her hands on her hips, chin up.

Atlas stands too now and begins to roll up their blanket as I do with mine.

"Time to continue looking for the biggest tree so we can find that gnome," I say, tucking my blanket back into my satchel now. "I say we eat some food while we search, so we don't waste any time."

"Fine," says Rhea, drawing out the word in a groan. "I am pretty hungry." She walks over to me, holding out her hands. "Food please, friend."

I take a small bread loaf out of my satchel and tear it in two, laying half in her open palm. She quickly begins biting into it and lets out a moan. "This is delicious! What is it?" she asks, spinning to Caspar and Atlas.

"It's oat bread," says Caspar, tearing his loaf to share with Atlas. "It's best for travel because it's very filling. A little goes a long way."

I take a bit of the bread for myself. Wow, Rhea was right. It is delicious. The texture is dense, but not dry.

"Alright. Eat and walk, people," I say, striding forward, Rhea falling into step beside me. "Keep an eye out for the biggest tree."

* * *

"This bread is going to pass its way through my entire freaking system before we find this stupid gnome," Rhea says with a huff.

"For real," I say, frustrated. I turn to Atlas. "How long do you think we've been searching now?"

Atlas thinks and then holds up his fingers.

"Four hours?" I ask, stunned. "Has it really been that long?"

"It's felt like even longer than that," Caspar says a few feet over from me, shoving his hands in the pockets of his vest.

I shoot him a glare. "Could you at least *try* to be helpful?"

"Hey, I've been searching the same as everyone else," he says, splaying his arms with his hands still in his pockets, flaring the leather fabric of his vest out to the sides of his chest. He rolls his eyes before spinning away from me.

Why is he acting like my attitude is coming out of nowhere? You can't just tell a woman that kissing her was a mistake and then expect her to take it gracefully. He hurt my feelings *and* my pride and I won't just let that go. At least not without a few sarcastic quips.

"Any luck up ahead, Rhea?" I call to her from where she stands searching up ahead of Caspar and me with Atlas.

She spins slowly back to face me, her face solemn. "Nothing here," she calls back, but suddenly Atlas's face perks up and he points excitedly off towards the right a ways away. Rhea's eyes wander till they see whatever Atlas must have noticed. Her face lights up, mirroring his hopeful expression.

"There's a huge tree over there!" she says, pointing. "Come on!" She grabs Atlas's hand, who looks startled at the physical contact, and starts running off towards the tree.

Caspar and I quickly run after them. After a minute, and a veer to the right, following their lead, I see the tree that Atlas pointed to. It's massive. Its trunk is gigantic in width and its height scales the tallest tower of the palace. I've never seen a tree so large in all my life. The sight of it takes my breath away and I turn to see a similarly awed expression on Caspar's face.

Rhea and Atlas near the tree before us.

"This has to be it!" Rhea yells, but as soon as the words leave her mouth, I hear a snap and watch as suddenly both she and Atlas are swept up in what appears to be a net made out of woven vines and they are cast upwards where they're left dangling from a high tree limb.

Rhea lets out a scream from up above. Caspar and I run beneath the net and peer upward.

"Are you alright?" I yell out, but Rhea can't hear me over her screams. I try again, but louder this time, shouting at the top of my lungs. "Rhea!"

She's still wailing, but thankfully, Atlas hears me and gently covers Rhea's mouth to silence her. I see her shoot him an annoyed look through the netted vines from where I stand below. He slowly lowers his hand and points down to me with the other.

"Are you two alright?" I ask, again. "Are you hurt at all?"

They both take a moment to look themselves over before Rhea calls down with a shaky, hysterical voice, "I think we're okay physically, but mentally I'm shot!" She huffs. "I have had it with this fairy-forsaken forest!"

"We'll try to get you down!" I yell back. "Just stay calm!"

She whimpers and begins trying to move in the netting to a different position above. Her pulling on one side of the net forces the side against Atlas to push him forward, flopping on top of Rhea, who lets out a pissed yelp before huffing, "If you try to cop a feel scholar-boy, then your lost vocal cords will be the least of your concerns!"

Atlas quickly tries to get off her, but the two have a hard go about it, the net only further entangling them. Caspar turns away from the disaster of the two of them to look for a way to help. I follow his lead and turn to search on my own. We search for a few minutes, as Rhea finally quiets up above, but our search is to no avail.

I meet Caspar's side and place my hands on my hips with a huff. "I thought there would be a tether or something holding them up that we could cut, but I can't find anything of the sort."

He nods, slowly, scratching the back of his head. "Me either."

We stand in silence for a moment, trying to think of any other options.

Suddenly, a rustling noise sounds from the bushes a few feet behind us and we both spin towards it, Caspar laying a hand on the dagger at his hip as he turns.

I don't know what I'm expecting, really. Perhaps a forest creature, or Effie's spirit back to seek revenge on me as in my dream, but what emerges surprises me entirely.

Out of the thorny pickets of the bushes, comes a small old man.

Chapter 19

A *gnome* old man.

He shoves his way through the bushes till he's fully emerged. He's incredibly short, not even reaching my hip in height, and has on a tall blue hat that comes to a stark point. The wooden staff he's using as a cane would give away his age if it wasn't for the pruning of his skin. He looks like he was put out in the sun to dry and someone forgot that they left him there for far too long. His small eyes peek out above what is the largest and roundest of noses I've ever laid eyes on, but the rest of his face is entirely hidden behind a thick grayish-white mustache and long, fluffy beard. His brown-colored robe drags on the ground as he hobbles with his cane toward us, a basket of produce nestled into the crook of his other arm.

He stops, plucking stray pieces of branches from the sleeve of his robe before he turns and takes in the sight of Caspar and me with our suspended friends above.

"Oh, bugger," he says, his voice soft and ripe with age, sounding both tired and wise. He looks up at me. "I do apologize, dear. That trap was meant for the drats that keep eating my tomatoes."

"Drats?" Caspar asks, beside me.

The gnome fellow nods. "Annoying things. Like rats, but worse cause they can fly. Quite the devilish little creatures. This here net was meant to get them, not your friends. Again, I apologize."

"Um, it's alright," I say, slowly. "Apology accepted."

I can't see his mouth buried under his thick beard and mustache, but I know he's smiling by the way his droopy eyes turn up at the ends. I extend my hand.

"I'm Luna," I say as he shakes my hand and I try not to show my surprise at the size of his hand being about a third of my own.

"Hodgington," he says, softly, "but you may call me Hodge."

I smile at him. "Thank you. This is Caspar," I say, gesturing to him, "and up there are our friends, Rhea and Atlas."

"Nice to meet you!" Rhea calls down, with a wave of her hand which makes the net swing a little, before she gestures around. "Quite the sturdy net you've constructed here."

"Thank you, dear," he says, with a humble nod. "Let me get you younglings down and then how 'bout I brew us all some tea? I made fresh scones just last night."

Rhea lets out an excited gasp up above. "I love scones!"

"It's settled then," says Hodge. "Just one moment."

Caspar and I watch him hobble over slowly around a nearby tree, muttering, "I know it's somewhere over here." His voice dwindles as he rounds the tree.

I spin to Caspar, my voice low. "Do you think he could be the gnome that we need? That'd be almost too perfect of luck."

Caspar shakes his head. "I'm not sure, but at the very least he may know the gnome we're looking for."

I nod. "Good point."

I hear a loud snap and then look up to see the net become loose from the tree limb and begin to descend quickly. Rhea acts fast. The previously cinched opening at the top of the net has loosened and she grabs onto Atlas before pulling them up and through it, flapping her wings so they remain safely suspended in the air as the rest of the net falls to the ground with a light thud.

"Great job, Rhea!" I call up to her where she's clearly struggling to hold onto Atlas.

"My gosh, how much do you weigh?" she groans out, her voice strained in effort, as she lowers Atlas slowly to the ground, who shoots up a glare at her. Once they've touched back down safely, she lets go of him, bending over with her hands on the tops of her knees, trying to catch her breath. Atlas smacks her arm, but she stands up, holding an index finger out towards him.

"Don't you give me a hard time," she says, plainly. "This reaction is

Chapter 19

justified. You sprite men are dense."

"In more ways than one," I mutter under my breath.

Caspar's head spins to me. "What was that?" he asks, an inquisitive look on his face, but thankfully Hodge returns from around the corner and saves me from having to form a response.

"Alrighty, kiddos. Follow me," he says, with a motion of his tiny hand and we all fall into step behind him. However, due to the small size of his feet and legs, the rest of us are left feeling like we're walking in slow motion as we try not to make him feel hurried.

He leads us around the other side of the large tree, which takes a decent minute considering its extreme width before we finally reach a small door. A really small door. Grabbing the wooden handle, he swings the door inward, walking through with a wave of his hand.

"This way," he chimes.

I bend down, crouching to the ground, and crawl through the small entryway with my wings tucked flat to my back. As soon as I've passed the threshold, I'm forced to sit back on my feet, the ceiling so low that I can hardly do more than kneel. The most pleasant of aromas hits me and I close my eyes, inhaling with a smile.

"The scones?" I ask when I open my eyes to see Hodge peering before me.

He gives a knowing nod. "Precisely. Take a seat over here and I'll bring a plate for you to nibble while I put the kettle on."

I watch him turn to go fetch the scones and take in his humble abode. Burrowed into the wide tree trunk, he has made a cozy oasis. Books line a shelf spanning the entire left wall, spines worn with age. A small, roaring fire sits in a stone hearth with rocks and crystals on the mantel. To the right is a small bed, and I do mean small since it is Hodge-sized, with a wooden nightstand. The bed is made, the quilted blanket tucked in neatly. It's the most wholesome thing I've seen in so long that it makes me want to cry.

The nightstand's top surface is crooked, and I can tell that the little candle that sits lit atop it is mere moments from sliding clean off and potentially burning this entire home to the ground. Hodge seems completely unbothered by this though as he hums to himself in the tiny kitchen straight across from the doorway whilst filling a small tea kettle with water from a tap in the wall.

His kitchen cupboards are all crooked, some leaning into each other as if hugging, the others facing away as if they prefer to be alone, but the counter top is what truly draws my attention since it's covered in moss. I feel like this would make it impossible to clean, but far be it for me to enter into a friendly stranger's home and immediately berate it. His kitchen curves along with the rest of the circular outline of the quaint home, and in between the crook of his kitchen lies a small table with four colorful pillows splayed around it on the floor.

There's a loud thunk and the house shakes, dust and things flaring up into the air from the rattling movement. I turn quickly behind me to see Caspar outside through the small doorway rubbing one shoulder and swearing under his breath. Atlas and Rhea have made their way inside now, scooting over toward the fireplace and small shelves of books.

I turn to Rhea, arms out at my sides in question and she shrugs. "Man child can't fit his fat shoulders through the door."

"I heard that!" Caspar calls through the opening with a huff.

"I don't care!" Rhea calls back.

I hold an index finger in front of my mouth in an attempt to hush her as I look over my shoulder to see that our gracious host is thankfully too occupied with making tea to have heard their sassy banter.

I crouch down slightly more now, peering through the doorway to him. "Caspar," I call, waiting to continue till I see his frustrated face before me. "What's the problem?" I ask, mindful to keep my voice down so Hodge doesn't hear.

Chapter 19

"The door is too small," he complains.

"You really can't fit?" I ask.

He groans at this, standing back up and walking far enough back from the outside of the door that I can see his full form.

"Look at me!" he says, exasperatedly, gesturing up and down the length of his body.

I groan. "Hang on."

I pull my head back inside to find Atlas and Rhea seated on two of the tiny pillows around the small wooden table by the kitchen, Hodge handing them each a teacup.

I clear my throat. "Mr. Hodge?"

His head tilts up at the mention of his name, the tip of his tall, blue hat poking the ceiling. "It's just Hodge, dear. No one's called me Mr. Hodge since the Mrs died."

Rhea lets out a sympathetic, "Aw," placing her hand on his shoulder, comfortingly.

He whips his long beard her way as he turns to face her. "No need to pity me, dear. 'Twas the best day of my life."

"Oh," Rhea says, attempting to hide her surprise as she slowly lowers her hand.

Hodge turns back to face me.

"Okay, then, Hodge," I continue. "It appears that our friend, Caspar, here is too large to fit through your doorway. Do you happen to have another entrance by chance?"

He shakes his head. "I'm afraid not. I'm not usually one for large company, so I've never needed a bigger entrance."

Shoot. Okay.

"Well, he doesn't mind staying outside until we're done visiting. Right, Caspar?"

I hear him sigh on his side of the open doorway. "Not at all."

I crawl over and take a seat on another of the small cushions surrounding the table with Atlas and Rhea as Hodge fills up a teacup and walks over to the entrance.

"Here you are, big fella," he says, pushing the tiny teacup through the entryway. "Make sure you blow on it before you sip. I always make the tea hot," he turns to face Rhea at the table as he adds, "just like the women."

Rhea hiccups into her tea at this, launching into a coughing frenzy. Atlas pats her back in an attempt to help. I swallow my smile.

"My kinda man," Caspar calls from outside.

Hodge chuckles as he returns to pouring the tea at the table; a small candle lit at the center, adding even more so to the cozy ambiance. I expect him to strike up a conversation again once he has poured and passed small cups of amber tea to both Atlas and myself, but instead, he begins to sip his tea in complete silence, releasing a heavy sigh after his first gulp.

Alright. I guess the conversation is left for me to generate.

"You have a lovely home," I begin. "How long have you lived here?"

Hodge tilts his head in thought for a moment. "Oh, about 900 years now," he finally offers, leaving us all shocked. Noting our expressions, Hodge continues. "That's nothing! I'll live for easily another 3,000 years or so. Most gnomes do."

Atlas and Rhea nod as if they are perfectly accepting of this information, but it only fills my head with more questions. Firstly, if most gnomes live to be almost 4,000 years old, then how come his wife is already dead? Was she just a lot older than he was? And secondly, if he already looks this aged at 900, what in the realm will he look like at almost 4,000 years old? Or when he reaches halfway, do they start going backward? It is the Bog, after all. Anything is possible. None of these though are questions I'm actually willing to ask because, for the first time since starting this fairy-forsaken adventure, I'm finally in a position where being well-mannered is coming in handy.

Chapter 19

"Wow," says Rhea, flabbergasted. "That's a long time."

I shoot her a glare over the rim of my teacup as I bring it to my lips, but my eyebrows pinch together as soon as I register the taste of the tea.

It's horrendous. Easily the most bitter substance I have ever tasted. I will really have to pull off my very best acting for this one. I swallow the tea, which is no easy feat. Searching for something to omit the taste, I nonchalantly grab one of the small scones off the plate Hodge has set out and am utterly relieved that it tastes pleasant. Taste buds relieved from their misery, I turn my attention on Hodge again as he sits across from me now at the little table.

"These scones are delicious," I say, honestly, "and the tea is exquisite," I say, less honestly. "Thank you for sharing with us."

"Oh, it's my pleasure," he says, politely. "One can grow tired of gnomes after a while. We are quite the cumbersome bunch, so visitors are always a delight."

We all smile at this.

Rhea and I have each had two scones, their size being about one regular bite for us, but three for Hodge. When he reaches for his second one, he finds an empty plate.

"Oh, I'm so sorry!" says Rhea, apologetically. "I ate the last one. They were just so delicious!"

"No need to apologize," says Hodge with a wave of his hand. "An empty plate is the best compliment to a baker."

I raise my teacup to him. "I couldn't agree more."

He takes the empty plate and heads to the kitchen. "Luckily for you, I put a few more in the oven to warm up in anticipation of my guests being hungry."

"Oh, thank you!" Rhea chimes, happily.

Anything to help me down this tea.

"You're most welcome," he says, removing a tray of scones from his small oven. He refills the tray with them and rejoins the table.

Atlas grabs one, taking a quick bite, but he quickly drops it from his hand. It clatters onto his plate and he fans his mouth. "Ouch! Hot! Too hot!"

Rhea chokes on her tea once again as I whirl towards him.

"Atlas, your voice is back!"

Chapter 20

Atlas's face becomes overwhelmed with a gloriously surprised expression as he grabs at his face and throat. "I can talk! I can talk!" he yells about happily.

Rhea claps her hands, cheering, and I fear that my smile is so wide it will cause my dimples to cramp.

Hodge sits on his stool, his thick brows furrowed under the rim of his blue, pointy hat in complete confusion. "I beg your pardon, but could you not talk before?"

"No!"Atlas says, panting still from the shock, but with the brightest of grins plastered to his face. "We had an encounter with these two horrible wisp sisters a while back and they burned my vocal cords."

"Oh my," says Hodge. "I just assumed you were a quiet fellow, but that sounds quite unpleasant indeed."

Atlas's eyebrows shoot up in a knowing expression. "You could say that again. Worst pain in my life."

"This is fantastic!" Rhea exclaims, excitedly. "Caspar!" she says, spinning in her seat to yell towards the doorway. "Atlas can talk again!"

"For real?" he calls back, his voice faintly heard with us sitting so far inside the burrowed house.

Rhea rolls her eyes. "Like I would ever joke about that!" she yells, annoyed before suddenly spinning back to the table with wide eyes. "Wait! How is this possible?"

"Twas probably the scone," says Hodge, taking another sip of the awful amber tea.

Our heads all swivel towards him.

"The scone?" I ask, confused.

"Yes," he says. "The elderberries in them were from my garden."

I slowly make eyes with both Rhea and Atlas to make sure I'm not the only one confused as to how that answers things.

Thankfully, seeing our expressions, Hodge continues. "There are two kinds of gnomes. Miners and creators. Some of us mine for crystals underground in the forest and others are in charge of using the crystals in helpful ways. I am clearly not rugged enough to be a miner, so I incorporate crystals into my gardening by grinding them up into a powder that I infuse with my soil. This leads all of my produce to have different magical enhancements. My carrots help with stress, my strawberries emphasize beauty, and so forth, but my elderberries heal."

"The elderberries in that one bite of hot scone that I had healed me?" Atlas asks, clarifying.

"One bite is all it takes. There's a reason my produce is the best in the business," he says, with a wink.

"This hardly seems scientifically possible," Atlas says, dumbfounded, before adding, "but I have never been so grateful. I can't thank you enough."

Hodge waves his hand, dismissively. "Oh, hush. No need for thanks. It was fate! It just so happened that the elderberry scones were the ones I currently had on hand and it was just what you needed. Fate's timing, my boy, is never up to us, but we must accept what it brings

Chapter 20

nonetheless."

Atlas nods with a content smile.

"Now, I highly doubt you younglings decided to venture into the Bog together for fun. No one enters unless something outside has left them with no other option. So, why don't you tell me what you're up to?" Hodge says, taking another sip of his tea.

Rhea and Atlas turn, ushering for me to take the lead. I clear my throat. "We are here on a quest to obtain an amulet that has the power to undo anything."

"Ah," Hodge muses, knowingly. "I'm familiar with the legend."

"You are?" Rhea asks.

Hodge nods. "A fellow came long ago on the same journey you are venturing now."

"We are familiar with whom you're speaking of," Atlas says. "He recorded his expedition in a journal and we are following it as our guide."

"I see," says Hodge. "Well, when the gentleman came before he claimed he needed my most magical item. I knew, as soon as he said it, that it was the Red Beryl."

"The what now?" Rhea asks, confused, but Atlas interjects.

"Red Beryl is one of the rarest gems in all the realm," he says to her before turning back to face Hodge. "One of your miners found some?"

"My father found one when he was about my age. He was quite rougher around the edges than I, you see, and was widely known as the best miner in the Bog. When he found the Red Beryl, it only solidified that title even more. When my father passed, he left the gem to me and it was easily my most prized possession."

"But you gave it to the other gentleman who came searching for the amulet?" I ask. "Even though it was the most important thing to you?"

"I certainly did, dear." He sets down his teacup softly before meeting my eyes again. "It's hard to understand at a young age, but throughout your life, you will accumulate what you regard as the most important things to you. They will be your everything. Then, one day, by some stroke of fate, something will come along and make you realize that what was your everything could be someone else's everything and more."

"Wow," I breathe, my heart reeling with his wisdom.

"So, the man who came here before made you realize that the crystal would be more useful, or valuable, to him than it was to you?" asks Rhea, propping her head in her hands, elbows on the table.

Hodge nods. "He did indeed."

Wait, if he gave the crystal to the man, then what can he give us?

"That's beautiful," I begin. "Truly, but I have to ask. If a rare Red Beryl gem is what we need, and you've given yours away, then what are we to do now?"

Hodge picks back up his teacup, slurping another sip down under the tuft of his mustache, before answering calmly. "Another one has been found."

Rhea, Atlas, and I all perk up at this.

"Seriously?" Rhea asks, excited.

"That's incredible considering the extreme rarity of it," Atlas muses to himself, pushing his glasses up.

"That's fantastic!" I say. "How might we get it?"

Hodge picks up the teapot, walks back to the kitchen, and begins to brew a fresh batch of tea. "You'll have to fight for it," he calls over his shoulder, before proceeding to hum a little tune to himself.

I turn to Rhea who shares my confused expression.

Atlas pokes my shoulder. "Did he say fight for it?" he asks in a whisper.

"Like a physical fight?" Rhea adds, leaning in.

"I don't know," I say, voice hushed in our huddle as Hodge hums to himself. "Maybe we misheard him." I clear my throat and motion for

Chapter 20

them to sit back. "I'm sorry. Would you mind clarifying exactly what you mean when you say we have to fight? Do you mean a physical fight?"

Hodge turns, holding a fresh pot of tea in his hands to set on the table. "Well, of course. A fight of intellect or something would be quite silly."

Atlas, Rhea, and I exchange looks again before turning back to Hodge.

"I'm sorry, but I think we're all still a bit confused," I say.

Hodge pulls our teacups towards him. When he notes that mine is still half full, he tosses the rest of it over his shoulder onto the floor, emptying the cup, and I try not to show my surprise.

"I'm afraid I can't give away all of the information as it's pretty top secret," he says, beginning to pour a teal-colored tea into the cups now. "You must simply be in or out."

"It's the only way to get the gem?" Atlas asks, warily.

Hodge nods, pushing a teacup in front of each of us now. "I'm afraid it is."

A wave of silence falls over us as we all consider this. Are we crazy for even considering this?

Hodge takes the teapot over to the doorway, calling out, "Are you out there, big fella?"

Caspar's head appears on the exterior side of the entryway. "I am, sir."

"Let me refill your teacup for you."

Caspar extends his arm through the doorway, teacup in hand, and Hodge refills it before coming back to take a seat at the table.

Atlas, Rhea, and I all begin to sip the new tea that fills our cups, which I'm pleased to find practically flavorless. I ponder his vague proposal as we all sip in silence. Would our group be able to win a physical fight for the gem? I think Caspar would do alright and Rhea can throw down if irked in the right way. However, Atlas looks like he would have no clue how to use the muscles of his tall body in a fight. He's far too gentle a creature. Caspar may have taught me a thing or two about fighting, but I haven't had the chance to really use any of that new knowledge yet. Wait. Would we all have to fight or just one of us?

I set down my teacup once it's empty, which takes only about three small sips given its tiny proportions similar to the rest of Hodge's home. "Would we all have to fight or just one of us?" I ask.

Hodge stares at me calmly from across the table. "I'd only need the big fella outside," he says, motioning to the door.

Rhea lets out a scoff. "Well, then we've got a deal."

"Hey, hold on a second," I tell Rhea before addressing Hodge again. "It would be just him and one opponent?"

"Precisely," Hodge responds.

I turn to Atlas at this. "You know him best, do you feel like he could do that?"

Atlas puffs out a laugh. "He's the strongest and most agile sprite in all of Durand. If he can't do it, no one can."

"Alright, then," I breathe, turning back to Hodge. "We'll still need to run this past Caspar to double-check, but I'd say we have a deal."

Hodge claps his tiny hands in front of him. "Marvelous!"

A large thud sounds from outside the front door and we all spin towards it.

"Caspar?" I call out, quickly crawling from my seat over to peer out the doorway where I find him flat on the ground. "Caspar?" I call again, but he doesn't move or wake. I turn back to face everyone inside. "I think he's unconscious!"

"Unconscious?" Atlas asks.

Rhea rubs her temples with both hands, squeezing her eyes shut. "Guys, I don't feel so good."

Chapter 20

"It's just the tea," Hodge says, coolly. "I'd honestly expected it to hit the big guy last, but," he shrugs, "magic never acts exactly as expected."

"What do you—" I begin, but my voice fades as soon as I notice that Hodge never poured a cup of the new blue tea for himself. "Did-did you drug us?" I ask, horror lacing my tone.

Hodge waves a small hand. "Drugged is far too harsh a term. I've merely given you a tea made from the blueberries of my garden that make you fall asleep painlessly."

Atlas's eyes bulge out of his face from behind his lenses. "I've been drugged!" he exclaims. "But I don't feel anything—" and just like that, his eyes roll back and his body goes limp, slumping forward onto the table.

I go to move towards him, but suddenly feel so fatigued. I fight it. I will myself to keep moving, but I can feel my limbs going slack.

"Why would you—" I start, but my voice trails away as I quickly become too tired to speak. I watch Rhea fall back onto the floor of the home, sound asleep.

Hodge's small feet pitter-patter from under his robe as he walks to where I flop onto my side on the floor.

"You'll all be perfectly fine, my dear," he says, patting the top of my hair comfortingly. Both he and his tall, pointy hat start to look very fuzzy as he adds, "I just can't let you see the pathway to the underground ring."

Chapter 21

"My head is woozy," Atlas says, lifting his head slightly from where he's sprawled on the floor.

"Consider yourself lucky then," says Rhea, pulling herself up into a sitting position to rub at her temples. "My *everything* feels woozy."

I push myself up from where I lie face-down on the soil to peer at them, noting Caspar flat on his back to my left. The dark room, lit only by two lanterns on the far wall, has surprisingly tall ceilings and is empty other than a door off to my right; a door that is thankfully much larger than at Hodge's residence. This and the lack of wood and coziness affirm my guess that we are no longer in Hodge's home.

I gradually work my way into a sitting position, my head pounding like a drum, and reach my hand out to nudge Caspar's shoulder. He shifts but doesn't wake.

"Caspar," I say, this time slapping his shoulder.

The hand of his opposite arm flies to the shoulder I hit as his eyes flutter open. "Ow!"

"You have to wake up," I encourage him as Rhea and Atlas both stand.

Rhea offers me a hand up and Atlas does the same for Caspar, who grabs at his forehead once he's fully standing, eyes winced. "What the hell was in that tea?"

"A sleeping potion, apparently," Atlas says, pushing his glasses up. "Honestly, for the speed at which it was able to put us all to sleep, we should consider ourselves fortunate to not have worse symptoms upon awakening. In fact, there is another sleeping element I've heard of before, but—" he's cut off as Rhea slaps her hand across his mouth.

She lets out a groan, looking at Caspar and I. "This is insane. We don't even know where we are and we're trusting an old gnome man we've never met before today." She pauses, tilting her head in thought. "If it *is* still today."

Suddenly the door opens, and Hodge's head peaks through. "Oh, good! You're awake!" he says, cheerily, before making his way inside. Once the door is shut behind him he turns toward Caspar, bunching his hands together in excitement. "Are you ready big fella? Time to make us all proud!"

Caspar towers over Hodge as he peers down at him, a confused expression on his face. "Sorry, what are you talking about?"

"Your fight," says Hodge, plainly, his mustache still turned upward with a grin.

Caspar blinks at him. "Again, sorry, but what are you talking about?" This time he turns to me, asking again, "What is he talking about?"

I hold my hands together behind my back. "Um, we may have agreed to have you fight an opponent for the gem that we need to get the amulet."

His mouth drops open for a moment before he takes on a straight face, pointing a finger at me. "You mean *you* agreed to it."

I scratch the back of my head, averting my eyes to the ceiling as if in thought. "I'm having trouble remembering exactly who said what. My head's still pounding from the tea."

"Mhmmm," Caspar muses, rolling his eyes. "I bet I could guess exactly how that conversation went." He looks back down at Hodge before him. "I'm just fighting one guy?"

Hodge nods. "That's correct." He looks at the bunch of us. "I apologize for the tea, but I couldn't simply lead you here and have you see where the ring is located."

"You can't tell us anything about where we are?" Rhea whines.

Hodge tilts his head. "Well, I can tell you that we are in the underground roots of the Bog trees, and," he points back towards the door, "that out there lies the top secret fighting ring that we gnomes organized for sport as a way to barter off high-demand crystals and gemstones that arise in the mines. It's a full house out there tonight. Should be a jolly good show."

"Wow," Atlas breathes, hands on his hips, and we all turn to face him. "Oh, sorry," he mutters. "It's just that given your calm and homely demeanor, one would never expect you to help orchestrate an underground fight club."

Hodge lets out a chuckle. "I like to remain somewhat of a mystery; defy expectations and whatnot. It is customary though for the fighters to be introduced before we begin, so can I go ahead and bring him by now? We don't have too long."

Caspar nods, hands on his hips, his chest puffed slightly as he huffs, "Sure. Bring him by."

"Excellent," Hodge says, before hobbling off with his cane back through and out the door.

Caspar turns to me as soon as he's gone. "Are you freaking kidding me, Red? You entered me in a fight without even telling me?"

"Hey!" I say, jutting a finger towards Atlas. "He said if you couldn't do it, no one could!"

Caspar swivels towards Atlas now, who blushes. "I may have said that, but Rhea here agreed as soon as the suggestion had left Hodge's mouth!" He nudges Rhea with his elbow, who turns, smacking his arm.

"So, what if I did?" she says, crossing her arms over her chest now. "Out of all of us, you're definitely the most physically capable, and we need the Red Beryl, or else we have to give up."

"I can take him," Caspar says to her. "I'm a trained fighter. That's not my issue. My issue," he continues, turning and walking closer to me now, "is that this little arrangement was agreed upon without my input."

"Look, I'm sorry, okay? I told him I still wanted to check first with you, but the next thing I knew, we'd all been drugged and then we woke up here! There wasn't time to sit down and have an in-depth discussion about it."

Why is he arguing with me? What in the realm does he expect me to do about it now?

"Oh, sure," he says with a scoff. "Of course, the one time you don't freak over thoroughly detailing out a plan before committing is when it's only my life on the line."

My mouth drops open at this, fury sparking in my core. "Hey, I may not have discussed it with you yet, but I sure as hell did think it through. I wouldn't put you in danger so carelessly like that."

He steps closer to me, towering down at me, his eyes dark and tempting. "Oh, really? And why is that?" he says it as a question but it feels like a dare.

"Because," I begin, annoyed that my words are coming out slightly shaky, "as much as I hate to admit it, we need your help on the rest of our quest."

"Are you sure that's the only reason?" he asks. I see his eyes drop to my mouth momentarily and it makes the ground beneath my feet feel unsteady.

"I—" I begin, looking down, my voice coming out far quieter than I meant it. I gulp before meeting his eyes again, frightened at the intensity I find there. "What other reason would there be?"

His eyes dip down to my lips again and for a brief second, I think it might actually happen. Maybe he's going to tell me he feels something, too; that it's not just me and that our kiss wasn't a mistake. Maybe he'll say that all of this isn't casual, meaningless flirting and that it means something more. Maybe he'll say that he doesn't hate me as much as I think he does.

Instead, I'll never know because there's a knock at the door and Rhea breaks from her trance of watching Caspar and me, yelling, "I'll get it!" and running over.

She opens it slightly and I hear a low, husky, "Hello, there."

Rhea's eyes widen and she twists her head to me mouthing, "Wow," with raised, suggestive eyebrows before turning back to whoever is on the other side. "Come on in."

She swings the door open and I swear I hear Caspar curse under his breath.

In walks the tallest man I have ever seen. Long, blonde hair frames firm eyes and a jawline sharp enough to cut, atop a body that looks chiseled by gods. His black pants are cut off at the ends and his bare chest shows off a tattoo across his heart of two flowers. However, it's his ears that truly catch my eye.

He's a sprite.

"What's your tattoo of?" Rhea asks.

The spriteman points to the art on his chest. "They're two white roses," he says.

"Aw," Rhea says. "Why white roses?"

"To signify each one of my kills. Seemed appropriate since they're all sure as hell pushing up flowers now."

Rhea does an excellent job at maintaining a straight face as she takes a gulp, letting out a shaky, "I see."

His eyes begin to move past Rhea, catching on Atlas, who looks

Chapter 21

terrified. He scoffs. "Well, I know I'm not fighting you. Gnomes aren't that unfair."

I see hurt flash across Atlas's face and hear him mumble under his breath, "A fight of intelligence wouldn't be fair either, so—" but our menacing-looking visitor takes a step towards him.

"Try saying that again to my—" he begins, but Caspar walks forward, laying a hand on his arm and turning him slightly away from Atlas to face him instead.

"Lay off him," Caspar says, voice commanding.

Our visitor takes a step back, shifting his body slightly so Caspar loses his grip on his arm. His eyes scroll over Caspar, sizing him up. "You're the fresh meat for tonight?" he asks before letting out a low chuckle. "Guess the gnomes really *are* unfair."

It's so strange for me to see Caspar look small next to someone, him having been the tallest person I'd ever seen till about 30 seconds ago.

I see Caspar bunch his right hand into a fist at his side. For a moment, I fear that he'll start the fight right here, right now, but instead, as quickly as he clenched his fist up, he releases it with a breath. He plasters on that cocky grin of his that I know all too well.

"I'd save the smack talk for in the ring, bud. Pride does come before a fall," he stops, touching a finger to his chin in thought. "Or was it an ass-whooping?" He meets our visitor's eyes again with a satisfied grin, tucking his hands in the pockets of his vest. "I'm not one hundred percent positive, but I'm pretty sure it's the latter."

Our visitor lets out another low chuckle. "Lot of tough talk," he says, reaching out a hand and shoving Caspar's shoulder roughly, "for a King."

I feel the vertebrae of my spin lock in fear and see a hint of equal unease on Rhea's face, but Caspar remains calm.

"Lots of talk for a runaway," Caspar says, his face set strong as he takes a step up towards the spriteman, whose face becomes enraged.

He shoves again, this time with both hands, forcing Caspar backward, his back hitting the wall with a hard thud.

"Don't you dare call me a runaway!" he yells at Caspar now, his voice enraged. "You banished me and you know it!"

"Ah, still making excuses for ourselves, are we?" Caspar asks, tauntingly. "You know you've got to stop playing the victim at some point, Helix."

I see Helix's nostrils flare.

Do they know each other?

"You know each other?" I ask, but as soon as the words leave my mouth, I wish they hadn't.

Helix's eyes turn to me and where there was anger only a moment ago, a devilish smile now creeps across his face.

"My, my, my," he says, clicking his tongue after the last word. "Honey, you've got me feeling all messed up and I haven't even messed you up yet."

Now it's Caspar's turn to deliver a firm shove. "Leave her alone, Helix." He walks to stand in front of Helix, blocking him from where I stand.

Helix's eyes dart between Caspar and me before his face takes on a knowing expression.

"Ah, I see," he says, letting out an amused snicker. "You've already tapped that." He takes a step forward, towering down at Caspar while standing so close to him I'm sure he can feel his breath. "Don't worry. I wouldn't want your sloppy seconds anyway."

Both of Caspar's fists ball at his sides now. "Get out of my face," he spits.

"Gladly," Helix says with a chuckle. He begins taking steps backward towards the door. "You know, I've had a lot of pent-up energy lately. And while I'd love to take it out on *you*," he says, shooting me a wink that makes my stomach pull into a knot. His eyes avert back to Caspar.

Chapter 21

"I guess I'll just let it all out in the ring," he finishes.

With that, he turns to exit, allowing us a full view of his back, *covered* in roses.

Chapter 22

As soon as Helix leaves, it's like the whole room releases a breath. I spin to Caspar. "Thank you."

He waves his hand. "Don't mention it."

Rhea puts her hands on her hips. "How do you know each other? He was *banished*? I'm gonna need all the juicy details."

Atlas raises an index finger, shooting Caspar a look of question. "If I may?"

Caspar nods.

"Helix is the bastard son of Durand's previous King," says Atlas.

Both mine and Rhea's mouths drop open as if our jaws have become unhinged.

"For *real*?" Rhea asks, dumbfounded.

Atlas pushes his glasses up the bridge of his nose. "Precisely."

"So, the previous King *did* have an heir, just not a *legitimate* one," I say, putting everything together out loud.

Beside me now, Caspar nods. "He was always a jackass. Merciless and cruel, just like his father. When his dad died, he didn't even mourn. All he did was bust into the palace like he was already King."

"So, you banished him?" I ask.

Chapter 22

Caspar scratches the back of his head, exasperatedly. "I didn't get the chance to, officially. Not yet, at least. Word spread that he had barged into the palace and people were scared. He wasn't a legitimate heir so he had no legitimate claim to the throne." He sighs. "The people didn't want to go through the same thing they did under his father's rule. It was horrible and he's so similar to his father that things definitely would have taken the same ruthless course. Late one night, the kingdom held a meeting in the town square and I was voted into rule. I went to the palace to break the news to him myself and he got rather violent. He was mad that the people had voted someone else into the position of King, especially because it was me. We got into quite the bloody fight and it ended with me saying that I would banish him if he didn't get his act together." He meets my eyes now as he draws his story to an end. "He was gone the next morning. No one could find him. Now, I know where he's been."

"Am I the only one even more excited to see this fight now, or what?" Rhea asks, raising her hand into the air with a chuckle. Caspar, Atlas, and I all shoot her an are-you-kidding-me-look and she slowly averts her eyes, lowering her arm back to her side. "Too soon to joke. Got it."

I groan, putting my head in my hands and rubbing at my temples. Why did this have to happen? Of all the horrible, stupid luck we could run into, this has got to be the worst.

"You okay?" Caspar asks.

"He's going to kill you," I say, voice hushed to a breath.

Caspar turns towards me, eyes caring. "No, he's not."

"I'm sorry, *did you not see the roses?*" Rhea exclaims, voice borderline hysterical. "He looks like he could eat you alive."

"I'll be fine," he says, voice insistent.

"You have to be alright," I say, feeling tears brim my eyes. I blink them back. I need him for this quest and I need to see what this thing is that I feel for him. I'll never get that chance if something happens to him. And if something happens to him because of me, I don't know how I'll forgive myself.

"Hey," he says, voice comforting as he gently grabs me by my shoulders, turning me towards him as he bends down to be eye level with me. "Nothing is going to happen to me."

"You promise?" I ask, and in that one simple question, it feels like I just told him everything. I can feel it in my eyes, shining out, and I know he feels it, too. He can feel the emotions I have there, the way I hold onto our kiss like a best-kept secret and the way I care for him.

I see the moment he reads it all on my face because his eyes soften and I swear I feel him reflecting those feelings my heart is sharing. When he looks into my eyes, it's like he's looking into the deepest parts of me.

"I promise," he says, and I know he means it because his thumb scrapes gently over the bare skin of my shoulder where his hand rests.

Just then, a knock sounds at the door and Hodge's head peeps inside. "Ready, big fella?"

Caspar turns to him and nods, giving my shoulder a slight squeeze before letting go.

Hodge smiles, ushering us through the door with a wave, and I take a deep breath as I fall into line behind the others. I've barely stepped through the entryway when the sound of yelling and cheering meets my ears. Hodge leads us in a small rooted hallway around a long bend of a corner and suddenly I'm greeted with a roaring crowd of gnomes.

The end of the bent hallway opens into a tall arena with a domed ceiling. On a raised platform lies the ring. Although, now I don't understand why they call it that because its actual shape is square. Thin, thorny vines are braided and intertwined together snaking along the border of the ring from the muddy floor of it to just about two feet shy of the ceiling. Surrounding the square ring is a crazed chorus

Chapter 22

of gnomes, both male and female, in tiered wooden stands, screaming at the top of their lungs for blood. The room is dimly lit with lanterns that have tinted cases around them, turning the hue that they cast into an ominous shade of red, only adding to my sense of unease.

I feel like my brain can't comprehend what's before me. This is the furthest thing from what I was expecting when Hodge first proposed the fight. Fears of this brawl going south, and having only myself to blame, once again flood my thoughts and I feel like I'm going to hurl.

Rhea must see it on my face as she turns from ahead in our line as we follow Hodge to check on me. She slows her steps till she's fallen back beside me and takes my hand in hers, giving it a comforting squeeze.

"It's going to be fine," she says.

"It better be," I breathe, "or else I don't know what we'll do."

Hodge leads us to a dark, wooden bench along the floor at the side of the ring, and Rhea, Atlas, and I sit. Hodge opens his mouth to speak, but just misses his chance as the previous chanting of the crowd suddenly increases tenfold in volume as Helix enters from the opposite side of the room. Two gnomes flank his sides and he puffs his chest, beating his fists on it, and belting a war cry that only riles up the crowd further. Even through the thorny thicket, across the large expanse of the ring, I see the moment he locks eyes with Caspar, an unsettling smile snaking across his face.

"I'm coming for you," he mouths.

Hodge taps Caspar's leg, since that's about all he can reach, turning his attention away from Helix. Hodge bunches his hands together excitedly. "Alrighty. It's time! The first one to knock the other out wins!"

"What?" asks Rhea, horrified. "That seems rather extreme!"

A male gnome sitting on the lowest level of the tiered wooden stands behind us overhears her comment, leaning forward to offer, "Honey, this is a *man's* sport. It's meant to be extreme."

While I expect this to set Rhea off in an impulsive fury, she instead stands, calmly turning back to face him with an innocent grin. "Sorry, *honey*," she says, drawing out the pet name, "guess I couldn't tell since, where I come from, the men are at least three feet tall."

His eyes widen, his face taking on a furious blush as he sits back down in his seat. Rhea takes her seat again, crossing her legs and folding her arms across her chest with a satisfied smile.

A bell dings and the crowd roars.

"Are you ready for the show of the century?" booms a voice and I turn to see that it's originating from a gnome woman sitting in a high chair on the outside of the ring, yelling into some sort of wooden cone thing that amplifies her voice to a whole new register. The crowd cheers, but she says it again. "I said, are you ready for the show of the century?" The room goes ecstatic now, raging away in a frenzy. She smiles beneath her tall, purple hat, finally satisfied. "Opponents, make your way to the ring!"

Helix walks, following a different gnome, up to the edge of the raised ring's vine exterior, and through a door his guide opens.

Caspar turns towards us and Atlas stands, placing a hand on his shoulder. "Knock him dead, dude."

Rhea smacks his behind from down where she sits on the bench and Atlas recoils, spinning back to her. "Don't touch my bottom!"

"Well then, don't say stupid stuff!" counters Rhea. "We don't want to promote killing! We just need a gem. This isn't war!"

"It's just an expression!" Atlas fires back, cheeks flaring as he angrily shoves his glasses up his nose and sits back down.

Normally, I'd laugh at an interaction like that between them, but right now I can't seem to find humor or amusement in anything, fear and unease clouding my mind. Caspar must sense this in me as he turns my way. His face softens and he reaches out, fingertips lightly

Chapter 22

brushing a strand of red hair back from my face. I'm shocked at the contact, but even more surprised at how natural it feels.

He opens his mouth to speak, but I miss the opportunity to hear what he has to say as the gnome woman with the cone shouts, "New guy! I said get in the ring! We don't have all night!"

Caspar releases a short sigh. His eyes graze over the features of my face as if memorizing them before he turns to make his way over. Once he walks into the ring with Helix, the assisting gnome closes the vine-covered door, sealing them in. With the look on Helix's face, you'd think it was his birthday or something, but I know the horrible truth. I set Caspar up for his sworn enemy to have him trapped and ripe for revenge. I offer up a prayer to the rainbow that Caspar will be able to smack that horrible expression right off Helix's chiseled face.

Suddenly, perhaps prompted by some kind of cue I missed, the crowd of surrounding gnomes begin chanting, counting down from 10. With every number shouted, I feel my stomach coil further into itself. I really feel like I might be sick.

When the gnomes hit the number six, Caspar peels off his vest, tossing it to the side, before slowly removing his shirt, grabbing the bottom left of it with his right hand, pulling it over his shoulder and off his torso in one fluid motion. I hear female gnomes begin shrieking in the stands at the sight of his strapping torso. While I already expected him to be muscular and strong, having seen the way his sleeves fit so tightly before, I'm still floored at the sight now. While all the gnome women in the arena seem to have trouble making any noise other than a squeal at the sight of him, I can't seem to remember how to take a breath. I know it starts with breathing in, but somehow I'm getting lost after that.

Three.

I feel Rhea, beside me, jut an elbow into my side. I swat at her, but can't seem to avert my eyes off of Caspar's form. Rhea snickers.

"You okay there, Luna?" she asks, voice teasing. "You look a little flushed."

I lightly shove her knee beside me, my eyes still spanning Caspar's chest as he stretches out his neck before crouching down across from Helix in the same beginning fight stance he taught me just the other evening. The dark veins from ripping out Seraphina's heart are on full display now and I can see the way they snake up his arm and bicep before swirling to an end at his shoulder.

Two.

His torso begins broadly at his shoulders, narrowing slightly at his waist. Staring at his firm pectorals and sculpted abs any other time would have given me full confidence that he'd be able to take someone in a fight. However, knowing that the opponent he's facing now is Helix, makes doubt creep into my heart.

One.

A bell dings, signaling the beginning of the match, and Helix wastes no time in launching the first punch. He swings for the face, but Caspar smoothly avoids it, angling his body to the right.

"What's the rush, Helix?" Caspar asks with a grin.

His confidence eases my worry slightly.

"Revenge waits for nothing," Helix says, lunging forward, bent down, grabbing Caspar around the waist, and pushing him back against the thorny vines. He can't pin him for long though because with a swift, hard knee to the inner thigh, Helix's arms turn soft in a moment of pain and Caspar shoves him off, circling towards the other side of the ring, all the while never taking his eyes off of Helix.

"Nope," Caspar says, "but it does take at least one decent punch, don't you think?"

Helix lets out a war cry, similar to the one upon his entry into the arena, before locking eyes with Caspar again, face menacing. "I think you should focus less on your trash talk and more on actually throwing

Chapter 22

a punch yourself. Or is this whole fight going to be me swinging and you just running away every time?"

"I don't know," Caspar says, arms out at his sides, but legs still slightly bent in a crouch. "Why don't you come find out?"

They circle, shuffling around the ring in an intense staring match for another moment before Helix charges towards Caspar, fist raised, and I don't know how he does it, but Caspar slithers around the side of Helix, and in doing so, lands a firm punch to the side of his ribs. Helix's hands go to the tender spot before he turns back towards Caspar, furious.

"You little—" he begins, but Caspar's fist collides squarely with his jaw as soon as he turns towards him.

The crowd roars as Helix lands on his back, eyes shut, and for a moment, I wonder if it's over. Has Caspar bested him this quickly? The audience creates a thunder-like sound with their cries, and I know they're sharing my thoughts. Suddenly the tone of their chants changes as Helix's eyes open and he lets out an angry groan, pulling himself back up to a standing position, which allows me to see the bleeding cut along his jaw where Caspar's fist made contact.

"No!" Rhea and Atlas both cry out beside me on the bench, all of us having hoped that one punch could have been all it took.

"You think one punch is all it's gonna take? I'm not letting you get away with what you did." Helix spits, eyes enraged with sweat beading on his chest. The way he says this is unsettling to me. The pure fury his words are laced with seems fueled by something otherworldly; as if his anger runs so deep that it goes beyond the realm.

Is there more to their story than I was told?

Rhea and I both turn to look at Atlas on the end of our bench and he bunches his lips inward, eyes coy. I narrow my gaze at him.

"What is he talking about, Atlas? Caspar becoming King?"

Atlas gulps, still looking straight ahead. "Yup," he says, voice higher than usual. He clears his throat. "That's all."

Rhea reaches, bunching the material of the collar of his shirt into her fist, lurching him forward till he's inches from her face beside her on the bench. She juts the index finger of her other hand at his nose. "You are the worst liar ever. Now you tell us what he's talking about or so help me, I will—" she halts in her words as the crack of fist colliding with bone rings out and the crowd suddenly roars.

We all spin back to the ring to find Caspar wiping away a trail of blood that drizzles now from his nose. Helix is shaking out his fist, looking satisfied, but still hungry for more.

"What?" Rhea yells. "I look away for *one second!*"

My heart's beating so fast, pounding away in my chest like a drum. *Is he okay? He has to be okay.*

Caspar finishes wiping the blood from his face, mouth open, taking deep breaths. "I hope you enjoyed that one," he says, shooting Helix a low stare, "because that's the only one you're going to get."

Helix chuckles, eyes wild, before swinging for another blow that Caspar parries. After that, it's like they've begun a makeshift dance. Attack, counter, parry. Attack, counter, parry. Their feet shuffle as they skirt around the edges of the ring in between advances.

Caspar lands a firm kick to the side of Helix's torso that distracts him enough for him to land another jab to his jaw, the same cut spot from before. The force of Caspar's blow is so strong that it sends Helix flying forward onto his stomach. He pushes, getting up slowly, shaking his head in an attempt to shake the dizziness from the hit. Once he gets to his feet, I see his eyes are bloodshot, full of tears.

"I won't let you win, Caspar. Not this time," he says, voice hauntingly threatening. "Not after all you've taken from me!" he cries now, fists bunched at his sides.

I see Caspar's face take on an almost apologetic look from where I sit. "Helix, none of it was personal. You know I never meant to—"

Chapter 22

Helix cries out in rage, racing forward suddenly and landing a firm punch under Caspar's jaw. Caspar stumbles back, eyes winced for a moment, but when he opens them again as he shuffles across from Helix, he seems to have locked back into focus. "Helix, I mean it!"

"Shut up!" Helix shouts in fury as he lunges towards Caspar. Caspar manages to dodge it alright, but Helix spins back sooner than he anticipates and lands not one, but two swift punches to the gut. Caspar swings for him, but his feet are unsteady and he misses, Helix landing a blow to the side of his torso. Caspar keels forward slightly from the startling blow, but Helix immediately meets his face with a high knee, sending Caspar sprawling onto his back with a hard thud.

"You're not getting out of this one, Caspar!" Helix cries. Angry, hot tears stream from his eyes down his sweaty face as he turns. He stalks towards the door of the ring and in one swift, downward jut of his elbow, bashes in the hatch of the door; locking both him and Caspar inside the ring.

Rhea, Atlas, and I all jump to our feet, the crowd in a concerned frenzy as the realization hits us simultaneously. Helix has absolutely no intention of letting Caspar walk out of that ring.

I grab Rhea's arm beside me. "Rhea, what do we do?" I cry. "We have to help him!"

"I—" she stutters, dazed in fright. "I don't—" she tries again, but she can't find the words.

Atlas stands beside her, frozen in fear.

Caspar groans, trying to push himself upright from where he lays on his back, but Helix stalks towards him, before lifting his leg and stomping a foot down with a mighty thrust straight onto the center of Caspar's stomach. The crowd of onlooking gnomes cries out as Caspar's body jerks, folding into itself from impact as blood spurts from his lips.

I realize I'm screaming now. "Help! Somebody help him!" I shout, my voice pleading.

Caspar looks like he's trying to speak, but Helix doesn't give him the chance, putting a leg on either side of Caspar's body, before bending and firmly grabbing him by the throat with one hand. He pulls Caspar's head slightly off the floor, by his neck, to peer into his eyes.

"The only way to get revenge for a King killed is to kill another King," Helix sneers before using the left hand wrapped around Caspar's throat to turn his head to the right just to use his right fist to deliver a punch in the countering direction, knocking Caspar's head back with a crack. He lets go, Caspar falling backward slack to the floor, but I see his eyes flutter, rolling back into his head.

How is he still conscious?

I don't have time to wonder. I have to do something. Anything!

But *what*?

Helix stands smug over Caspar, arms out to his sides. "You'd think this was the grand finale, right?" he shouts down at Caspar, who seems barely awake, bleeding from his mouth with another deep gash above his eyebrow. A spot along his jawbone is already turning a shade of purple.

Gnomes are working at the door along the ring's edge, but they're not fast enough. They're taking too much time and we don't have any time to spare.

"But didn't anyone ever tell you, Caspar," he says, pulling the dagger from the side of Caspar's pants. "I'm a *carver*."

Blood rushes to my brain and I feel an overwhelming sense of protectiveness rise inside me. I don't even stop to think about it. As soon as the thought enters my mind, I act. I fly upward, squeezing through the shallow opening between the roof and the top of the thorny edge of the ring, and dive straight for Helix.

Chapter 23

I hear a revolution in the roar of the crowd as I make contact, latching onto Helix like a backpack.

"Luna!" Rhea's voice rings out, coated in pure fear and disbelief. "What the hell are you doing?"

But I barely register her above the loud audience, my focus solely on Helix who seems completely taken aback at my interference. As he should be. I'm even surprised at myself.

"What the—" he begins, but I act fast, thinking that if I'm quick enough, it can be over before it even begins. I wrap my arms up, nestling his neck into the crook of my elbow so that I can apply maximum force as I begin to squeeze. I barely get the chance to even start though because he stops trying to swing me off and reaches up over his shoulder to grab my hair tightly. I cry out as he yanks hard and I have no choice, but to relax my grip and let him pull me off his back lest he pull all my hair out.

Once I'm off, he holds his grasp on my hair, pulling me to stand in front of him. His face is surprised when he registers that it's me.

"Well, well, well," he muses, voice haunting. "You couldn't even wait till I'd finished knocking his lights out to pounce on me, sweetheart?"

His words are laced with so much innuendo that I could barf, but instead, I will myself to play along and keep the upper hand, playing on his interest. I flutter my eyelashes for a quick second and, with all my self-control, reach out to place a hand on his gleaning chest, trying not to cringe at the excessive sweat I find there. I toss my other hand coyly in front of my mouth as if suppressing a flirtatious smile.

In my peripheral vision, Caspar struggles to hold his head up from off the ground, face bloodied and concerned when he sees me. "Luna? Get out! You shouldn't be here!"

"Didn't you say you wanted to get all messed up?" I ask Helix, ignoring Caspar to truly sell this performance.

His brows shoot up, his eyes widening in surprise before settling into delight. His grip on my hair loosens slightly, his hand sliding down to the back of my neck, pulling me so close to him that I can not only see the sweat, but smell it now as well, and I try not to gag from the overwhelming stench.

"Oh, baby, I want you to mess me up bad," he says, biting his lower lip. "Let me make you feel things that Caspar never could."

His other hand reaches out to slither around my waist and I do my best to not recoil from his touch, keeping my expression light and flirtatious.

Caspar tries to push himself up from the floor of the ring, concerned and outraged. "Don't you touch her, Helix! Luna, get out of here! Let's go." He can't lift himself though. His body is too exhausted and weak.

Helix goes to turn towards Caspar, but I reach out, guiding his face back to mine with a hand on his jaw. "How about I make *you* feel things that you have never felt before?"

Helix lets out a pleased groan.

I tilt my head, inching my face closer to his and lowering my voice. "Only if you say please."

He closes his eyes. "Ple—" he begins, but I don't even let him get the

Chapter 23

whole word out before I grab hold of his shoulders, keeping him in place, and quickly jerk my knee up into his groin with all of the might I can muster.

He cries out in pain, folding forward and I use the opportunity to deliver a shove with the side of my body, sending him onto his back in front of me where he rolls back and forth, cursing under his breath and holding the area I've treated quite the opposite of what he was hoping.

I rush over to Caspar on the ground and will myself not to cry at the pain I see on his face as I try to help him to his feet.

"Come on, Caspar. We have to get you out of here," I say, as I link my arms under his shoulders and attempt to pull him up.

He shrugs out of my hold though and I turn to peer at his face, my brows bunched together in question. "What are you—" I start, but he grabs my hand in his, cutting me off.

"Luna, you can't carry me over the ring's wall. I'll be too heavy. Just go. Please. Save yourself," he coughs out, more blood spurting from his lips.

"No," I say so quickly that it's like a reflex. "I can't leave you. I won't leave you."

I hear a sweet sigh released from the crowd before it suddenly turns to screams and I spin to see Helix hurdling for me at Caspar's side. I duck to the left, barely skirting out of the way in time; ever grateful for the crowd's warning.

I stand, turning to face Helix. I'm surprised to find him with a waiting hand that slaps across my face so hard that I cry out. My footing wasn't prepared for his hit. I stumble to the right side of the ring into the thorny vines which prick at my skin but do not pierce. My cheek is stinging and my head is spinning.

Is that drumming from the crowd or the pain on the side of my face?

Helix holds his arms out at his sides, flames in his eyes, but a maniacal grin on his face.

"You think you're quite the little actress?" he asks, dropping his arms, and stalking towards me. "Then, let's see how well you can play *dead*."

My heart is thrumming at my chest and my head still feels dazed from his slap. I'm so scared. What was I thinking flying in here like that? I can't do this. Now, I've set both Caspar and myself up to die at Helix's calloused hands.

"Luna!" Caspar cries, drawing my attention back to him over the top of Helix's shoulder as he moves towards me, creeping slowly. Caspar's eyes soften when they meet mine for a moment before his face talks on a determined look. "Remember what I taught you," he yells over the crowd. Helix ignores him. "You've got this," he mouths silently now.

His words coat over my fear, silencing it enough to allow me to take a full breath. I turn my attention back to Helix, summoning up Caspar's words from before. "Gauge what their physical strengths are so that you're aware of what they'll be trying to utilize against you. Use that information to predict their next move," his voice flows like a guiding melody in my mind.

Focus, Luna. Focus.

Helix is tall and seems to rely the most on his upper body. How can I deal with his height? He towers over me and I can't just magically grow six inches taller. A thought suddenly occurs to me. I don't have to necessarily *be* as tall as him. I just need to keep the high ground, meaning that I need to take to the air. I need to fly up and stay at least eye level with him to give myself a fair chance.

Now, to predict how he'll use his upper body strength against me. He'll probably go for some more swings, but if I stay higher, that should be slightly more difficult.

Wait. Perhaps I can use his large upper body to my advantage. His

Chapter 23

back is so broad, and his neck is so thick from his muscles, that I'm sure he has difficulty seeing what's behind him.

His back is his biggest blind spot.

Feeling slightly more prepared with this information, well, as prepared as I can be, I avert my attention back to Helix right as he approaches me, right hand raised for another ripe slap. I act fast, flying up and around behind him. He turns back and forth, whipping around to try and see me, but I stay with him, squarely in the center of his back, silent.

The crowd begins to cheer now, which only makes Helix grow even more irritated as he whips around faster. This makes him harder to keep up with, but I still manage to stay in the blind spot.

He roars now. "Give it up, sweetheart! Show yourself!"

I flip upside down in front of his face. "Here I am," I say, before mustering all my courage and strength to deliver a firm punch of my small, bunched first right into the bridge of his nose. I hear a crack. His head knocks back slightly and this is the part where I'd be proud of myself, but instead, I'm blinking back tears. The pain emanating from my fist is so horrible, that I begin to fear that the crack I heard was from one of my fingers breaking instead of his nose. How can Caspar make punching look so easy? Apparently, when I'm involved, it feels horrible for both parties.

Helix uses a hand to wipe under his nose, which flows blood now, his eyes registering shock at the crimson before turning enraged back to me.

"Come on, Luna!" Caspar yells from the ground, still trying to get to his feet, but failing. It's for the best. If he got up, Helix would revert his anger back to him and finish him off. I just have to keep him distracted long enough for the gnomes to pry the door open somehow.

Helix lunges for me, raising his right arm as he does. I go to swerve to the left to avoid him, but he delivers a quick punch to my jaw with his left hand just as I try to do so. He played me. He sent me to the left by making me think he was coming from my right.

The punch knocks me back slightly, but I don't fall, and the crowd roars. I don't have to check to know that his nail cut along my jaw. I can feel the trickle of blood landing on the base of that side of my neck like warm raindrops. I'm seeing spots in my vision from the combination of adrenaline and pain. I don't know how much longer I can do this. He could end this at any moment, only growing angrier with each flying fist.

How can I possibly beat someone so much taller and bigger than me? I've been doing my best, but I need something better. *Think, Luna. Think.*

Suddenly, it hits me. I take a deep breath and move my body into the fighting stance Caspar showed me. I pretend I'm back there. I'm beside the dying fire in the misty woods of the Bog. Caspar's in a mirrored stance before me and silence blankets the air around us. I don't feel afraid. I see his eyes, looking at me like he saw potential in me. And I feel confident.

"Ahhhh!" Helix roars and begins to charge at me, just as I see the gnomes successfully open the door behind him.

In a flash, I use the speed at which he's charging at me to the advantage of my momentum, and I beat my wings as strong as I can. Grabbing his left arm with both of my hands and mustering all the might I hold in my body, I cry out from the effort and flip him over me.

He lands with a loud thud and everyone falls silent. I stand, resting forward with my hands on my knees to try and catch my breath. The gnomes in the ring don't run to Caspar, or me, they all just stand still, eyes behind me. I lift my head a little higher after a moment for my breathing to slow, just to find that the audience beyond the ring shares their shocked stares.

I turn slowly to look at Helix behind me and find him flat on his

Chapter 23

back, unconscious.

I didn't just distract him away from Caspar long enough for the gnomes to open the door.

I won the fight.

Chapter 24

I caress the side of Caspar's face in an attempt to wake him slowly, happy when it works and his eyelids gently lift. His pupils dart around the dark interior of the cave, lit only by a candle from Hodge, before landing back on me. He smiles softly, lifting a hand to cup the side of my face. "Luna?"

"I'm here."

His eyes dart around, warily, before circling back to me.

"Am I dead? Are you dead?" He pauses, his brows furrowed. "I thought it'd be nicer over the rainbow."

I nudge his arm, playfully, with a chuckle. "Glad to see he didn't knock your wit out of you."

He starts to chuckle, but quickly stops, his hand flying to his abdomen with a wince where he lays on the floor beside me.

"Here," I say, opening my satchel beside me on the floor and taking out two scones. "Eat these. They'll heal you."

"The gnome man?" he asks, brows raised.

I nod, extending the scones to him. "Hodge. And yes. Now eat."

He takes the tiny scones from my hand, plopping them both in his mouth at once. I sigh with relief as he chews them and the bruises on

Chapter 24

his face begin to fade.

When he's finished, he looks me over. "You're okay?" he asks.

I turn and gesture to the side of my jaw. "Helix gave me a pretty good gash along my chin here, but one scone from Hodge, and I'm good as new."

He releases a deep sigh. "That's good." He pauses, moving his extremities slowly one at a time. "I think that stuff already worked," he says, amazed.

"Hodge says his stuff is the best," I say, with a shrug.

"I see why," he says, moving into a sitting position beside me. He turns to peer out the opening of the cave into the darkness beyond. "We're in a cave?"

"Well, you wouldn't exactly fit in Hodge's house," I pause, chuckling. "Or the house of any of his friends for that matter."

He rolls his eyes with a quick laugh, stretching his legs out in front of him and leaning back on his hands. "Where are Rhea and Atlas?"

"They're still at Hodge's house."

He nods, before turning to me slowly out of the corner of his eyes. "Why aren't you there?"

Because I didn't want to leave you, I want to say. It's the truth. I skipped dinner at Hodge's house because I knew I wouldn't be able to eat anything until I knew he was awake and alright. I've been sitting here for the last four hours completely consumed with thoughts only for him.

I shrug. "I came to check on you. I had to see how you were doing after the fight."

"Yeah, about that," he stands, running a hand exasperatedly through his hair. He paces beside the candle centered on the cave's floor before turning back to me, hands on his hips. "What the hell were you thinking?"

My mouth drops open from my utter shock.

"You almost got both of us killed, Luna."

I blink. He can't be serious. "Are you kidding me right now?"

He gives me a condescending glare from where he stands before me, towering over where I sit, before throwing his arms out to his sides. "Are you seriously surprised at my reaction?"

"Well, yeah!" I shoot back. "It's not exactly the *thank you* that I was expecting."

"Thank you?" He turns away with a scoff before spinning back to me and coughing out a laugh of disbelief. "Thanks for putting yourself into an enclosed ring with that violence-driven maniac? That's completely idiotic!"

His words make my chest hurt as if taking a physical blow, but the words quickly twist from hurt to anger as I fire back, "Well, you put yourself in that ring with him, too. So, I guess I could only be as idiotic as you are." I pause tilting my head before leveling my eyes back up at him with a glare. "And that's a *lot*."

His nostrils flare. "My word. You are unbelievable."

You know what? Enough with this. I'm done letting him stand over me, talking down like he's scolding a child. I rise to my feet, planting my own hands on my hips, mirroring him. "*I'm* unbelievable? You're the one who's mad at me for *saving* you!"

"I had it under control!" he yells now and I flinch, momentarily, from the surprise of him raising his voice. He seems surprised, too, for a moment, but then keeps at it. "You shouldn't have gotten involved!"

"Really?" I ask, with a scoffing smile at how ridiculous he sounds. Does he even hear himself? "What would you have suggested I do then, huh? Just sit there and watch Helix hack you apart?"

He takes a small step towards me, eyes set. "That wasn't going to happen, I—" he starts, but I cut him off, raising my hand.

"That was *exactly* what was going to happen, Caspar. Don't be so naive."

Chapter 24

He stares at me dubiously for a moment, mouth agape, shaking his head slightly.

"What?" I ask loudly with a stomp of my foot as I take another step into him.

"I've never argued with anyone like this before," he breathes.

I let out a laugh, throwing my hands in the air. "Well, gee. Sorry, Your Highness. Your subjects might just abide by your asshole tendencies, but I—" I raise my voice even more now, "a soon-to-be-Queen, will do no such thing."

"No, of course not. You have your own to live with!" he fires back.

My mouth flies open and I ball my hands into fists at my side, fury running through me. "What is your problem?" I yell.

"My problem?" he asks, eyes wide, gesturing to himself.

"Yes!" I shout.

"*You!*" he shouts before backing up and turning away from me.

He can't be serious. He's the one who's been difficult since the moment we first met and he has the balls to say that *I'm* the problem here?

He runs his hands through his air with a loud groan. "Gosh! Why are you so irritating?"

My nostrils flare. "Irritating? Oh, please! Tell me what about me is *so* irritating."

He spins back to face me, putting a hand on his chin as if in thought. "Gee, I don't know," he says. "How about the fact that you're the most stubborn person I've ever met? How about the fact that you hardly ever agree with a word I say? Or," he pauses, his voice growing airy, as if struggling to get the words out. "Or the fact that I can't stop thinking about you?"

I still, sucking in a breath for a moment, wondering if I heard him right. "What?"

"I can't," he says, looking down and shaking his head. He grows quiet for a moment before peering up, and meeting my eyes. "You consume my *every* thought." He throws his arms up with a huff of frustrated laughter. "It's messed everything up," he says, raising his voice again, "because I can't think straight!"

"Oh, so you're trying to pin all of this on me?" I throw back at him. "It's not my fault if you can't focus!"

"Yes, it is!" he shouts at me, voice thundering. He moves suddenly, grabbing me by the outsides of my arms and turning, pinning me up against the wall of the candlelit cave. "You don't have to *look* like that and look *at* me like that!"

"What?" I ask, confused and frustrated. He holds me off the ground, my back to the wall, wings flat as if I weigh nothing. He moves into me where I'm pinned. The feeling of his strong chest against me sends my stomach into a woozy state.

Traitorous body. Now is hardly the time!

"What do you want me to do?"

"I—" he hesitates. "I don't know. Just stop it!"

"Stop?" I ask.

"Yes!" he shouts, voice growing husky from the strain of the yelling.

"Stop what?" I yell.

"Stop making me *want* you!"

I am still in his hands where I'm pinned as he grows silent, his breaths heavy.

"You can't want me," I say, my voice barely a whisper. I drop my eyes. "We hate each other."

"Yeah," he huffs, staring at me with raging intensity. "But you know that line between love and hate?"

I nod.

"Well, it just blurred," he breathes. His eyes darken as his hands begin to move down the length of my arms till he reaches my legs, which he pulls around his waist. Each touch of his fingertips leaves a

Chapter 24

warm patch on my skin and it feels like time has slowed. I feel so tiny wrapped around him like this.

He leans forward, pushing my back into the wall even more, and bringing his face closer. I go to suck in a breath, but his lips are on mine before I can.

Chapter 25

His kiss is strong, but his lips are soft as he pushes me against the wall. There's static in my brain like there's no logical explanation for what's happening, but my body knows exactly what to do as I tighten my legs around him and wrap my arms up behind his neck to coax him even closer.

My wings are ablaze with a glowing light that fills the space around us. His kisses keep coming and I welcome them, having held our first kiss in that pool deep in my heart, wondering what it might be like to do it again and do it right. The memory of our first kiss suddenly reminds me of him saying that kissing me was a mistake and my heart plummets.

What if this is just another moment he'll call a mistake later?

He feels me start to falter in my reciprocation of his kisses and pulls his face back, tilting his forehead into mine.

"I'm sorry," he breathes, panting slightly. "We should take this slower. I just—"

"It's not that," I half-whisper, upset to ruin the moment, but knowing I won't be able to move on otherwise.

"Oh," he says, his expression slowly fading into worry. Slowly

Chapter 25

releasing his grip, he brings me back down to the floor. He takes a small step backward. "Was the kiss not good?" he asks, nervously.

I reach with my hands to smooth the back of my hair out, avoiding his eyes. "No." I clear my throat. "It was—"

"Amazing," he breathes, his face cracking into a grin as I look back up at him.

"Yes," I say with a sigh, an equal smile on my face for a moment before it falls as I continue. "But you said our kiss before was a mistake—"

His face falls into a state of concern, brows furrowed. "Wait, Luna—"

"I just don't want you to look back and call *this* kiss a mistake later, too," I say, peering into him. "It was hard for me to hear you say that before and I don't know if I could handle that again. I've got to be honest with you and honest with myself." I pause, drawing in a shaky breath. "I didn't have the same idea as you when we were trapped in that awful pool of blood."

I see surprise dart across his features, but I can't tell if it's good or bad.

"I lied. I didn't kiss you back to help create more light," I continue, not understanding where the courage is even coming from to allow me to get this out. "I just said that because I didn't want you to know that I had kissed you back because," I shrug, feeling so exposed by the words, "I wanted you."

His lips part.

"When it was made clear that you did not kiss me as some sort of desperate attempt to share a moment before our compounded drowning, I didn't want to tell you. I was too embarrassed and realized what I'd felt had been one-sided."

He opens his mouth to speak, taking a small step towards me, but I raise a hand, taking a step back.

"It's okay that it was just me who cared about that kiss," I continue, trying to get everything out before I lose my momentum. "But I don't want to be the only one affected by any more of them. It's," I stall, searching for the right words, "difficult to handle. And all of this, right now," I say, gesturing to him and around the cave, "is only confusing me more and making things even more complicated."

He opens his mouth to speak again, but I'm still not finished.

"I mean, how can I even feel this way?" I ask the universe in general, rather than directly to him, with a crazed laugh of disbelief. "I mean, you're the King of a kingdom estranged from mine."

He nods, crossing his arms over his broad chest.

"And you are incredibly stubborn."

He rolls his eyes slightly, but nods again, a grin beginning to brim on his lips. The lips that were just on mine.

"And you hate my tarts!" I finish, raising my voice now and throwing my hands up to rub at my eyes. I groan. "It just doesn't make sense at all! There's no logical reason behind this and that makes it very unlike me." I huff out a breath with the last of my bluster.

He waits a beat before raising his eyebrows with a smirk. "Can I speak now or is there more?"

I rub my eyes with my hands, uttering a groan.

"Not that I couldn't listen to you rant about me all night long," he says, "even if they weren't the nicest remarks."

I narrow my eyes at him, trying to suppress the smile that brims on my lips.

"But I do have some things to say, myself, that I feel might be beneficial for you to hear," he continues.

I throw my hands up at my sides in surrender before crossing them over my chest.

He sucks in a breath, allowing his arms to drop at his sides. His eyes darken as he looks at me and I brace myself for whatever words he's about to share.

"I know there's nothing logical about this," he says, gesturing

Chapter 25

between us, "but this still makes perfect sense to me."

My shoulders relax as I release a breath I didn't realize I was holding. "But—"

"Shh," he says, walking forward and silencing me with an index finger to my lips, a grin on his face. "I let you have your monologue and now it's my turn."

I narrow my eyes at him, but stand straighter, pulling my shoulders back to show that I'll abide.

He lowers his finger with a smile and moves forward to take my hand in his. I watch our fingers intertwine. The contact is so simple compared to the moment we shared against the wall just a few minutes ago, yet this somehow feels incredibly more intimate. The sensation makes my heart teeter on its axis. I tilt my head back to peer up at him as he continues.

"Look, I didn't mean to get so mad earlier. I was just scared." His eyes gaze into mine and I can tell that whatever he's about to say next, he's never told anyone else. "My father was not a good man. When you're done working all day, you're supposed to come home." I watch him draw in a shaky breath, averting his eyes to the floor. "He'd stumble home right before the sun would rise again, smelling of rich tonics so strong that the stench would hit you as soon as he'd walk in the house. I watched Mom run herself ragged. She was convinced that she could fix everything by fixing the little things that she could control since she couldn't control him. She'd polish the silver till her fingers were bloody so that he could dine on the best dinnerware, that is if he ever made it home early enough for dinner. I'd watch her spend hours on her makeup, or picking out her clothes, but he'd always saunter home too drunk to do anything more than tolerate her, let alone appreciate her."

He drops my hand, gently, taking a step back. He fidgets with his hands in front of him for a moment before turning to peer out the black abyss at the cave's opening. I know he's picturing his mother there. The sight of how difficult this is for him to say, makes me ache to reach out and embrace him.

"I could see how sad it made her. She was breaking before my very eyes. Breaking with him and breaking *for* him, but she'd never tell. I'd ask her a million times over if she was okay and she'd always say, 'Of course, Cas. Of course.' Then she'd try to take my mind off of everything with her stories. She'd sit me down in the garden and she'd say she had another story for me. I'd always ask if it had a happy ending. I wouldn't let her tell it to me otherwise. I suppose I was craving the happiness in stories that my reality wouldn't gift me."

He pauses now and sucks in a deep breath. I can't take it any longer. I walk forward and use a hand on each side of his face to gently guide him back to face me. "What happened?" I whisper.

He tilts his forehead to touch mine as he slowly lets out the breath he's been holding. I move my hands from his face to slide them down his arms until I find his hands. Our fingers lock together and only then does he continue.

"It'd be late, but he'd always come home. Then one day, when I was older, he didn't return. It was my mom's birthday. She got so worked up worrying about him that she started throwing the furniture. I knew she'd been breaking, but that night she finally snapped. I couldn't take it anymore. I left the house and went to all the taverns till I found him. He was upstairs in a bed," his voice growls with a huff, "not alone."

My breath hitches in my throat.

"I walked over and I grabbed him by the throat and I said that if some part of him still loved mom, that if he loved her at all, he'd leave and never come back because that was the best thing he could do for her." He sighs. I feel a drop land on our intertwined hands and realize he's crying.

"He never came back," he utters now. "And instead of getting better,

Chapter 25

my mom just withered away with each passing day. She died a few years before I was voted King."

"I'm so sorry," I breathe, giving his hands a comforting squeeze that I hope truly expresses the depths of my sympathy.

"It is what it is, but here's where this pertains to you," he says, tilting his head slightly to look down at me now as he explains. "Throughout my entire life, I admired my mom's level of commitment. She woke up every morning and chose my dad despite all the odds. Sure, she probably should have left at times, but she never did. And she wasn't just committed to my dad. She was also committed to me, to our home, to Durand, to generating happiness. She was so inspiring in her loyalty. Nowadays, people have trouble committing to what kind of house or shoes they want, but not you."

"What do you mean?" I ask, lifting my head further back to look up at him, confusion and wonder swirling in my eyes.

A smile brews on his lips. "Luna, look at what you have been doing for Celestia. You traveled into the Bog, ripped out a wisp's heart, and jumped into a fighting ring to save me."

"Aha!" I say, letting go of his hands to jab a finger into the center of his chest. "So, you admit, I saved you?"

He rolls his eyes, letting out a chuckle. "I'm not one to openly admit things." He grows serious now, but a pleased and sincere expression remains on his face. "Luna, I admire your loyalty to your people. It's what I try to have for Durand every day. I never thought that I would find someone with the loyalty of my mom's spirit, but I've fallen for you more with every selfless act you've done."

I feel my heart skip a beat in my chest. "You've fallen for me?"

And right then, Caspar does something I've never seen him do before. He blushes. His face is crimson as he shrugs before reaching up to scratch the back of his head. "I do believe that's what I said."

"But—" I stutter. "But we only just met a few days ago. How can you fall for someone so fast?"

Caspar takes a tiny step forward and his eyes peer into me like he never wants to look at another soul, and I believe him. "Because it's *you*, Luna. My preconceived notions about you were so far from the truth. Then when I first met you? I denied what I was feeling, thinking it was some sort of lustful crush and it would go away with time, but every moment with you has only made all my feelings grow stronger. I've been falling for you and falling *hard*."

His voice grows low and even though we're alone and no one is around to hear us, he hushes his voice to a whisper. "I think that from the moment I locked eyes with you over that last tart, part of me knew I'd be standing here telling you this one day."

He's had feelings for me since the moment we met? This whole time I thought he hated me.

"If you've felt this way for so long, why are you just telling me now?" I ask, genuine curiosity ebbing my tone.

He smiles. "Do I look like someone who shares their feelings easily?"

I can't help, but chuckle. I nudge his arm playfully. "I'm serious!"

He reaches out to gingerly tuck a strand of hair behind my ear. "Because everything got messed up after our kiss in that pool," he says, his brows bunching together at the memory of it all. He looks into my eyes and sighs a deep breath. "Luna, I didn't kiss you to create light. I kissed you because I thought it was the end and I didn't want to die without having a chance to let you know how I feel about you."

His confession casts a dizzy spell on my head as I struggle to add everything together in my brain. "But—" I stutter. "But you said it was for the light."

"Atlas said I did it for the light. I looked to you to try and gauge your reaction because I knew I'd felt you kiss me back, but you wouldn't meet my eyes. I wasn't about to hash it all out with you in front of Rhea and Atlas, so I just said I was 'happy it worked' and went along

Chapter 25

with it. What a colossal mistake that was. But now I know you kissed me because you wanted to and I want you to know that it was the same for me."

Everything he's saying sounds so wonderful and fills me with a joy I've never experienced before. He *did* kiss me because he wanted to. We *both* kissed each other because we *wanted* to. "Then why did you say that kissing me was a mistake?"

He reaches out, grabbing my chin gently in his hand, to tilt my face up towards his. "I only called it a mistake because our first kiss should have been more like this." The hand on my chin steadily moves to cup the back of my neck as his other arm reaches around my waist, drawing me into him slow and sweet like honey. His lips hover over mine, like waiting for permission and I reach out, wrapping my arms around him in answer.

He lightly brushes my lips with a kiss and the sincerity I feel there, him treating me so gently and respectively, is somehow a thousand times more passionate than our kiss against the wall earlier. The tenderness of his hand on my neck as his fingertips slide into the base of my hair is all too delightful and I can't help it when a small sigh escapes me onto his lips.

Suddenly, I don't care where Rhea and Atlas are. Celestia, my mother, the messy events of the last few days all fade away. Everything fades away. There is nothing but Caspar and I, and this moment.

I tell myself I don't care what happens next. I wouldn't even care if he forgot all about this tomorrow. I'll keep this moment in my heart like an expensive tonic; only to be opened on the most special of occasions.

I accept each of his kisses like precious gifts, savoring each small minute detail, like unwrapping a present slowly.

His lips part from mine for the briefest of seconds, only for him to utter words that melt my inhibitions even more. "Kissing you could never be a mistake, Luna. Not when it feels this right."

I smile, my lips pulling thin as he meets mine again in the candlelit cave. Although I haven't voiced it yet, I know it in my heart. Caspar isn't the only one who's falling.

I am, too.

Chapter 26

"Wait!" I say, reaching out to grab Caspar's arm where he lays beside me on the stone floor of the cave, my smile wide. Is the ground uncomfortable? Absolutely. Do I care with Caspar beside me? Not one bit. "This whole time?"

He nods, letting out a laugh. "It's true," he says, propping his head up slightly by curling his elbow up under it. "I liked your tart."

I make a musing sound stroking my chin before turning back towards him, his face even more handsome in the candlelight. "You liked my tart or you *loved* it?"

He rolls his eyes at me now and the action makes my stomach flip. He's too cute for his own good. All I want to do is reach out and touch him when he looks like that.

And now I can.

I smile, dimples pronounced, as I reach out to take his hand in between us. He watches me lace our fingers together before meeting my eyes again. "I loved it," he answers.

I squeeze his hand as I let out a giggle. A freaking *giggle*.

What is this man doing to me?

"Now, that sounds more like my baking," I say, proudly.

He stares at me for a moment, a cheeky smirk on his face. "Has anyone ever told you that you're adorable when you're being smug?"

"Hmmm, not smug," I say, before narrowing my eyes at him and adding, "but confident? A thousand times. Or at least, that's when I stopped counting."

He chuckles before leaning forward slightly to deliver a light kiss into the center of my forehead that sends butterflies whirling through my abdomen. We sit in complete silence for a moment, but it's not awkward. It's comfortable.

Right when I'm about to, he speaks. "What are you thinking about?"

"This," I breathe. Our gazes simultaneously drift back down to our hands locked together.

"I know what you mean," he says before growing serious. "Luna, I want to apologize for everything I said before about being mad at you for jumping in the ring to help me. I was just upset because you put yourself in danger." He hesitates. "Or rather, I put you in danger."

"Hey," I say, holding his gaze with mine. "You didn't put me in that ring. I flew in there all by myself. I wasn't going to sit by and watch Helix kill you. I couldn't do that."

He tilts his head for a second, pinching his eyes shut in thought. "I remember you flying into the ring and the crowd just roaring. Then Helix slapped you or something and I don't remember much besides that. My head was throbbing so much from the pain that it felt like someone was just hitting my head repeatedly with a hammer."

I wince at the image.

"Next thing I knew, I was waking up here," he concludes with a shrug of his shoulders. His face turns downwards and he averts his eyes. "I'm sorry we failed, Luna. It's all my fault."

"What?" I ask, confused. "Oh, wait!" I let go of his hand to flip onto my other side and pull my satchel over across the floor to me by the strap. I rifle through the contents, my hand immersed in the bag until

Chapter 26

I find it.

"About that," I say, spinning back over to face him with the Red Beryl in hand. "We didn't fail."

His eyes widen at the sight of the gem, mouth agape. "But how? How did—"

"Honestly, I got lucky," I say with a chuckle, passing the gem over for his inspection. "I flipped Helix like I flipped you that one night and I guess he hit his head and got knocked out cold."

Now, Caspar's mouth gapes even more. "Are you serious? So, you didn't just save me, you *won* the fight?"

I nod, happily. "I sure did!"

His lips turn upwards before they're on mine as he leans forward to deliver a laugh of a kiss. "You're incredible," he breathes. "Is there anything you can't do?"

Be Queen, my thoughts supply and I hate how I can feel it alter my entire mood. Caspar must see it in my face because his expression changes, ebbing with concern.

"Are you alright, Red?"

"Yes," I breathe, trying to focus on the cute nickname and not on the self-doubt I feel creeping in.

He grabs my chin gently in his hand, tilting my face up at him. "Don't lie to me," he says, voice commanding yet caring. "Tell me what you're thinking about. Maybe I can help."

I stare at him, nervous at the level of vulnerability that telling him would require of me. But then again, he said he's falling for me. If he can't handle hearing about what weighs on my heart, then maybe his hands aren't where my heart should lie. Only one way to find out.

"When you asked if there was anything I couldn't do, I thought 'be Queen,'" I say, sending my eyes downcast, but not so fast that I'm unable to register the shock on his face.

"What? Luna, why would you think that?"

"Hardly a day goes by that I don't think about it," I say and it feels amazing. I always thought it was easiest to hold the thing that scares me close but spoken aloud, it seems slightly less daunting. There's so much power in sharing. I draw in a shaky breath. "I can't draw on the people for confidence because they don't even want me to be Queen."

He hesitates before finding the words. "Maybe it's not as bad as you think."

"Oh, it's true," I say, wiping a tear from my eyes before it's able to fall down my cheek. "My mother has been an incredible Queen and I'm so proud of her for that. It's truly inspiring, but she's also just set the bar so high that now the people think no one can live up to her."

He opens his mouth before closing it again and moving to sit in a cross-legged position, which I rearrange to mirror.

"Luna," he says, voice low and eyes intensely peering into mine as if he never wants me to forget what he's about to say.

I already know I won't.

"You are not your mom," he says, plainly, and I feel my heart fall into my stomach, his words echoing what I know is the complaint of the majority of Celestia. Yet, he continues, reaching out to stroke my cheek. "That's the best thing you have going for you."

"What?" I say, pulling my head back in surprise.

"You're not her because you're *you*," he says, emphasizing the words with his tone. "Your mom may be a good Queen, Luna, but you're going to be an amazing ruler in your own way. You know what you're capable of, and how much you care for your kingdom, but the people just don't know that yet. You have to let them see that."

"But how can I do that?" I ask in question.

"Luna," he begins, eyes clouding with sincerity. "You're doing it right now! What do you think this quest is all for? You jumped into action to save your people. When you return and stop Amyra, there will be no one to question your ability to rule."

Chapter 26

Is he right? Will everyone believe in me once they see and hear what I've been doing on this quest for them? "Are you certain?"

"I've never been more certain of anything," he says, smiling. "Well," he says, leaning in to brush a kiss against my lips, "besides this."

* * *

"Tell me you're seeing this, too," says Rhea's voice softly beyond the darkness of my closed eyelids. "I'm not imagining this, right?"

"If the sight before you is Luna and Caspar asleep with her wrapped in his arms," says Atlas, "then yes, I do believe that is our reality. Although, I agree it is quite surprising to witness."

A moment passes before I feel a poke to my shoulder. "Pst! Luna," says Rhea's hushed voice.

My eyelids flutter open, the light streaming in from the cave's entrance causing my retinas to sting as they adjust. Finally, Rhea's hovering face before me comes into focus. "Rhea?"

"*Girl*," she says, eyes bulging. "You're in Caspar's arms right now."

A smile lifts my lips as I recall the warmth of him as he curled me in against his chest last night as the conversation dipped and we gave into our fatigue. "I sure am."

Her eyes get even larger at this as both shock and realization dawn on her face. "Oh, wow. So—"

"Yup," I say, with a curt nod.

She lets out a deep sigh, a grin brimming. "I see."

I reach, slowly untangling Caspar's strong arm from across my waist, and begin to sit up. He stirs as I do, rubbing at his eyes. Surprise dawns on him as he registers our company. "I don't remember ordering a wake-up call."

"Well, we fell asleep at Hodge's place and when we woke up and saw you two still hadn't returned, we came to check on you," says Rhea, standing over us before clasping her hands behind her back, smiling suggestively. "Although, now I see we were worried for nothing. Looks like Luna was taking care of you *quite well* all on her own. *Ow!*" she finishes as I slap her ankle from where I sit on the floor next to Caspar.

Oblivious to Rhea's sly comment, Atlas speaks. "Also, Hodge is making us all breakfast."

At this, Caspar and I both bolt up.

"Oh, thank goodness," I utter. "I'm absolutely starving. Did he say what he was making?"

"No, but if it's anything like his scones, I'm sure it will be delicious," Rhea says, turning with Atlas and heading out the opening of the cave.

I smooth out my dress as Caspar twists his neck next to me, which emits a resounding crack. I wince at the sound.

"Turns out the rocky ground of a cave," he begins, twisting his back now which also makes a crack, "is not the most comfortable of places to sleep."

I stretch out my limbs, not hearing any cracks, but feeling an ache in certain joints that hopefully won't linger too long. "Agreed."

We head out of the cave behind Atlas and Rhea. I feel almost sad to go, stealing a glance back over my shoulder, and recalling the moments Caspar and I shared. Our stolen kisses and conversations will stay in my heart and mind, no matter how far we venture from the cave where they took place.

I turn, facing forward again, and find Rhea flying in front of Atlas, turning back to tease him. "Keep up, scholar sprite!" she taunts, spinning around him now.

He swats at her like a fly, a grin on his face, and she laughs. I can't help but smile at the sight of them playfully teasing one another. It makes it hard to believe they met just a few days prior.

I'm suddenly jolted from my thoughts as I feel Caspar's hand graze

Chapter 26

mine as if asking for an invitation. I glance over at him, but he's looking up at the sky as if he has absolutely no idea what his hand is up to. I fight to suppress my smile as I keep walking. I stare forward but feel him glance sideways at me momentarily before his pinkie wraps around mine now. I feign shock.

"Um, excuse me, sir, but I think your hand is trying to grab mine."

We continue walking forward, but he turns to look down at his pinkie twirled around mine with a surprised expression. "Oh, my!" He shrugs his broad shoulders. "My apologies. I'll take care of this right away." Yet, instead of retracting his pinkie, he envelops my whole hand in his.

I gasp, playing along, and fight the urge to laugh. "Now, you've taken my whole hand!"

"Hmm," he muses, peering down at the sight between us with eyebrows raised. "It would appear so."

I tilt my head, pouting my lips ever so slightly. "Might I ever get it back?"

He strokes his chin with his free hand, bunching his brows with eyes cast upwards. He makes the sound of one in deep, tumultuous thought before facing me again. "Nope," he finally supplies with a cheeky smirk. His eyes flash something sweet yet wild at me, like a dare.

"Hmm," I say, my turn to fake consideration now. "Well, I suppose I do have a spare."

"Perfect," he says, giving my hand a gentle squeeze as we walk onward.

We walk in silence for a few more minutes, simply enjoying each other's company and the small form of physical touch, before the large tree of Hodge's home comes into view. I fear our arrival at Hodge's will prompt Caspar to retract his hand, but he continues holding mine contentedly.

"There he is!" yells Hodge as he emerges from the entrance of his humble home with a platter of colorful muffins, eyes fixed on Caspar. "You took quite a beating, boy, but it's nothing to be feeling ashamed about," he says, eyes sympathetic as he sets the muffins down, blending them into the picturesque picnic set up right outside his front door.

"Oh, I wasn't feeling ashamed," says Caspar with a flick of his free hand. "Until now," he adds, glancing over at me from the corner of his eye, voice hushed.

I chuckle and squeeze his hand once.

"I became quite concerned once Helix began gaining the upper hand," Atlas says as he plops down onto a corner of the large blanket spread out beneath a slow-raised wooden table. "I honestly became a bit worried that you'd wake up with some serious cerebral damage after that one blow caused you to fall back and hit the lower part of your skull." He narrows his eyes at Caspar intently. "You're sure your memory and cognitive abilities are fully intact?"

Caspar shoots him a look, pulling me down to sit beside him across the small table from Atlas. "I'm perfectly fine."

"You're certain?" Atlas asks, mouth bunching speculatively.

"Yes," Caspar drawls. "I know my name, your name, my age, the reason and details behind this quest, and I know your ointment is for—"

"Okay!" Atlas shouts, eyes nervous. Caspar smirks and Atlas's cheeks flush. "No need to continue," he says, taking a deep breath. "I see you're alright."

"I am," Caspar smiles. "But thank you for worrying about me."

"Always," Atlas says before sliding me a glass of juice.

I sniff the beverage, inspecting the aroma before bringing it to my lips. A sort of cherry scent greets me and I eagerly take a sip. It's as delicious as it smells.

Rhea crawls out of Hodge's small doorway with a bowl of what

Chapter 26

appears to be grits and Hodge hot on her tail. "Okay, this is the last of it," she says, plopping the dish down on the table. "Thank goodness, too, because everything smells so good that I'm not sure I have the self-control to wait much longer."

"Based on previous behavior, yes, you likely do not have the self-control to proceed patiently," says Atlas, but he quickly shuts his mouth as Rhea snaps her head his way, plopping down on the blanket beside him.

Hodge chuckles at them, a smile creeping between his thick beard and full mustache, as he takes a seat on the side in between Atlas and me. "Well, let us all dig in then!"

The words have hardly finished leaving his lips before Rhea is scooping heaps onto her empty plate. Atlas, beside her, jumps, startled at the sudden movement, and the rest of us can't help but laugh.

I fill my plate with two muffins, and an assortment of fruits, but avoid the grits. Having tried them on a separate occasion, I found the texture to be a bit tough for my taste. However, Caspar beside me, gingerly squeezes my hand once more before letting it go to fill his plate with a large serving of grits. We all begin eating and for a moment, the only sound to fill the air is that of chewing and the occasional moan derived from a particularly delectable bite.

I ponder our progress as I eat, still struggling to believe how successful our quest has gone so far. Yes, everything has been a tad rocky, but we've gotten through every challenge. Only one more to go.

I finish chewing the bite I have before I speak. "Atlas, did you have a chance to read up on the final challenge we must complete?"

Atlas nods, swallowing his bite with a loud gulp. "I did," he says, pushing up his glasses, but his face turns wary. "I'm afraid it's quite unlike the others."

Chapter 27

"How so?" Rhea asks.

Atlas scratches the back of his head, shooting Rhea a nervous glance before she turns to face us. "The challenge is to find a special object within a memory."

Caspar and I both jut our heads forward slightly in disbelief with raised brows. "I'm sorry," Caspar says. He clears his throat. "Did you say a *memory*? As in an actual memory of the past?"

"That would be correct," says Atlas. "Apparently, there is a large hill that has an enchanted tunnel. The journal says the rest of the instructions will be written upon stone at the tunnel's entrance."

I blink, trying to process. Caspar sets his spoon down beside me, clearly dazed as well.

Hodge burps suddenly, breaking the unease, and all our heads spin to him. While I can't see his eyes under his tall, pointy hat, I'm sure they're wide with embarrassment as his hand flies to his chest. "Oh, my! I do apologize."

I begin to open my mouth to let him know there's no need for embarrassment, but a burp from Rhea shuts me up. Hodge spins to face her, surprised. She simply smiles at him. I watch the ends of

Chapter 27

Hodge's mustache flit upward.

"I always knew I liked you," he says, reaching over to pat her arm. Suddenly, he jolts slightly in his seat, raising an index finger towards the sky. "Wait! I think I know where you're talking about with this enchanted tunnel thing!"

"You do?" I ask, fingers gripping the edge of the small table. I'm grateful for any insight as to what we might be walking into.

"Yes," he says, nodding curtly. "I believe it's just a tad bit north of here. My neighbors who used to live just a few trees over yonder," he gestures widely off towards the right of the forest, "ventured there once together. They were the sweetest of couples. Went there for one of their elaborate date nights."

"They went to an enchanted tunnel for a date night?" Caspar asks, tone dripping with disbelief.

"Not your preferred idea of romance?" I ask, leaning to bump his shoulder gently with my own.

He chuckles. "Well, I'd say it's definitely unheard of."

"I couldn't agree with you more," Hodge says, nibbling on a muffin, causing crumbs to get lost in his beard. "Honestly, I think they may have just run out of ideas. They'd been together, and in love, for the longest time; as long as I'd known them at least."

"I'm sorry," Atlas says, cutting in, "but you're speaking of their love in the past tense?"

Hodge nods, using the long sleeve of his robe to wipe crumbs from his face. "I'm afraid I am. They went their separate ways after the tunnel."

Rhea's face contorts with concern. "Wait, what? Like they broke up?"

"Unfortunately, yes," Hodge says, setting the remaining portion of his muffin back down. "After they ventured into the tunnel together, they were torn apart. They split and moved away. As far as I'm aware, that was the last they saw or spoke to one another."

Well, gosh. If I wasn't already wary before, I certainly am now.

Caspar's hand searches under the overhang of the small table till it finds mine and grasps it tightly. I know he's thinking the same thing I am.

What happens in that tunnel? What does it do to you?

Rhea locks eyes with me across the table and my heart pinches. *What will it do to us?*

* * *

"I thought Hodge said it wasn't that far north," says Rhea, throwing her head back with a groan as she flies in the front of our group.

"He did say that, but he's also like a billion years old," says Caspar up beside her.

When we first began traveling onward after breakfast, I did start at the front with Caspar, but I reluctantly freed his hand to allow him to jump ahead and walk with Rhea a little while ago. He said that if we let her lead the group any longer, we'd get lost for certain. After many failed attempts to keep her flying straight north, I'm beginning to think that whatever inner compass she possesses is quite broken. While traveling in one direction wouldn't usually be so difficult, since one could just use the setting sun for reference under normal circumstances, Hodge informed us not to try as the sun in the Bog is incorrect.

"I'm afraid I have to echo Rhea's comment," Atlas says from where he walks alongside where I fly, hovering just a few feet off the ground. "We have been traveling for much farther than one would classify as a short distance. I'm worried we're lost."

I breathe a sigh. "I'm worried you're right."

His eyes fall to the ground and I see a sense of unease in the way his

Chapter 27

shoulders slack. I drop down onto my feet to walk beside him.

"Anything on your mind?"

His eyes dart to me for the briefest of seconds, but he stays quiet.

"Whatever it is, you can talk to me about it," I say, clasping my hands behind my back as we walk now, the sun setting.

His head turns to me slowly now, a distraught look on his face. "I just wish I could be of bigger help."

I'm not sure what I was expecting him to share, but it wasn't that. "Atlas, what do you mean? You've been a huge help to us on this quest. I mean, without you, we wouldn't even know where to go for these challenges."

"Thanks, and yeah, I know I'm the only one who can read the journal, but—" he falters, drawing in a slow breath. "I don't know anything really about the Bog, or gnomes, or wisps, and it's been bothering me this whole trip." His eyes peer at me, sincerely. "It's not my intention to sound pompous by saying this, but I usually know pretty much all there is to know about," he shrugs, "everything."

I nod, processing his words. "So, it's been bothering you that in this new environment we're in, there's a lot you don't know or understand?"

"Precisely."

"Atlas," I say, leaning a hand onto his shoulder. "You have been so helpful on this trip with reading the journal and in being here for Caspar as he goes through all this. Heck, not even Caspar. Rhea and I are thankful you're here, too."

His eyes widen slightly at this. "You mean that?"

"Of course," I say, nodding. "We've all been through so much together already on this quest of ours and everything we've gotten through has been as a team. We're like a little family."

He nods slowly, a smile brimming as he turns forward to glance at Rhea and Caspar up ahead. "I suppose we are. A non-biological one, of course."

The mention of family brings my mother to mind and my heart immediately aches. Gosh, I hope she's alright. What has it been now? Two and a half days? So much time for Amyra to fill with more destruction and death.

The wave of emotion that hits me must be written across my face because Atlas's eyes catch on me as he scans the forest. "Are you thinking of your mother?"

His question is so on the nose that I'm shocked. "How did you know?"

"I'm very family-oriented, myself," he says, casually scratching the back of his head. "As I mentioned prior during our encounter with those two wisps, I come from a rather large family."

"I remember. You said you're the youngest of six, right?"

He nods. "I sure am. I don't know how my parents have managed us all these years. The house has been packed my whole life, but I've learned to love it that way," he says with a smile.

"You're so lucky," I admit, tucking a loose strand of hair behind my ear. "My mother's the only family I have. My dad died before I was born and I've always wished I had a sibling. Someone who would share my point of view on stuff, you know?"

"Well, you have Rhea," he says, gesturing ahead towards where she and Caspar are arguing and pointing towards different directions of the forest.

"I do, but it's not the same."

"Do you mind if I ask how so?"

"We just come from very different backgrounds. Rhea's not a family-oriented person because she has no family. She doesn't remember them at all." I pause, dissecting my thoughts. "Because of that, I feel like I can't talk to her about missing my mother right now."

"Because she does not have a mother?"

Chapter 27

"Exactly. I just feel like she can't relate, so I don't talk to her about it. She wouldn't understand," I sigh.

"Well, if it's any consolation," he says, turning to flash me a smile, and pushing his glasses upwards. "I understand how you're feeling. My family is back in Durand. I keep pondering the horrible possibility that Amyra has moved from wreaking havoc upon Celestia to Durand as well. I desperately hope everyone is safe. Not just my family, but—"

"Everyone else, too," I finish for him. "I know the feeling. It's always on my mind. I worry for the safety of everyone. Not just my mother."

His fear for his family reminds me of my fib that Durand will be next on Amyra's list, which I can't actually know for certain, and it sends a pang of guilt through my gut that I fight to ignore.

"Your people are lucky to have you," he says.

I turn towards him to thank him for his kind words, but Caspar suddenly appears in front of me. "Hop on, Red," he says, standing in a crouch with his back facing me.

I stop walking and tilt my head. "I don't understand."

"Hop on my back."

"But why?"

Caspar groans. "I can't stay in a crouch forever, fairywoman."

Atlas clears his throat beside me. "I believe he's attempting a sweet gesture by offering to carry you so you don't have to walk on your own. It's just coming off strange because it's quite unlike him to be so affectionate."

Caspar whips his head over his shoulder to shoot Atlas a glare. Atlas merely shrugs. "Just stating facts."

I chuckle. "Alrighty," I say as I climb onto Caspar's back. I wrap my arms around his neck, over the tops of his broad shoulders, and he pulls my legs around his sides before standing and walking onward.

Caspar must shoot Atlas a look because suddenly he becomes stiff and quickly says, "I believe I'll just go on ahead and keep Rhea company."

"Oh, because we know she'll love that," I whisper sarcastically in Caspar's ear as Atlas jogs to meet Rhea.

He chuckles before growing serious. "Are you doing alright?"

"Yes."

"You're not nervous about the tunnel?"

"Not as nervous as I was a few minutes ago," I say with a smile as I nuzzle my face into the crook of his neck, the warmth of his body providing me with a sense of peace.

"What happened a few minutes ago?" he asks.

"I chatted with Atlas about our group and how much we've gone through together already on this quest. We agreed that we've all become like a little family."

"We really have," he says in a tone that lets me hear the smile he's wearing even though I can't see it with him facing forward.

"I was worried about the tunnel after Hodge's story, but after talking with Atlas, I know we're going to be fine."

"We are." He stops walking suddenly and loosens his grip on my legs to slide me down and off his back. He turns to face me, gingerly holding me by my shoulders, crouching so he's at eye level with me. "I wanted to have the chance to tell you before we got there that nothing that happens in the tunnel could ever change the way I feel about you and I hope you feel the same way." He lowers his voice slightly. "I promise I'll never forget our time together in that cave if you won't."

A smile erupts on my face, pulling my lips tight and I reach out, wrapping him in my arms, my head on his chest. "Of course. I could never forget that."

He plants a kiss on the top of my forehead and I'm certain there is nowhere else I'd rather be and no one else I'd rather be with.

"Save the smooches for later, you two. We've got more important matters at hand right now," Rhea calls from the front with Atlas.

Chapter 27

Caspar and I turn to face her, but he holds onto my hand with his. "What do you mean?" he asks.

But Rhea doesn't even have to answer as our eyes lock onto the sight before us.

Just beyond where Rhea and Atlas stand rests two large trees that tilt inwards like leaning in for a kiss, and the roots from their trunks poke out of the ground before curling down the long opening of a tunnel into the mountain behind them. The moss blanket that covers patches of the mountainside also extends into the tunnel which glows from a deep source of light hidden within.

The enchanted tunnel.

"We're here," I breathe.

Chapter 28

"All who enter, their memories they must surrender. One tunnel each, we beseech you to explore. All must reminisce like never before. The memory of another, you will discover. Not all secrets are ours to keep. But as you search, keep high alert, for a baby bird that is soundly asleep."

We all stare at the words, etched into the stone across the tunnel's entrance as Atlas finishes reading it aloud.

"The memory of another?" Rhea asks, hands on her hips, head tilted to the right. "As in like I could see a memory of Atlas's?"

"And I could see one of yours," I supply. "Yes, I think that's what it's saying."

"I believe it's saying that we will each enter into our own tunnel and experience one memory from one other person in our group. Quite bizarre," muses Atlas.

A wave of silence collectively falls over the four of us as we process this. I see Rhea and Atlas share a nervous look. When I turn to face Caspar, he gives me a small shrug of his shoulders.

I know the thoughts that are going through our minds.

What memory of each of ours will be exposed? And what kind of effects

Chapter 28

could that exposure bring about?

I shake my head slightly to rid my mind of those anxious thoughts. What everyone needs right now isn't uncertainty and worry. It's confidence.

"I know we're all concerned about what we're heading into here," I begin, turning to face everyone individually as I speak. "But this is *us*, you guys. We can do this."

There's a quiet beat before Rhea begins to nod. "She's right. Look how far we've come."

Smiles break out on our faces as we look at one another, our confidence levels rising.

"We can do this as long as we do it together," Caspar says, squeezing my hand gently.

"Hands in," I say, throwing my hand, palm down into the center of the circle of us.

Rhea's hand flops on top of mine before Caspar and Atlas join in. Everyone looks at me and I begin to tear up. I couldn't have come this far on my own. There's no way I would even have this chance at saving Celestia if it wasn't for all of them.

"I love you guys," I say.

Caspar's eyebrows shoot up and I roll my eyes at him.

"This is different!" I insist, quickly.

He smirks and I know he understands what I mean.

"Now, what should we yell together before we enter?" I ask, looking at the others.

Everyone thinks for a moment before Atlas happily suggests, "Into the hole!"

Caspar, Rhea, and I all share a grimace. "Sorry, bud, but I'm not yelling that," says Caspar with a chuckle.

Rhea and I giggle before Atlas speaks again. "How about this? In together, out together!"

Rhea slaps her free hand over his mouth as Caspar and I outright laugh now. "Okay, you are officially no longer qualified to give suggestions," she says, before slowly lowering her hand.

Atlas pouts before flashing a smirk.

I think to myself. *What can we say that would reflect us as a group?*

Suddenly, it hits me. "Together through every endeavor."

Smiles bud on everyone's faces as they turn to me. Caspar leans down to plant a kiss on my temple. "That's the one."

"I agree," Atlas says.

Rhea nods excitedly beside him.

"Then, on three," I say.

We all chant together. "One, two, three. Together through every endeavor!"

The smile on everyone's faces and the energy as we cheer fills me with a rush of confidence to take on this tunnel. We all drop our hands and turn toward the entrance.

I take a deep breath. "Let's go guys."

We walk through the tunnel's entrance, twisted tree roots lining the sides and curling up across the ceiling as well. Atlas and Rhea lead the way while Caspar and I carry up the rear. The warm inner glow of the tunnel casts dimly around us like a rising sun.

Caspar's hand finds mine and he stops walking, turning me to face him. I peer up at him as he cups my face in his hands. "Don't forget everything in the cave, alright?"

In his face, I find a tenderness, but his eyes are lined with worry and I feel it shake my confidence ever so slightly. Yet, I nod with a smile on my face. "Alright."

He smiles before one of his hands slides down and around my waist, pulling me to him. I stand on my tip toes to wrap my arms around his neck, but I still fall short. He notices and uses one arm wrapped around me to hoist me up, his other hand still caressing the side of

Chapter 28

my face, his thumb landing softly behind my ear.

The kiss is sweet but passionate in an entirely new way, and my wings glow. His lips meet mine tenderly yet earnestly. Like he's drowning and I'm the last breath of air he'll get. I can feel him trying to savor every second. I'm sure he feels how I try to, too.

"I think this is it, guys," Rhea calls.

He breaks our kiss and gently lowers me back down to the ground, still holding my hand. We turn and walk to where the tunnel splits into four in front of Atlas and Rhea. Each tunnel emanates a faint light.

Rhea points up to the ceiling as we reach her and Atlas. "I'm not finding the repetition of this line very comforting."

Caspar and I tilt our heads upwards to see what she means. Sure enough, etched into the stone above us is the line from the instructions, "Not all secrets are ours to keep."

I take a deep breath. In and out.

Beside me, Caspar pulls Atlas in for a hug. While Atlas seems startled at the physical contact at first, a smile slowly brims his lips and he wraps his arms around Caspar. I decide to take this moment to do the same.

I turn to Rhea and pull her into me. Unlike Atlas, there is no hesitation of reciprocation and she squeezes me tightly, her head nuzzled into the crook of my neck. My eyes brim with tears at the scent caught in her hair. She smells like home. Celestia. The scent is the perfectly timed reminder of why we must do what we're all about to do.

"I love you," she whispers to me, the crack in her voice signaling she's struggling to hold it together.

"I love you, too," I whisper back. I squeeze her once more before she pulls back, wiping a stray tear from her eye and smiling at me. While I had so many other things to say to her, somehow it all seems mute now.

Love is enough.

We turn back to face the boys.

"Aw, what the heck," Rhea says, throwing up her arms before embracing both Atlas and Caspar, one arm around each. "You too sure are wearing on me."

The men envelop her, their large forms towering over her, but they both have nothing but sweet smiles on their faces.

"You're wearing on me, too," says Caspar.

They pull back from their hug and Atlas crosses his arms over his chest with a shrug of his shoulders. "I'm still deciding."

Rhea laughs a scoff, poking him in the side, playfully.

Atlas laughs before his eyes land on me and I smile at him. I open my arms and he walks forward, wrapping me in the softest of hugs, like if he squeezes me too tightly, I'll break.

"I'm not still deciding with you, Luna," he whispers and I smile.

We pull back and all move to face the entrance of each of our tunnels. When I stare down the barrel of mine, it appears to travel so deep that I can't see the end. Everything leads to a faint, glowing abyss and I don't know whether to find it comforting or terrifying. I turn and share one last look with everyone.

"We've got this," I say, and we all step into our tunnels.

The walls of my tunnel start to shimmer and brighten. Everything begins to dazzle so intensely that I'm forced to shield my eyes with my hand.

"It'll be okay, you guys!" I call.

It has to be.

The shimmering of the tunnel walls around me becomes so bright that everything grows stark white and I cry out from the intensity of it. Suddenly, the shimmering dissipates slightly before me and amid the white, I see a room full of books. I fly through the hole quickly,

Chapter 28

desperate to escape the blinding light.

I pass into the room and turn to see the portal to my tunnel close slowly until only a few specks of sparkles flitter to the floor where they melt away. I survey my body to make sure I'm still me, and I'm still perfectly intact, before twisting around to survey the room.

Where am I?

The small wooden room is dark and candlelit. Shelves line the walls stuffed to the brim with books and before me lies a humble desk with a chair and an open book.

The door suddenly opens and, not seeing anywhere to hide given the utter lack of furniture, I fly upwards, flattening myself across the ceiling, facing downwards so I can still observe who this mysterious visitor is.

A man walks in down below, closing the door behind him with his free hand, the other holding a stack of books. He sets the books down on the table with a loud thud. He heaves a sigh before using the back of his hand to swipe under the ashen hair that falls across his forehead. The movement allows me a peek at his pointed ears and the rims of his glasses.

It's Atlas. He doesn't look much younger, so this must be a fairly recent memory.

Why would the tunnel bring me here?

Atlas sits at the table and begins rifling through the new books he brought in with him. He takes a sip of the contents of his mug but looks more distraught than I've ever seen him. He flips through pages sporadically before suddenly stopping, peering intensely at one page and I wish that I wasn't too high up to read what it says. He rubs at his temples and then scratches the back of his head as he stares at the page before him.

Why is he acting so strange?

Slowly, he peers towards the doorway of his little study. After a moment of silence, he pulls the book towards him on the desk. His chest shakes slightly as he gingerly grabs the top inner portion of the page with his index and thumb fingers and begins to tear the page out. He only creates a small crack before a knock sounds at the door and he practically jumps out of his chair, swiping a hand across his forehead again before frantically shutting the book, and shoving a piece of paper in to keep his place.

"Come in," he says, voice slightly shaky.

The door creaks open and in walks Lennox, the young guard from when Rhea and I arrived at the palace in Durand. He stands in position just inside the doorway.

"His Highness wants to know if you have found it yet."

Atlas nods, curtly. "I have."

"He asks that you please bring it at once to present to his guest."

Atlas nods, again. He peers nervously at the book before picking it up and clutching it to his chest.

"Alright," he says.

He stands and follows Lennox out the doorway. Thankfully, they leave the door open and I fly through silently behind them, careful to stay tucked up against the ceiling.

Silly sprites. They never think to look up.

I follow Atlas and Lennox down the hall before moving up a flight of stairs before I realize we're in the Durand palace as we pass a portrait of Caspar's mother. We approach the dining room and I hear chatter emanating from inside. Caspar, whose voice I'd recognize anywhere now, says something I can't quite make out and it's followed by a woman's laugh.

Did I get it wrong? Maybe this is an older memory and I will get to see Caspar with his mother. A smile brims my lips as I think of the happiness he'll feel when I get back and tell him that I was able to see her. It's the closest I can get to meeting her after all.

Chapter 28

Lennox and Atlas slip through the doorway in the dining room. I wait for a short beat before following them in, but once I do, I halt quickly in my tracks, flying backward into the wall with a painful thud. For there, sitting across the table from Caspar, is Aunt Amyra.

I'm sure that the thud I caused by hitting the wall will draw everyone's attention to me, so I wince, waiting, but no one looks at me.

Can they not see me?

I bravely clap my hands in front of me a single time and no heads turn my way. They can't see me *or* hear me. I release a sigh and allow myself to drop down to a standing position.

"Here he is. Amyra, this is Atlas, my best scholar," Caspar says, gesturing to where Atlas now stands beside him at their table.

Atlas nods his head politely but doesn't meet Amyra's eyes.

"My, my, my!" Amyra coos, looking Atlas up and down. "So, all you spritemen are dashing." She shoots a wink Atlas's way that he doesn't notice as he taps Caspar on the shoulder.

She seems so normal, not whispering over her shoulder to any voices in her head. Perhaps she hasn't gone crazy yet?

"Your Highness, might I please have a word with you in private?" Atlas asks, clutching the book tightly to his chest. I walk closer to him, making sure not to touch him, as I steal a look at the book's title peeking out above the top of his arm.

Impermissible Legends.

Impermissible? That sounds familiar. I think hard, trying to remember the meaning of the word from my school days. Suddenly, it comes to me.

"Impermissible," my teacher had said. "Too evil to be allowed."

I feel my heartbeat quicken in my chest.

What could Caspar possibly want Atlas to find in this book?

"Atlas, we've discussed this already," Caspar says, an edge to his tone.

"Now, please read to our guest what she's asked for."

Atlas draws in a shaky breath, still not meeting Amyra's eyes, but turns his body to face her again. He opens the book slowly, looking pained as he begins to speak.

"The legendary potion of withering can be found by collecting the following items. You will need one wisp's heart, one wild rabbit's tear, two—" his words fade out as a ringing forms in my ears and I stumble forward, gripping the edge of the dining table to balance myself.

"No, no, no," I say, out loud. It doesn't matter. No one hears me.

This can't be happening. It's a trick. It must be a trick.

"Stop," I say, turning to Atlas as he continues to read, telling Amyra exactly what she needs to do to gain her evil power. The power she'll use to kill my people. "Stop it!" I yell at him.

Amyra sits in her chair, soaking up all the information with her signature, sinister smile. I turn to where Caspar sits, staring at his plate in silence. I don't know what lies she fed him to get him to share this legend with her, but whatever she did worked. He has no clue what wicked he's unlocked.

"Stop him!" I scream, running over to the side of Caspar's chair, but he doesn't even turn to me. "You don't know what you're doing! She's going to use this against my people! She's going to—" my screams die out as I grab his shoulder and shudder at the cold touch of him.

Atlas shuts the book, clutching it back to his chest and I think I see a tear stuck in the corner of his eye.

Caspar sits up straighter in his chair, turning flat eyes to Amyra. "Will that be enough for you?"

An evil, coy smile twists across Amyra's face and she pushes back her chair to stand up from the table. "That's perfect, Your Highness. I will send word once I have reclaimed my throne in Celestia."

I feel the blood in my body turn ice cold as a shiver runs down my spine so starkly that I have to fight the urge to physically shudder. No.

Chapter 28

No, I must have misheard. I must have.

"I look forward to doing away with the estrangement of our kingdoms," Caspar says before, to my very horror, he stands and shakes Amyra's hand.

He *knew*. He knew what she was going to do to me and my kingdom. He didn't just know, he *helped* her.

For what seems like the longest moment of my life, I feel like I can't breathe. I'm gasping for air and failing. I've never had an all-out panic attack before, but it feels like I've always guessed it would; like drowning on everything and nothing all at once.

Finally, I find my voice, but all that comes out are screams. I grab Amyra's glass of tonic from the table and I chuck it at the wall with all my might. It shatters into a thousand little shards, just like my heart, and no one cares.

How? How could I have been so foolish?

It all makes sense now. The wisps said another woman had taken their sister's heart. *That's* how they recognized Caspar. Amyra must have told them about him. And when Atlas first met me in the garden, he said, "Another legend?" *Another.*

I scream again with so much might that my throat hurts from the effort as I grab anything and everything I can off the table. I chuck food and dishes on the floor, dying for the destruction to ease my pain, but it doesn't.

Caspar bids Amyra farewell and Lennox escorts her out as I find my self-control enough to stop smashing things.

Atlas turns to Caspar as soon as Amyra is gone. "This is wrong, Caspar."

Caspar heaves a breath, leaning back against the wall by the doorway with his eyes shut. "Sometimes there is no right way to do things, Atlas. Amyra might be evil, but she will work with us and not against us if we get on her good side now. This Princess Luna could be a tyrant.

You've heard the rumors. Even her own people don't want her to be Queen. I can't take any chances with the stability of our kingdom. We can't repeat things like the last King. I have to try and take things in the direction I need them to go. No matter the cost."

It's at his words, that now, after everything, I finally begin to cry. Hot tears spill down my cheeks and drip onto my collarbone as I look at Caspar. The Caspar that told me he was falling for me. The Caspar that said I'd be a great Queen. The Caspar who took my first kiss.

I'd thought he was a dream come true, but now I know that he'll forever haunt my nightmares.

I gasp from a pain in my chest as if I can feel my heart breaking. I can't take any more of this.

"Let me out," I beg. I wait for nothing. "Let me out!" I scream now, more tears flowing. A shimmer draws my gaze to the right and I sigh in relief as I see the portal back into my tunnel appear. I stride for it quickly, desperate to run away from this awful memory, but something blue catches my eye on the nearby windowsill.

A baby bird, fast asleep. Just like the tunnel's instructions said.

I won't let Caspar, Atlas, or any of this stop me from finishing what I've started. I walk over and gingerly scoop the baby bird into the palm of my hand before returning to the portal. I walk through the shimmering entrance, desperate to feel the relief of escape, but knowing I'm heading back to face the worst of it now.

Chapter 29

I stride through my tunnel, feeling like my body's not my own until I see a bright opening and walk through it into a forest clearing. I survey the land as I tuck the sleeping bird into my satchel. How can it not be waking? It must be magic. The large grassy area is surrounded by a handful of scattered trees with limbs that climb up towards the sky.

I hate that they can look so beautiful when my world has never felt uglier.

I hear a shimmering noise, like crystals tinkling together, off towards my right and I turn to see Rhea emerge from it, her eyes red and puffy.

An idea occurs to me. *What if I can spare myself from confrontation all together and Rhea and I can leave now and leave the spritemen behind?*

"Rhea, I—" I begin, reaching for her arm, but she recoils away from my touch, turning her eyes on me like I'm a predator she didn't notice sneaking up. I'm startled at her reaction, but I continue. "Rhea, Atlas and Caspar lied. They've been lying since the moment we first met them. They're in on everything with—" I start, but my words fall away as she raises a hand abruptly, taking another step back from me.

"I don't want to hear it," she says, plainly. Her body language is cold and distant yet her eyes have never looked more on fire.

"What?" I hold my palms open out to my sides in question. "Rhea, you have to listen to me!"

"Why?" she asks, crossing her arms over her chest now. "Why do I have to listen? And why would you want to tell me anyway? It's not like I could even *understand*, right?"

She turns and begins walking away. I grab her forearm in an attempt to make her stay, but she rips away from my grasp. "Rhea, what are you—"

"*I saw you!*" she turns and screams at me.

Her outburst is so sudden that I flinch, stepping back away from her.

Her fists are balled at her sides so tightly that her knuckles turn a lighter shade against the dark cocoa of her skin. "The memory I saw was yours," she spits at me with gritted teeth. "I heard you tell Atlas that you don't talk to me about things, like your mom, because how would I understand?" she screams at me. "You know, I've been treated differently because I've been an orphan my whole life and the *last* person I would have expected to receive that kind of treatment from was you." She raises her arms before letting them fall, her face contorted in disgust. "I guess you're not the Luna I thought you were."

"Rhea—" I begin, but she marches forward till she's so close to my face I can feel the heat of her breath.

"You told me in Durand that I'm like the sister you never had," she breathes, her voice breaking as tears fall from her eyes. "Now, I truly wish you were the sister I *never* had."

I gasp, her words hitting exactly where she wanted them to. Tears fall from my eyes as she turns and flies off into the forest, to who knows where, while the last bit of my heart breaks.

A shimmer sounds behind me and I turn, wiping away my tears,

Chapter 29

and see Caspar and Atlas both emerging from their tunnels. Caspar locks eyes with me and I raise my hand. "Don't even talk to me."

"Like I would want to talk to you right now," he spits back.

My jaw drops and my eyebrows shoot upwards. "Excuse me? I'm the one who was played this whole time and just had it thrown in my face, so don't even try—"

"Actually, no. Both of us were played," Caspar says, back straight.

I narrow my eyes at him. "What the hell are you talking about?"

"I'm talking about the fact that I just saw Rhea's memory of you and her chitchatting before meeting me at my palace about how you were going to tell me that Amyra was coming for Durand after she took over Celestia. How could you lie to me like that?"

My jaw clenches and I muster a stiff shrug. "I don't know. How about you tell me? You're the bigger liar here."

He stills for a moment before finding his words. "What did you see in the tunnel?"

I take a deep breath and feel tears line my eyes. "I saw Atlas's memory of you making him find the legend for the potion of withering for Amyra. I saw you talking with her about her taking my throne and I saw you give her everything she needed to come ruin not just my life, but the lives of all my people! My mother could be dead right now because of you! *Lita is dead because of what you did!*"

I watch as his face flushes and he struggles to find his words. "Luna, just let me explain why I did it," he breathes, his shoulders sagging.

"No," I sigh, my tears finally falling. "There's nothing you can say that would justify this; that would make it go away. Yes, I lied to you, and that was wrong of me, but I had to do it for my people."

His brows bunch together and he juts a finger towards himself. "I did *this* for my people!"

"*No, you didn't!*" I scream, startling him so much that both he and Atlas take a step back. "I lied because I knew you wouldn't help me otherwise and I had lives on the line. *Your lie is what put those lives on the line!*" Slowly, I feel my anger turn into disbelief. "How could you?" I breathe. "How could you do it when even Atlas knew it was wrong?" I flit my eyes to him. "I saw you try to rip out the page before you found it." I see Caspar's eyes flit to him momentarily in surprise, but I continue. "I know you didn't want to help Amyra and I thank you for that."

Atlas gives me a small nod.

I avert my eyes back to Caspar. "You acted based out of fear of what I'd be like. You said you'd heard rumors and that I could be a tyrant. You went out of your way to aid evil measures before even trying to know me!"

Caspar stalks forward, grabbing my hands, and I hate that I still feel heat in his touch. "Luna, none of this matters now. We both lied to each other, so let's just call it even and let it go. Look how far we've come together! Luna, I—" He stops, drawing in a breath. "Luna, I love you."

His confession startles me, sending a wave of butterflies through my stomach, but I push them away, ripping my hands from his.

"No, you don't," I say, shaking my head.

His brows furrow. "Yes, I do."

"*No, you don't!*" I scream at him now, grabbing fistfuls of my hair in my hands. "I may not know much about love, but I know that it means *nothing* without trust."

Despair clouds his eyes as he sees me slipping away.

"No, Luna. Please," he reaches for me and I step back, distancing myself both physically and emotionally from him as best I can. He looks pained and I think I see tears line his eyes. "You can't forget about everything in the cave, Luna. You promised. You can't throw away what we have."

"You're the one who threw us away," I spit at him, anger and hurt seething my words. "And I know that what we had will be hard to forget," I breathe, feeling like I'm suffocating even though I'm outside in the open. "But I'm going to give it my *very* best try."

With that, I turn and fly, as fast as I can.

* * *

It feels like I've been crying forever where I sit at the edge of the watery stream. I take a deep breath to try and steady myself, straightening my posture on the bank with my feet dangling in the water. I close my eyes and will my tears to stop, but so many emotions are overloading my system that it feels like an impossible endeavor. I ache from the hurt of Rhea's words and the hurt of knowing how much my memory hurt her, but most of all, I pain from Caspar's betrayal.

How could I have thought I was really falling in love with him? We've both been lying to each other since the beginning. Actually, I'm not sure if I would even classify what I did as lying because it very well could be true. No matter what promises Amyra made to Caspar about reuniting the kingdoms, she could very well grow hungry with power and come after Durand next.

I hear a twig snap behind me and whip my head in the direction of the sound to find Atlas. He holds both hands up in front of him.

"I understand you are upset and I promise I come in peace," he says.

While part of me wants to turn him away for knowing about giving Amyra the legend and not telling me, the other part of me feels so alone. I pat the grass beside me and he slumps down cross-legged with a plop.

I lift a brow at him. "You don't want to put your feet in the water?"

He glares down at me, incredulously. "Do you have any idea how much bacteria running creeks contain? The stream of water is consistently flowing and passing more germs through it. One kind of—"

I hold up a hand, silencing him. "Okay, I get it. I get it. I'm sorry, but I'm just not in the mood right now." I breathe a sigh and we both face forward with nothing but the slight breeze rustling through the trees filling the silence for the longest time. "How did you find me?" I finally ask.

"Well," he begins. "I headed off in your same direction shortly after you left. Thankfully, you flew fairly straight, or else I'd probably be quite lonely and astray right now."

I peer down at my feet beneath the surface of the flowing water. "Why aren't you with Caspar?"

Atlas flicks a small bug off of his pant leg. "I left him behind at the tunnels."

I jolt with surprise, turning to face him. "You just left him?"

"I did," he answers.

"Why?" I ask.

Atlas straightens his back. "For two reasons. First, I wanted to apologize to you. While I never outright lied, I also haven't been entirely truthful."

"Yes," I say, bunching my lips. "I am upset with you for not telling me, but I'm not mad." I sigh. "I can't be mad. Not when I saw firsthand how horrible you felt handing it over. I mean, you even tried to get rid of it."

He nods. "I did and I still wish I could have. I was just in a very difficult position. I became torn between my ethics and my best friend to whom I attributed my success."

"I could see how torn you were, Atlas. I know you're sorry."

He turns his head to peer at me, cautiously. "Does that mean you forgive me?"

"I do," I say, heaving a breath before flashing a small smile at him. He mirrors my expression. "Thank you."

Chapter 29

I nod and we sit in a window of quiet for a moment before I remember apologizing was only part of why he tracked me down.

"What's the other reason you wanted to find me?"

I watch him take a deep breath, chewing nervously on his bottom lip for a moment before he turns to meet my eyes. "I need your help."

My eyebrows shoot up. "My help?"

"Yes. You see, while intelligence may be my strong suit, I am aware that I lack a solid knowledge of social or emotional construct."

I stare at him, blankly. "What?"

Atlas heaves a breath, his gaze forward. "I don't always know the right way to say something and sometimes it comes across wrong. I saw a memory of Caspar's in the tunnel and I am afraid to tell Rhea about it."

"Why are you afraid to talk to Rhea about it?"

Atlas turns to me with a distraught expression. "Because it was about her parents."

Chapter 30

Searching for Rhea takes what feels like an eternity since I have to stay close to Atlas and can't fly at my own free will. I release a breath I didn't realize I was holding as we finally find her. Sitting with her legs tucked into her chest atop a tall, mossy boulder, she feels so close yet so far away. I feel a distance between us now and I hate it with every fiber of my being, wishing I could rip it away like a band-aid.

I wish it were that easy, but I know it isn't. I hurt her deeply. The only way to recover is to truly talk it out and remind her of how much I love her. I pray to the rainbow that we can get back to the bond we had and not let this break us.

I place a hand out in front of Atlas's chest to still him in his tracks beside me. "I think I should talk to her alone. Would you mind giving us a bit of privacy?"

Atlas nods. "Not at all. I'll be right over here."

I squeeze his shoulder. "Thank you."

I fly over to Rhea and lower myself down beside her onto the boulder at a steady pace. Her eyes flicker to me above her arms crossed atop her kneecaps before she turns her head in the opposite direction. The action chips at my heart, but I press on.

Chapter 30

"I know you don't want to talk to me right now," I begin.

"Got that right," she mutters into her arms.

I take a deep breath, trying my best to continue. "But I really need to talk to you. Atlas asked me to."

"The tunnel already showed me enough of what you and Atlas talk about, alright? I'm not in a hurry to hear anymore."

I sigh. I wanted to ease her into the news, but it doesn't look like it's going to work. I opt for bluntness.

"Rhea, Atlas learned information about your parents."

Her head whips up and towards me in a flash. "What? How?"

"He saw a memory of Caspar's and your dad was in it."

She sucks in a small breath. "Really? Atlas actually *saw* my dad?"

"Yes," I say. I move to slide my hand atop hers resting on the rock's surface, to try and provide some comfort through this, but she pulls away. "Caspar attended a city hearing a few years ago at the palace. The old King was supposed to be hearing the requests and needs of the sprite people. Although, Atlas says he did this as a mere formality and usually just mocked everyone. Anyways, it was a spriteman's turn to speak and he said it was an important matter, but it was private, so he wanted to speak to the King alone. The King refused and told the man he'd have to say whatever it was in front of everyone."

I meet Rhea's eyes now and can tell from her expression that she's never listened more intently than she is at this moment.

"He said he'd been with a fairywoman a long time ago and had just discovered that she had died giving birth to his child. I guess he worked as a guard outside the front gates of Durand, so he wanted the King to excuse him from his guard contract so that he could go to Celestia to raise you, now that he knew about you. The King refused."

Rhea closes her eyes, tears cascading from her lids as she soaks up my words. She opens them, peering at me, her emotions swirling before me in her eyes. "How did Atlas know that it was my father

Caspar saw?"

The corner of my mouth tips upwards. "Because Atlas said he looked just like you."

A small smile brims her lips, too. I reach for her hand again and this time, she doesn't pull away.

"Rhea, I'm so sorry for what you heard me say to Atlas in that memory. I just haven't wanted to talk to you about my mother and have you feel like I'm waving my family in your face or something. I just wanted to be sensitive to your situation. I never want to make you feel like I'm treating you differently, but then I went and said that and that's exactly how I made you feel." I sigh, my shoulders sagging with the weight of all the emotions hanging in the air. "Please know how sorry I am for what I said and I never, ever meant to hurt your feelings because I love you. You're the last person I would ever want to hurt."

She gives my hand a squeeze, her eyes more their usual glow. "I know that and I love you, too. Luna, the part that bothered me was that you felt like you couldn't talk to me about that stuff. I'm your best friend! I want you to know that you can talk to me about absolutely anything. It's what I'm here for."

She's right. Hearing her say it all now, I wonder how I ever began worrying about talking to her about my mother in the first place. Of course, I can always talk to her about everything. It all makes me feel so silly now.

She lays her other hand on my shoulder, gently. "I may not always share your exact situation on things, but I will always understand them because I understand you. So, please tell me everything, always. Alright?"

I nod and smile before we embrace each other. In her arms, I feel like maybe everything will be alright after all. Suddenly, I remember what else I have to tell her.

Chapter 30

"Rhea," I begin, pulling back from our embrace and holding her by the shoulders. "I have something else to tell you. It's about what I saw in the tunnel and you're not going to like it."

She narrows her eyes at me. "Okay," she says, drawing out the word.

I take a deep breath in and release it. "Atlas and Caspar gave Amyra the legend she needed to find the potion that gave her her withering abilities. Amyra told Caspar that she would close the gap between Durand and Celestia once she had reclaimed her throne. It was all Atlas's memory." Her face is stone as I finish and I'm shocked at her lack of reaction. I drop my hands from her shoulders and peer at her. "Rhea?"

Suddenly, I watch a look of pure, fiery rage envelop her features and she flies up and past me. Before I can even turn around, I hear Atlas scream.

Uh oh.

I spin around quickly on top of the rock, climbing to a standing position, to see Rhea latched onto Atlas like a backpack, banging a wooden twig on the back of his head.

"You helped Amyra?" she screams at him through his calls for help. "You helped her and you kept it from us this whole time, you lying piece of—"

"Rhea!" I yell, cutting her off. Her head spins my way, but her arm keeps whacking Atlas with the twig as he runs around in a small circle trying to reach his arms around to swat her off. "Please just let him explain!"

Her arm stalls in the air, poised for another firm whack, but she slides off Atlas's back slowly. He turns to face her, holding both arms out to protect himself, as if that would be enough. Rhea points the end of her twig in his face, her other hand on her hip, eyes narrowed. "You better talk fast, spriteman, or else this twig is gonna meet a place where the sun doesn't shine."

I watch Atlas gulp and a bead of sweat drops down the side of his temple. "Caspar instructed me to find the legend and read it to her. I didn't want to. In fact, I attempted to rip the page from the book when I found it, but a guard came into my office and interrupted my efforts. I told Caspar it wasn't right to help aid Amyra like that, but he said it was necessary. I still feel awful about it, but I felt like I had no choice. I was torn between my ethics and my best friend and that was a horrid place to be."

He stops, but Rhea hasn't had enough. She points the tip of her stick into the center of his chest, raising her brows.

"I'm sorry!" he quickly adds. "I shouldn't have helped Amyra and shouldn't have kept it from you. You have my deepest apologies."

Rhea narrows her eyes at him before turning to face me. "He already apologized to you?"

I fly over beside her and nod. "Yes, and I forgave him. I saw him in the memory, Rhea and he was miserable giving her that legend. I believe that he's truly sorry."

She turns from me back to face Atlas, slowly. "Since Luna has forgiven you, I suppose I can forgive you, too." She quickly moves the end of her twig from the center of his chest to the tip of his nose. "But so help me, if I find out you're keeping any other secrets from us—"

"I'm not," he says, quickly. "I assure you."

"Alright," she says, throwing her twig off to the side and crossing her arms over her chest with a small huff.

"No more secrets," I command, hands on my hips. "Sound good?"

They both nod.

"Okay," I continue. "Then let's hear how you guys escaped when you fell into that pool of tree sap."

Rhea's cheeks shimmer furiously as Atlas's eyes widen. He looks to her as if in permission and she closes her eyes, giving him a nod. Atlas turns back to face me, heaving a heavy breath.

Chapter 30

"The tree sap was difficult to get out of because it was of such a thick density. While we were stuck, I remembered that warm liquids can break up sticky substances."

I tilt my head, furrowing my brows as I wait for him to continue.

"I'm afraid I had to pee on us," he finishes.

My hands fly to cover my gaping mouth as Rhea covers her whole face in her hands and lets out a pained groan.

"What?" I ask. "No, no—"

"Oh, yes," Rhea says, lowering her hands now to show her face fully shimmering.

I peer back and forth between them before their embarrassed expressions suddenly seem so comical and I begin to laugh.

"*Do not laugh!*" Rhea commands, balling her hands into fists at her side. "It was absolutely horrific and I will not have you finding entertainment in my misery!"

Now, at her outburst, Atlas begins to chuckle as well.

"Both of you, *stop it!*" Rhea yells now, stomping her foot on the forest floor.

"Careful there, Rhea," I say through my laughter. "Don't get so *pissed!*"

At that, we all laugh.

A few moments later, we're finally able to calm ourselves, stomachs cramping from laughter. I sigh, bracing my hands on my hips. "I don't know what to do now, you guys."

Atlas's face flicks to mine, sadness edging his eyes. "Well, did either of you happen to find the baby bird while venturing through your tunnel's memory?"

Rhea shakes her head at the same time that I nod mine. "Oh, yes! I did," I say, pulling the bird out of my satchel to show them.

"Wow," Rhea muses, rubbing the top of the sleeping bird's head with the tip of her index finger. "How is it still asleep?"

I shrug, placing the bird safely back in my bag. "I'm not sure. I figured it must be some kind of magic."

Atlas nods. "Most likely. This is the Bog, after all. Now, let's head out."

Rhea and I spin our heads towards him.

"Head out?" she asks.

Atlas nods. "Yes. We have all the items we need to get the amulet."

My eyes widen as I realize he's right. Yes, Caspar took one wisp heart, but I have the other, the Red Beryl gem, and the baby bird. We have everything we need to go on and finish our quest.

Rhea and I quickly fall into step behind Atlas as he turns and starts walking away.

"Wait, I know you've said we had to collect these items to get the amulet, but now that we have these things, what do we do with them?" I ask.

"The journal says we must venture to the heart of the Bog to visit the swamp monster. Then we trade the monster the items that we've collected for the amulet," Atlas says, plainly, not bothering to even look back at us.

Rhea and mine's eyes fly to one another in a panic.

"I'm sorry, did you say *swamp monster?*" Rhea asks, head jutted forward in question. "Yeah," she huffs in a frightened laugh. "I don't do swamp monsters and I most definitely do not want to get anywhere near that thing."

"Well, you're in luck then," Atlas says, "because the journal clearly states that one person must enter alone. The monster only hosts one visitor at a time."

Rhea turns to face me, putting the tip of her index finger on her nose in a lightning-quick movement. "Not it!"

I shoot her a glare and she chuckles, looping her arm through mine. I know it should be me, but that doesn't mean I'm not afraid to visit

Chapter 30

the monster. My heart pangs with the feeling of wishing Caspar was here. His presence used to fill me with an overwhelming sense of comfort and safety. Now, the memory of him fills me with regret.

Why regret?

I know I should feel angry and part of me still does, but the other part wishes I would have heard him out. I allowed Atlas the opportunity to explain, but not him. That wasn't fair of me, but the cut from the betrayal was just too fresh. I couldn't think straight. Now, all my thoughts are dedicated to wondering if there's any possible chance that what we had could be salvaged.

People do bad things sometimes, but that doesn't make them bad people. If that was all it took, then I think everyone would be a bad person. Even me.

"What about Caspar?" I ask before I can stop the words from leaving my lips.

Rhea practically growls. "You mean he who shall not be named?" she spits, jaw clenched. "He lied to you, Luna."

"Yes, but so did I and she forgave me," Atlas says with a shrug.

Rhea sends a glare at the back of his head in front of us.

"That's true, Rhea," I say, turning my conflicted eyes onto her. "I allowed Atlas to apologize, but not Caspar. I could have at least let him try to explain."

I see Rhea fighting with herself in her mind for a beat before she finally shrugs with a huff. "I suppose."

Tears suddenly line my eyes and I let out a small sniffle. Rhea notices, but Atlas doesn't. He continues walking onward as we stop in our tracks and she turns me by my shoulders to face her. "Luna, I know how much you cared about him. The way you looked at him?" She stops to give her head a small shake, lips pressed. "That was love if I've ever seen it."

Her words finally give me the courage I need to allow my tears to fall. "Why are you telling me this?"

"Because," she begins, squeezing my shoulder, "you looked so happy and I loved seeing you like that. While I am possibly even more mad at him than you are for what he did, I do think that if there's even a possible chance you could get what you guys had back, you should at least try to explore it."

She's right. If I don't even try to let him explain or apologize, I'll always wonder what if. That could make me go mad. I'd rather go mad from love than go mad from missing out on it. I nod my head at her slowly. "Thank you, Rhea."

"Of course," she says, pulling me in for a hug. "I love you."

"I love you, too."

Up ahead, Atlas turns back; finally realizing that we're falling behind. "Are you crying?" he asks, spotting my eyes as he walks back towards us.

I nod, wiping my face. "Yes. I just wish I could talk to Caspar."

"Oh," Atlas says. "Well, then you're in luck. He promised to meet us in the heart of the Bog to see the swamp monster."

I feel my heart skip a beat. "Really?"

Rhea nudges me with her elbow. "See?" A grin breaks across her face. "I knew he wouldn't let you go that easy."

* * *

The sun is finally setting as we reach the heart of the Bog. Walking here took forever. I kept telling myself that finally reaching our destination would be a wonderful sight. Instead, I find the view before me to be one of the worst.

Before us, the land breaks into a sea of murky, hazy water that's tinted a deep shade of tan. Dark-trunked trees with cracked bark protrude up out of the scummy water's surface every few feet or so

Chapter 30

with long-hanging vines that flow above the water with the chilling breeze of the fog that rolls like a blanket across the swamp.

Somewhere, a frog ribbits.

"What an ugly heart," Rhea says beside me as the three of us stand peering at the sight before us.

"The air feels heavy here," I say, turning to Atlas. "Is it—"

"It's humid here, yes," he confirms. "Similar to in Durand. It's a standard element for this kind of ecosystem."

"Well, it means no flying for us," Rhea huffs, crossing her arms over her chest.

The sun is casting lower and lower by the minute. The rays shining through the misty trees of the swamp slowly die out; darkness takes up the space they leave.

"Wait, where's Caspar?" I ask, turning to Atlas at my side. "Didn't you say he was going to meet us here?"

Atlas nods. "We probably just beat him here, but he has a great sense of direction from hunting in Durand. He couldn't have gotten lost. I'm sure he'll arrive any moment now."

"Okay," I breathe out with a sigh. "So, what now?"

He shrugs, peering at the related page of the journal. "I'm afraid the journal only says the location and the fact that only one person may speak with the swamp monster to get the amulet. Do you have all the items on you?"

I nod. The wisp heart, gem, and baby bird are all in the satchel strapped across my body.

"Alright, then," he says. "Perhaps, we can walk around. Maybe if we explore the area, we can find the—"

Atlas's words die in his throat because, before us, the murky water begins to ripple and a hiss of a voice rings like a whisper into my ear.

"You must drown yourself to see me."

My eyes bulge with both shock and fright at the chilling sound of the voice in my ear. I whip my head to Rhea beside me and she shoots me a look, tilting her head.

"Luna, are you alright?"

"It-It spoke to me," I stammer, my skin growing cold.

Rhea's face adopts a scared expression, similar to mine, and she places a hand on my shoulder. "The monster?"

"What did he say?" Atlas asks now, turning toward me with concerned eyes.

"He—" I stop, drawing in a shaky breath. "He said I have to drown myself to see him."

I watch all the color drain from Atlas's face. Beside me, Rhea's eyes gawk wide and she begins shaking her head.

"No," she begins saying quietly before progressively getting louder. "No, no, no. You can't."

"But, Rhea—" I start.

"No," she says again, voice firm with terror in her chocolate eyes. "You can't. I won't let you. What if it's a trick?"

"It is the only way," the voice rings suddenly into my ear again, causing me to stumble back a step.

Rhea's grasp on my shoulder tightens to help straighten me. "Luna?"

"He says it's the only way," I say to the ground before turning to peer at both of them. "I have to do this."

"No. No, you don't Luna. It's too dangerous. You—" Rhea begins, but I reach up to my shoulder and take her hand in mine.

"Rhea, we did not come this far to stop now. We're so close. I can't let everything we've done be for nothing," I say, eyes sincere.

We have come so far. We're so close to saving my mother, my people; all of Celestia. I don't want to follow the monster's instructions, but if he says it is the only way, then that's the way it must be.

"Just trust me," I tell them both, giving them a small smile. "I've got this."

Chapter 30

Rhea stares at me for a solid moment before slowly beginning to nod. Tears line her eyes and she wraps me in a tight embrace. Atlas stands beside us and I turn my head to him over Rhea's shoulder. "Get in here, Atlas."

Atlas slowly steps forward before wrapping both Rhea and me in his arms, pulling us into him and I can't help but think to myself that if this really is the last moment of my life, it's a pretty good one.

"I love you," Rhea whispers into my hair. "Please be careful when you see the monster. Come back as soon as you can."

"I will," I assure her as I pull out of their arms. I relax my shoulders and draw a deep breath in, turning to face the swamp.

Slowly, I begin wading into the water, happy to find it on the warm side versus the cool temperature that I was expecting. The water is thick from the gritty dirt swept up into it from the floor and banks of the swamp and it feels rough as it brushes against my legs the deeper I wade in. Thank goodness I kept my shoes on or else I'm sure I would have horrible traction against the muddy floor of the water.

The fabric of my satin dress sways in the gentle current of the water as it surpasses my waist. The confidence and assurance I had when entering the water fades with each inch as I move further out. Only when the hazy fluid meets my chin do I steal a glance back at Atlas and Rhea up on the bank. Rhea's wiping at tears that fall from her eyes as Atlas stands tall behind her, an arm wrapped around her that she clutches to for comfort. I feel tears begin to bud along my own eyes now, but I blink hard, forcing them away.

I turn back towards the water and I keep walking, forcing my legs onward even though all my limbs want to do is turn back to my friends and the safety of the shore. I dig the heels of my feet into the ground beneath, propelling myself forward. I take one last deep breath of air in and hold it as the water lapses up over my face now as I become submerged beneath. The current sways me, but I walk on. Forward,

forward.

Just keep walking, Luna.

I have to do this. I think of my mom, my people, my friends, and everyone who's counting on me. This is for them.

My pace has slowed significantly since becoming fully submerged below and when I crack open my eyes, I find that barely any light penetrates the swamp water's surface. All I can see is a murky wall of brown. The dirt in the current stings my eyes and so I squeeze them tightly shut. My lungs begin to strain, my throat tightening from holding in my breath already longer than I thought I was capable of.

I try to hold it just a second longer, but I can't and my lips part with my release. The murky water of the swamp stings as it fills my mouth and throat. I begin coughing instinctively, my body wanting to rid myself of this horrible fluid, but coughing only allows more to slither in. A stinging sensation expands in my chest like someone has set me on fire and I will now burn from the inside out. My body screams at me as I begin to convulse deep below the hazy water's surface.

I try to think of Atlas, Rhea, and my mom, but all my mind fills with is Caspar. Even with everything going on between us right now, he is still the thought that brings me peace. Flashbacks of us in the cave fill my mind as black fills my sight and I succumb to the fluid waves that fill my chest.

Chapter 31

I lurch forward, coughing and hacking with such force that every muscle in my body screams at me. I wheeze until I'm finally able to take in full breaths again; my chest heaving from the effort. I'm sitting in a thick mud, at least six inches deep, and soaked from head to toe. I lift my head slightly more to survey my surroundings, but all my eyes find is darkness. In front of me lies stark nothingness; an endless pool of black. It reminds me of the dark bleakness of death.

Am I dead or alive?

"Neither, I'm afraid. You're sort of in between," comes a voice from behind me and I flip over quickly, turning to see it, but immediately wishing I hadn't. If all of the deepest shadows of the realm formed together, they still wouldn't come close to creating the wretched nightmare my eyes fall upon now.

Towering at least ten feet tall, is hell incarnate itself. The swamp monster stands before me composed of protruding bones wrapped in thin skin pulled so taught that it looks as if the slightest movement could cause it to rip. I only manage mere peaks at the skeleton makeup of the creature though due to the ever-flowing mud that emanates from somewhere atop its head. Thick, dark mud flows from the top of its frame down the length of its body, coating long hair and creating a wall to block the monster's face.

I scurry backward in the mud, coating myself more in the thick substance from the splashes my effort creates. My blood runs cold and chills lace my limbs even though the mud I lay in is warm.

"You-you're the swamp monster?" I stammer, barely finding the words.

The creature lets out a low rumble from behind its wall of hair that I take as a makeshift laugh. "That's rather tame," it hisses, voice as low and chilling as it was when whispered in my ear earlier.

It stands taller, making me feel smaller and smaller with each inch it grows before me. A hand stretches out from its side, webbed fingers, long and thin, with nails that resemble the talons of birds, curling in on themselves. The creature gestures to itself with the frightening hand.

"They called me the Marsh Reaper."

"Who-who did?"

The Marsh Reaper releases a low grumble of a laugh again and a dim light ignites above us in the dark. "They did."

I tilt my neck back to peer up and feel my stomach lurch as soon as I do. Above me lies the bodies of fairies, sprites, and other varied forest creatures suspended by their ankles from some unknown tether; decaying and rotting away. A drop of something warm falls onto my cheek and knowing it came from one of the hanging bodies above is enough to send me into a heaving spell.

"You're all too weak to stomach death. That's why I only let you see what I want you to," the Marsh Reaper says in a hiss. I see the light above dim and fade out. The monster keeps speaking as my stomach continues contracting from knowing what lies above me, even if I can no longer see it.

"They were all a particularly weak lot. Thought they could come

Chapter 31

to take something from me without giving me the items I asked for. What fools." The Marsh Reaper takes a step closer to me as I finally stop heaving. "They were merely proof that fate experiments with mistakes." It's dripping form looms over me. "Are you a mistake, too?" It seethes.

"No," I say, surprising both myself and the creature with my fast response.

"Then stand," the Marsh Reaper commands, "and tell me what you've come for. No one visits me for pleasure; only a last resort."

I slowly push myself to a standing position, my eyes pinned on the monster's wet, hair-covered face dripping before me. My dress is raked with mud and my legs and hands are coated too, making them feel slightly heavy as I force myself to straighten my back and stand tall. "My name is Luna and I'm the Princess of Celestia. Someone has taken over my kingdom with a deadly power and I need to undo the damage they've done and save everyone."

"Ah," the Marsh Reaper breathes in a daunting sigh that sends a chill through the air. It stalks slowly towards me before coming so close I can smell the reeking odor of its form and see dark veins running beneath the patches of skin that peek from the flowing mud. "You want the amulet."

"Yes," I breathe, "and I have all the items you ask for."

"Give them to me."

Slowly breaking my gaze from the monster, I grab the items out of my satchel and place them all into the giant, webbed palm of its hand. Long fingers curl around them once they're all within his grasp and they suddenly begin to melt into mud, dripping down from the Marsh Reaper's hand.

My head whips from the hand to its hidden face as if searching for an explanation in the expression I can't even see. "What? Why are you doing that? Don't you want these things?"

The monster simply watches the last of the newly-formed mud drip from his hand and become one with the rest that encircles my ankles. "Do you think I have a use for them?"

I shrug, my mind too confused to formulate an answer as I think of all the hard work we went through to get those things just for them to melt away into nothing.

"They are not turning into nothing. They were always nothing," the monster hisses.

Can it hear my thoughts? If it can, it doesn't say so as it continues.

"They were merely tangible things and tangible things are worthless. It's the intangible things in life that are priceless, don't you think?" The mud-coated head turns my way, the wet wall of hair swinging slightly from the movement, waiting for my answer.

"I suppose so," I say, trying to force my shoulders to relax from where they sit high by my neck in my frightened stance from the creature's presence. "But you can't take intangible things. They're intangible."

"I thought the same as you once upon a time, but I was wrong," the monster muses, its spine letting out a chorus of small cracks as it bends to hover slightly forward towards me even more now.

"You had something intangible taken from you?"

"I did."

I hesitate, not sure if I should ask, but my curiosity wins out. "What did they take?"

"All of the euphoria I kept within my heart," it breathes. "I was in love once." The Marsh Reaper's voice turns raspier and huskier as if pained to continue. "But that love was taken from me. My heart was shattered and broken. I ran away into the Bog, thinking that maybe something within this forest could cure me of my misfortune, but I found nothing capable. When I reached the center of the Bog, I collapsed. I cried so hard that I died."

Chapter 31

A beat of silence passes between us before I speak. "I'm sorry—"

"Do not give me your mortal pity!" the monster spits at me, turning from me and stalking a few strides away.

I'm left heaving deep breaths from the surprise of his outburst, but I will myself to calm down once again. A few more moments of silence float by before the monster continues speaking.

"Yet, while I died, my heartbreak did not. It escaped with my spirit as it left me and it rooted itself into the magical soil of the Bog. Thus, creating the swamp that I am tethered to for all of eternity, receiving only the rarest of visitors." It whips its head over its shoulder at me. "All the most precious of intangible things are fragile and can be taken away. Now, those things are what I seek. Intangible things are the true price to be paid for my magical accessories and tools, like the precious amulet you so desire. The only price I require is something priceless to its beholder."

I feel my frightened heart sink into my chest. "What? But the items I just brought you were the price! They were—"

"They were merely a test!" the monster reels at me. "Visitors must bring me those things to show me how much they want it; how much they need what they ask of me. But once that test is passed, there is still a price to be paid. I do not give gifts, girl. I only make *transactions*. Now, do we have a deal?"

I falter back a step. "A deal? What's the price you seek? What intangible thing? I wouldn't even know how to give that to you."

The Marsh Reaper turns, stalking towards me before it crouches to be level with my face. A talon on the end of a long, webbed finger juts into the base of my chin, tilting my head upwards into its curtain of wet locks. "You will not give me anything. I will take it from you. The price will be paid when you use the amulet. One use and one price. Then the amulet will return to me."

"You're asking quite a hefty price for a *loan*," I spit, pissed at the fact that I'm now being forced to sacrifice even more when I've already sacrificed so much.

"You're asking to use a powerful thing. Everything has a price to be used."

"Fine," I huff. "What intangible thing do you want?"

"I can't say," the monster says, pushing the tip of its talon so firmly into my chin now that I worry it will pierce my skin.

"You can't say or you won't tell me?" I ask.

"Smart girl," the Marsh Reaper muses, drawing back its hand. "I don't tell you because you don't want to know."

"But I'm telling you I want to know."

"And I'm telling you that knowing will only make things harder. Now, do we have a deal or not?"

I tear my eyes away from the monster to peer at the muddy ground while I think.

I have to say yes, don't I? I mean, if I don't then everything we've done up to this point will have been for nothing and there will be no hope left for saving Celestia and my mother.

Thoughts flood my head of Atlas, Rhea, Caspar, and all of the challenges they've overcome with me on this journey. Lita may be lost, with nothing I can do to save her now, but I have no desire for my mother or anyone else in Celestia to join her beyond the rainbow.

I have to do this for my people.

"Yes," I hear myself say. "We have a deal."

As soon as the words leave my lips, I feel a heavy energy pass through me. Some omnipresent, cosmic transaction has now been promised and the feeling of its finality leaves me breathless.

The Marsh Reaper lets out a sound similar to a purr of delight. "Wonderful. Here you are, dear."

The monster's webbed hand unfurls outwards towards me, the amulet within its open palm. I feel myself sigh with relief. The amulet

Chapter 31

is finally mine. Finally, I can begin to mend things.

At the end of a small gold chain, resembling a thorny rose stem, lies a deep fuchsia crescent moon with a single gem dangling from its tip like a turquoise teardrop. Gold trails along the outer shape of the moon, emphasizing its beauty and color.

"Wow," I breathe. "It's beautiful."

"Beauty hides power like nothing else," the monster muses. "Now, turn around."

While the last thing I want to do is turn my back to the most terrifying creature I've ever seen, I'm more afraid of what will happen if I refuse. I slowly spin on my heels in the mud to face away from the Marsh Reaper. The reeking odor of the monster becomes stronger as it stalks up to me and brings the necklace over my head to hover it in front of my face.

"Only one use, girl. Don't waste it."

I nod as wet, muddy hands wrap the chain of the amulet around my neck. I hear a click at the base of my neck before forcing myself not to physically shiver at the feeling of the monster's talons as they pull my mud-soaked hair to fall on the outer side of the amulet's chain.

I turn back around, the Marsh Reaper looming before me. "Our visit ends here," the monster says. "May we never meet again."

With that, I begin to sink into the mud. My head whips down towards my feet as I become consumed by the thick fluid. "Wait!" I cry, searching for something to hold onto, but of course, there's nothing. I watch as the Marsh Reaper turns on its heels and begins walking away from me. "Am I going back? Will this—"

The monster's head whips slowly over its right shoulder just as my shoulders sink beneath the mud. "Be wary, girl. Darkness is afoot." I gasp for my last breath as I hear the Marsh Reaper's voice add, "And it's closer than you think."

Chapter 32

I expect to wake up beneath the muddy water of the swamp, but instead, my eyes snap open and my head lurches forward, smacking into something hard. I wince, throwing a hand to my forehead, before taking in my surroundings. I'm standing inside a dark wooden cylinder.

"What in the realm?" I ask aloud to myself. I press my hands to the coarse wood in front of me, feeling the messy lines of it.

Did the Marsh Reaper lie and trap me?

Quickly, my hand flies to my chest and I sigh with relief when I feel the amulet there. Perhaps the monster didn't trick me after all. I just need to get my bearings.

I begin to press along the wood to the sides of me as I thank the rainbow that I didn't have to wake up hacking and coughing up mud yet a third time. Nothing in front or to the sides of me gives way, so I do my best, wings pinned to my back, to shimmy around and face the opposite direction within my wooden capsule. If it wasn't for how mud-soaked I was, I might have an easier go of it, but finally, I manage to face the other way. Immediately, I notice a thin trail of light in a large rectangular shape. I press on the wood it outlines and

Chapter 32

feel an overwhelming sense of joy when it swings open like a door, showing the forest of the Bog just outside, cast dark with a low hue of moonlight.

I walk out and turn back to discover that my wooden entrapment was the trunk of a swamp tree. How odd that the monster would return me inside a tree instead of to the swamp water I originally ventured into. My eyes drift from the tree to the surrounding ones instead and my confusion grows. I'm certain I'm still in the swampy heart of the Bog, but the area around me looks unfamiliar. I must be on the opposite side of the swamp from Atlas and Rhea.

I close the door of the tree trunk and begin walking forward through the dark terrain until I find the edge of the large swampy sea. I squint my eyes to peer through the thick of the night. Through the trunks of the scattered trees, far across the water, I see a flash of Rhea's bright, tangerine dress and a smile immediately breaks out across my face. I hasten my pace and begin lightly jogging around the swamp's edge, thinking of how happy both Rhea and Atlas will be to see the amulet.

I haven't felt this light and excited in what feels like forever and the emotions are downright cherished as they flow through me. I want nothing more than to get to the other side of the swamp as quickly as possible to reunite with everyone and celebrate. If it wasn't for the sticky mud lacing my wings and limbs, or the humid air of the swamp, I'd fly right across the water and be with them now.

I hope Caspar is there so that we can finally talk all this drama out and move on. The relief of the amulet and the completion of our quest overflows my heart with a wave willing to wash everything away. Caspar and I have both made mistakes, and while we still need to talk things through, the bottom line is that if he truly has fallen for me, and I for him, then we should be willing to give each other a second chance.

I try to keep my eyes pinned on the tiny slip of color from Rhea's dress as I make my way around the sea of the swamp, but I stop dead in my tracks as I see a flash of red hair, just like mine, through the trees beside her. Carefully, I crouch down and begin to tiptoe through the remaining area of trees till I'm close enough to get a better look. I halt behind a particularly large trunk before peeking my head around the side of it.

Amyra is there, standing beside Rhea, who sits with her arms bound behind her on the ground. I count not three, but four Celestia palace guards scattered around Amyra. My mind begins racing with a million questions as my heartbeat hastens tenfold.

How the hell is she here? How do I help Rhea? What do I do?

Amyra looks even worse than when I last saw her at my party. Before, there still appeared to be some sense of life behind her eyes. Now, I can sense the pure rage and darkness that she dispels, even from the distance of my hiding spot. It's as if the evil power she possesses consumes her heart and now there's hardly any of her left. She wears a dress with an emerald green, robe-like cloak that's floor-length with bell-shaped sleeves. She pulls the hood of it over her head, slightly shadowing her face, which only ages her complexion more. Her red hair peaks forward, protruding from the hood as she stands, arms crossed, facing the swamp's sea.

"How much longer, child?" she growls at Rhea.

Rhea flips her head up towards the side of her where Amyra stands. "I told you the truth. I don't know when, or if, she's coming back. She walked into the water and drowned." Her defiant tone changes to one of sorrow. "She could be dead right now for all we know."

Amyra lets out a cackle before her face returns to its cold front once again. "No, it can't be that easy." Her head ticks, slightly. "But I wish, I wish, I wish."

"You know, I'm curious," Rhea says, narrowing her eyes at Amyra. "Of all the voices in your head, have none of them told you that you're

Chapter 32

a psycho—" Rhea's words warp into a gasp as the back of Amyra's bony hand smacks across the side of her face.

My hands fly to cover my mouth in an attempt to stifle my own gasp.

Rhea is still for a moment, other than the heaviness of each breath she draws in, before she turns back to Amyra with a smile on her face; my ever-strong best friend. "I'll take that as a no."

Amyra tilts Rhea's face upwards with a finger forced under her chin. "That mouth of yours would have you lying dead and prostrate right now, in this very swamp, if it wasn't for the fact that you are playing the very necessary role of bait in this little game I'm hosting."

Okay. *Think, Luna.*

I've got to get a grip and assess the situation.

Amyra's trying to lure me to her with Rhea, but she doesn't know I'm aware that she's here. For all she knows, I'm still away visiting the Marsh Reaper. She thinks she has the element of surprise, but I've got her right in my line of sight. Maybe I could try to sneak around and get to Rhea from behind Amyra, but Amyra's team of palace guards would make that plan have a very, very slim chance of success.

Why in the realm would my palace guards be helping Amyra anyway?

Ever so slowly, I move closer to them to get a better look. The moon is shining a bright cast of hazy yellow across the swamp as it reflects off the murky water. Normally, the sight would be rather beautiful, but now it feels more eerie than anything I've encountered before. I'm thankful for the cloak of darkness though, provided by the trees, as I snake my way through them.

I get about as close as I dare, before the underside of my foot lands on a twig I hadn't noticed, which now emits a loud snap, sending everyone's heads spinning toward the direction of my hiding place.

I plant my back, wings pointed low, against the bark of the closest tree, and hold my breath. While no one says anything, I hear movement and wonder if one of the guards is coming to inspect the area I'm in. Briefly, I consider moving to a tree further away, but I'm afraid of what noises that movement could cause, so I opt to stay in the dark pocket of shadow I'm currently in. The tall grass and reeds spark an idea in my mind. I slowly slide down and submerge myself beneath the tall grass. Crouching forward onto all fours, I lower myself to the ground as much as possible. Then, I focus on breathing as slowly and quietly as I can. I pray to the rainbow that the guards don't find me.

At least they're Celestia palace guards and not guards from Durand. If a sprite guard found me, I'd have even slimmer odds against their strength and tall height. I still remember how shocked I was at the tall height of Caspar and Atlas when I first met them.

Wait, where is Atlas? Did he leave? Did Amyra kill him already and dump his body in the swamp or something?

I shake my head to disrupt my thoughts. Now is not the time to assume the worst.

Maybe he got away? Perhaps he ran to find Caspar or something? Oh, how I wish Caspar was here to help me figure out what to do.

A grunt sounds out as something hard collides with the side of my ribs and then tumbles over me. I don't have time to inspect my now possibly broken rib as I quickly move to escape the grasp of the guard who fell over me. It's the guard who used to be posted outside my chambers. He's never been anything, but kind to me.

"It's me!" I half-whisper, half-shout at him, but as soon as his eyes meet mine, I know that I can expect no mercy from him. The skin around the guard's eyes is tinted black like a mask similar to the dark shade that graced Amyra's fingertips when she first unleashed her power at the palace. It's as if permanent shadows have clouded his vision. He's no longer in there. He's just become an extension of Amyra.

I quickly stand to try and run, but he grabs hold of my ankle. I trip,

Chapter 32

falling forward onto my stomach with a hard thud. I gasp, the wind knocked out of me, as the guard begins to pull me back towards him by my ankle. Quickly, I flip around onto my backside and then jab the foot of my free leg squarely into his jaw. I hear a loud crack and feel like I may hurl as he slowly spins his head back towards me and I can see where his jaw has broken. The right side of it hangs slack, yet he shows no signs of pain. I stare at him, my brows bunched in disbelief. It's as if he has no feelings at all, just like when Amyra smashed that glass cup in her hand at my coronation party and didn't even care.

My plan to force him to loosen his grip on my ankle failed as he didn't even let go with my swift kick. He gives me a hard yank, pulling me the rest of the way to him. He pushes himself to a standing position, pulling me with him, before pushing me up against the nearest tree and binding my hands in front of me with a thick, twine rope.

No, no, no. My mind reels, feeling my hope diminish.

After he finishes tying my hands, the guard grabs me and takes me out into the clearing. Amyra's face becomes overcome with a pleased smile as she sees me, but Rhea's face falls with despair.

"Well, well, well. Hello, dear niece," Amyra coos. "How nice of you to join us." She adds to no one over her left shoulder, "Finally, finally."

When we get close enough, the guard lightly kicks the backs of my knees to force me to the ground in front of Amyra and Rhea. I tilt my face up to Amyra's, hoping she can see the fire in my eyes.

"How did you find us?" I ask.

"It's no secret that desperate people run into the Bog," she says, bringing her fingertips together in front of her. "My guards and I ventured into the forest where we met a stupid, gullible, little birdie who told me exactly where I could find you." She pulls something blue out of her pocket, throwing it onto the ground between us.

Hodge's hat.

"No," Rhea breathes across from me. Tears begin to fill her eyes and

I blink hard to force back the ones that threaten to form in my own.

"You're a monster!" Rhea screams at Amyra.

"Aw, thank you," Amyra says with a chuckle. "Oh, don't worry. He went quickly. Didn't he?" she twitches her head to the side, answering her own question. "He certainly did." Her neck snaps straight on her shoulders again as she locks her dark eyes on me. "Faster than you'll get."

"Why are you doing this, Amyra?" I ask.

"Killing you? Taking over Celestia? You'll have to be more specific," she maniacally chuckles, giving me a wink.

"All of it!" I shout at her now, my emotions overflowing. She came back and ruined everything, and I refuse to die without at least knowing why. "Is this really all because they never found you after the fire?"

"They never even tried to find me!" Amyra yells at me.

Something moves in the trees behind Amyra and my eyes zip to it. Atlas's head pokes out from around a tree trunk and I try not to show relief on my face. He brings his finger to his lips and I quickly turn my gaze back onto Amyra, who thankfully didn't notice my distraction. "How do you know that? Maybe they—"

"Because I saw them!"

Rhea and I both flinch at her outburst before furrowing our brows as her words sink in.

Rhea gulps before finding the words. "How could you have seen them—"

"—unless you were there," I finish for her, eyes wide.

Amyra's shoulders hunch forward as she rolls her neck, but says nothing.

"You said you escaped and waited just outside the kingdom for someone to come find you," I breathe heavily, thinking out loud. "You said you waited there two days before you heard the coronation bells

Chapter 32

and knew they'd crowned my mother."

Amyra spins towards me at a frightening speed, her teeth bared like a predator. "I lied," she hisses. Suddenly, her eyes tick back into her head. "Secret. Don't tell."

"Haven't you heard, Amyra?" I ask, setting my hard gaze on her as I recount the words from the tunnel. "Not all secrets are ours to keep."

Amyra squeezes her head from the outside of her hood as she lets out a pained groan, as if the voices in her head are speaking too loudly.

In my peripheral vision, I see Atlas hiding just a few trees behind Amyra now, a large, thick stick braced in his hands like a club. On his face, I see a look of both bravery and fear, and the combination is so uniquely suited to him.

"What's not yours to keep, precious niece, is that shiny new accessory you've picked up," Amyra says, standing tall with the moonlight casting over the top of her hood. "I heard all about the amulet. Now, hand it over." She extends her open palm. "Family is supposed to share."

"No," I breathe, willing myself to be strong and not show how terribly and completely frightened I am.

I have to do it. I have to use the amulet *right now*.

I don't have time to before panic ensues.

"I said give it to me!" Amyra screams. She moves to lunge towards me, but Rhea moves swiftly, kicking a leg out sideways from under her to trip Amyra, who lands forward with a hard thud. I quickly scurry to my feet as best I can with my hands bound, before the guards come at me. I turn to Rhea to try and help her, but it's at this moment that Atlas chooses to charge out with a battle cry and land a hard blow to the back of the nearest guard's head. The guard crumples and I can tell from Atlas's expression that he hates being the one to deliver the blow. I wish he didn't have to do it either, but I appreciate his help more than he'll ever know.

He unties Rhea's hands quickly as I sidestep to my left, dodging one of the guards as they reach for me. Amyra pushes herself up to a kneeling position on the ground and I see a trickle of blood coming from the corner of her mouth. Her face is one of absolute rage as she locks eyes with me and lets out a shriek so unbridled that it spreads goosebumps across my arms.

"Run, Luna!" Rhea screams from across the small clearing beside Atlas as he fights off another guard.

I blink, my brain barely even able to process all of the different things happening at once as I turn and flee back into the crowded trees. I run as fast as I can, wishing I'd had the chance to have Atlas untie my hands as well before fleeing. I weave around and behind different tree trunks, hiding in the darkness.

I stumble on something and fall sideways down into the tall grass of the swamp, unable to catch myself with my hands bound, but thankfully, I'm uninjured. I lean against the nearest tree to help push myself back up to a standing position and then I continue to run as far and fast as possible. When I finally steal a glance back over my shoulder, the two guards that were hot on my tail are nowhere to be seen. I slow my pace to a light jog as I try to catch my breath.

I startle and halt starkly in my path when I suddenly notice a figure hidden in the dark shadow of a nearby tree. It's so hard to see with the minimal moonlight that peaks through the swarm of trees, but the tall height of the figure sends recognition through my system, and a wide smile breaks across my face. Tears of relief bud in my eyes as I quickly run to him. "Caspar!"

I duck into the shadows and embrace him around his waist. Strong arms wrap around me and a tear falls from my eyes. He squeezes me tighter. And then tighter. "Caspar," I whimper. "I can't breathe."

I try to twist free, but the arms around me somehow get even more constricting and I gasp, feeling like my rib cage could shatter.

Chapter 32

"Good. I could use another rose tattoo."

Chapter 33

I've had nightmares before, but none compare to this. My blood runs cold and my breath gets caught in my throat. I can barely draw another one in with Helix holding me so tightly as he walks forward, pressing my back up against the nearest tree in the pocket of shadow. His breath is hot against my forehead as he chuckles, watching me struggle.

Suddenly, I miss being in the clearing with Amyra.

"What's wrong?" Helix asks, his voice dripping with mockery. "Can't catch your breath? Here. Let me help you with that."

His arms loosen around me and I manage to take in one large breath of air before his fingers wrap firmly around my throat. Tears bud in my eyes as I try to squirm free, but it does nothing. He's too strong. The small moonlight grazing through the trees of the swamp hits him where he stands now. Wearing a long-sleeved shirt and dark pants, his expression is crazed. He's out for blood and he wants me to see it in his eyes.

I do.

"I didn't expect to run into you tonight, but now I can't believe my good fortune. Don't think I've forgotten about you crashing my fight

Chapter 33

with Caspar," he seethes. "But you got lucky before." He grabs at his back pocket before bringing a dagger out, twirling it in his hand. As black begins to cloud the edges of my vision, he trails the tip of the blade down the side of my cheek. "Where's your luck now?"

"I'm right here."

Helix moves quickly. His hand releases my neck and moves us both. Spinning me around, he wraps an arm around me, pinning my back against his chest. He presses the edge of the dagger's blade along the base of my throat. "Good. I always do my best work when I have an audience."

"Go to hell," Caspar growls.

Helix chuckles before tilting his mouth down beside my face. "If I do, I think I'll take her with me."

"Let her go, Helix."

"Please," I breathe, but he only presses the edge of the blade further against my neck and I tilt my chin up instinctively as if that will help me get away somehow. My eyes lock with Caspar and I become even more scared seeing the look of fright he's trying to subdue in his eyes. The situation is truly dire if even Caspar is concerned.

"This is between us. It's not about her," Caspar says, his arms out in front of him.

"You're right," says Helix. "You're the one I want. But," he says, tilting his head to the side, "she's the one you want, so no, I'd say she's fairly involved."

"I thought this was about your dad," Caspar says, letting his arms fall to his sides as his shoulders go slack.

I feel Helix's arm around me loosen ever so slightly. "Of course it is," he growls. "You killed him."

My eyes flit to Caspar in question. He gives me a solemn nod of confirmation before his gaze reverts to Helix. "He was going to kill that man, Helix."

"He disobeyed the King's direct orders," Helix seethes.

"He still didn't deserve to die," Caspar says.

"It doesn't matter what you say," Helix says, teeth bared. "Nothing you say can make me feel better." He pauses, chuckling as he flashes an evil grin at Caspar. "But killing her in front of you might."

Helix moves the dagger into the air, poised to stab right through my heart, but as soon as the edge of his knife leaves my throat, I act. I bend forward without any warning, sending his torso forward over me, just in time for me to raise my head backward, with all the strength I can muster, smack into his face.

He cries out, his limbs releasing me. The dagger drops from his hand. I scurry away quickly. Helix blinks hard from the pain of his head; the same pain that now plagues my skull. Caspar is on him almost too quickly for me to register. One second he's in front of me and then the next he's landing a punch to Helix's jaw. Helix falls disoriented to the ground and Caspar climbs over him.

Desperate to help somehow, I quickly untie the rope around my wrists with my teeth.

He lands another blow to Helix's face, but then I see Helix reaching for something out to the side with his arm. It's the dagger.

"Caspar!" I scream in warning just as Helix's fingers wrap around the dagger's handle.

Caspar's head turns towards me, and Helix uses the window to slice across Caspar's thigh. Caspar cries out but remains focused. He tries to grab the blade out of Helix's hand as I see blood begin to stain his pants where the dagger cut him. Helix fights against him, refusing to give up the blade.

With my hands finally free, one flies to my chest in fright as I watch them struggle. It's then that I feel the bare skin of my chest and realize that I'm no longer wearing the amulet. My eyes go wide and I grab at my neck, confirming that it's gone.

Chapter 33

No! Where could it have gone?

Helix lets out a grunt, drawing my focus back to them, as he flips them over so he's atop Caspar. Helix grasps the handle of the dagger with both hands trying to force it downward into Caspar's chest, but Caspar pushes back against Helix's grip with all his might.

I run to them and try to grab Helix by his shoulders and pull him backward off of Caspar. At first, it begins to help, but then Helix lets go of the dagger's handle with one hand to swing his elbow back up into my face. It hits me along my temple and I fall backward onto my side as my eyes water from sudden pain.

"*Luna!*" Caspar cries.

I push up off the ground with my arms and turn back to face them just in time to see Helix push the dagger dangerously close to Caspar's chest.

"Tell my dad I say hi," Helix seethes.

In one swift move, Caspar swings his arm up across Helix's neck as he rolls them over. Once he's atop Helix, Caspar firmly headbutts him squarely in the center of his forehead where I did earlier. It disorients Helix enough to make him loosen his grip on the dagger and allow Caspar to flip the blade in their hands before ramming it through Helix's heart.

"Tell him *yourself,*" Caspar says as Helix's eyes bulge. Blood pools from where the dagger pierces him, and he gasps for breath for all about two seconds before his mouth relaxes agape and his whole body goes slack beneath Caspar.

"Is he—" I start to ask, but can't find the words.

Caspar lays his fingers along Helix's throat as he climbs off of him. "Yes," he nods, standing up.

For a moment, we both just stand there, breathing heavily from the adrenaline still running through us from the perilous moments before. Then, I rush over to him as I remember that he's injured.

"Is your leg alright? I hope it didn't cut you too deeply," I say. I crouch down slightly to get a better look at it, but his hands cup my face and lift me back up. He brings his forehead to mine and I close my eyes at the peace I feel with him so close. I welcome it like rain in a drought.

"Luna, can you ever forgive me?"

I open my eyes and my mouth to speak, but he gently lays a finger on my lips. "Wait, please. Luna, What I did was wrong; so utterly wrong. I never should have helped Amyra. You were right. I was acting out of fear. I am part of a kingdom still recovering from a tyrant ruler and with the rumors I'd heard, I was scared of a relapse of things. I knew Amyra could only want that legend for something bad, but I thought at least I'd know what I was dealing with and I could make a deal with her now to get her in Durand's good graces and ensure the safety of my people."

He stops to heave a breath with a frustrated roll of his dark eyes. "Of course though now I know what an absolute lunatic she is and that no one is safe from her." He trails his thumb along my cheek. "I never should have helped her, Luna, and I never should have hid it from you either. I also shouldn't have believed the rumors I'd heard about you because not a single thing I'd heard was true and every second with you has only made me believe more that you were *made* to rule. You will be the kindest and most favored ruler the realm has ever seen."

He looks down now and lowers his hands to intertwine our fingers. "I know this apology doesn't erase everything." He sighs, his eyes desperately searching mine. "I remember you saying love means nothing without trust, but Luna if you let me, I will spend forever working on rebuilding that trust. Because I do love you, with every fiber of my spirit, and I want that love to mean not just something, but everything to you."

I smile, my heart a thousand pounds lighter as I feel the courage to

Chapter 33

finally tell him how I feel. "I love you too," I say and his eyes widen along with a smile across his face. He looks downright cheerful and I can't help but chuckle at him before I continue. "And I'll forgive you if you forgive me for lying to you. Yes, it's true that Amyra might very well come for Durand next if we don't manage to stop her today, but I did say that at the time just to get you to help us. I shouldn't have done that and I'm so sorry. If you can forgive me—"

"Yes," he breathes, happily, cutting me off. "I do forgive you. Now, can I kiss you, please? Cause it's killing me."

I nod and his lips are on mine in an instant. His hands grab my waist and pull me into him as I run my fingertips up into the back of his hair. This is love, I tell myself; this right here. Being willing to forgive each other and put the past in the past, all for the knowledge and hope of what you could share if you do. I know that what I feel with Caspar is worth anything. It's a priceless, incandescent love and I know, in this moment, that neither of us will ever let the other go.

It's simply me and him. And him and me. Forever.

A scream slices through the air around us from off in the distance and I break free of our kiss, drawing back into the present, as I remember that Helix was only one of our present enemies.

"What was that?" Caspar asks brows furrowed.

"That was Rhea," I tell him with panicked eyes. I move to grab him by the shoulders. I have to catch him up. "Listen to me closely, Caspar."

He nods, assuring me that I have his full attention.

I speak fast, knowing time is of the essence. "Amyra is here with a team of magically brainwashed guards. She traveled into the Bog looking for us and killed Hodge after she got him to tell her where we were. She showed up while I was getting the amulet from the swamp monster. Atlas already killed one of the guards, but there are still three left."

I grab his hand now and we break into a run as I try and retrace my route back to the clearing where Amyra is.

"That's a lot of information to take in all at once," Caspar pants as he runs alongside me. But he turns his head to me, flashing me a smile and a nod. "I'm here for whatever you need, though. We can do this. Let's use the amulet and get rid of her power."

I stop dead in my tracks and he quickly halts too. I groan, slapping my forehead. "I lost the amulet!" I cry, remembering.

"What?" he asks. "How?"

"I don't know!" I say. "I had it on when I was running away from two of Amyra's guards earlier—" my face falters as I remember my fall. "Wait! I tripped and fell when I was running from them. It was somewhere right around this area."

"Okay. I'll help you look," Caspar says with a nod.

"No!" I say, grabbing his arm. "Rhea sounded in trouble and she comes first. You go on ahead and I'll search for it."

Caspar cups my face with both his hands, forcing me to peer up into his dark eyes. "I'm not splitting up with you. We are going to do this together, every step of the way. Got it?"

Realm, help me. I'm so in love with this man. "Got it."

He takes my hand in his again and we begin running off towards the direction of Rhea's scream, but a thought pierces my mind.

"Caspar, who was the man you were talking about before? The one Helix's father wanted to hurt?" I ask as we run.

"Some sprite who'd asked before if he could leave to Celestia to help take care of a child he'd had with a fairywoman. Helix's father had told him no, but the man got caught trying to run away anyway."

I give his hand a firm squeeze and shoot him a glance sideways as we sprint through the tall grass and maze of trees. "Caspar, that's Rhea's dad!"

His eyes widen. "Seriously? How do you know?"

"From the memory that Atlas saw in the tunnels! Is he still alive?"

Chapter 33

"Yes," he nods. "Helix's father, the King, tried to beat him to death for disobeying direct orders. I got into a fight with the King trying to get him off the man, but at one point, I punched him and he fell back and hit his head on a rock. It killed him instantly."

I knew it. Deep down, every time I heard Helix talk of how Caspar had killed his father, I knew that he hadn't killed him out of spite. He wouldn't do that. That's just not Caspar.

"But if Rhea's dad is alive, why did he never come to Celestia after all?" I ask.

Caspar's face falters slightly as I shoot another glance his way, while still making sure to retrace my steps back to Rhea as we run.

"The King had already broken both his legs by the time I got there. His injuries were beyond repair. He hasn't been able to walk since."

A piece of my heart cracks with the news, but the other is uplifted. I can't wait to tell Rhea how hard her dad tried to be with her and how she still has a chance to be with him.

That is, if she's okay.

Chapter 34

We finally reach the clearing and the sight before us is chaos.

One palace guard has Atlas in a headlock on his stomach in front of Amyra and Caspar quickly runs over to help. I scan the area for Rhea and finally spot her up in a tree. She's holding onto a high branch with one hand and swinging a sword at two guards who stand at the base of the tree, trying to climb up. How she stole a sword from one of the guards, I have no clue, but I couldn't be more thankful that she's alive and in one piece.

I quickly run over to her tree and I hear her yell, "You want a piece of this? Come at me! I dare you!" as I approach.

I stop a few paces away behind the guards and call her name, turning both her head and the guards' towards me.

"Luna! You're alright!" she calls, a smile breaking out across her face. But one of the guards suddenly charges in my direction. Wanting to stay on offense this time rather than defense like with the guard earlier, I quickly drop low to the ground right as he approaches and kick my leg out to the side, tripping him. He falls forward, landing on his stomach, but as soon as he rolls onto his back to try and stand up, I act.

Chapter 34

I swing my leg and let my foot connect firmly between his legs before balling my first and colliding it with his temple. He flops onto his side and I let out a loud groan from the excruciating pain that now radiates off my knuckles. I shake my hand out and get into the fighting stance Caspar taught me as I wait for the guard to get back up. Except he doesn't. I stretch my leg out, poking him with my foot. Sure enough, he's out cold.

"That's my best friend!" Rhea shouts proudly from her spot up in the tree.

Suddenly, I hear a commotion and I spin to see the cause of it. Behind me, across the clearing, the guard Atlas had been fighting is now taking quite the pummeling from Caspar. Amyra stalks toward Atlas a small ways away from them, arms extended straight ahead.

"Come here, little thing," Amyra coos, a devilish grin on her hooded face. "I promise it only hurts," she cocks her head to the side, "a lot."

Atlas, with wide eyes and furrowed brows, walks backward away from her carefully, but suddenly, he trips on something and falls onto his backside. He scurries on the ground to move away from her, but she nears him in an instant.

"Atlas!" Rhea shouts, hopping down from her tree, and barely missing the harrowing hands of the other guard as she begins to try and run to Atlas's aid. I fall into step behind her, knowing the guard from the tree is surely close behind, but I fear we'll be too late.

Atlas backs up against a large boulder. He can't go any further and even from where I run towards him I can see the panicked look in his eyes as he realizes he has nowhere left to go.

Fight, Atlas! Fight!

But he looks too frightened to.

Amyra's fingertips turn black as she cackles like the sound of hope shattering. Just when I think Atlas is a goner, lost to her darkness like Lita, Caspar appears to the side and pushes the guard he's been fighting between Atlas and Amyra. Amyra's blackened fingers collide with the body of the guard, instead of Atlas, and the guard's body begins to wither. His skin turns ashen and his eyes sink in as we all watch his skin shrivel and decay into nothingness. I haven't been able to forget the sight of Lita and the palace guard that Amyra withered before, but somehow, seeing it again, it's still even worse than I remember.

Amyra groans as the guard's body finishes rotting away. "What a waste."

Three guards down. Only Amyra and one to go.

Atlas pushes the guard's fallen body off of him in a hurry. His eyes are wild and scared beyond belief. His reaction reminds me of the fact that he and Caspar haven't seen Amyra's power in action before, since they left my coronation party before she crashed it.

Caspar helps Atlas to his feet as Rhea and I approach them, but Amyra swivels towards us, her arms outstretched.

"Take one step towards me and it will be your last," she says.

"Likewise," Caspar says, tilting his neck with a crack.

Atlas comes up beside me and I grab his arm, pulling his ear down by my mouth. "I lost the amulet. I think it came off my neck when I tripped and fell earlier over towards the right side of the forest. Please find it." I let go of his arm and he gives me one swift nod before turning and running off.

Behind me, Rhea swings her sword at the remaining guard, who pulls his sword out to fight back. Their blades collide and Rhea holds firm, but I can see her arms waver slightly. She's not used to maneuvering the weight of a sword and I can tell she's growing weaker by the second.

Caspar and Amyra move around in a semi-circle slowly and I approach them with my arms stretched out in front of me.

"Amyra, explain to me how you lied," I breathe.

"I don't have to explain anything to you," she insists, straightening

Chapter 34

her back to stand tall.

"Yes, you do," I say with a huff, balling my fists at my sides. "Because no matter which one of us dies today, the truth deserves to be told."

Amyra stares at me for a moment, her eyes narrowed, as she mulls over my words.

The guard Rhea is fighting slices the side of her outer shoulder with his sword and she cries out, dropping her sword to cover her now bleeding arm. Caspar wastes no time in swooping in. He quickly grabs the fallen sword before the guard can. The guard ducks as Caspar swings at him, before launching his blade straight forward towards Caspar's side. Caspar barely dodges it and the blade goes between his torso and inner arm, along the leather of his vest. He flattens his arm to his side, trapping the sword, and turns in a half-circle. The action forces the guard to lose hold of his sword so that when Caspar turns back to face him, he now holds both swords out towards the guard.

Rhea has backed up to sit along the front of a tree just behind them. She's far enough away to be out of range for any fighting, but close enough that she could come running if we needed her. Though, I doubt we'd call for her help with her arm so injured.

The guard turns away, rotating at his waist as if he's going to walk away, but suddenly he recoils with a dagger he must have pulled from his belt. He lunges forward, slicing through the air towards Caspar's abdomen, but Caspar steps backward just barely enough to be missed. Panic flashes through the guard's widened eyes as he realizes the mistake he's made. His neck is now stretched out perfectly at waist level in front of Caspar, and Caspar seizes the opportunity, bringing one of the sword blades down and through the neck of the guard in one clean motion.

I gulp down the bile that rises in my throat from the sight as the guard's body falls limp to the ground and Caspar gently nudges the fallen head away from us. He turns back to face me and I see a look of pain in his eyes. He's not a killer. He's a protector. And I can tell how much he hates it when one turns him into the other.

I spin back to face Amyra who stares over my shoulder now at Caspar with wide eyes. "You're alone, Amyra. No more guards," I say, crossing my arms over my chest. "Now, are you ready to talk?"

"Are you ready to *listen?*" she hisses.

"Yes," I huff. "Now, tell me. How did you know that the fairies never tried to find you after the fire?"

She slowly lowers the hood of her cloak, the wrinkles of her face highlighted in the moonlight adding to her eerie presence. "The people had never wanted me as their Queen," she begins, her eyes set like stone off towards the distance. "I trained for it my whole life. I learned everything there was about diplomacy and etiquette. I know I wasn't born it, but I made myself beautiful. I became my biggest critic and I nit-picked every little thing about myself. I was determined to be perfect. I told myself that I had to be."

I turn my head slightly and lock eyes with Rhea, who shoots me a solemn glance, knowing this part sounds a bit familiar.

"But I was never enough," Amyra continues, "and no one saw me as enough. I knew the fairy people wanted your mother over me. Marigold was prettier than me, sweeter than me, smarter than me, and to top it all off, she had fallen in love and had already gotten married. She was even already pregnant with you! Just when I thought she couldn't possibly get any better than me, she did. She had everything to offer them, and all that I had to offer was my effort; the fact that I tried every day. One night, I simply couldn't take it anymore."

Her head ticks to the side like a clock and she whispers to no one over her shoulder, "Lit a match. Flames on flames on flames."

Lit a match?

"Amyra—" I begin, but the words vanish in my throat.

She whips her head back towards Rhea, Caspar, and me now at a

Chapter 34

frighteningly quick speed and I jump slightly.

Her eyes are like fire; alive but deadly. "I lit a match and I walked into your mother's bedroom. I stood over your father and her, with you in her womb, and I saw the life I could have had if only fate didn't pick favorites. I kissed her forehead lightly and whispered that she deserved it. Then, I let the match fall from my hand onto the pillow and I ran."

The fire that we all thought killed Amyra with my father, she started herself? She tried to kill her sister, her brother-in-law, and her niece all at once *in their sleep?*

I feel Caspar's hand rest on my shoulder and it's only then that I come back from my thoughts and realize that tears are flowing down my face.

"How could you?" I breathe, wiping my tears away with the back of my hand.

Amyra struts forward towards the edge of the swampy water now, overlooking the murky scenery before us. "I thought the people would finally see me as enough if they stopped having something better to compare me to," she says over her shoulder with a shrug.

"You're a *monster*," Caspar seethes at her from beside me.

Amyra turns to face us now, the span of the swampy sea behind her, as she shoots him a glare. Finally, she averts her eyes back to me. Her face is entirely unapologetic. "It would have worked if it had gone as planned, but alas, " she lowers her voice to a menacing whisper, "only one out of three."

I take a step backward, her words hitting me like a physical blow.

"I ran and hid in the closet of my parents' chambers. I figured I would hide there till the fire was put out and you'd all been successfully declared dead. Then, I planned to make a grand return." Her eyes somehow darken even more than the night sky above us and the fog of the swamp swirls around her. "I could hear the commotion of the fire. Then, a while later, my parents walked in. They talked about your father being dead and Marigold being in the infirmary. Then, my father turned to my mother and asked if they should send some guards to look for me since my body hadn't been found."

Amyra pauses, closing her eyes. She squeezes them tightly as she heaves a breath, as if by reciting the words she's forced to relive it.

"My mother said, 'Why would we do that? Fate treated us poorly when I birthed Amyra first, but perhaps now we have a chance to give the kingdom the Queen they truly want.' It was then that I knew not a single person believed in me; not even my parents. I'd never felt more worthless. So, I decided to stop being a burden to everyone and I fled. I went into hiding and when I caught word that my parents had both died of old age, I didn't shed a single tear for them."

"But why return now?" I ask with an exasperated shrug of my shoulders.

Her eyes gaze off into the distance once more. "Because one day, I decided that I no longer cared if they didn't want me on the throne. I still wanted it. So, I set out to take it by force. I'm sure the same idea has occurred to you before, too."

My brows furrow together and I narrow my eyes at her in question. "What? I would never—"

"Oh, please," she spits, before rolling her eyes at me. "You of all people should understand what I'm going through. The people don't want you either. *They still prefer her!*"

"It's not the same," I say, straightening my back to stand taller. "Yes, the people love my mother, but they will love me too once they give me a chance and see me as Queen."

Amyra's head cocks to the side and she whispers into the air, "Delusional child. So naive." Her eyes flit back to me as if remembering I'm there. "They will always prefer someone else. You'll never be enough, just like I never was."

Chapter 34

Caspar's hand moves from my shoulder down to intertwine fingers with me. He gives my hand a comforting squeeze as if to help me find the words, but I don't think I need any help. Amyra's speech unlocked something deep inside of me and I think that possibly for the first time, I know exactly what to say.

"Amyra, I'm already enough."

She lets out that maniacal cackle of hers as she shoots me an amused expression.

"I used to think similarly to you," I continue. "If you'd talked to me a few days ago, I probably would have better understood how you feel, but I know now that I've always been enough. I've been tested on this quest in countless ways. I've proven to myself that I am brave, courageous, smart, and determined; all qualities that make a good leader."

I glance to my side, locking my eyes with Rhea again. A tear falls from her eyes as she stares at me with a look of pride.

I draw in a deep breath and turn back to face Amyra. "I kept thinking I wasn't enough because the people didn't see me as such, but I'm done placing my self-worth in the hands of others. All I can do is trust in myself and realize that my imperfections are part of what makes me the perfect me; the me that's going to be a great ruler."

Amyra's eyes burn into me now.

"You can't expect others to see you as good enough, Amyra, if you don't even see yourself that way."

She cries out, lunging for me, but Caspar grabs my arm and pulls me off to the side with him, out of the way. We lose our balance though, with our sloppy effort to get away, and fall into the tall grass. Amyra pulls a long-bladed dagger out from somewhere beneath her cloak and throws it towards us. The blade flies through the air, piercing Caspar through his shoulder. He cries out, but I have no time to help him before Amyra is on me. She latches one black-rimmed hand around the back of my neck and lays her other flat over my heart.

Instantly, I feel a stinging, burning sensation from deep within my chest, as if someone has set my very soul on fire. Every nerve in my body feels pained yet alive, and I realize this is the end. If I must go, at least I can go knowing that I tried my very best. And at least I knew love before I left.

My eyes are frozen on Amyra's face. I'm sure Rhea is trying to run to my aid, even though she's beyond my sights. Caspar rips the dagger out of his shoulder, letting out a sound of utter pain, before trying to stand, but he can't. His foot is caught on something that he struggles to unlatch.

They won't get to me in time. I know it, but it means the realm to me to see them try.

"*Luna!*" calls Atlas's voice through the muggy air of the swamp. I turn my eyes slightly toward the direction of his voice and see him sprinting out from the trees across from us, with the amulet in hand. Realizing he won't get to me in time, he halts his steps and throws the amulet towards me. It falls onto the ground beside me as Amyra's mad eyes pour into me and my body feels alight with a blazing fire.

Channeling her power into me seems to take all her concentration and she doesn't notice as I slightly move my hand to place a finger on the amulet beside me.

I open my mouth to speak and my voice emits barely a whisper. "I wish to drain you of your power and undo your withering ability."

Amyra's eyes go from pleased to pained above me and her hands release me. As she lets go of my body, I feel a magical, fulfilling sensation in my chest. I look at my hand to see the shriveled limb become, once again, full of life and color. Amyra lets out a scream as she looks at her own hands, averting my eyes back to her.

"What have you done?" she wails as the black tips of her fingers slowly vanish. She pulls her cloak down over her face roughly,

Chapter 34

shouting, *"No! No!"*

She sloppily steps around me as she cries. I try to flip onto my side to then push to a standing position, but she turns and trips over my ankle. Amyra screams out as her cloaked body is thrown into the murky, moonlit-coated water with a resounding splash. Rhea and Atlas both reach me, flanking my sides now. We all watch as Amyra resurfaces with hair soaked, and a look of pure rage upon her face.

"This isn't over!" she cries, pointing her index finger out of the mud towards me on the shore. "I will rule Celestia if it's the last thing I do!" Hysterical sobs now flood out of her and she begins to whisper into the surrounding air. Although, I'm not certain if her words are meant for us or the voices that fill her mind. "It can't end like this," she hauntingly chants. "It can't end like this."

Rhea, Atlas, and I all watch from the shore as the Marsh Reaper's spine-chilling figure silently surfaces behind Amyra. Rhea grabs my arm with the hand of her uninjured shoulder in fright, while beside me, Atlas's mouth drops agape. Amyra, however, doesn't notice the monster's presence till it lays a hand on her shoulder.

She stills instantly at the contact; her words catching in her throat. She turns slowly around to face the Marsh Reaper and her face falls as soon as her eyes take in the sight before her. "No," she whispers. "No. Leave me, please. This can't be the end."

"This is the end," the monster's chilling voice hisses at her. Then we all watch as the Marsh Reaper's eerily long fingers grab Amyra by the back of her soaked, red hair and begin pulling her slowly under the water. She screams out for help, thrashing her arms about in the hazy water.

Images of the bodies from the monster's lair flood my mind and I realize that as much as I hate Amyra for all that she has done to my family and my people, I do not wish that fate upon anyone. I move to try and go help her if I can, but Rhea's grip on my arm is firm. I turn my face back to Rhea to tell her to let me go, but then I hear Amyra's cries vanish beneath the water's surface.

I face the water once again to confirm that she's gone. The Marsh Reaper has dragged her beyond death and even after all she's done, I still feel sorry for her.

Rhea suddenly grabs me by my shoulders, turning me to face her. Her eyes are alight with sheer joy. "Luna, we did it! She's gone! Amyra's gone!" She pulls me into a tight embrace and it begins to sink in. She's right. Amyra's gone. Our quest is over. We can go home.

I can finally be reunited with my mother.

The realization makes my heart swell with joy. Tears of happiness and relief begin to descend from my eyes as Atlas pulls Rhea and me into his arms, making it a small group hug. But then, I realize that Caspar is still missing from our huddle and I absolutely cannot wait a second longer to bask in this moment with him.

We all relax out of our embrace and I spin around. I don't see the amulet on the ground where it last was. The Marsh Reaper did say it would return to him after a single use.

My eyes land on Caspar, his eyes winced and his shoulder bleeding from where Amyra's dagger pierced him. He's sitting with his legs out in front of him and his back resting against a nearby tree. I sprint to him as fast as my legs can go and I waste no time when I reach him. I fall onto my knees and throw my arms around him, pulling him to me as more joyful tears fall from my eyes.

"Oh, Caspar. We did it. We actually did it! Thank you! Thank you so much for believing in me and for all of your help."

I pull back, wiping tears from my face, but I still instantly at the blank look in his eyes.

"Um, you're welcome," he says, brows furrowed, "but who are you?"

Chapter 35

Mother fixes a few stray hairs from the long locks of curls that cascade down the back of my golden dress.

"Are you ready, sweetheart?"

I catch her face over my shoulder in the long mirror in front of me. She looks so proud and it fills my heart with warmth.

"Yes, I'm ready," I say, with a nod.

"Did you know that this is the same dress I wore when I was crowned?"

"It is?" I ask, smiling.

She nods, a nostalgic joy shining across her face. "I remember it like it was yesterday. I was so nervous. I was shaking like a leaf so terrible that I could hardly stand. You could have tipped me over with the slightest nudge!"

We share a chuckle before her smile falters. I turn around to face her with concerned eyes as she begins to well up.

"Mother, what's wrong?"

"It's just—" she starts, heaving a breath and blinking back tears before she can continue. "When Amyra locked me away in that cell, I had no idea what happened to you. I spent every second praying that you were alive and that we would get to be reunited somehow. I suppose I just feel overwhelmed with thankfulness that we are both here; alive and well."

My own eyes get teary now at her words and I pull her into an embrace. "I'm thankful for this, too, Mother. I thought of you every day we were apart."

We pull back from our hug and dab at our eyes, carefully.

"I still don't understand why Amyra kept you locked away instead of killing you, though," I say, thinking out loud.

Mother's inner brows raise as she thinks back. "She told her brainwashed guards to lock me away because she knew the people might leave if she had nothing to hold over them. I was her hostage for leverage."

The image of my mother being locked away, for all those days I was hunting for the amulet, chips at my heart and I pull her in for a hug once again.

"I'm so happy you're safe. Keeping you alive is the one thing I am grateful to Amyra for."

"Whatever happened to her?" Mother asks, pulling back from our hug. "You never did say, exactly."

I could tell my mother of Amyra's demise, but I know that even with all the havoc Amyra brought upon us and our kingdom, the image of her within the Marsh Reaper's grasp would haunt my mother terribly. It already haunts me, along with Amyra's truth about starting the fire all those years ago. Those things don't need to haunt my mother, too. She's been through enough already. Now, all she needs is peace.

"She's gone, mother. Let's leave it at that, alright? Please just trust me."

She peers into my eyes for a moment before she grabs my hand and gives it a slight squeeze. "I trust you. And I'm so proud of you, sweetheart. I love you."

Chapter 35

"I love you too," I say, squeezing her hand back.

A knock sounds at the door and Rhea pops her head in.

"Can I come in?" she asks.

"Of course," mother says. She turns to me, kissing my temple. "I'll see you out there, darling."

"You look absolutely breathtaking," Rhea gawks at me with wide eyes, as soon as my mother exits.

My cheeks shimmer at her compliment, but the truth is that I've never felt more beautiful than I do today. The gold dress of my mother's is made of a material that shimmers when I move and it hugs my body in all the right places before flowing down to the ground. The top comes to tie around my neck and I wear long, cream-colored gloves of a semi-translucent, tulle fabric. As if the outfit isn't enough, my long, red hair has been transformed into a waterfall of curls; the soon-to-be resting place of my mother's crown.

"Me? Look at *you!*" I say throwing my arms open towards her.

Her short black hair is pulled back into two small buns and she's wearing a mint green dress that is fitted at the top before puffing out to all sides like a daisy. She gives me a twirl.

"Oh, this old thing? I just threw this on," she says with a smirk.

I roll my eyes at her, suppressing a smirk of my own. "Is Atlas here yet?"

She nods. "He's sitting with my dad." Her whole face lights up and she lets out a joyful chuckle. "Gosh, it's still so wild saying that. I have a dad. I have a *parent*," she says, throwing her arms up in the air.

I chuckle at her glee. "I know! I'm still not used to hearing you say it myself."

When we all realized, back in the Bog, that Caspar had no idea who I was, we decided to split up. Rhea and I flew back to Celestia on our own and Caspar and Atlas returned to Durand. As soon as Rhea and I began our journey home, I told her of her father and she wept tears of joy. She was saddened to hear of his legs, of course, but overjoyed to discover that she wasn't an orphan after all.

Atlas met Rhea's father after returning to Durand and wrote to Rhea about his condition. Caspar was right. Her father, a kind man named Roland, no longer had the use of his legs and was currently getting around Durand in a wooden wheelchair. Rhea and I sent some guards to Durand to pick him up and fly him back to Celestia.

Rhea and her father have been inseparable ever since. The girl who usually hardly touched the ground, now walks, pushing her father's wheelchair, everywhere she goes. You've never seen two people happier in each other's company.

"I think I might be even more excited about this ceremony than you are," Rhea says, jolting me back to the present. "I mean, after all, my title is changing today; not just yours. I will finally be Lady Rhea; Incredibly Beautiful and Talented Best Friend to the Queen of all Celestia."

I laugh at her. "You're right! Congratulations. This truly is *your* day," I say, flashing her a wink.

She walks over, bracing her hands on the windowsill to steal a peek outside. "Seems like the whole kingdom has come out for this!" she exclaims, happily, as she turns back to face me. "Everyone is here."

Not everyone.

Rhea sees my face fall as soon as the words leave her mouth. She walks over, taking my hand.

"I'm sorry," she says, with a huff. She hesitates for a moment before pressing on. "I know you miss him."

"Terribly," I answer immediately, the words tumbling out of my mouth. "And it's horrible knowing that while I'm miserable missing him, he isn't missing me. He can't be when he doesn't remember me at all."

Atlas drilled Caspar with questions as they traveled back to Durand,

Chapter 35

studying him like he would a scholarly project. He found that Caspar remembers our whole quest. He remembers Hodge, Helix, beating Amyra, and everything else, except me. When Atlas asked him who had been on their quest, he said Atlas, himself, and Rhea. When Atlas asked him about moments, or things, directly corresponding to me, Caspar said his brain felt fuzzy. His mind is now full of blank patches that used to be filled with memories of me; memories of us.

Little did I know that the amulet's price, which the Marsh Reaper warned me about, would be the most priceless thing I had. Our love story is completely forgotten.

"Why don't you go after him then?" Rhea asks, thwarting me back to our conversation. "It's been two weeks."

"It's complicated, Rhea," I groan at her.

"It is not!" she insists, hands landing on her hips. "You love him and he loves you. You're meant to be together. Simple!"

"He doesn't love me anymore, Rhea!" I snap at her, my eyes watering from having to say the truth of my new reality out loud. "He doesn't. I love him and he doesn't even know me."

Rhea grabs me by my outer shoulders, forcing me to face her. "Luna, listen to me. You might no longer be in his mind, but I guarantee you are still somewhere in his heart."

"Rhea—" I start, but she cuts me off, holding up a finger.

"Let me finish. I know why you're scared to see him again. It would be incredibly painful to face the love of your life and have them not even recognize you. And it would be an incredibly daunting task to try and get to know them all over again, but Luna?"

My eyes are sincere as they pour into hers. "Yes?"

"You have to try. Go to him and remind him of your love. Make him remember!"

"You really think that will work?" I ask.

She shrugs. "Nothing is guaranteed, but I know you'd rather fail than live wondering what if."

Her words sink into my heart like a rock in the ocean. I know she's right, about all of it. If there's even a chance to still be with Caspar, I need to take it. No matter how hard it may be, what we had is worth it.

"Okay," I breathe, a hopeful smile blossoming on my face.

Her eyebrows raise. "Okay?"

"Okay!" I exclaim now, breaking into a full grin. "I'll do it. I'll go to him and try to remind him of us."

"Yay!" Rhea screams, throwing her arms around me and jumping up and down.

We're still reveling in our happy moment when a knock sounds on my door.

"Yes?" I call.

"It's time, Your Highness," calls a guard and chills descend my spine. It's time to become Queen.

"I'm gonna go back to my seat," Rhea says, happily clapping her hands in front of her. "You look great! It's going to be amazing! I love you!" she yells as she flies out.

The guard stands in my open doorway and holds his arm out to usher me through. "This way, Your Highness."

"Thank you," I say, following him out.

We fly down the halls of the palace till we reach the throne room's tall double doors. The guard knocks twice, signaling a choir of trumpets on the other side to ring out a joyful melody.

The doors swing wide as the music sounds and a different guard off to my left announces, "Her Royal Highness, Princess Luna of Celestia."

I fly down the deep, fuchsia-colored carpet that has been splayed down the length of the room from the entrance to the throne, which sits on a risen platform. Wisteria flowers descend from the ceiling around a sparkling, gem chandelier. My mother stands beside the

Chapter 35

throne, wearing her crown. Her white dress is cast in a hue of rainbows from the light streaming through the massive stained-glass window spanning the wall behind her.

Palace officials, dignitaries, and select close friends are gathered to my left and right. They all stand as I fly slowly past them. When I pass Rhea, she gives me a wink. Her dad and Atlas wave next to her with beaming faces. Only when I reach my mother does everyone take their seats. She takes my hand in hers and we face the room.

"My people," she begins, ever the regal host, "thank you for being here for this exciting day. After serving the majority of my life as your Queen, today, I will be stepping down and passing the crown to my beloved daughter. I could not be more excited," her eyes flit momentarily to mine, "or proud."

I squeeze her hand before letting go as we turn to face each other. A palace official walks up with the ceremonial sapphire and flower bouquet on a velvet pillow. One at a time, my mother removes them from the pillow and places them into my open palms.

When the man once again takes his seat, she proceeds to the vows.

"Princess Luna," she begins, and instinctively, I stand taller; straightening my back. "Do you vow to govern the fairypeople of Celestia fairly and justly?"

"I do."

"Do you vow to keep us connected to our roots so that we may never lose our spirit and gentle way of life?

"I do."

"Do you vow to put the needs of the kingdom above all else?"

"I do."

"And finally," she pauses, tears welling in her happy eyes. "Do you vow to love and care for the people as every ruler before you?"

"I do."

A tear falls down her cheek and I blink the ones that threaten to descend from my own eyes.

She gestures to the throne and I move to take my seat.

"It is my privilege and greatest honor," she says, lifting the crown from her head, "to crown you, Queen Luna of Celestia."

She slowly lowers the crown onto the top of my hair and I can't help but notice that it doesn't feel as heavy as I thought it would. Rhea jumps from her seat with a holler, the rest of the party follows in turn until the whole room is in an uproar of cheers.

A joy encompasses me unlike anything before and it overflows from me into laughter. My mother claps beside the throne, only pausing to wipe her tears.

When the applause finally begins to die down, my mother raises her arms.

"It is now time for Her Majesty to take her first flight as Queen through her kingdom!"

The cheering kicks up again as I stand and hand the flowers and sapphire back to the palace official. Mother and the rest of the attendees fall into step behind me as I make my way to the front gates of the palace. Guards stand ready at the entrance and they swing the gates open as I approach, revealing the citizens of Celestia all lined up throughout the kingdom for me to fly past.

The sight of them all is so overwhelming that I suddenly feel called to speak. I halt in my tracks and turn back towards my mother. "Is it alright if I say something first?"

She nods.

I turn back to face the people, holding my head high. "My people," I begin, speaking as loud as I can to allow everyone to hear me. "I'm aware that many of you have doubted my ability to be Queen and I'm here to tell you that you are not alone. I, also, doubted myself greatly, but I've realized that filling my mother's shoes is an impossible feat. Instead of trying to be someone else, I will aspire to be the best version

Chapter 35

of myself and the best Queen that I can be for you."

I stop to draw in a breath.

"I know you have all heard the story of my venture into the Bog where I fought alongside Lady Rhea and two spritemen from Durand, to obtain the amulet of undoing and defeat Amyra. We faced countless horrors in those woods, but trust me when I say that I would do it all again for Celestia."

Confidence fills me as I realize that I sound like the ruler I've always dreamed of being. "I can't promise to be perfect, for I am not perfect, but I can promise that I will put this kingdom first. I will foster friendship with Durand, who we now know was not responsible for the fire, and seek only peace during my time on the throne. I know I will be a great Queen, but only if I have your support for my reign as you are all the spirit of Celestia."

The words leave my lips and I pray that they properly convey to everyone the dedication and confidence I have.

Slowly, I begin my solo flight through the kingdom. I pass only a few fairies before someone chants, "Long live, Queen Luna!"

I twist my head in the direction of the voice as I fly, but a chorus of chants rises up to meet it.

"Long live the Queen!"

"Long live, Queen Luna!"

"Hooray for the Queen!"

Every uplifting chant makes my heart swell. My arms rise to wave at everyone and soon people begin throwing flower petals over me as I fly past. Their support is like music to my ears and happy tears flow from my face.

I never want to forget this moment. The smiling faces of the people, the raining flower petals, or the cheers of the crowd. I commit them all to memory as best as I am able.

I fly through Celestia, embracing every part of the kingdom that

I now rule. I reach the end, the setting sun before me, and my eyes drift far off into the distance. I long to fly onward; to fly right to his door, take him in my arms, and never let him go.

But today is my moment. Tomorrow will be ours.

Epilogue

I peer out the window over Durand, watching the lanterns of the homes flicker off with the rising of the morning sun. Oh, how lucky I am to call this place my home.

A knock sounds at the door to my chambers and a guard pops his head in.

"Yes?" I ask, turning from my spot along the windowsill.

"You have a visitor from Celestia, King Caspar."

My eyebrows heighten in surprise. Has Rhea come to visit me? I haven't seen her since our journey into the Bog with Atlas. My head aches trying to recall the memory of our adventure. I get the oddest headache every time I try to think back on it and while many doctors in Durand have looked me over, no solutions or causes have been found. I can remember Rhea, Atlas and I meeting Hodge and gathering items to get an amulet to stop Amyra, the woman I wrongfully aided, but everything is so fuzzy. There are blank bits and gaps in between scenes that flash through my mind.

I shake my head to rid myself of my thoughts as I follow the guard. Oh, well. Hopefully, it will all come back to me.

I round the corner into the throne room to find Atlas embracing a woman. Her bright red hair stands out like a beam of sunlight in the room and the freckles of her face splotch about in a pattern across her skin like paint on a canvas. Yet, as she retracts from their hug and turns to face me fully, I feel floored; like the very ground beneath me has dissipated from her sheer beauty. She's lovely in a way I didn't know creation was capable of and I'm suddenly finding myself wishing that I had the time to study her every feature and devote it all to my memory.

Who is this iridescent fairywoman?

Could it be the girl who hugged and thanked me in the Bog? It was the oddest encounter, yet it somehow burned its way into my mind.

A smile breaks out on her face, that threatens to melt me right where I stand, as she looks at me.

"Hello," she breathes.

"Hello, there," I echo.

Atlas smiles between us before joining his hands behind his back and clearing his throat.

"Your Highness, this is Queen Luna of Celestia." He grins, patting her once on the shoulder. "I'll let you two have some privacy," he says before he exits.

"A fellow ruler, I see. It's nice to finally meet you," I say, walking up to her, arm extended. I see what I think looks like a flash of pain cross her expression as she hesitates to take my hand. "Are you alright?"

"Oh! Yes- yes, I'm fine. Sorry," she says, putting a smile back on her face as she peers up at me, her blue eyes piercing. We shake hands and I feel like we both hold on a second longer than most. "I've just been looking forward to meeting you." She hesitates, before adding, "very much."

I smirk at her as I say, "Oh, really? And why is that?"

"Well," she begins, but it's then that I notice that a strand of her hair has fallen forward.

Epilogue

Some inner force makes me instinctively reach out and tuck it softly behind her ear. The movement catches her by surprise as she stops mid-sentence and I apologize.

"I'm so sorry," I say with a nervous chuckle. "I'm not quite sure why I—"

"It's alright," she says, a more genuine smile on her face now as her eyes scan my face. "I don't mind. Thank you."

A beat of silence passes before I clear my throat. "Sorry, you were saying you were looking forward to meeting me because?" I trail off, waiting for her to jump in.

"Oh, yes!" she says, clasping her hands together in front of her. "Might we sit down first?"

I nod, gesturing to two chairs surrounding a small table in the corner. We go to take our seats, but as I sit, she bolts back up.

"Oh! Wait," she exclaims, rushing over to the long, thin table pushed against the opposite side of the room to retrieve something. "I brought these for you."

She turns and walks back to our table, placing down a tray of what appears to be some sort of dessert.

"What are these?" I ask, inspecting the food with a sniff.

"They're lavender tarts," she says, softly. "I made them for you."

I flash her a smile, not wanting to taint her generous gesture by telling her I don't usually care for sweets.

She takes a seat across from me with a grin. "They might be sweet, but something tells me you'll love them."

I narrow my eyes at her with a smirk. It's like she heard my very thoughts. "Confident, are we?"

"Very," she says, placing her hands in her lap.

A moment passes between us as a bird chirps outside the nearest window and I search her expression for some sort of clue as to what she's thinking, but her eyes tell me a million things all at once.

She's both unnerving and welcoming; beautiful and intimidating. Something within me feels pulled to her like a magnet and I long to explore it.

"You came to Durand just to bring me a dessert?" I ask.

She laughs and I'll be damned if it's not the most melodious sound I've ever heard.

"No, no," she says, smoothing her dress before looking back up at me. "I came to," she hesitates, drawing in a deep breath, "tell you a story."

I lean forward towards her, bracing my elbows on the table. "Does it have a happy ending?" I ask with a smirk.

She leans forward onto her arms, her stark blue eyes locking on mine. She stares at me for the briefest of moments before she sighs, a hopeful smile on her face. "Yes, I believe it does."

Luna's Lavender Tarts Recipe

Created by Brenda Mandelis

CRUST

Ingredients:

1 cup room-temperature unsalted butter
1/2 cup sugar
1/2 tsp salt
1/4 cup culinary-grade dried lavender buds
1 tsp vanilla extract
2 cups all-purpose flour

CRUST DIRECTIONS

Preheat your oven to 300 degrees Fahrenheit and line the bottom of your tart pan with parchment paper. (You should use a tart pan with a removal bottom. If you do not have one, line the parchment paper higher up the sides of your pan to use for easy removal once the tart crusts have cooled.) In a stand mixer, or mixing bowl, combine the unsalted butter, sugar, salt, and lavender buds for approximately five minutes or until all ingredients are thoroughly combined. Then add in the vanilla extract and flour. Mix until combined. Press the dough into your parchment-lined tart pan. Bake on the middle rack of your preheated oven for 30 minutes, or until golden brown. The tart crusts will continue to harden as they cool. Allow them to cool completely before adding the lemon curd filling and whipped cream.

LEMON CURD
Ingredients:
1/2 cup fresh-squeezed lemon juice
2 tsp finely-grated lemon zest
3 large, room-temperature eggs
1/2 cup sugar
1/3 cup room-temperature unsalted butter

LEMON CURD DIRECTIONS

Begin simmering a small amount of water in a pot or double-broiler. (Not enough for the water to touch the bottom of the bowl of ingredients you will place later on top of the simmering water.) Whisk the lemon juice, lemon zest, eggs, and sugar together in a heatproof bowl or double-broiler bowl. Once mixed, place the bowl of ingredients atop the simmering pot of water and stir the ingredients steadily for 10 minutes while being careful not to "cook" the eggs. Add in the unsalted butter and stir until combined. Remove from heat and strain with a fine sieve into the cooled tart crusts. Place the tarts into the refrigerator and allow them to cool for at least two hours.

WHIPPING CREAM
Ingredients:
1 cup heavy whipping cream
1 tsp vanilla extract
2 tbsp powdered sugar

Luna's Lavender Tarts Recipe

1 tsp culinary-grade, finely-ground lavender (optional)

WHIPPING CREAM DIRECTIONS

Use a stand or electric hand mixer to combine the heavy whipping cream, vanilla extract, powdered sugar, and ground lavender until light and fluffy. Add the whipped cream atop the tarts immediately before serving.

Enjoy! Though be sure to grab a tart while you can. If you forget, you might discover that there's only one left and lose it to a wickedly handsome sprite...

Acknowledgments

I had the idea for this book almost four years ago and finally started writing it around April 2023. Now, here I am writing the acknowledgments?! Gosh, it's so wild how fast time really does fly by when you're having fun. This book is my proudest creative accomplishment.

Knowing that YOU, whoever you are, are reading MY book right now is so surreal. That's all I've ever wanted. I hope you loved it, or at least could detect all of the love that I interwove into it for you over these last few years. From the bottom of my heart, **thank you**.

Next, I have to thank God. Do you have any idea how many times I thought about giving up on this story? There was not one, but many nights I cried or wanted to scream because I was struggling to get the story out of my head and onto paper. I didn't get through those hard moments by myself. I got through them by leaning on Him for strength. Without the imagination, creativity, and stubbornness that He instilled in me, none of this would have been possible.

I absolutely must thank Mrs. Downer, my high school English teacher, for showing me that books can be so much more than stories and that words are the most powerful tool at my disposal. She

Acknowledgments

awakened my creative passion within me and showed me how to harness it for good. Everything I write is tied to her. On behalf of myself and every student who has been blessed to experience her teachings, I want to thank her for showing us the true beauty of literature.

I'd like to thank my husband for showing me what a true love story is. I know I'll never be able to write anything as perfect as ours, but at least this one is pretty close. Here's to all the dreams we have supported each other through and all the ones to come, Hubby. Thank you for inspiring me daily. I love you with all my heart.

Many thanks to my best friend Tori who would come to my house and read aloud every chapter as I wrote this book. She'd give me all of her honest compliments and criticisms and for that, I am eternally grateful. Tori, you were the first person to read this book and you will be for all the books to come, too. Thank you for letting me be your Rhea.

Did you notice how gorgeous the cover of this book is? That's the work of Sarah Moon! Not only is she one bad-ass and incredibly talented graphic designer, but she's also the best college roommate a girl could ever ask for. I won the jackpot with her. Sarah, thank you for everything you've done for me, girl. And I don't just mean with this book.

Louis, who's a good boy? You are! *gives pumpkin biscuit*

Finally, I'd like to thank all of my many family members for loving me and letting me write my little fairy books. You give me the space I need to independently pursue dreams like this one, but you're always there to celebrate with me at the finish line, and I appreciate that more than you know. All my love.

begins working on next novel

About the Author

Kasey Safford lives in Washington with her husband and corgi. When she's not writing, you can find her reading, binge-watching FRIENDS, baking, and drinking too much coffee. Her articles have been published across many media platforms, including NCWLIFE, the Wenatchee World, and Gleaner Magazine. The Amulet of Undoing is her debut novel.

Fellow book enthusiasts can join her literary journey by following her at @kaseysafford on TikTok.

Made in the USA
Monee, IL
02 February 2026

43109960R00198